A Twist of Hate

A TWIST OF HATE

VR BARKOWSKI

FIVE STAR
A part of Gale, Cengage Learning

GALE
CENGAGE Learning®

Farmington Hills, Mich • San Francisco • New York • Waterville, Maine
Meriden, Conn • Mason, Ohio • Chicago

LIBRARY OF CONGRESS CATALOGING-IN-PUBLICATION DATA

Barkowski, V. R.
    A twist of hate / VR Barkowski. — First edition.
      pages cm
      ISBN 978-1-4328-3018-2 (hardcover) — ISBN 1-4328-3018-X
(hardcover)
      1. Art theft—Fiction. 2. Family secrets—Fiction. 3. Mystery fiction. I. Title.
PS3602.A77556T95 2015
813'.6—dc23   2014047853

First Edition. First Printing: June 2015
Find us on Facebook– https://www.facebook.com/FiveStarCengage
Visit our website– http://www.gale.cengage.com/fivestar/
Contact Five Star™ Publishing at FiveStar@cengage.com

Printed in the United States of America
1 2 3 4 5 6 7 19 18 17 16 15

For my parents, Robert and Barbara.
Not a day goes by when I don't miss you.

ACKNOWLEDGMENTS

Deepest gratitude to my longtime critique partner, Rochelle Staab, a wonderful writer whose keen eye and infinite patience made A TWIST OF HATE a better book; to my agent, Christine Witthohn, for her faith, wisdom, and tenacity; and to Steven Appel, who shared both his knowledge of wartime France and his considerable library. That said, any errors herein are solely my own. Fist-bumps, thank yous, and hugs to the online writing/blogging community for their continued support and encouragement. Finally, at its core, this is a book about loyalty. I would be remiss if I didn't thank Laurie West, who, during our thirty-five-plus-year friendship has never failed to demonstrate this most rare and precious quality. I am indeed fortunate.

PROLOGUE

21 JANUARY 1943
THE EVE OF "ACTION TIGER"
MARSEILLES, FRANCE

"They're coming," Max said from his vantage point at the front window. It didn't matter there was no one but little Samuel to hear. Max needed to say the words aloud to make them real.

A pair of Gestapo agents marched up the steep, cobbled street. Behind them, two soldiers, Mausers resting on their shoulders, muzzles pointed toward heaven. They were rounding up Jews. Three days ago, these same agents took Émile Singer, the old man next door. Even then, Max knew they'd be back. He should have run.

Samuel stood beside him. "Who, Papa?"

Max stroked the boy's downy head and pulled him close as they watched the agents climb the steps to the Gilbert house. The thinner of the Gestapo men pounded on the glossy door, then waved one of the soldiers forward. The young man—not much more than a boy, really—jogged up the stairs, shot the lock, and kicked open the door. Max knew they'd find the house empty. Terrified Singer might talk, the Gilberts fled Marseilles three days earlier.

A cold sweat crawled down Max's back. Had the secret police tortured Singer? Made promises to go easy on him if he gave up friends and neighbors?

Max had secured false identity documents for the old man

just as he had for the Gilberts, but Singer had refused them. He was a Frenchman and a Jew, too proud twice over. What use pride if you were dead? Max wanted to know. With the bitter taste of guilt burning the back of his throat, he'd watched, helpless, as the Gestapo marched his friend and neighbor away at gunpoint.

He recalled his own easy camaraderie with the officers, their pleasure at finding *ein Deutscher unter das meer der dummen Franzosen und der schmutzige Juden*— a German among the sea of stupid Frenchmen and filthy Jews—and another rush of shame shook him. His own forged papers guaranteed execution if the Gestapo learned the truth. As if being a Jew wasn't enough of a death sentence.

He let the curtain drop and knelt before three-year-old Samuel. The boy blinked, fixing wise brown eyes—his mother's eyes—on Max. Saying goodbye to his son was like losing Adèle all over again. Max swallowed tears.

"It's time to go, little man. Remember what I told you? You must be very quiet." Max put his finger to Samuel's lips.

The child nodded, eyes wide.

Max wrapped a blanket around the boy and gathered Samuel's slight frame in his arms, tenderly placing him in the worn canvas duffle in which their few valuables lay packed and waiting. Having no time to think, only to do, was a blessing. It meant no chance of being pulled under by the waves of despair that now lapped at his heels.

"Scared, Papa."

"Shh, little man. Be brave." Max took a sugar cube from his pocket and slipped it into the boy's mouth. "Once we're away from here, you can make all the noise you want."

He folded back the rug and felt for the hidden edge of the trapdoor leading to the cellars. The dark, dank smell of saltwater and earth wafted into the room as he lifted the hatch. He'd chosen the house because of the interconnected cellars and months ago mapped their escape. The Gestapo would figure it out, of course, but not until it was too late. Max bent and kissed the top of the boy's head and closed the flap protecting the precious bundle. After testing the straps one last time, he carefully slung the bag over his shoulder and started down the ladder.

There was a hard fist on the door. *"Aufmachen!"*

Max positioned the rug to camouflage the opening, secured the trapdoor from below, and dropped down to the dirt floor just as he heard the crack of a gunshot. With the duffle held tight against his body, he ran.

CHAPTER 1

*Our passions are the true phoenixes; when the old one is burnt
out, a new one rises from its ashes.*—Goethe

Ten a.m. on a Wednesday and the place was already total
pandemonium. How the hell had he let himself be dragged out
of the office for this? Right, Mom. Tough to get a bitch on when
Mom called. Del pushed through the human throng on the
sidewalk, ignored the queues at the entrance, and stepped into
the lobby of the California Museum of Fine Art. CaMu, San
Francisco's timorous answer to The Met.

The attractive blonde—Christa, Chrissy?—behind the admission desk smiled and waved. He'd given her a ride home after
CaMu's Art of Masquerade Ball last fall. She'd dressed as Ki-
zette from the Deco painting by de Lempicka, short pleated
skirt, knee socks, and little girl shoes. Amazing legs, long,
slender, strong as a vise. He smiled and waved back.

The museum required all visitors be wanded before entering
the exhibition floors. Del stepped into the shortest security line
to wait his turn. Although CaMu stood virtually unchanged
since it opened its doors more than a century ago, each passing
year its marble columns, crystal chandeliers, and grand staircase
seemed to grow more imposing. Having triumphed over two
major earthquakes with Beaux-Arts splendor intact, the
museum had earned its status as a San Francisco legend, and
legend eclipsed reality every time.

The security supervisor caught Del's eye and gestured him forward. "How ya doin', Del? Don't see much of you anymore. Here to visit your mother?"

"Less social call, more summons. Place is a friggin' zoo, Amos."

"Opening day of the Post-Impressionists, hottest ticket in town." Amos surveyed the crowd and rubbed a hand over his forehead as if massaging out the wrinkles. "Lucky us," he said under his breath.

"What's with the lines? Thought this exhibit sold out months ago."

"Advance ticket holders waiting their turn. Fire marshal will only allow so many art lovers into our quaint little establishment at one time."

"Good to hear Van Gogh and Gauguin can still draw a crowd."

"Nah, those guys are second string. These folks are here to admire your parents' Cézanne—that's their reward for running the gauntlet."

A security guard checking backpacks at the end of the line caught Del's eye, then looked away. She was cute, dark haired and doe-eyed. When she glanced up, Del winked, then struggled to refocus his attention on Amos. "The gauntlet?"

The man slapped Del on the shoulder. "New hire. Pretty little thing, isn't she? What was I sayin'? Yeah, yeah, the gauntlet. First we make 'em stand in line at the door, then at security, then on the exhibition floor. I don't even want to talk about the wait for elevators and the john."

Del stepped forward to allow a woman with a squalling toddler in tow to pass behind him. He watched the pair walk away. "Poor little guy. Why would anyone expose a two-year-old to this? Can't blame the kid for crying, I might join him."

Amos laughed. "I remember your mama bringing you in here

when you were that age. You always looked like someone just stole your favorite toy. Fess up, what was it like growing up around a gen-u-ine Cézanne? My mama's house, all we had was a picture of Jesus and a poster of dogs dressed in tutus."

Del released a breath. He could take or leave the Cézanne, but the shitload of family baggage that went along with it made him nuts, memories so overused they felt more myth than reality. "Between you and me, Amos? I'd rather have had the dogs." He forced a smile. "You need to wand me?"

"Depends. You packing, Mr. fancy-schmancy security consultant, or did the SFPD take away your carry permit when you ditched their sorry asses?"

"Nothing on me, although a weapon might make it easier to move through this mob."

Amos smiled and jerked his thumb over his shoulder. "Go."

Del pressed through the crush to the bank of elevators beyond the lobby. After ignoring the first four jammed cars, he forced his way onto number five. The elevator reeked of stale perfume, sweat, and accumulated halitosis. He fixed his spine along the rear wall and held his breath. This juxtaposition of fine art and teeming humanity was a dozen kinds of wrong. Art should be passion, a marvel of the human heart and soul. When had it become a substitute for mass entertainment?

The last of the museum visitors emptied off on the fifth floor, and Del surrendered his frustration to worry as he rode alone to the administrative offices. His mother's earlier phone call planted a tiny seed of dread that had taken root. Her words carried an uncharacteristic panic, and her refusal to discuss whatever was bothering her over the phone only added to his unease.

The elevator doors slid open onto a long, narrow reception corridor with a desk at one end and a set of enormous double doors at the other. The incongruous blend of plush carpet, stark walls, intricate Beaux-Arts woodwork, and minimalist furniture promised nothing if not ascetic indulgence.

The guy behind the front desk nodded. "May I help you?"

Del struggled to hide his surprise. What happened to the cute redhead with the amazing tits? This joker needed a barber. "I'm Del Miller, here for Hanna Rosen Miller. Can you buzz me into the offices?"

"She'll have to escort you back." He paused, then added, his voice apologetic, "The director told me not to let anyone back without an escort."

"No problem. You can ring her in the docent office. She's expecting me."

The phone console chirped. The receptionist held up a finger and answered the line.

Del plucked a membership brochure from the display and settled into a chair to wait.

"There you are, Mendel. What took you so long?"

Del winced and glanced up. How two people as intelligent and caring as his parents could come up with a name like Mendel boggled the mind. He stood to meet his mother's smile and intense silver gaze. Tall and striking in a dark tailored suit, no one could argue that Hanna Miller had presence, but her smile was what people remembered—warm and generous, just like the woman herself.

"Got here as fast as traffic allowed." Del kissed her cheek, noticing the grooves etched between her brows and around her mouth, the dark smudges of fatigue under her eyes. She looked old. He'd never thought of her as old before, and a tiny fear slid through him. His mother was mortal. "What's so urgent?"

She flashed him an inscrutable warning glance and nodded to the receptionist. "I'm glad to see you back at the front desk, Carter. You had us all worried."

"I'm fine now, thanks. Asthma attack. Guess I just need to be more careful what I inhale." He chuckled.

Hanna smiled. "Carter, this is my son, Mendel."

The receptionist removed his headset and pushed a lock of blond hair away from his pockmarked face. A scar ran along his jaw, and a row of piercings fringed his right ear. He nodded. "Nice to meet you."

"You too. *Please,* call me Del."

Del's mother put a hand on his back. "Let's walk down to special exhibits. I want to show you something. We can take the back stairs." She leaned over the reception desk. "Page me as soon as Director London is in the building. It's important."

She hooked an arm through Del's and guided him along the corridor to the locked stairwell, ran her key card through the reader, and opened the door. Gone were the lavish carpet and pristine walls. In their place, cinder block, concrete, and the sharp tang of disinfectant.

Del stopped her at the foot of the stairs. "Are you going to tell me what this is about?"

She cocked her head to one side and narrowed her eyes, lips turned up at the corners. "When you were little, I tried to teach you patience. I'm convinced it's an inherited trait. You acquired yours—or more accurately, your lack of—from you father."

He grinned and squeezed her arm. "So you've mentioned several thousand times. You look tired, Mom. I'm concerned. Sue me."

They exited the stairwell on the fourth floor and shouldered their way to a small cordoned alcove. A half-dozen museum visitors crowded into the niche and several score more lined up behind the stanchions waiting to view the Cézanne.

Hanna signaled to the security guard. "Can you help me close off this area after the patrons exit?"

"What do I do about the line?" the guard asked.

Hanna nodded. "I'll take care of it."

She turned and addressed the waiting queue. "Ladies and gentlemen, my apologies, I'm afraid we need to close this portion of the exhibit for a short time."

A collective groan erupted from the crowd.

"It will be for no more than ten minutes, I promise. You will all have an opportunity to view the Cézanne."

She put her arm around the shoulders of an elderly woman and guided her to a bench to wait while Del helped move the stanchions and cordon off the area. The sooner they had the space secured, the sooner he'd find out what was going on.

With the alcove emptied, his mother guided him to the Cézanne. "What do you see?" she asked, her voice just above a whisper.

"Mom—"

"Dammit, tell me what you see."

His mother never swore, and apprehension eddied around him like toxic gas; something was very wrong. "A still life by Paul Cézanne. The painting that's hung in Dad's study for as long as I can remember."

"No, what you see is a forgery. A brilliant forgery, but a forgery nonetheless."

He studied her. *She was sixty. Could she go senile at sixty?* "I don't understand—"

"That Cézanne is your legacy, your father's legacy. The painting was with him when he was smuggled out of France during the war. Your grandfather sacrificed his life—"

"Stop." Del blew out a breath. "I know Grandfather died in a concentration camp." He kept his eyes on her, searching for some sign she was unwell, but her face shone with its usual clear intelligence.

"Listen to what I am telling you. The painting that left your father's study was the Cézanne. The work was authenticated. I watched the canvas crated for delivery to the museum. This is not the same painting."

Her words landed like a body blow. "Have you notified the police? The FBI?"

"Shh, keep your voice down." She peered over her shoulder at the crowd standing near the stanchions. "No one's been notified."

Del pulled his cell from his jacket pocket.

She blinked hard. "What are you doing?"

"I'm calling the FBI."

She took the phone from his hands. "You can't. If CaMu's internal security is called into question, no other institution will agree to lend us art, individual donors will withdraw, the endowment will wither and die. It could ruin the museum. I love CaMu too much to stand by and watch it destroyed."

"Mom, ninety percent of all museum thefts are inside jobs. The FBI will interview every employee, every trustee, every volunteer."

"The museum runs full background checks on staff. Its holdings are under constant scrutiny. We've never had a theft here."

"Before now, you mean."

"Only a fraction of the collection is on display. Why would someone inside risk taking the Cézanne when there are so many valuable lesser-known pieces that would be far easier to sell? It doesn't make sense."

"It does if whoever took the painting already had a buyer lined up. Someone replaced the Cézanne with a copy, *a brilliant forgery,* you said. This wasn't a smash and grab, it was planned. The thief had to have access." Del pinched the bridge of his nose trying to suppress a burgeoning headache. Why were they even discussing this? "I know a local Fed who works with the Bureau's Art Crime Team—"

"Mendel, I called you because I want *you* to find who's responsible. You were a detective. Detect."

CHAPTER 2

It took a beat before her words registered. Del couldn't hold back a laugh. "I was a homicide detective, Mom. I don't know anything about art crime. I understand you want to protect CaMu, but the Cézanne is not only a family legacy, it's a cultural treasure. If someone is replacing art with forgeries"—he dropped his voice, trying to ignore the growing number of onlookers—"how can you be sure none of the other paintings brought in for this exhibit weren't *exchanged*?"

"Because someone had to produce the forgery. As soon as the Post-Impressionist exhibit was on the museum's calendar, there was no question we would lend the Cézanne, no question the painting would be the highlight. Your father and I were scheduled to be in Paris when the exhibit was mounted, so CaMu took possession of the Cézanne several weeks in advance and held the painting in secured storage, allowing ample opportunity to make the switch. Every other piece of art brought in for this exhibit was logged and unpacked in front of cameras, then delivered directly to the exhibition floor." Sadness rippled across her face.

His mother had always been fueled by an unbreakable resolve to see only good in the people around her. He loved her for that. "I know you want to believe no one associated with the museum had a role in this," he said gently, "but explain to me what about the scenario you just described suggests the disappearance could be anything other than an inside job? And how can you be sure there haven't been other thefts? Lesser pieces from the museum's own collection you haven't discovered yet?"

"The museum will take care of authenticating the collection. Help us locate the Cézanne, Mendel. Do it for your father. That painting is his heart and soul." She drew in a long shaky breath. Del touched her cheek, and she covered his hand with hers and held it there.

"Who else knows about this?"

"I haven't told anyone. That's why I asked Carter to page me. Thurman needs to be briefed as soon as possible, told you're looking into it. You know how highly he thinks of you."

Del knew no such thing. He took his mother's hands in his. "Mom, there is no way I can investigate an art theft. How did you talk Dad into going along with this?"

She lowered her head, eyes downcast. "Your father doesn't know."

Del stared at her, disbelieving. "For God's sake, why haven't you told Dad?"

"*Please* keep your voice down." Her eyes flicked to the sea of waiting faces. "Let's find somewhere less public to talk."

She signaled the guard to reopen the viewing area, and Del followed her back to the stairwell, down three flights to the entrance level. She slid her key card through the reader and led him out to the large cement loading dock. The delivery bay along the back wall was empty and its metal roll-up door closed. Adjacent to the bay was a glassed-in security cage, beside it, the staff exit. Hanna and the security guard in the booth exchanged waves.

Near the cage, a rangy guy, thirtyish, with bleached hair and cheekbones sharp enough to cut glass, sat bent over a cluttered desk. He looked up and a grin broke across his face. "Help you with something, Hani?"

Even the dock operator called her by her nickname. Del smiled.

"Walt, this is my son, Mendel. He'll be doing some security work for the museum."

Del gave his mother a sharp glance. He had no intention of doing anything for CaMu.

"Walt is our loading dock operator. He can tell you everything there is to know about shipments into and out of the museum," she said.

The man peeled off a leather work glove and extended his hand for Del to shake. "Not much to tell. This is the loading dock. It is, as they say, where the magic happens."

Del chuckled, then realized the man wasn't smiling.

Walt scratched his jaw with an index finger. "Museum loading docks differ from your standard dock in that the bays are large enough to enclose the delivery vehicle. This isn't Walmart. You can't have the truck cab hanging out the front while you're unloading the Mona Lisa. Mona doesn't travel, of course, but you get the picture." He grinned. "No pun intended."

"So the vehicle is completely secured within the building?" Del asked.

"You got it. Every piece of art that comes in is protected. This outer section of the dock stays sealed until every item on the bill of lading is confirmed and logged in the uncrating area."

Del surveyed the dock. "Where do you uncrate?"

"Behind that door there." Walt pointed to a large seamed steel panel at the back of the dock. "We receive a delivery, the door rolls open, and someone from Exhibitions comes up from the basement to confirm receipt, unpack, and examine the art before it enters the museum. Once everything is checked in, checked out, and secured, the roll-up door comes down, the exterior door goes up, and the freight truck is allowed to leave. This all happens on camera."

"The art stays on the dock?" Del asked.

"Hell, no." A pink flush crept into the man's honed cheeks.

"Pardon my French. I deliver the art to its designated location, sometimes to the exhibit floor, sometimes to storage or conservation. That's what the freight elevator is for." He gestured to where several empty wheeled carts waited outside the elevator's massive iron grill.

"What about trash pickup and deliveries to the café and store?"

"This dock is only for art. There's a half-bay for the mail van and other non-art deliveries near the café. As for security, there's a guard in the booth twenty-four/seven. That glass is bullet proof. Most of the staff thinks the cage is there to keep an eye on their comings and goings, but it's really security for art shipments. At least that's what they tell me." A flicker of a smile played on Walt's lips.

An old bicycle, half red paint, half rust, sporting Cadillac fins over the back wheel, leaned against the wall near the staff exit. Walt noticed Del's stare and said, "Doesn't look like much but it gets me here, gets me home, and you can't beat the gas mileage."

Del's mother pulled the pager from her pocket, looked at the screen, then at Del. "Let's go. Thurman is in his office."

A collision of clean lines and absence of color, Dr. Thurman London's office mimicked an exhibition space with a desk in the middle. CaMu's director smiled and crossed the room, hand extended. "Good to see you, Del. Been far too long."

"You look well, sir." It wasn't total bullshit. London, a tall, silver-haired, hawk-featured man in his mid-sixties, did look well; in fact, energy rolled off the old fart in waves.

Hanna squared her shoulders. "Thurman, sit down. We have a serious problem."

"Well, Hani, if you're in charge of finding the solution, I doubt any of us need to worry." London flashed a mouthful of capped teeth.

With a vague sense of satisfaction, Del watched the director's bronze skin blanch to the color of spring slush as he learned about the missing Cézanne.

"You're absolutely certain the painting is a forgery? We must be discreet, of course, but we can call in an expert to confirm," London said.

Hanna bristled. "I am an expert, Thurman. I'm a docent, an artist, and I've admired that Cézanne every day for more than forty years. I'm familiar with every brushstroke, every plane of color, every nuance of line and composition. This morning I examined the painting on the exhibition floor and noticed the hesitation in the stroke, the absent *sweep of freedom*. That's when I checked the provenance markings. Make no mistake, we are talking about a superb copy, but it is not the Cézanne." She closed her eyes. "When I think of Samuel, my heart aches. He cherished that painting."

"Is there a way to determine when the substitution took place?" London asked, his tone brisk.

Hanna shook her head. "Sometime after the painting left Samuel's study and before it arrived on the exhibition floor. I saw no evidence the canvas was cut from the frame. It was simply replaced. It's possible the Cézanne never reached the museum. I've asked Mendel to investigate."

"And I explained that I know nothing about recovering stolen art. It's critical you turn this over to the FBI," Del said, fighting to keep his voice even.

The director leaned across his desktop. "I agree with your mother. Making this public could devastate the museum, bring the provenance of every piece of art into question. This institution is dependent on public support predicated on trust. Should word get out, the damage to CaMu's reputation would be irreparable.

"Take the recent Paris MOMA theft. Five canvases, one hundred million Euros in art gone, museum staff left looking like a clutch of bumbling idiots. Can you imagine the fallout if the media were to discover a painting borrowed by CaMu was replaced in situ with a copy? Beyond shattering public confidence, the endowment would never recover."

"MOMA admitted their security system failed," Del said. "That's not the case here. Someone inside CaMu has to be involved. And with all due respect, Dr. London, what do you think the *fallout* will be if the media gets hold of this story and discovers the museum took no action?"

"A private investigation *is* action. I have every confidence you can track down who's behind the theft. Once you identify the perpetrator or perpetrators, if necessary, we'll call in the FBI to handle recovery of the painting."

His jaw clenching against a rising tide of frustration, Del said, "That's not the way it works. The Cézanne is priceless."

London laughed, clearly amused. "Hani, I believe we've just been dressed down by a police officer for not knowing the value of a Cézanne still life."

Condescending dick. Del felt his anger as hard and sharp as splintered bone. "I am no longer with the SFPD, and this is about more than CaMu's reputation. That painting is a part of my family's history."

His mother flinched as if he'd struck her. "Thurman is aware of that, Mendel."

The director folded his hands in front of him on the desk. "I apologize, Del. I didn't intend to patronize. I'm aware you've been around museums all your life. You're no doubt better versed in art than many of my staff. Hani, what does Samuel say? Does he agree this should be handled privately?"

She let out a small, pained rush of air. "Samuel knows nothing about this, and that's the way I intend to keep it."

"Dad deserves to know," Del said, his fingers curling into fists, the nails biting into his palms.

"It will break his heart. I can't bear that."

Del stood, braced his hands on the edge of London's desk, and leaned toward the director. "Where are your art experts? Curatorial staff? Exhibitions people? Why is my mother the only one who noticed the star of your lauded Post-Impressionist exhibit is a fake? If the freight company was involved, wouldn't someone on staff have picked up on missing provenance markings?"

London's voice was tight, his words measured. "Yes, of course. But for good or ill, there is an assumption the art is genuine. When we check in a work, we're primarily concerned with the condition of the piece, confirming no damage in transit. What do you need to begin your investigation? When can you start?"

Del shook his head. "You aren't hearing me. I'll do what I can, but you have to bring in the FBI."

London's eyes locked on Del's. "You realize if we involve the FBI, their initial line of investigation will be your mother and father? The Feds will assume insurance fraud. To someone who doesn't know your parents, the story of the painting leaving their home as an original Cézanne and reappearing on the exhibition floor as a fake is suspect at best. Especially given your mother's ties to this institution. Keep in mind, a lesser Cézanne still life sold at auction for sixty million dollars ten years ago. In today's market, the painting is, as you say, priceless."

"Mendel, please," his mother whispered, her face twisted with misery.

Del studied her. The light gone from her eyes, she appeared unimaginably fragile. He reached for her hand. "The FBI will investigate anyone who has had access to the painting. They'll find who's responsible."

Her voice trembled. "If the FBI looks to your father and me first, it could cost valuable time. Possibly even alert whoever *is* responsible. Investigate the theft, Mendel. Two days, that's all I ask. Follow the path of the painting. Please."

"Under what pretext, Mom? You think my running around grilling museum staff isn't going to raise antennae?"

"You're a security expert, aren't you?" London asked with undisguised contempt. "I'll announce you've been hired as a consultant to revamp the museum's system. I'll make certain you're given access to records and to all secured areas."

"Won't your chief of security wonder why he wasn't brought in on this surprise overhaul?"

"Ray's on medical leave—surgery. He won't be back for at least two weeks."

"Dr. London, I understand your position—I do—but it's impossible. I have a contact at the FBI who works major theft. His name is Neil Sobol."

Del's mother's fingers tensed in his. "Sobol? He's Jewish?"

Del stared at her hard. "Why would you—?"

She bowed her head. "I thought if he were Jewish, he might understand the insurance money means nothing. That painting is all your father has left of his family."

Del released her hand, turning his attention to London. "I'll contact the FBI on your behalf. You'll need to alert the museum's attorneys. Bottom line, you're perpetrating a fraud."

"Now wait just one minute—" London said, rising from his chair to face Del, his voice taking on a dangerous edge.

Del ignored him. "Patrons paid to see a Cézanne. You know the painting is a fake. Find out the legal ramifications. Your attorney will likely advise you to pull the forgery from the exhibit."

"We can't. The press, patrons, they'll all want to know why." London picked up a special exhibit brochure from his desk and tossed the flyer at Del. A close-up of the Cézanne graced the cover.

Del studied the familiar tapestry-draped table, the open book, the tipped basket of overripe pomegranates and oranges, the striking pyramid of skulls gracing the milk-glass *compotier.*

His mother touched his arm. "Mike Gabretti's firm represents the museum."

Great, Mike. Exactly the guy they didn't need in the middle of this mess. Del said to London, "I'll call Neil Sobol, you call Mike. Make it clear to Mike he's permitted to talk to me."

"I thought you two were friends," London said.

"Mike takes client privilege seriously, and I don't want to be stonewalled."

London heaved a sigh of resignation. "Agreed."

"And Mom?" Del said, keeping his voice soft. "Tell Dad about the painting. If you don't, I will."

CHAPTER 3

Paint and synthetic. The air was caustic with the smell of new office. Elbows resting on his desk, Del held his palms against his eyes to ease the burning. Brand-new office, brand-new job, same old Del—sounded like a punch line. Guess that made him the joke.

The Cézanne gone; he couldn't believe it. His mom was right, the money didn't matter, but then neither did CaMu's reputation. This was about family, about his father.

He blew out a breath and skated his finger across the letter in front of him, then folded the sheet in thirds and slid the page back into its embossed envelope. Guardian Piedmont Global LTD. A job offer out of the blue, the last thing he expected. Less than three months ago he'd quit the force and turned security consultant. He didn't know if he was ready to throw it all away for another job, another life, on the other side of the country. He turned in his chair and stared out the window. A layer of fog as thick and hoary as sheep's wool blanketed the landscape, the Golden Gate rising from the murk like some furtive dragon. San Francisco was in his blood, as much a part of him as an arm or a leg.

A sharp rap sounded on the half-open door. Mike Gabretti stuck his head into the office. "I'm here to talk to a man about a painting." He pushed open the door and not so much walked as strutted into the room, decked out in the same designer shit he'd been wearing since he passed the bar. "Reeks in here. New paint or did someone die?"

Del put his hand over his heart. "Ouch, I'm wounded. Let me guess. You had a word with Dr. London?"

"Many words. Had more pleasant words with your charming mother. I even had a chat with your stand-up FBI buddy, who, if I'm right—and I always am—suspects your parents may be hinky." Mike gazed up at the ceiling and shook his head. "Hope Samuel and Hani never cheated on their taxes, because Special Agent Snowball is a bulldog."

"Sobol's only doing his job. You were a prosecutor. You remember how things work. Everyone's a suspect."

"What happened to the presumption of innocence?"

Del snorted. "Don't ask me. I was a cop. Different rule book. We leave it to you lawyers to sort that muck out." Del pointed to the chair across from his desk. "Take a load off. Did you tell London to pull the painting from the exhibit?"

"Not yet. Mr. G-man wants to keep things quiet until he double-checks backgrounds. Thinks it will be easier to figure out who's had their hand in the CaMu cookie jar if staff aren't on the alert. Who would be stupid enough to try and sell a fucking Cézanne still life? Talk about your white elephant."

"Not if whoever took the painting already had a buyer lined up."

"You've been watching too many old movies, bro. I guarantee the painting was not stolen to"—Mike stiffened his upper lip and affected a British accent— "*assuage the compulsive obsessions of a wealthy private collector.*"

He reached over, grabbed the stress reliever ball from Del's desk, and worked the foam rubber with his left hand. "More likely it'll be used to finance drugs, terrorist activities, or both. If your Fed pal doesn't come up with a solid lead within twenty-four hours, he'll set up a tip line and take the story to the media. London about peed himself when he heard. Fun to watch."

hell missed his partner. Twenty years on the force, shot twice, d she dies of fucking cancer. So much for justice. "I take it u and Sophie haven't spoken?"

"Alexa isn't keen on my maintaining a close relationship with y ex." Mike paused, then added, "And Sophie made it clear e'd prefer I keep my distance."

There it was. "Thought you worked things out. What happened to all that forgiveness shit?"

"Forgiveness is one thing. Forgetting is a whole other story. I heated, and that, my friend, is that. Now, with Amy—" He hook his head and gave a caustic laugh. "Talk about a catchwenty-two. If I leave Alexa, Sophie would look at it as more roof I can't be trusted. She'd never take me back."

Del's stomach did an unpleasant flip.

A hard edge crept into Mike's voice. "Why haven't *you* seen er? I thought you and she were tight."

Del shrugged. "I told her to call if she needed anything. She never called."

"So what exactly does she *need* tonight?"

"She asked me to dinner. She wants to catch up."

"Catch up, my shiny white ass."

Del stood. "Drop it, okay? How about you shifting your *shiny white ass* toward the door? It's getting late and these fumes are killing me. Let's get out of here while I can still see to drive." He grabbed his jacket and shoved Mike toward the office door.

"Let me know how your date goes."

"It's not a date, and it's none of your business."

The Bay Bridge was closed again. He'd have to take the long way around, over the Golden Gate, up through Marin and across the Richmond–San Rafael Bridge into the East Bay—all during rush hour. Del glanced at his watch, then down at his

Mike leaned back in his chair, stretching out his legs. "I totally get your mother's misguided attempts to protect the museum, but any guess as to why London would object to the theft being made public? He was so busy being indignant. I didn't want to interrupt him to ask. Frankly, when this breaks, the story is going to mean major media attention. Tourists will be flocking to CaMu in even bigger droves for years to come."

"According to London, 'the scandal will reflect badly on the museum.' "

"And according to P.T. Barnum, 'All publicity is good publicity.' Nope, something else is tweaking the director's tits."

"Did my mother mention she and London wanted me to investigate privately?"

"Yeah, well, your mom's upset. She's worried about the Cézanne. She's worried about CaMu. Mostly, she's worried about breaking the news to your old man. She told me Samuel wasn't happy about lending the painting in the first place."

"Then why the hell didn't she listen to him?"

Mike rolled his eyes. "Do you always have to be such a prick?"

"Pisses me off. Dad should have been the first one she told."

"Instead, she told you. Maybe she was looking for an ally. Did you ever think of that, genius?"

Del pressed thumb and forefinger to the corners of his eyes, remembering the anguish on his mom's face, and his heart clutched. He blinked at Mike. "Okay, so I am a prick."

Mike smiled like a kid who'd just gotten what he wanted for Christmas. "Love it when we agree. On the upside, you're flush whether the painting comes back or the insurance pays." His gaze slid around the office. "Leaves you free to try your hand at the crap job of your choice. You've done cop and consultant. What next, mall security guard?"

Del wasn't up to talking about the letter from Guardian Piedmont, not with Mike, not yet. "That painting means a lot to my dad."

Mike's smile faded. "I'm aware of that. Means a lot to you, too, whether or not you want to admit it."

Del's eyes broke away from Mike's and he held up his hands. "Not my problem. The case is in the capable hands of the Federal Bureau of Investigation."

"Special Agent No-Balls to the rescue."

"Really, Mikey, Sobol is a stand-up guy."

"Whatever." Mike brightened. "Fuck Cézanne. Let's talk real art. How'd you like to feast your eyes on the most beautiful girl in the world wet and naked? Got photos, and they're hot, I promise you."

Del raised a brow. "Bring 'em on."

Mike pulled a cell from his pocket and passed the phone across the desk. Del focused on the tiny screen. Amy Rebekah Gabretti was indeed naked and beautiful, all nine pounds of her.

"Took them this morning. Can you believe she's two months old already? Time flies when you're a parent."

"Right. Only seventeen years, ten months, and she'll be out of the house. You're practically an empty nester."

Del scrolled through the photographs. Although her head was cut off in every shot, he recognized Mike's wife, Alexa's, long slender hands bathing the baby. Even at two months, little Amy had a smile for the camera, or at least for her photographer. "You're right, she is the most beautiful girl in the world."

"She's getting her bath," Mike said, with a lopsided grin.

He looked so damned goofy, Del laughed. "Yeah, I figured that out."

"God, I love her." Mike said, taking the phone from Del. "She is so much more than I deserve. I'm not going to fuck this up, Delbo. Swear I'm going to be a good dad."

Mike stared at the tiny screen, then slipped the cell back in

his pocket. "I realize this is last minute, but A   as
wondered if you could come to dinner tonight. Wipe   an
horror off your face. She isn't cooking, we'll order   yo
play with the baby. For reasons I can't fathom, An
about you."

"I have a way with women," Del said. Or at least   sl
women, with the exception of the second Mrs. Gabr
who never missed an opportunity to show Del how   p
resented the time he spent with her husband. "Alexa
there?"

"It was her idea. Says she needs some adult comp   s
you're the chosen one. She won't invite any of *her* frie   t
Don't think she trusts me around other women."   p

Mike laughed as if it were a joke, but Del was pretty
friend had hit close to the mark. "I would, but I alre
plans. Thanks for the offer, though, and thank Alexa fo

"Bring your date along. You can take her home and
after we eat."

Heat rose up from Del's collar. Showing up for a
party with the host's ex-wife on your arm was a br
etiquette even in open-minded San Francisco. "M
awkward. Sophie invited me over."

Mike tilted his head and studied Del. "So, how is o
Sophie?"

And they were off and running. Del blew out a long
This was a perfect example of why men didn't discuss an
personal. Male friendship was about moving through li
by side, private lives never intersecting, a tacit agreement
to talk things out.

"I don't know how she is. I haven't seen her since E
funeral. She sounded fine over the phone." The menti
Barb brought an unexpected lump to his throat. He lo
away and swallowed. Didn't much miss being a cop, but he

jacket, khakis, button-down, and loafers. There wasn't time to change.

He grabbed a hand full of Tic-Tacs out of the glove compartment and shoved them in his mouth. Sophie would have to take him as he was.

Fog still hugged the city, and traffic was even slower than usual. It wasn't until he exited I-580 to the parkway that he remembered the bottle of Sophie's favorite pinot gris left behind at the loft. He'd thought he'd have time to run home before dinner. Horns blaring, he cut across three lanes of traffic, pulled into the parking lot of a convenience store, and ran inside to buy more wine.

Five minutes later, he pulled through the Promontory Pointe gate and parked in front of Sophie's house, a shoebox of a place that backed up to Richmond's Marina Bay. The neighborhood was quiet and peaceful; the only sounds the soft whistling of the wind off the bay and the distant whoosh of BART.

Del rang the bell, the door opened, and there she was, cat in her arms, dog by her side. Barefoot, she wore a short white dress, her russet curls tied with a green ribbon halfway down her back. Not a single one of his fantasies stood up to the real thing. She was exquisite.

When she smiled, the oxygen disappeared from the air and his voice along with it. "Hi. Late. Traffic." *Smooth, Miller, very smooth.*

"Hi, you. It's been too long. Thank you for coming." She put the cat down and stepped forward to wrap her arms around him. She was five foot nothing, and the embrace was around his waist.

Holding the bottle of rosé behind her back, he returned the hug, feeling her soft curves and delicate frame beneath the silk, smelling her light spicy scent. What would she do if he refused to let her go?

She stepped back and held the door open wide. "That for us?" She pointed to the wine.

"Yeah. Maybe. Probably not. It's only a rosé. Chilled. It was all they had. I meant to ask what you were serving." He handed her the bottle to shut himself up.

She glanced down at the dog and cat. "You two go upstairs. I don't want you underfoot." Then to Del, "Tenderloin in bourbon sauce, which I hope is still one of your favorites? I trust you haven't gone vegan on me?"

"No, sounds great. Smells terrific."

"You want a glass of wine? I can open this now," she said, holding up the bottle, "or there's some of the Lagavulin scotch you and Michael like so much."

Somewhere between the car and the house his throat had gone as dry as chalk. "Water would be perfect."

"Water I can do. Hang up your jacket and have a seat. I'll be right back with the H2O. You okay? You look a little, um . . . frayed?"

Del had already spent too much of the day talking about the Cézanne. "Fine. Crazy afternoon."

She nodded. He watched her pad into the kitchen, unable to pull his eyes away from the fabric hugging her small, perfect ass. When he saw the scar, guilt burned through him like acid. The mark ran to mid-thigh, a thick pink seam that bisected the perfect flesh and pulled and puckered the skin. A souvenir of her run-in with a madman that had left her shattered and peeled raw, an encounter Del should have prevented.

She returned armed with a tray, two glasses of ice, and a large bottle of Pellegrino. "Could you hold this for a minute?" She handed the tray to Del and scooped up the tarot cards spread across the glass coffee table.

"I thought the tarot business was too much to handle with teaching and your dissertation."

Mike leaned back in his chair, stretching out his legs. "I totally get your mother's misguided attempts to protect the museum, but any guess as to why London would object to the theft being made public? He was so busy being indignant. I didn't want to interrupt him to ask. Frankly, when this breaks, the story is going to mean major media attention. Tourists will be flocking to CaMu in even bigger droves for years to come."

"According to London, 'the scandal will reflect badly on the museum.' "

"And according to P.T. Barnum, 'All publicity is good publicity.' Nope, something else is tweaking the director's tits."

"Did my mother mention she and London wanted me to investigate privately?"

"Yeah, well, your mom's upset. She's worried about the Cézanne. She's worried about CaMu. Mostly, she's worried about breaking the news to your old man. She told me Samuel wasn't happy about lending the painting in the first place."

"Then why the hell didn't she listen to him?"

Mike rolled his eyes. "Do you always have to be such a prick?"

"Pisses me off. Dad should have been the first one she told."

"Instead, she told you. Maybe she was looking for an ally. Did you ever think of that, genius?"

Del pressed thumb and forefinger to the corners of his eyes, remembering the anguish on his mom's face, and his heart clutched. He blinked at Mike. "Okay, so I am a prick."

Mike smiled like a kid who'd just gotten what he wanted for Christmas. "Love it when we agree. On the upside, you're flush whether the painting comes back or the insurance pays." His gaze slid around the office. "Leaves you free to try your hand at the crap job of your choice. You've done cop and consultant. What next, mall security guard?"

Del wasn't up to talking about the letter from Guardian Piedmont, not with Mike, not yet. "That painting means a lot to my dad."

Mike's smile faded. "I'm aware of that. Means a lot to you, too, whether or not you want to admit it."

Del's eyes broke away from Mike's and he held up his hands. "Not my problem. The case is in the capable hands of the Federal Bureau of Investigation."

"Special Agent No-Balls to the rescue."

"Really, Mikey, Sobol is a stand-up guy."

"Whatever." Mike brightened. "Fuck Cézanne. Let's talk real art. How'd you like to feast your eyes on the most beautiful girl in the world wet and naked? Got photos, and they're hot, I promise you."

Del raised a brow. "Bring 'em on."

Mike pulled a cell from his pocket and passed the phone across the desk. Del focused on the tiny screen. Amy Rebekah Gabretti was indeed naked and beautiful, all nine pounds of her.

"Took them this morning. Can you believe she's two months old already? Time flies when you're a parent."

"Right. Only seventeen years, ten months, and she'll be out of the house. You're practically an empty nester."

Del scrolled through the photographs. Although her head was cut off in every shot, he recognized Mike's wife, Alexa's, long slender hands bathing the baby. Even at two months, little Amy had a smile for the camera, or at least for her photographer. "You're right, she is the most beautiful girl in the world."

"She's getting her bath," Mike said, with a lopsided grin.

He looked so damned goofy, Del laughed. "Yeah, I figured that out."

"God, I love her." Mike said, taking the phone from Del. "She is so much more than I deserve. I'm not going to fuck this up, Delbo. Swear I'm going to be a good dad."

Mike stared at the tiny screen, then slipped the cell back in his pocket. "I realize this is last minute, but Alexa and I wondered if you could come to dinner tonight. Wipe the look of horror off your face. She isn't cooking, we'll order in. You can play with the baby. For reasons I can't fathom, Amy is crazy about you."

"I have a way with women," Del said. Or at least with most women, with the exception of the second Mrs. Gabretti, Alexa, who never missed an opportunity to show Del how much she resented the time he spent with her husband. "Alexa wants me there?"

"It was her idea. Says she needs some adult company, and you're the chosen one. She won't invite any of *her* friends over. Don't think she trusts me around other women."

Mike laughed as if it were a joke, but Del was pretty sure his friend had hit close to the mark. "I would, but I already have plans. Thanks for the offer, though, and thank Alexa for me."

"Bring your date along. You can take her home and nail her after we eat."

Heat rose up from Del's collar. Showing up for a dinner party with the host's ex-wife on your arm was a breach of etiquette even in open-minded San Francisco. "Might be awkward. Sophie invited me over."

Mike tilted his head and studied Del. "So, how is *our* little Sophie?"

And they were off and running. Del blew out a long breath. This was a perfect example of why men didn't discuss anything personal. Male friendship was about moving through life side by side, private lives never intersecting, a tacit agreement never to talk things out.

"I don't know how she is. I haven't seen her since Barb's funeral. She sounded fine over the phone." The mention of Barb brought an unexpected lump to his throat. He looked away and swallowed. Didn't much miss being a cop, but he sure

33

as hell missed his partner. Twenty years on the force, shot twice, and she dies of fucking cancer. So much for justice. "I take it you and Sophie haven't spoken?"

"Alexa isn't keen on my maintaining a close relationship with my ex." Mike paused, then added, "And Sophie made it clear she'd prefer I keep my distance."

There it was. "Thought you worked things out. What happened to all that forgiveness shit?"

"Forgiveness is one thing. Forgetting is a whole other story. I cheated, and that, my friend, is that. Now, with Amy—" He shook his head and gave a caustic laugh. "Talk about a catch-twenty-two. If I leave Alexa, Sophie would look at it as more proof I can't be trusted. She'd never take me back."

Del's stomach did an unpleasant flip.

A hard edge crept into Mike's voice. "Why haven't *you* seen her? I thought you and she were tight."

Del shrugged. "I told her to call if she needed anything. She never called."

"So what exactly does she *need* tonight?"

"She asked me to dinner. She wants to catch up."

"Catch up, my shiny white ass."

Del stood. "Drop it, okay? How about you shifting your *shiny white ass* toward the door? It's getting late and these fumes are killing me. Let's get out of here while I can still see to drive." He grabbed his jacket and shoved Mike toward the office door.

"Let me know how your date goes."

"It's not a date, and it's none of your business."

The Bay Bridge was closed again. He'd have to take the long way around, over the Golden Gate, up through Marin and across the Richmond–San Rafael Bridge into the East Bay—all during rush hour. Del glanced at his watch, then down at his jacket, khakis, button-down, and loafers. There wasn't time to change.

He grabbed a hand full of Tic-Tacs out of the glove compartment and shoved them in his mouth. Sophie would have to take him as he was.

Fog still hugged the city, and traffic was even slower than usual. It wasn't until he exited I-580 to the parkway that he remembered the bottle of Sophie's favorite pinot gris left behind at the loft. He'd thought he'd have time to run home before dinner. Horns blaring, he cut across three lanes of traffic, pulled into the parking lot of a convenience store, and ran inside to buy more wine.

Five minutes later, he pulled through the Promontory Pointe gate and parked in front of Sophie's house, a shoebox of a place that backed up to Richmond's Marina Bay. The neighborhood was quiet and peaceful; the only sounds the soft whistling of the wind off the bay and the distant whoosh of BART.

Del rang the bell, the door opened, and there she was, cat in her arms, dog by her side. Barefoot, she wore a short white dress, her russet curls tied with a green ribbon halfway down her back. Not a single one of his fantasies stood up to the real thing. She was exquisite.

When she smiled, the oxygen disappeared from the air and his voice along with it. "Hi. Late. Traffic." *Smooth, Miller, very smooth.*

"Hi, you. It's been too long. Thank you for coming." She put the cat down and stepped forward to wrap her arms around him. She was five foot nothing, and the embrace was around his waist.

Holding the bottle of rosé behind her back, he returned the hug, feeling her soft curves and delicate frame beneath the silk, smelling her light spicy scent. What would she do if he refused to let her go?

She stepped back and held the door open wide. "That for us?" She pointed to the wine.

"Yeah. Maybe. Probably not. It's only a rosé. Chilled. It was all they had. I meant to ask what you were serving." He handed her the bottle to shut himself up.

She glanced down at the dog and cat. "You two go upstairs. I don't want you underfoot." Then to Del, "Tenderloin in bourbon sauce, which I hope is still one of your favorites? I trust you haven't gone vegan on me?"

"No, sounds great. Smells terrific."

"You want a glass of wine? I can open this now," she said, holding up the bottle, "or there's some of the Lagavulin scotch you and Michael like so much."

Somewhere between the car and the house his throat had gone as dry as chalk. "Water would be perfect."

"Water I can do. Hang up your jacket and have a seat. I'll be right back with the H2O. You okay? You look a little, um . . . frayed?"

Del had already spent too much of the day talking about the Cézanne. "Fine. Crazy afternoon."

She nodded. He watched her pad into the kitchen, unable to pull his eyes away from the fabric hugging her small, perfect ass. When he saw the scar, guilt burned through him like acid. The mark ran to mid-thigh, a thick pink seam that bisected the perfect flesh and pulled and puckered the skin. A souvenir of her run-in with a madman that had left her shattered and peeled raw, an encounter Del should have prevented.

She returned armed with a tray, two glasses of ice, and a large bottle of Pellegrino. "Could you hold this for a minute?" She handed the tray to Del and scooped up the tarot cards spread across the glass coffee table.

"I thought the tarot business was too much to handle with teaching and your dissertation."

"Summer. No teaching. The tarot's my only source of income. And if California doesn't figure out its budget issues, teaching opportunities this fall will be slim." Then, under her breath, "Not that they want me back, anyway."

"Sophie, you were a victim. What happened wasn't your fault—"

She held up her hand. "Don't. I don't want to think about any of that right now. Let's just have a nice evening. Like we used to."

She poured the drinks, climbed onto the sofa, and kneeled next to him, her backside resting on her heels.

"So how are you doing?" he asked. "You look amazing." *Stunning, luminous, breathtaking.*

"I'm okay." She set her glass on the coffee table, and held her fists in front of her, unfurling her fingers one by one. She stared, then reached out to Del with both hands as if she were begging. Pale red lines, shiny and fierce, crisscrossed both her palms. Another souvenir. He swallowed, took both her hands, and met her gaze. "I'm sorry."

"Why? It's not your fault," she said quietly. She glanced at her hands again and cleared her throat. "Del, did I do something wrong? Say something?"

"What?" The conversation had changed direction, and he'd apparently missed the turn. "What are you talking about?"

"Why didn't you call after I got out of the hospital? You stopped coming to visit."

He exhaled. "I wasn't sure you . . . You didn't call me either, Sophie. You and Mike had things to work out. I didn't want to get in the way. Not that I could." *Shut up, Miller. Jesus.*

"Michael has a wife and a new baby. I'm no longer part of his life. But even if I were, it wouldn't matter, because you and I are friends, right?" Her eyes searched Del's as if looking for some hidden truth.

He reached for the right thing to say but settled for a nod.

"Michael's mother told me they named the baby in memory of your sister. Is she as beautiful as Peg says?"

"Amy is gorgeous, and Mike is so in love with her. Funny thing is, I don't think anyone is more surprised than he is."

"Michael is a good person, much better than he gives himself credit for." She lowered her head and pressed her lips together. "But I'm preaching to the choir."

He grinned, and for an instant it felt like old times, like he didn't have to be careful with his words. "You should see Mike with Amy, you wouldn't believe it."

She smiled, but tears filled her eyes. She wiped at them with the back of her hand.

He reached out and touched her arm. "I'm sorry. I wasn't thinking." Why the hell couldn't he stop apologizing?

She squeezed his hand. "These are happy tears. A little girl deserves a father—deserves someone—to love her unconditionally." Sophie had grown up with neither a father nor unconditional love.

"How about we try something new and not talk about Mike? Deal?"

"Deal." Her eyes darted away, then came back to rest on his. "I'm glad you're here. I missed you." She leaned in and kissed him quickly on the lips, her mouth soft and yielding, tasting of cinnamon.

"I missed you, too." The words barely scratched the surface of what he felt. She sat so close, he could feel her warmth, see the outline of her nipples beneath the thin fabric of her dress. The desire to fuck her had always been there, shoved on the back burner because of Mike. After her divorce and one disastrous night together, it was clear—to Del at least—Sophie wasn't ready to move on. Tonight the air was electric. She seemed different, and his hopes surged.

She kissed him again. His mind swam. A buzzer went off in the kitchen, and she sat back on her heels.

"I need to check the roast. Come with?" She took his hand and led him into the tiny kitchen.

"Hey, you have a new toy." Del gestured to a flip-down television attached to one of the upper cabinets. The set was on, but the volume was adjusted down. "Since when do you watch TV?"

"I won it in a raffle. Kind of like having a TV in here. Keeps me company. Wouldn't have bought the thing for myself, but it's convenient." She opened the oven and slid the roast back in. "Not quite done. You prefer medium, right? Maybe another fifteen minutes. Are you hungry?"

"Not really." *Not for food.*

She hoisted herself up on the kitchen island and sat facing him. "I think we need to get back to what we were discussing in the living room."

"What exactly are you referring to?" He could still taste her sweetness on his tongue.

Knees spread slightly, she crooked a finger and he pressed closer, kissing the side of her neck, running his finger along her delicate collarbone. "You are so beautiful," he whispered, wondering, even as he said the words, why the truth always sounded like a cliché.

"So are you." She took his face between her palms, looked into his eyes, and kissed him open-mouthed.

He slid his hand between her thighs, his fingers skimming the smooth skin and traveling up. She made a small sound deep in her throat and opened her legs wide, her dress riding up over slender hips. She wore no underwear, and he heard himself moan.

"Come inside me," she said, the words a soft vibration against his ear. "Now." Leaning into him, she reached down, unfastened his slacks and trapped him with her legs.

For a beat, he hesitated, confused and half-drunk with some emotion that went beyond lust. Then he took hold of her bare buttocks and carried her across the room, pressing her back against the wall, her legs locked high around his hips, his pants half-off, her dress rucked around her waist. He thrust inside her, and she gave a tiny cry. Loathsome, really, how much that small sign of pain aroused him. He slammed hard against her slight frame, only half aware of her arms and lips, her nails burrowing into his back, her words. His movements were uncontrolled, and he came too soon, gulping for air, his body spasmed with shudders.

He rested her against the wall and tried to breathe her breath, to kiss her, to apologize, to lie and tell her he wasn't like that. He wanted to make love to her, not fuck her against a goddamn kitchen wall. He'd make it up to her. "Did I hurt you? I'm sorry. I'm—"

"You didn't hurt me." She laid her head on his shoulder, her voice a murmur. "You were perfect. Don't pull out. Stay with me."

He would have stayed forever, but the oven timer went off again, and they both craned their necks toward the stove.

"We have options," he said, still trying to catch his breath. "I can put you down, I can carry you over to the stove, or we can let the meat burn."

She giggled. "The roast is an entire week's food budget. You better put me down."

He lowered her to the floor, his muscles jelly and his cock still hard. She whimpered as he withdrew, semen running down her thighs, both of them shaking and sweaty. She stroked his erection, then tore off a paper towel and pressed the sheet into his hand.

"What a waste," she whispered.

While he cleaned up and tucked himself back into his pants, she smoothed her dress and moved toward the sink to wash.

"Hey, isn't that CaMu?" Sophie pointed at the television. "What's going on?"

He squinted at the minuscule screen. Lit by the strobe of cop cruisers and emergency vehicles, the street clogged with onlookers, the museum looked like Times Square on New Year's Eve. Del moved closer to the TV to get a better look at the familiar figure hunched on the museum's steps. Even amid the lights and chaos, he recognized his mother.

Chapter 4

Mike Gabretti turned onto Shoreline and pulled around the circular driveway to the front of his house. Spending time with Thurman London always put him in a bad mood. Fucking asshole. Masterpiece goes missing and London wants to keep it a secret. Like it wasn't already going to take an act of God to get the underwriters to pony up. Sure, it was possible the FBI might recover the painting. It was also possible fairies might fly out of London's butt and hold a pancake breakfast at the Hall of Justice. Probable? Not so much.

Mike clicked off the ignition and sat, listening to the tick of the cooling engine and contemplating his house. *"Charming Mill Valley vintage home with huge state-of-the-art country kitchen,"* the property listing read. Alexa fell in love with the kitchen, had to have the place. The bitch couldn't even boil water.

He hated this house, hated his wife, hated everything but Amy. Wasn't fair. One wrong turn, one mistake, and you end up paying for the rest of your life. He thought about Sophie and Del together and slammed his palm against the steering wheel.

Alexa stared at him from the front window. Too late to escape. He braced himself for the inevitable argument, climbed out of the car, and headed for the front door.

The house was warm and smelled of yeast, garlic, and cigarette smoke. His anger arced. He'd told Alexa a dozen times he didn't want her smoking around the baby. He hung up his jacket and stepped into the living room. Alexa had vanished.

Then he saw Amy.

"Jesus Christ!" He ran to the sofa and plucked her up in his arms, held her close, swaying back and forth. "Are you okay, sweetheart?"

She cooed at him.

Alexa ran out from the kitchen, panting. "What's the matter? What's wrong?"

"You left the baby alone on the couch, Alexa. She could have rolled off. How stupid are you?"

"Fuck you, Mike. She can't roll over yet. How the hell is she supposed to roll off? And watch how you speak to me. You may have talked to Sophie like that, but I'm not going to put up with it."

He'd never had a reason to speak to Sophie like that. He drew a deep breath. "I'm sorry, okay? Seeing her there scared the shit out of me. Some babies learn to turn over at two months."

"Well, your precious Amy isn't one of them."

"Just don't leave her alone on the sofa, okay? Please?"

"Fine."

Mike studied his wife, her flawless face and corn-silk hair. Poured into a tight, low-cut, sequined dress that barely covered her ass and teetering on five-inch heels, her legs were endless. How could anyone be so sexy and so repulsive at the same time?

"What smells like shit?" he asked. "Jesus, Alexa, do you ever check her diaper?"

"You change her. This dress is brand-new and cost a fortune. When will Del be here?"

"He won't. He had a date. You might want to think ahead next time and not invite him the day of."

"Why didn't you call and let me know? I've been holding dinner for an hour. Did you tell him it was okay to bring someone? I was looking forward to some adult company."

He stared at her. What she was looking forward to was showing off her tits. "Whatever. I'm going to change Amy."

Alexa trailed him upstairs into the nursery. "I ordered enough food for six people."

Mike placed a fresh diaper on the changing table and laid Amy on top, chucking her under the chin.

"Mike, I'm talking to you."

"What? What do you want, Lex? You are talking *at* me. There is a difference."

She let out a frustrated sigh. "Did you tell Del he could bring a date?"

"Yes I told him, but he was having dinner with Sophie, and he thought just maybe things might get awkward."

She smirked. "So that's why you're being such an asshole. You can't stand the thought of someone else fucking your beloved Sophie." She spat out the name as if it were rancid.

Mike unfastened the diaper tabs and held Amy's feet together, lifted her bottom, and cleaned her.

"God, that is so disgusting," Alexa said.

"How would you know?"

"I'm a slave to her all day. You come home for a few hours, change a diaper, and think you're something special. You have no idea what it's like to be trapped with her day in and day out. We need a nanny."

"If you want a nanny, why don't you get a job and pay for one?"

Amy began to mewl. Mike blew on the bottoms of her feet and she blinked at him. He fastened her romper, picked her up, and kissed her cheek.

"I don't want to go back to work, but I don't want to be stuck here all day, every day, either. I need to get out of the house. My mom will be here next weekend. She's already agreed to take care of Amy. Let's go out on the boat, Mike. We'd have such a blast. You promised you'd take me one day, and we've never gone."

"This is Delbo's weekend for the boat."

"I thought you told me he wasn't using it."

"That doesn't mean he isn't planning to."

"Call him and find out."

A four-thousand-square-foot house wasn't big enough. Mike didn't want to think about being trapped on a boat with this woman. "If I see him, I'll ask. By the way, how many times do I have to tell you I don't want you smoking around Amy? This place reeks of cigarettes."

"Any chance you might get off my back for five minutes? All you've done is complain since you walked through the front door. And you didn't say a word about my new dress." She twirled around. "You like?"

He laid Amy in her crib, turned toward Alexa, and looked her up and down. "The sequins are on the skanky side for an evening at home and having to worry about your tits falling into the mashed potatoes will probably upset my digestion." They were great tits, but still.

"Mikey," she said in a baby voice, "do you realize how hard I worked to get my figure back for you?" She stepped toward him and unzipped his slacks, touching him.

He grabbed her wrist and held it while he switched on the baby monitor. Then he dragged her out of the room, closed the door, and pushed her to her knees. Watching his wife take him into her mouth, he studied her perfect face and felt nothing, nothing but the need for release. He closed his eyes. How had he fucked things up so badly?

The phone rang five minutes after they'd finished dinner. Alexa answered, rolled her eyes, and passed the handset to Mike, taking Amy from him. "It's Del. Something about an emergency. Some guy's dead." Her face lit up. "Hey, while you have him on the line, ask if he's going to use the boat next weekend."

CHAPTER 5

Del's fingers slid over the edges of Sophie's TV. "How do you turn this thing up?"

She reached around him and tinkered along the underside of the set.

". . . Dr. London's body was discovered in his office early this evening."

Del's breath caught. Not possible. Thurman London? The man was as resilient as a cockroach.

"More on this story when we return." An ad for an FDA-approved medication for growing longer eyelashes took over the screen

"Dr. London is dead?" Sophie left the stove and stood beside Del in front of the TV.

"You knew London?"

She nodded, her face sad and lovely. "Michael does quite a bit of legal work for the museum. I always thought London was charming. Michael detested him."

"Not to speak ill of the dead, but Thurman London could be a royal A-hole."

She gave Del a disapproving look. "He must have been close to retirement. You think he had a heart attack or a stroke?"

"Not a chance. Way too much press splash for death by natural causes."

The PSA for the eyelash-challenged at an end, Sophie increased the set's volume another notch.

"CaMu's director, Dr. Thurman London, is dead tonight of an apparent suicide."

"Bullshit," Del said. "London would never kill himself. I've known the guy my entire life. He worshipped the ground he walked on."

"Dr. London first came to the California Museum of Fine Art forty years ago, leaving two years later to become curator of European paintings at the Graigham in Philadelphia. He returned to San Francisco as lead curator in 1978 and became the museum's director in 1981. Dr. London is credited with establishing CaMu's Provenance Research Project and organizing the current sold-out Post-Impressionist exhibit, the most ambitious in the museum's one-hundred-ten-year history.

" 'The loss of Thurman London is a shock and tragedy for both the museum and for this city,' Trustee Hanna Rosen Miller said in a statement to reporters. 'It is impossible to imagine CaMu without him. San Francisco has lost a great benefactor, this museum has lost a fine administrator, and I've lost a dear friend.' "

The camera panned to Del's mother, in tears, as she watched the EMTs wheel the body from the building. Special Agent Neil Sobol stood beside her.

A priceless painting disappears from a museum and a few hours later the director is dead? Coincidence? Sure as hell didn't sound like a coincidence to Del. He guessed from Sobol's presence, the FBI agreed.

Sophie put her hand on Del's forearm. "Oh, my God, your mom. Someone should be with her."

Del dug his cell from his pocket and punched in his parents' number. His father picked up on the first ring.

"Good, you're home," Del said on a sigh of relief. "Thought you might still be at the hospital. Did you hear about Thurman London?"

His father's voice was as taut as guy-wire. "I heard."

"I saw Mom on TV, she looks ready to break. She and London—"

"I'm a physician, Del. I can't bring back the dead." Under his breath he added, "Just as well in this case."

His father had never got on with London, but still, the icy words sent a chill feathering down Del's spine. "I'm not calling about London. I'm calling about Mom. She shouldn't be alone."

Sophie stared at Del, her face a question mark. He shook his head and shrugged.

"I have a report due to the chief of staff first thing tomorrow. I can't run off to CaMu on a whim."

On a whim? Was he kidding? Del waited for him to apologize, to say he was on his way to his wife. Silence.

"Fine," Del said. "I'll go."

"Your mother is a grown woman. She can take care of herself."

"I understand you're angry about the painting—"

"What painting?"

Dammit. Mom didn't tell him. No way Del would step into that pile over the phone. "Dad, I met with London this afternoon. The man was not suicidal."

His father blew out an impatient puff of air. "Hadn't you ought to stop thinking like a homicide detective? As I said, I don't have time to discuss this right now."

Del's control slipped. "Guess what, Dad? I'm short on time, too. Apparently I need to rush to Mom's side because *you* don't give a flying fuck." Del disconnected the call and glanced at Sophie, her eyes wide.

"What was that all about? Your dad's not going to the museum?"

"No. He's too *busy*."

"That doesn't sound like Samuel. Are you sure he understood?"

"Oh, he understood." Del read the clock above the stove. "I better get on the road."

"Wait." She touched his hand. "What you said about Dr. London's death not being a suicide. You really believe that?"

"I picked out two guys from Homicide in the newsfeed."

"Isn't Homicide always present at a suspected suicide—just in case?"

"London wasn't suicidal, Sophie. Somebody needs to make sure the SFPD knows."

"By somebody, you mean you. I thought you were going to be with your mother." It was more accusation than question.

"I am, but—"

"You're not a cop anymore, Del."

"So if something smells like shit, I'm supposed to breathe through my mouth and get over it?"

A shadow crossed her face, and she dropped her gaze.

He put a palm on her cheek and lifted her face, his eyes finding hers. "I'm sorry about missing dinner after you went to all this trouble. I promise we'll reschedule. Dinner soon. On me. Many dinners."

She bit her lip, her face still troubled. "Can I go with you? Your mom needs someone. I'll stay with her while you talk to the police. I'm worried about her. She looked . . . she's always been so good to me."

Del eyed the stove. "What about the tenderloin?"

"The food can go in the fridge. Just give me two minutes to throw on warmer clothes."

He nodded. "While you change, I'll call Mike."

"Michael? Why?"

"He's CaMu's legal counsel, and the painting—" He stopped himself, realizing he hadn't told her about the Cézanne.

50

"The painting you mentioned to your father?"

"Change your clothes. I'll explain on the way."

"But—"

He put his hands on her shoulders, spun her around, and aimed her toward the stairs. "Go. Hurry. I promise to tell you everything in the car. And Sophie?" She glanced over her shoulder and he shot her his best wicked grin. "Wear some underwear. It's my mother."

She grinned back. "Killjoy."

He dialed Mike's number.

"Alexa said you were eating. Sorry to interrupt," Del said.

"You didn't; we're finished. What's the emergency and who died? Are your parents okay?"

"Thurman London is dead. They're calling it suicide. He apparently hanged himself."

"Fuck me."

"In your dreams. I'm heading over to CaMu to be with Mom. Sobol is there. Spotted him on the news."

"What the . . . ? I thought he was supposed to be undercover."

"Probably caught in the wrong place at the wrong time. It happens. Any thoughts about London and suicide?"

"London was a self-important sonovabitch who never took responsibility for anything. No culpability meant no pressure; he let the shit roll right off him. I admired the guy for that. He was a role model," Mike said.

"Exactly. Arrogant bastard. What if all that ego was an act?"

"Horseshit. You don't believe London would kill himself any more than I do. Gotta tell you, though, I don't like Special Agent Slow Boil hanging around. The Feds don't do suicide, not unless the victim is a terrorist and happens to take a few dozen innocent people along for the ride. Special Agent S. only fits if London's death and the Cézanne are connected."

Del's thoughts exactly. Sophie sailed down the stairs, hair

loose, wearing jeans, a thick sweater, and a smile. His heart lifted. He spoke into the phone. "Like I said, Neil could have been caught up in the press mess. Regardless, I'm worried about Mom. The possibility that London's death had something to do with the Cézanne does not give me the warm fuzzies."

Understatement. The possibility scared the holy shit out of him.

CHAPTER 6

Del turned the corner and slammed on the brake, swerving into the left lane to avoid the string of news vans lining the front of CaMu. Bystanders spilled into the street, and parking was non-existent. The Porsche crawled forward. Nothing in the next block or the one after.

Sophie pointed through the passenger side window. "There's a spot."

It was a commercial driveway for a bakery, probably empty until morning. Del backed in and set the car alarm. A funk of gasoline, stale grease, and unremitting fog hung in the night air. Despite the chill, sweat trickled down his back. He took Sophie's hand, and they jogged up the dark street in the direction of the museum, their feet beating a frantic tattoo on the pavement.

Half a block from CaMu, Sophie stopped dead. "There she is, at the top of the stairs, under the lamp post." They sprinted.

Hanna sat alone just outside the vivid yellow line of police barricade tape, a blanket around her shoulders, hands in her lap, fingers worrying at her key card. She looked worn. Her usually bright eyes, glazed, her mouth slack. A small thread of panic unraveled at Del's core.

He sat beside her on the stone steps, the cold seeping through the thin fabric of his khakis. Without a word, she slumped against him, her body as stiff and brittle as a bundle of twigs in his arms. He took the key card from her and slipped it into her jacket pocket. "Mom, we need to get you home. There's nothing you can do here."

She wiped at tears with the back of her hand and shook her head. "The police want to talk to me again."

Sophie knelt in front of Hanna and cinched the blanket tighter.

"Later," Del said. "They can question you at the house, or we can arrange for you to go into the Hall of Justice tomorrow. Are you okay to walk?"

Sophie's eyes lifted to meet Del's. She raised her brows and nodded to a small cabal of uniformed officers and men in suits street-side.

Del studied the faces. Neil Sobol was not among them.

"Why don't you get the car and drive it around? I'll stay here with Hani," Sophie said.

His mother made a small wordless noise. "I found him, Mendel. I found Thurman."

Del's heart pitched. No wonder she was a mess.

"It was horrible. The police questioned me, but the big one said they'd want to talk to me again, that I shouldn't leave the scene." She squeezed her lids shut and buried her face in Del's shirtfront.

Sophie dropped down next to Hanna and began to massage small circles on her back. "It's going to be okay, Hani."

She turned as if noticing Sophie for the first time and said, "You found your grandmother, didn't you, when you were just a bit of a girl?"

Del cast Sophie an apologetic glance, but she was too focused on his mother to notice.

"I was nine. I'd just come home from school."

Hanna reached out and touched Sophie's cheek. "I'm so sorry. I can't imagine how awful that must have been for you."

Sophie squeezed her hand. "I think you probably can."

Homicide Inspector Charlie Kralmer lumbered up the stairs.

He was a fat, sullen man, his belly wide and round, the buttons on his jacket only for show. Halfway up, he leaned against the iron railing to rest. By the time he reached the top step, sweat streamed down his face and he panted like a rabid dog. Wouldn't have surprised Del to see flecks of foam on his lips.

His voice wheezed. "Miller, what are you doing here? This is a *police* investigation. Forget you jumped ship?"

Del got to his feet, blood throbbing in his temples, eyes level with the top of Kralmer's receding hairline. "I'm here because my mother found the victim. What's your excuse? The body's gone. Looks like the techs are done. If this is a suicide, shouldn't you have it wrapped up by now?"

"Del," Sophie said, her tone sharp. She shook her head, her eyes flicking to his mother.

Right. "Why don't we go downstairs and talk?" Del said to Kralmer.

Kralmer glanced at Hanna, then at Del. "So, all those rumors about you coming from money were true. Why am I not surprised? Explains why you think your shit doesn't stink. As for the victim—"

Del touched Kralmer's arm hoping he'd take the hint and step away.

Kralmer jerked his enormous body out of reach. "Take your fucking hands off me. Don't even think of sticking your nose into this investigation. Take care of your mother and stay the hell out of my way."

"Hey, Charlie." Homicide Inspector Terry Molina trotted up the stairs behind Kralmer. He was as compact as Kralmer was obese, with dark slicked-back hair and a perpetual grin. "Brady wants to talk to you."

"Who the fuck is Brady?" the fat man asked.

"Brady. The uniform? First officer on scene?"

Kralmer squinted toward the street. "Oh, right. Thanks,

Terry." Kralmer turned his back on Del and started down the stairs.

"You partnered with that asshole?" Del asked Terry when Kralmer was out of earshot.

"Give him a break. He's going to AA. He's trying. I think Cap wants me to keep an eye on him."

"You get hazard pay?"

Molina chuckled. "He's not all that bad once you get to know him."

"Glowing endorsement." Del looked down at his mother. "Terry, can I have a word with you privately?"

"Sure, up here." He gestured to an alcove at the top of the stairs out of hearing distance of the women.

Del knelt in front of his mother. "I need to have a word with Inspector Molina. Sophie will be right here with you. Will you be okay?" He pulled the edges of the blanket close around her, and she gave him a slight nod.

Del followed Terry to the recess at the far edge of the barricade tape.

"My mother's in shock," Del said. "I'm taking her home. You can either question her there, or I can bring her to the Hall in the morning, but making her sit and wait in this cold is bullshit."

"Take it easy, Del. She may be in shock, but that's one feisty lady. Charlie tried to convince her to sit in a squad car to keep warm, and she'd have none of it."

"About that. What's with all the Homicide presence? If London hung himself—"

"You know the drill. Unattended death, prominent citizen, we have to make a show."

"Don't jerk me around, Terry. I was in Homicide while you were still in Cub Scouts. I've known London a long time, and he wasn't suicidal."

Terry chewed the inside of his cheek, not meeting Del's eyes.

"What did your mother tell you?"

"That she found him. She's in no shape to talk."

"Nothing about *how* she found him?"

"What the hell is going on?"

Terry's sigh bled resignation. "Okay. You know what scarfing is?"

"I assume you're not talking about scarfing down dinner. You mean autoerotic asphyxiation? Thurman London? Are you fucking crazy?"

"Your mother found London in his office, naked, jaw-breaking rictus smile, cord around his neck, pussy magazines spread all over his white shag rug, boner intact. You do the math. You're the one who said he wasn't suicidal. Here's the thing. Until the medical examiner makes a determination, we're going to call it a suicide, because suicide is less of a scandal than autoerotic asphyxiation."

The thought of his mother walking in on London like that made Del lightheaded. "Jesus. We're talking an old man, Terry."

"Even old men get hard, my friend. Gives them something to live for, keeps the little blue pill folks in business"—his grin widened—"and gives us poor bastards hope."

"Autoerotic asphyxiation would mean accidental death, which doesn't explain why you and Kralmer are still hanging around. You suspect someone else was present?"

"Let's just say, we're not completely sure how London got himself into the position he was in when your mother walked into his office. As you say, he was an old man."

"So you're investigating this as a suspicious death?"

Terry's eyes narrowed and his face shuttered. "Any unattended death is suspicious." He looked over Del's shoulder toward the street. "Here comes trouble."

Kralmer slogged up the stairs again.

"Probably more exercise than he's had in a year," Del said.

Terry chuckled and shouted down the steps. "Gonna make it, Charlie?"

Kralmer grunted and gasped for air as he reached the top. "Getting tired of going up and down these fucking steps. What are you telling Mr. Miller about our *suicide*, Terry? Did you forget he's a private citizen? His right to know is in the shitter."

"His mother discovered the body. You think she won't tell him what she found?"

"What Mrs. Highfalutin does or does not tell her offspring is not my concern. Information leaked by an SFPD homicide inspector to a private citizen is. Mr. Miller here can watch the story unfold on TV like everybody else."

Del was tempted to step forward and give Kralmer a push, an experiment to see whether the lard-ass would bounce or roll. The thought made him smile.

Kralmer turned toward the street. "Perfect. What the hell is that wop attorney doing here? This is supposed to be a crime scene."

Mike raced up the steps. "Hey, Delbo, got here fast as I could."

"*You* phoned this ass-wipe, Miller?"

Del ignored the question. "I'm taking my mother home. You already have her statement. If you need to talk to her again, you know where to find her."

Mike smiled and held up a finger. "Excuse me. One correction." He aimed his grin at Kralmer. "If the SFPD wishes to speak with Mrs. Miller again, you go through her attorney. That would be me."

Kralmer shook his head. "Wow, this just gets better and better. Mrs. Miller doesn't need a lawyer, Gabretti. She's not suspected of anything."

"You have a problem with English, Inspector? I said if you want to talk to Mrs. Miller, you go through me. You want to wave hello or blow her a kiss, you go through me." Mike's smile never wavered, but his voice was barbed as razor wire.

Mike handed Kralmer his card and patted him on the shoulder. "No hard feelings about that little mix-up a few months ago. You remember, right? How you tried to get me fried for a murder I didn't commit?"

"I heard you were attorney of record for the museum," Kralmer said. "You ever hear of conflict of interest?"

"I handle intellectual property matters for CaMu. Did your victim violate copyright law when he offed himself?"

Molina chortled and Kralmer shot him a ball-shriveling glare. "For chrissake, shut up. You sound like a goddamned hyena."

Del still hadn't spotted Neil and wondered if the Feds were inside the museum. That would explain Kralmer and Terry cooling their heels out on the street. "Come on, Mike. I need to get back to Mom. Good to see you, Terry." Then, sotto voce, "Kralmer."

Mike gave the inspectors a mock salute, clicked his heels, and followed Del. Once they were out of earshot he said, "Suicide? What a bunch of BS."

"What if I were to say autoerotic asphyxiation?"

"Now that, I'd believe."

"You're kidding?" Del said, but Mike wasn't smiling.

The two women sat huddled together under the blanket. Mike walked ahead of Del and crouched in front of Hanna, his voice gentle. "Hani, anyone tries to talk to you, don't say a word. You send whoever it is to me. I'm your legal counsel."

"Mike, thank you. You're very sweet, but I don't need a lawyer."

"Of course you don't." He kissed her cheek. "If you did, I'd call my dad. I haven't practiced criminal law in ten years. But you don't want to ruin my fun, do you?"

Mike's gaze drifted to Sophie. "Delbo told me about your big date, but I didn't expect to see you here. Now I understand where he gets his reputation for showing a girl—lots of girls"—he grinned up at Del—"a good time."

The remark irritated the hell out of Del, but he wasn't about to take the bait. With his jaw clenched so hard it ached, he said, "Mom, I'll get the car and pick you and Sophie up at the curb. We need to get you home. Dad has to hear about the Cézanne before the FBI releases the story to the media."

"I can't talk about the painting tonight, Mendel. I'm not up to it. And you don't have to drive me. I have my car."

"We'll pick up your car tomorrow. The painting can't wait. I saw Neil Sobol with you earlier. What did he say?"

Her lids dropped, shielding her eyes. "What about my purse? It's in the docent office. I need my glasses and my wallet."

Del took a long breath and softened his voice. "The museum is a crime scene. You'll have to get along without them."

Mike squared his shoulders. "Maybe I can use my considerable charm to talk Inspector *Krawls-up-my-ass* into getting her purse. The sonovabitch owes me. London's office isn't anywhere near the docents'."

"Don't waste your time. The bastard wouldn't do it even if he could," Del said.

Mike eyed Sophie. "If you don't want to wait for Delbo, I can drive you back to Marina Bay."

Sophie stared at him with the eyes of a cornered animal and Del intervened. "I'd appreciate it if you could meet us back at the house, Mike. Dad may have questions about CaMu's liability with regard to the Cézanne. That is, if you're not in a hurry to get back to your wife and baby?" *Touché.*

Mike's eyes skated from Sophie to Del, a muscle twitching in his left cheek. "Not much I can tell Samuel at this point, but okay," he said, tone even. "I can do that."

Hanna swayed as she pulled herself to her feet, and Del took her elbow to steady her. "Not tonight, Mendel. I told you, I'm not up to it. I will tell your father first thing in the morning."

The Cézanne disappears, and now London is dead? His father would hear about the painting tonight if Del had to break the news himself. He put his arm around his mother's shoulders. "For now, let's just get you out of here."

She nodded, closed her eyes, and laid her head on his shoulder. The four of them walked down the steps side by side.

Out on the street, the press still twiddled their thumbs. Del peered over his shoulder at the museum. A uniformed officer moved out of the way as both entrance doors swung wide. A tall, middle-aged woman with a helmet of ash-brown curls and a boney frame stepped out onto the portico and into the light. Neil Sobol stood next to her.

Del said to Mike, "My car is three blocks north of here. Where are you parked?"

"Back of the museum, right outside the loading dock. London's spot. Hey, don't give me that look. I knew it'd be empty. London hated city traffic. He always took a cab to work."

"I need to talk to Sobol." Del thumbed over his shoulder. "Can you drive Mom and Sophie over to the house? I'll meet you there."

Sophie's head jerked up. "I don't mind waiting," she stammered, teeth chattering from the cold.

"You go get warm. I'll be five minutes behind. Promise." Del kissed her forehead and whispered in her ear that he didn't want his mother to be alone. "You don't mind if Mike drives you, do you, Mom?"

Hanna shook her head, eyes fixed on something in the distance.

Mike put an arm around each of the women, and Del watched as they walked to the end of the block and slipped behind the museum.

"Miller?" boomed a voice behind him. Del started and whirled around. Neil Sobol and the tall woman were marching toward him.

CHAPTER 7

Mike kept up the small talk, but the tension in the car was so thick, it was difficult to breathe. It started to rain as soon as they'd pulled out of the museum parking lot. "You think San Francisco will have summer this year? I wouldn't mind some sun. It's July, for chrissake." He studied Sophie's reflection in the rearview mirror. Trembling slightly, she gnawed at her lip and stared out the window. Maybe she was just cold.

"Do you want me to turn the heat up?" he asked.

"I'm fine," Sophie said.

Standard response. Trap his ex in a burning skyscraper with no escape, she'd holler out the window that she was fine.

Hani sat in the passenger seat. He reached over and squeezed her hand. "How about you, beautiful? Warm enough?"

A quick nod. She hadn't uttered a single word since they'd left the museum.

What the fuck was he doing here? He should be home with Amy, keeping his little girl safe from her mother. He stole another glance at Sophie's reflection and felt that tiny, familiar tug at his heart. She was the last person he'd expected to run into tonight.

A low stone wall topped with an iron fence and joined by security gates surrounded the Miller house. Mike pulled up to the gate and put on the parking brake. Delbo had a remote, but the guy was such a fucking grandma behind the wheel, they'd probably be sitting here for hours if they waited. Leaving the engine running, he climbed out of the car and sprinted to the access keypad. The gate stuttered open.

The Millers' house—mansion, really—was enormous, a dark gothic revival eyesore designed by Hani's father as a wedding present to his bride. At least he'd gifted her with something unique. Other than Willis Polk's Tobin House, Mike couldn't think of another gothic revival in San Francisco. He didn't understand why Hani and Samuel kept the place. Although most of the living spaces had been brought to human scale, more than half the house was closed off. And the public rooms? Mike was as intimidated by them at thirty-eight as he'd been at five. The Millers had no servants other than a housekeeper who came in once a week to tidy up the parts of the house where Hani and Samuel never went. Mike's own parents had a live-in maid, a gardener, a pool boy, and a house one-quarter the size of the Miller Monstrosity.

Mike opened the door and helped Hani out of the car.

"You still have your key, don't you?" she asked, her voice rough. "I don't want to disturb Samuel."

Mike had seen the determination on Del's face. Samuel would be disturbed tonight one way or the other. "How did you know I had a key?"

A brief spark lit her silver eyes. "You fibbed to your parents all through high school about staying here when you actually sneaked out of *our* house to be with your girlfriend. Wasn't hard to figure out Mendel gave you an extra key so you'd be able to come and go as you pleased."

And he thought they'd been so freaking stealthy. "You never said anything."

Sophie chuckled, and the corners of Hani's mouth turned up slightly. "Of course not. Would it have made a difference if I had?"

Mike doubted his very Catholic parents would have viewed

things that way. Sophie and Hani hung back while he turned the key in the lock and held the door open. Cavernous and gloomy, the foyer resembled some kind of medieval aircraft hangar. High stone walls topped with massive wood beams, and circled with slivers of mullioned window.

"I'm exhausted, I have to go to bed," Hani said, her words nearly lost in the expansive space.

The door to Samuel's study was ajar. Mike stepped back to steal a glance through the opening. He caught Samuel's eye and nodded. The old man stood and moved to the entrance to meet them.

A soft-bodied, soft-spoken man with round, well-etched features and a tangle of silver hair, Samuel Miller displayed none of his wife's panache, but Mike never doubted the steel under the man's gentle exterior. Mike grew up wanting Samuel for his own father, wishing it were possible to exchange loud, obstreperous defense attorney Mick Gabretti for this humane man of letters. Sometimes he still wished it.

Samuel looked his wife up and down. "I trust you're all right?" he asked, his voice unreadable.

"I'm fine," she said, weakly.

"Good, good." He turned to Mike and Sophie and smiled. "It's fine to see you two. Reminds me of old times. Especially you, my beautiful Sophie. It's been too long."

She grinned and hugged him tight, and Mike felt a faint pang of jealousy.

"How are you? Let's have a look at those hands," Samuel said.

She colored but held out her hands, palms up. For the first time, Mike saw the scars. So that's what that bastard did to her. A shame reared up in him so ferocious, he wanted to run and hide.

"They're doing astonishing things with lasers today," Samuel said. "Let me do some research, talk to my colleagues." He squeezed her hands and kissed her on the cheek.

"Don't bother, Samuel. I won't ever be a hand model but everything works okay." She wiggled her fingers. "Laser surgery is expensive."

"You let me worry about the money." His eyes skimmed the room. "Where's Del?"

"He stayed behind to talk to talk to someone—the FBI?" Sophie looked toward Mike for confirmation. "He should be here in a—"

The door crashed open, and Del stormed into the foyer. "Complete waste of time. I got more information out of Terry than out of the Feds. Neil and his bitch of a partner wouldn't tell me shit."

Samuel's face darkened. "What does the FBI have to do with a suicide?"

"I'll explain later, Dad," Del said, his voice tight as a fist.

"Fine. You do that. Now if you'll all excuse me, I need to get back to work. Good to see you Mike, Sophie." His tone went flat. "Hanna, I'm glad you're all right."

Del blocked his way. "Did Mom tell you she found London's body?"

"I don't want to talk about this, Mendel. I'm very tired right now. Please." Hani's voice broke in a sob.

Mike kept his gaze on Samuel, waiting for him to speak.

"I'm sorry to hear that, Hanna," Samuel said finally. "It must have been unpleasant. I think rest is an excellent idea."

"What the hell is the matter with you, Dad?" An angry red flush rode Del's cheekbones.

"Don't speak to your father like that," Hani said, her voice stronger now.

Del looked back and forth between his parents. "Would one of you please tell me what is going on?"

"I'm sorry your mother's had a bad day, but it's too late to change anything," Samuel said.

"*A bad day?* Thurman London is dead."

" 'We reap what we sow,' " Samuel said, skirting Del and entering his study. He clicked the door shut behind him.

"Goddammit." Del slammed his fist against the mahogany slab. "Dad, I'm coming in." He turned the knob and disappeared into the study, the crash of the door echoing off the foyer walls.

What *was* going on? Unlike Mike's dad, who kept a stable of girlfriends, Samuel had always been devoted to Hani, and treated her like a queen. Samuel took this marriage crap seriously. When he'd learned Mike had cheated on Sophie, the old man had practically torn him a new one. "What's the matter with you? Marriage is sacred. You don't want to be faithful, you little shit? No problem. Don't get married." It was the only time Samuel ever raised his voice to Mike, and Mike's face still flamed at the memory.

He told Samuel that Sophie would forgive him. Hadn't Mike's mother always forgiven his father?

Samuel scoffed. "Forgiving is not the same as forgetting. It would serve you well to remember that, Mike."

He had. Mike glanced over at Sophie, her arm tight around Hani's waist, gray-green eyes filled with concern. Samuel had been right. Sophie forgave, but it was too late to put the marriage back together. And forget? Sophie never forgot anything. He'd been so fucking stupid.

Out of the corner of his eye, Mike saw Hani's knees buckle and he lunged forward to catch her.

She moaned. "I have to lie down."

Sophie, who barely came to Hani's shoulder, couldn't steady her. "Michael, help me get her upstairs."

Hani leaned heavily on Mike while Sophie kept an arm

around her waist. They climbed the wide stone staircase.

"I'll stay in one of the guest rooms," Hani said. "I won't sleep tonight. I don't want to disturb Samuel."

Mike and Sophie exchanged a glance.

"Won't you rest easier in your own bed?" Sophie asked.

"Right here. This is fine." Hani gestured to the first room at the top of the stairs. She pulled away from Mike and Sophie, opened the door, and walked in.

Mike flipped on the light behind her. The scent of gardenia hung heavy in the air, and despite the cold, he was tempted to open a window. The bedroom was long and narrow, decorated in cool shades of green and white. A mirrored armoire sat against one wall, and opposite, two chests of drawers painted with silvery vines sprouting from Grecian urns. The tops of both chests were covered with framed photographs. From an eight by ten, Del smiled at them through a sepia haze. Mike picked up the photo. "I've never seen this picture of Delbo before. Looks like an antique."

Hani chuckled softly, stretching out on the bed. "Everyone thinks Mendel takes after my side of the family, but that's a picture of Samuel's father, Max, taken before the war."

The man in the photo looked exactly like Del. Gave Mike the creeps. He returned the picture to the chest of drawers.

"Hani, can I get you something to sleep in?" Sophie asked. "You'll be more comfortable."

Hani's curls rustled against the white pillowcase. "No, dear. I'm too exhausted to change, but will you help me with these pillows?"

Sophie propped the pillows behind Hani's head and helped her under the coverlet. Then, sitting on the edge of the bed, she took the older woman's hand.

Mike studied Hani, the gray skin, the deep grooves etched around her mouth and forehead, the circles under her eyes.

Hani was always so alive, vibrant. Now she seemed . . . what? The word *broken* popped into Mike's head. Hani seemed *broken*.

"What can we get you?" Sophie asked. "Something to drink? Shall we leave you alone so you can rest?"

"I have two of my favorite people in the world here with me. Come, Mike. Sit." She patted the side of the bed opposite Sophie. "Are you two being kind to each other?"

Mike sat on the edge of the mattress. From the crease in Sophie's brow, she had no idea what Hani meant either.

"I think we're trying to be," Sophie said finally.

"Mike, do you have any photographs of that beautiful baby of yours?" Hani gave him a wan smile. "A rhetorical question. I know you do."

Mike grinned and stole another glance at Sophie, trying to read what she was thinking. He pulled out his cell, switched on photo view, and passed the phone to Hani.

Sophie maneuvered herself on the bed so she, too, could see the tiny screen. Her smile was radiant. "Michael, she is absolutely gorgeous." Her eyes found his. "Amy is very lucky to have you for a father."

The warm words were so unexpected; he had to swallow a lump in his throat. Uncomfortable, he shifted his attention to Hani. She'd been so quiet, he hadn't noticed her tears. He touched her arm.

"I'm sorry." She wiped her cheeks. "It's just the baby reminds me so much of *my* Amy. I still miss her, my little girl. Foolish. She wouldn't be a child anymore. She'd be a grown woman."

Mike shouldn't have shown her the photos, not tonight.

Hani's silver eyes, still streaming, locked on Mike. "I thought God's taking Amy from me was a test. I didn't realize the true test would come after she was gone."

Mike felt the hackles rise on the back of his neck, a warning. Hani was about to say something he didn't want to hear. He took the phone from her, slipped it back in his pocket, and stood up. He had to get out of here, away from the cloying scent of gardenia. He needed fresh air. "Do you want me to get Samuel for you?" he asked.

She answered with a quick brittle laugh. "Maybe you can't understand, Mike, but I know Sophie can."

Confusion swam across Sophie's features. "Understand what, Hani?" she said, her voice just above a whisper.

"When you're betrayed, you can absolve, but the betrayal can never be erased. You can't go back, can't forget, even if you want to. Even if you want it more than anything in the world."

Mike returned to the bed and took Hani's hand. "I do understand."

She pulled her hand away and stroked his cheek. "You're a good boy, Mike. You have a big heart, but Sophie made the right decision to let go. Right for both of you." She turned her head away and sobbed. "It was just that I missed my little girl."

Sophie stroked Hani's hair. "I don't understand. Did someone betray you? Samuel—?"

"No!" Hani shouted so loud, both Mike and Sophie jumped. "Not Samuel. Me. I'm the one."

Hani's deep, guttural cries tore at Mike's heart. "It's all right, Hani," he said, not knowing what else to say but absolutely certain he was telling a lie.

"That's what Samuel said, but it never was. Not after he found out about Thurman. Samuel is a wonderful man, but he could never forget. So you see, I know." She lowered her lids.

"Forget what, Hani?" Sophie asked.

Mike didn't want to hear any more.

Hani's sobs quieted. "Losing Amy destroyed Samuel. He closed himself off. Wouldn't talk. Just shut himself up in his study. He couldn't understand why God would give him the power to heal but not allow him to save his own child. He cut me off, barely remembered he had a wife and a son. Samuel was alone because he chose to be. I was alone because he left me no choice. I needed my husband. And Thurman was there."

Mike's stomach hit the floor.

"The relationship was over as soon as it began," Hani said. "Thurman was married back then. Samuel found out."

"Samuel loves you," Sophie said. "I know he loves you." She said the words as if she couldn't bear to believe otherwise.

"Do you understand what I'm trying to say? Samuel forgave, but he never forgot. Just like you'll never forget how Mike betrayed you. Samuel should have left me. It's what I deserved. But he's an honorable man, too honorable. Watching his hatred for Thurman eat away at him was my punishment."

Hani glanced up and the sharp catch in her breath made Mike look over his shoulder.

In the doorway, Del stood watching.

CHAPTER 8

Del stepped into the bedroom, unable to gather his thoughts. His rage burned so hot and tangled, words wouldn't come. The scab of time had been ripped away and the pain and loss of his sister's death was fresh again. When he found his voice, it sounded alien, fierce but broken. "I was there too, Mom. Remember? Did you even think of me, or was fucking London less stressful than helping your sixteen-year-old son cope with the loss of his only sister?" She looked stricken, but he didn't give a shit.

"Mendel, I'm so sorry. I didn't—"

He moved farther into the room, closing the door behind him. "Don't lie. You were in your own little world. You think I don't remember? I didn't exist for you."

"That's not true." She raised her eyes to the ceiling, blinking to hold back tears. "It was a devastating time for all of us—"

"Were you still screwing him? Is that why Dad is being such a prick?" The thought of his mother and London together made him want to vomit.

"No, no, no," she said, her voice caught between a shout and a sob, the words layered with heartbreak. "Tonight I lost a friend. Try to understand, Mendel." She hid her face in her hands and burst into tears.

Del's gorge rose. "Must have been rough. I feel for you."

"Hey, bro, ease up. She's been through hell," Mike said.

An unexpected rush of fury caught Del off guard. "Well,

you'd know, wouldn't you? Seems neither you nor my mother put much of a premium on marriage vows."

Mike rose from the bed and confronted him. "Look, asshole—"

"That's enough," Sophie said. "Both of you, stop bickering or take it outside. You are not helping."

Del pushed past Mike to get to his mother. "I told Dad about the Cézanne."

She shook her head as if to clear the words from the air. "It's just a painting. A man is dead."

"The Cézanne means shit-all to you. Message received. How about you stop worrying about your dead lover long enough to remember that painting is all Dad has left of his father, the only thing he'll ever have."

Still holding Hanna's hand in hers, Sophie's hard, sharp gaze cut through Del like high beams on a dark night.

Shamed, Del flushed, heat stealing up from his collar into his cheeks. He looked away.

Mike took advantage of the opening, sliding into attorney mode, voice smooth and conciliatory. "It's been a long night. Why don't we give Hani a chance to rest? I'd like to hear exactly what Agent No Balls *didn't* say after we left the museum." Mike put his hand on Del's shoulder.

Del shook him off. "Later." He turned to Sophie. She needed to understand about the Cézanne, and what the painting meant to his father, to his family. "How much do you know about the Cézanne?"

She blinked, long black lashes brushing her cheek. "Just what you told me in the car. Someone replaced the real painting with a forgery. Hani and Samuel have a lot of art, and I've only been in Samuel's study a couple times." She colored. "To be honest, I'm not sure which painting we're talking about."

Del reached inside his jacket, pulled out the brochure London

73

had given him, and held the flyer out to her.

A flicker of recognition crossed her face. "The one with the skulls."

"The skulls symbolize the transience of human existence. Cézanne often painted still lifes with skulls," Hanna said, ever the docent.

"My grandfather fled Paris when Germany invaded France during the war. He packed up my father and headed south to Vichy—unoccupied France, the free zone. The Cézanne went with them." Del rubbed his temples to hold back the tension threatening to explode his brain. He hated talking about this. Hated it. Germans, Nazis, concentration camps, the Holocaust. Stories that festered and erupted out of nowhere, at camp, at school, at temple, always scraps and fragments, buried in secrets and sadness, wrapped in hushed tones, tears, and guilt he never understood and wasn't meant to. As far as his father was concerned, any topic to do with the war was off limits.

Sophie's brow furrowed. "I thought Samuel's family came from Germany."

"My grandfather came from Germany. My grandmother was French. Dad was born in Paris. His mother died giving birth." Del exhaled. "Anyway, the Nazis eventually occupied the free zone. My grandfather was caught in the net, sent to an internment camp, then back to Paris and deported." *To Auschwitz.* Those were the words left unsaid, the ones he could never seem to fit on his tongue. The words no one in this house ever uttered.

The room went quiet except for the steady sound of their breathing and the soft rustle of covers as Sophie let go of Hanna's hand and shifted on the bed. Her ocean eyes fixed on Del, expectant. "But your father escaped."

Del closed his fingers tight over the cold brass of the headboard; the metal felt hard and reassuring in his fist. He needed the solidity. "Dad was smuggled out of France to the

U.S., along with the Cézanne."

Hanna straightened, the corners of her mouth turned down, the muscles in her face suddenly taut with fury. "The Cézanne was considered degenerate art, socialist. The Nazis burned nearly five thousand works—Impressionists and Post-Impressionists, Cubists, Surrealists. Lost masterpieces. But as soon as they realized there was money to be had, they stopped burning and started selling the art overseas to finance their filthy war, their unspeakable *Final Solution.*" She shuddered with the force of her emotion, and the sobs came again.

Del's heart twisted. He let go of the headboard, sat on the bed, and took his mother into his arms. She cried silently. He'd never thought about how the war had affected her. Twelve years younger than his father and born in San Francisco, she hadn't suffered, hadn't been forced to flee her home, no threat of ghettos, or internment, or death. But if Del still felt the immense weight of the Holocaust growing up forty years later, what had it been like for her? A dark dragging sadness took hold of him.

"Did your grandfather collect art?" Sophie asked.

He had no idea how his grandfather had come by the Cézanne.

Hanna pulled away from Del, sniffled, and wiped her eyes. "Max, Samuel's father, worked for a gallery in Paris. My understanding is the Cézanne was a gift from the gallery owner to Max. Valuable yes, but worth only a tiny fraction of what the canvas is worth today."

Sophie's features clouded. "I can only begin to imagine how much that painting means to Samuel. I know his father died at Auschwitz."

"I'm glad someone understands," Del said, not able to keep the ice out of his voice. His mother went rigid beside him but remained silent.

Sophie got to her feet. "Why don't you and Michael go

discuss whatever it is you need to discuss? I'll stay with Hani until she falls asleep."

Mike had been so quiet, Del forgot he was in the room. They locked eyes and Mike nodded.

Hanna closed her lids. "Sophie, that's sweet of you, but I'd like to be alone for a while."

"You're sure you'll be all right?"

"Promise." Hanna reached out and squeezed her arm.

Del followed Mike and Sophie to the door but then walked back to the bed and kissed his mother's forehead. "Love you, Mom."

She stroked his cheek, her fingertips cool on his skin. "I love you, too, Mendel, more than anything else in the world. Never forget that."

Del trailed Mike and Sophie into the hallway.

"How about telling me exactly what your Fed pal said tonight?" Mike asked Del once they'd descended to the foyer.

"Keep your voice down, Mike." The door to his father's study was closed, but Del had had about all the family drama he could stand for one night. "Neil wouldn't talk to me, not about the Cézanne, not about London."

"Sobol's not an idiot. He must at least suspect a connection between the painting and London's death."

"Terry said London's death looked suspicious."

Mike barked a laugh. "You mean the story about the cops thinking he's a gasper? I'd believe it in a heartbeat if he were found at home, but seriously, in his office during business hours?"

"Technically, it happened after business hours."

"What exactly denotes suspicious? Is there evidence someone took him out? Not that he wasn't deserving, but still—"

"Why did you work for him if you disliked him so much?"

Mike shrugged but didn't answer.

"What are you talking about?" Sophie asked. "What's a gasper?"

Mike and Del both stared. Then Mike laughed. "That's why I love you, Sophie." He cleared his throat and stammered, "Love your naiveté, I mean."

She shot him a brutal glare. "I am not naive. Just tell me what gasper means."

Del dropped his voice to just above a whisper. "London was found in his office with pornography and a cord around his neck. He was—"

"Spanking the monkey?" Mike said. "Choking the chicken? Rubbing one out?"

"For chrissake, lower your voice, Mike." Del sighed and rubbed his forehead.

"You mean autoerotic asphyxiation?" Sophie said. "And Hani found him?"

Del had given as little thought as possible to what his mother witnessed in that office, and his gut heaved.

All three were quiet for a moment, then Mike said, "Something isn't right. I'm not saying London wasn't capable of a death jerk, but he wouldn't risk being caught in his office. Dr. Thurman Alcott London was all about appearances. When you talked to your mom at the scene, did you ask her what she saw?"

"Of course he didn't," Sophie snapped. "Hani was in shock."

Again, Del felt the tug at his core. "This is high profile. The medical examiner will rush the postmortem. As for Mom, she'll talk when she's ready. Didn't she prove that with tonight's little bombshell?" Despite his best effort, Del couldn't hold back his vitriol.

"What about the Cézanne?" Mike asked.

"What about it? Talk to the FBI." The study door opened, and Del made a quick cutting motion across his neck to silence

Mike, who changed the subject.

"Sure you're okay to drive Sophie home? You look like shit, Delbo."

"I shouldn't have suggested you bring me along. I'm sorry," Sophie said. "Having to drive all the way back to Marina Bay is a huge inconvenience."

"I'm fine and it's not an inconvenience. I appreciate all you've done tonight."

Samuel stood at the threshold of the study watching the three of them. "You are all more than welcome to spend the night. We have plenty of rooms."

Mike shook his head. "Thanks, but I have to get home to the baby, make sure Alexa hasn't painted her fingernails or tried to dye her wisp of hair. She was hoping Amy would be a blonde. Unfortunately"—he pointed to his head of black hair—"Italian genes."

Sophie glanced at her watch. "I need to get home, too. I didn't intend to be gone this long. Casper is probably desperate for walkies."

"Right, we should go." Del turned to his father. "Mom is in the room at the top of the stairs. If it's not too much trouble, would you mind looking in on her, make sure she's okay? Give her something to help her sleep if she needs it?"

The old man bristled. "Of course I'll check on her. I've been taking care of your mother for forty years. Why would I stop now?"

CHAPTER 9

Sophie slipped the key into the lock. Her body blocking the door, she turned to face Del. "Thanks for letting me tag along."

"Like I said, I'm grateful you were there, and I know Mom appreciated it."

"I realize it's none of my business, but you were pretty hard on her."

Del's defenses rose like battlements. "My only sister died, Sophie. I needed my mother. My father needed his wife. She had no time for us. She was off screwing London. Put yourself in my place."

"Sorry, I can't. I don't have a mother."

And with neither plan nor forethought the insensitive asshole strikes again. Del took a breath and cleared his throat. "Are you going to keep me out on the porch all night?"

Her eyes shifted past him to the dark street. "Don't you need to get home?"

A few hours ago they'd fucked in her kitchen. Now she wasn't going to invite him in? Drained beyond all measure, he swallowed his pride. "Would you mind if I spent the night?"

She pressed her lips together, her face inscrutable.

"I'm fine with sleeping in the guest room. Just not up to fighting my way across the bridge a fourth time today."

She cocked her head and leaned against the door, swinging it wide. "Of course you can spend the night. Come on, get in here."

In the entry, Sophie picked up Lucy and rubbed her cheek over the top of the cat's head. "How you doing, old girl?" Casper whimpered and put his paws on her thigh. "Okay, okay, message received. Come on. Let's have a tour of the backyard before bed."

Del trailed her to the kitchen and waited while she unlatched the slider and let Casper outside.

She glanced at Del over her shoulder. "We never had dinner. You must be starving. Help yourself to whatever's in the fridge. I'd avoid the tenderloin so close to bedtime."

As if on cue, his stomach rumbled. "This may be the first time I've ever left my mother's house hungry."

"You and me both."

He reconnoitered the refrigerator, found some fruit and yogurt, and set the kitchen table for two.

After they ate, she stood to clear the dishes. "You sure you had enough to eat? You're a growing boy."

She was achingly beautiful even in the kitchen's stark fluorescent light. He gently tugged on one auburn curl and rose in his chair to kiss her. Her mouth opened over his, warm and soft, tasting of peaches, cinnamon, and life. For that one moment, the rest of the day, the last shitty twenty-four hours, fell away. He pulled her onto his lap, buried his face in her neck, and inhaled her clean sweet musk.

"Well, well, what have we here?" she said. "I thought you were tired. Funny, you don't *feel* tired." She squirmed slightly and giggled, a fragile sound, as rare and ever changing as a flake of snow.

His longing for her chipped away at his exhaustion and nurtured him in a way food never could. He cupped her breast and tried to push his hand up under her thick wool sweater. She shoved his arm away.

"Not that I don't like kitchen sex," she murmured in his ear, "but let's try the couch this time."

Her slight weight pressed against him as he carried her to the living room and laid her down on the sofa. Her green eyes gazed up at him through a tangle of gauzy red curls and she held out her hand.

The empty ache of all the years wanting her when she belonged to Mike dissolved. He sat next to her, pressed his lips to hers, ran his fingers along the contour of her hip, across the flat of her belly, up over her breasts. Her nipples were hard as pebbles through the bulky knit, and he reached to lift the hem.

Her breath caught. "Leave the sweater, okay?" She moved his hand from her sweater to the fly of her jeans and began to fumble with his shirt buttons.

Del lowered her zipper, slid his hand down her warm stomach, and stroked the damp silk between her thighs. Her eyes never left his. She lifted her ass, and he tugged off her jeans and panties, his fingers grazing the snaking scar on her thigh.

"Lie down." She shifted into the corner of the couch to make room for him.

He did as he was told, and she straddled him. Another zipper, his, this time, fingers, cool, gentle, tentative, encircled his erection. She leaned forward, her hair falling like a curtain across her face. As she slipped him inside, the world around him softened and melted with the unhurried rocking of her hips.

"Slow and sweet this time, okay?" she said.

Anything. He nodded, lifting the hem of her sweater. "I want to feel you against me."

"No, leave it—please."

He chuckled at the tease and reached for the pullover again. Her hand came down hard across his face followed by the shock of cool air on his cock as she climbed off him.

"What was that for?" He sat up, holding his palm to his cheek. "That hurt."

"Good, it was meant to." She grabbed her underwear and jeans and began to dress. "When a woman tells you no, you think it's a secret code for yes?"

"What the hell are you talking about?"

"I said no. Don't you understand no?"

Del picked up his khakis from the floor and draped them across his waning erection.

"I thought you were teasing. First you shove my hand down the front of your pants, then you won't let me touch your sweater? Ever hear of a mixed signal?"

"No means no. Nothing mixed about it." There was no anger in her voice, only a ragged desperation.

He slumped against the back of the sofa. Maybe he'd heard what he wanted to hear. Self-reproach began to replace his confusion. "I'm sorry. I understand." True, he was sorry, but understand? He had no clue. His mind went over the evening's events and a piece of the puzzle clicked into place. *Mike. Wasn't it always about Mike?* "Is this about running into Mike tonight?"

She gave an indignant snort and rolled her eyes. "Men are such idiots. I'm going to bed. You know where the guest room is." She wheeled around and started toward the stairs.

"Sophie, stop. Come on, we have to talk."

She ignored him.

Del pulled on his pants and followed her upstairs, stopping at her open bedroom door. She stood with her back to him in front of the dresser. He took a tentative step into the room. "I would never force you do anything you didn't want to do. I thought you wanted me. I misread you. I'm sorry."

She swung to face him; her eyes glittering with unshed tears. "I did want you."

Hope sparked, and he took another step into the room. "Then

tell me what I did wrong, because I know damn well this isn't about the sweater."

"The sweater," she repeated, crossing her arms and hugging herself as if he might try to wrangle the garment off her. "I shouldn't have invited you in tonight. Please go to the guest room. I want to be alone." She lowered her head and tears slid down her pale cheeks.

He stiffened, her words falling harder than the slap. Never let it be said he couldn't take a hint. "Fine, if that's what you want. Is it?"

Lowering her arms she nodded and rubbed a scarred palm along the denim covering her ruined thigh.

Suddenly, there it was. *"Out of suffering have emerged the strongest souls; the most massive characters are seared with scars." Wise man that E.H. Chapin. Unlike me,* Del thought, drawing a breath before speaking. "This is about David, isn't it?" A gutless rhetorical question if ever there was one. Calling the bastard by name was bullshit. It implied David had been a human being rather than a sick fuck who'd tortured and nearly bled her to death. *Because you were too busy to take her call, Miller. Because you couldn't be bothered.* So much guilt with nowhere to go.

Sophie stared at the floor and said nothing.

"Talk to me, Sophie, please."

She lifted her head, her scalded gaze on his. "What do you want me to say? That he mutilated me? That no one with two eyes in his head would want me? Well, now you've heard it. You can go." She stormed past him into the bathroom and slammed the door so hard the walls shivered.

Fuck him blind for thinking he couldn't make things worse. He glanced around the room. Painted a shade of turned buttermilk, the bedroom was Motel 6 Spartan. A bed, two nightstands with lamps, a chest, and a few snapshots wedged into a mirror framed above a small dresser. All traces of Mike gone.

Apart from the photos and a faint scent of cinnamon and orange blossom, there was no evidence of Sophie, either. Del sat on the edge of the bed and waited.

The toilet flushed, the water ran. He listened to the hum of an electric toothbrush. Sophie stepped out of the bathroom dry-eyed, dressed in one of Mike's old Bradley University tees. *Gone but not forgotten.*

When she saw him, she sighed. "Go to bed, Del."

He walked over to her. "I am an idiot."

"Go to bed," she said again, head bowed.

He took her face in his hands, his eyes locking on hers. "Whatever it is, whatever he did, doesn't matter."

The defiant angle of her chin made her look proud and jaw-droppingly lovely. She pulled away from him. "Just so you know, what happened in the kitchen tonight? I planned it. I knew you wouldn't ask questions. All I had to do was keep my dress on so you couldn't see the . . . the rest. And I wouldn't be forced to witness your disgust—pity—whatever." Her face was white as chalk and her voice shook. "Why did you have to ask to spend the night?"

He tried to put his arms around her, but she was as unyielding as granite. "Sophie, we've been friends for more than half our lives. You think a few scars can change that?"

She wrenched away from him, stared down at her palm, tracing the marks with her fingertip. "Friendship, yes, but that's not what we're talking about. I can't be with you, Del. I want to, but I can't be with anyone. Not the way I am."

Frustration hit him with such force he wanted to howl. He gripped her shoulders and drew her close. "Listen to me. Stop punishing yourself for things, for people, you can't control. It's the same story over and over and over again, your grandmother's death, your mother leaving, Mike, and now David." He glanced up at the ceiling and took a long breath. "If you want to be with me, I'm right where I've always been—here waiting."

He let go of her, walked across the room, and flipped the light switch. In the weak, reedy glow of a streetlamp through closed blinds, the walls dissolved into a dark span of shadow and silhouette. Del's eyes adjusted, and he found his way back to her. She slipped her arms around his neck.

"Can I help you undress?" he asked softly. She nodded into his shoulder. Her skin was hot, electric, her body etched with fine grooves and ridges, like creases on velvet. The marked flesh felt foreign under his fingertips, and he tried to imagine what she looked like. But in his mind's eye, she was perfect. They made love, slow and sweet. Then did it again to make sure they got it right.

Afterward, unable to sleep, Del lay cupped around her, listening to the contrapuntal interplay of her easy breathing and the steady patter of rain on the roof. For the first time in decades he prayed. *Please God, let this be right.*

CHAPTER 10

When Del's cell woke him at 8:30 a.m., Sophie purred softly and stirred beside him. He vaulted from the bed and scuttled to the dresser. The bedroom was a fucking refrigerator. Summer in San Francisco. With his balls the size of peas and his mind filled with visions of his pleasure parts freezing off, he grabbed the phone and dived back under the covers. Awake now, Sophie lay on her side, head propped on an elbow, watching him.

"Miller," he said into the mouthpiece, too busy controlling his chattering teeth to pay attention to caller ID.

"Hey, Delbo. Tried you at home. No answer. Hate to interrupt." Mike paused. "So how was Sophie? Sorry. I mean how *is* Sophie?"

Del glanced over at her and smiled. "What do you want, Mike?"

"Have you seen the news?"

Del took a long breath and with more patience than he felt, said, "No, I've been asleep. Why are you calling?"

"The shit's hit the proverbial fan. The fake Cézanne is all over the TV."

"We knew that was coming."

"True, but what we didn't know is your law enforcement homies held out on you."

"Do you think you could quit screwing with me and explain why I'm wasting good sleep time talking to you?"

"Uh-oh, sounds like someone got up on the wrong side of

the bed. Better watch that. Sophie is a morning person. Okay, here's the deal. According to the news, before London shuffled off this mortal coil, he wrote a letter admitting culpability in the painting switch. In other words, the old sonovabitch confessed."

"Bullshit. There's been no postmortem. We wouldn't release a suicide confession until the medical examiner confirmed cause of death, and that's not taking the Feds into account. Even if London had a role in the theft, why would the FBI risk alerting co-conspirators?"

"Just a reminder, bro, you resigned from the SFPD. It's no longer *we,* but *they.* For what it's worth, the intel didn't come from your porcine pals. Channel Six broadcast the story during *AM San Francisco.* Nearly choked on my oatmeal. I assume the station believes the confession is genuine, or they wouldn't risk airing the report."

Del's heart jumped in his chest. "How the hell did Channel Six get hold of London's suicide confession?"

"He messengered a copy to one of their anchors."

"What the fuck?"

Sophie stared at Del, eyes wide, and he attempted another smile. "Did the broadcast mention my parents?" he asked Mike.

"Oh, yeah. The story detailed how Samuel and Hanna Miller generously lent their priceless Cézanne to the California Museum of Fine Art for its landmark Post-Impressionist exhibit. How the painting was stolen and replaced with a fake. And how, after meeting with the FBI and the museum's exemplary legal counsel—namely me—the director decided to off himself. My office phones are going nuts. The media is on this like a fat cop on a doughnut." Mike blew out an irritated breath. "Cop jokes aren't nearly as funny since you drop-kicked Homicide. You really should have thought this job change through better. There's nothing even mildly entertaining about a security consultant."

No shit. Del rubbed his palm over his face. "What is your office telling the press?"

"That Hanna Rosen Miller, docent, trustee, and lifelong pillar of the community, recognized the painting as a fake and immediately approached London about contacting the FBI. London argued the negative publicity would cause irreparable damage to the museum's reputation. Rather than call in the Feds, he tried to persuade her to agree to a private investigation. Implied but not stated outright: when Hanna refused London's appeals and demanded he call the FBI, the old man knew he'd be found out. He did himself in to escape the consequences. Of course I don't believe it, but it's a damn good story."

"Did you forget my mother was also bent on protecting CaMu's reputation? You work for the museum. This doesn't seem like a conflict of interest to you?"

"Doesn't hurt for anyone to believe London tried to manipulate your mom into keeping quiet. Bottom line, the museum will come out fine in this. Attendance will soar. My concern is Samuel and Hani. I guarantee the exhibit's underwriters are already looking for a way to avoid paying out a claim on the Cézanne if the painting is not recovered."

"Are you talking about the possibility of my parents suing CaMu? Not going to happen if my mother has any say. What a fucking mess." Sophie slid closer, her brow creased, concern clouding her face. Del said into the phone, "Just to be clear, neither of us believes London deliberately killed himself, right?"

"So that makes the suicide note what? A writing exercise?"

"Come on, Mike, suicide by autoerotic asphyxiation?"

"Could be he wanted to go out with a smile."

Del exhaled a long, frustrated rush of air. "I need to let my parents know."

"Done. I spoke with your dad. The press is already swarming

the Miller Monstrosity. I told him neither he nor Hani should leave the house today, but he insisted he had rounds."

"If London confessed, then where's the Cézanne?"

"About that, the note apparently neglected to mention the location of the painting." There was quiet on the line and Del heard a female voice in the background. Then Mike was back. "I have to go. The phones are lighting up like Vegas slots, and Susan is threatening to quit. So much for my loyal assistant. What's our next move, Delbo?"

"Not our show, Mike. All we can do is sit tight and wait for the results of the postmortem, but a suicide confession is cliché even for London."

"I hated the guy's guts, wouldn't put much past him, but I can't believe he'd ever do anything to intentionally harm the museum. Suicide or accident, a confession doesn't smell right. London was all about denial."

"If he confessed, it doesn't make much difference whether he killed himself on purpose or by accident while getting his jollies."

"Makes a shitload of difference if someone helped him, bro. You're the one who said the cops weren't sure the old fool could have gotten himself into that position without help."

"Thanks for the visual." Again Del heard Susan's voice in the background. "Take your calls, Mike. I'm fully aware of who does the work in that office. You lose Susan and you'll be slinging burgers at Bob's Big Boy by next week. Give me a buzz if you hear anything else."

"Roger that," Mike said, his voice suddenly businesslike. "Give my love to Sophie."

In your dreams, ass-wipe. Del closed the phone and caressed Sophie's cheek.

★ ★ ★ ★ ★

While it was cold upstairs, Sophie's first floor could have doubled as a walk-in freezer. They huddled under blankets on the sofa to watch the news, Sophie shivering, arms wound tight around Del's torso, assuring him the heat would kick in any second. After the broadcast, Del checked the Internet. According to the Channel Six website, the note had been overnighted to the station, presumably by London himself, but the idea of Thurman London committing suicide still rankled.

After breakfast, Del drove home, showered, shaved, dressed in a fresh shirt and slacks, and headed for his parents' house. A half-dozen news vans were parked outside the gate. He circled the block, tucked his car onto a side street, and approached the house on foot. Last night's rain had vanished, replaced by streams of clouds, brilliant white to the east, dark and threatening to the west. The air was sticky and damp and redolent with the scent of saltwater and eucalyptus. With the wind at his back, the bay lit gold in the morning light, his spirits rose.

He slid his key into the lock and crept in through the camouflaged back gate, the same one he'd sneaked out of in high school. That was irony for you. He leaned against a tree and punched his parents' phone number into his cell.

"Mom, I'm in the back garden. Can you unlock the service door? I didn't want you to think someone was breaking in."

Halfway up the path to the house, the door swung open and again a dark pall settled over Del. His mother stood at the threshold. Yesterday's dark circles now appeared permanent etchings in personal grief, the lines around her mouth deep and intransigent.

She stood on tiptoe to kiss his cheek as he stepped into the mudroom. The warmth and reassuring smell of food embraced him. He followed her into the kitchen and they sat at the wide oak table in the breakfast nook. This was his favorite spot in the house. His mother's art covered every inch of bare wall, portraits of family and friends, everyone he knew and cared about. Today, all those eyes on the back of his neck put him on edge.

"Have you had lunch?" she asked. "I made chicken soup and noodle kugel. I'm baking an apple cake for your father."

"I'm not hungry. Mike said he called and spoke to Dad about what's going on with London and the painting."

"He did. I've been watching the news people from the upstairs windows. I keep hoping they'll leave."

"Don't count on it."

She studied the table and took a shuddery deep breath. "Mendel, I hope you understand how very sorry I am. You were never meant to find out about my"—she pressed her lips together and lowered her gaze again—"my relationship with Thurman. I hope you know I wouldn't hurt you for the world. I didn't realize what I was saying last night."

Del ran his thumbnail inside a tiny moon-shaped divot in the wooden table unable to look at her. "How long did it go on?"

"It was a terrible time. After we lost Amy, part of your father died along with her. Our hearts broke into a million pieces. I lost not only my child but my husband. I needed someone to talk to, to reach out to, to remind me I was still here, still alive. I—"

His rage bubbled up. "What about me? You couldn't reach out to me? I needed you, Mom, and you were nowhere to be found. Answer me. How long did it go on?"

Her chin trembled, but tearless, her eyes met his, her gaze direct. "A few weeks. The affair meant nothing. I love your father. I always have. What I did was wrong. I'm not making excuses, but I pray to God you never know what it's like to lose a child."

"How did Dad find out?"

"He would never tell me. By the time he learned the truth,

both the affair and Thurman's marriage were over. Gitte filed for divorce."

"Perhaps if you'd been more discreet?" Del intended the words to draw blood, and she bowed her head as if in supplication.

"I made a mistake. I should have been there for you, for your father, instead of going off to lick my own wounds." She put her hand over his. "I'm asking for your forgiveness."

"Dad forgave. That's not good enough for you?"

She blinked back tears. "He tried. He loves me, but he could never really forgive, only accept."

"Did you ever think he might resent all the hours you spend at that goddamn museum? All the contact you had with your former lover?"

She wiped her eyes with the back of her hand. "I volunteered at CaMu before I turned twelve. In high school, I interned there. As an art student, I ran the museum's art education project for children. I became a docent long before Thurman London ever set foot inside CaMu's walls. The museum is part of me. Was I supposed to give it up? For what? If there'd been emotional involvement between Thurman and me, yes, but there was nothing."

She sighed deeply and sat back in her chair. "The affair happened so many years ago, I'm not certain Thurman even remembered. We were friends, remained friends for years, just like you and—" She stopped mid-sentence.

Del again felt the red zing of anger. "Who, Mom? Sophie? Because I never fucked Sophie while she was married to Mike."

She flinched. "It's not the same. You and Sophie have a special bond."

Yeah. Special. Sophie needed him to prove she wasn't damaged goods the same way his mother needed London to prove she was still alive. His stomach churned. He couldn't talk about this anymore. "When will Dad be back? You shouldn't be alone, not with all that shit going on out front."

"Language, Mendel, please?" she said weakly. "I'm fine. Your father had a meeting this morning and rounds at the clinic this afternoon. Did he tell you the hospital asked him to resign? They're concerned about his age. No one seems to care he's a brilliant physician, as sharp and capable as ever. I don't know what he'll do with himself. More volunteer work, I suppose," she said with a faraway look.

"I want to talk about what you found in London's office."

Her eyes sparked with indignation, and her voice went steely quiet. "No. That I will not discuss."

Not good enough. "When you entered London's office, did you realize what had happened?"

"The news reports mentioned a suicide note. He committed suicide."

"The note was a confession, Mom. Did you suspect London was behind the theft of the Cézanne?"

Doubt flickered across her face. "I don't believe Thurman would ever have done anything that would hurt the museum— not by choice."

"How did you find him? Did you knock? Was his office locked?"

Her nostrils flared. She turned away and shook her head violently.

"Was there padding around his neck?"

"Padding? What are you talking about?"

"Something to protect his neck from bruising. Padding would suggest he intended to produce asphyxia—deprive his brain of oxygen—for sexual gratification. That he hadn't meant to kill himself. I know the condition of the body when you found him. One of the detectives told me at the scene."

She clenched her jaw and glared at Del, biting off each word.

"I will not talk about this with you."

He rested his elbows on the table, leaned forward, and matched her tone. "Yes, you will."

She tried to stand and he caught her arm and held her in the chair. Maybe he wanted to punish her, or maybe he wanted to punish himself because he'd been duped. His beautiful, strong, perfect mother wasn't who he thought she was. "Was this normal behavior for him, Mom? Was this how he usually got his rocks off?"

"That's enough!" She slammed her palm on the table. "If you want to know about Thurman talk to one of his women, not to me."

"He had a girlfriend?"

"Or ask his ex-wife. Gitte lives up in Greenbrae. She'd probably remember you."

"How do you explain London's confession if he had nothing to do with the disappearance of the painting?"

Her shoulders slumped in defeat, and she buried her face in her hands. "I can't. Maybe someone forced him to write the note. All I'm sure of is he didn't kill himself, and he had no part in the theft of the Cézanne."

"On the news last night, I saw you standing with Neil Sobol. What did you two talk about?"

"Nothing. He had questions about the Cézanne, but I was too upset to talk." She exhaled and sat up straight, her eyes hard. "Are you finished interrogating me?"

Del didn't answer.

"The museum is set to reopen day after tomorrow," she said.

"To stellar crowds I'm sure. Now the theft rather than the Cézanne will be the draw."

"I'm not ready to go back."

"I doubt anyone would expect you to."

"I left my purse in the docent office. My wallet, glasses, keys."

"I know, Mom. You told us that last night."

"I wondered if you'd pick up my bag for me. You live so close." Her hand fluttered near her throat, her wedding band flashing in the light from the Palladian windows.

"I can, but why not send a courier?"

"You could talk to the staff about the painting."

Exasperated, Del let his chin fall forward and shook his head. "Mom, I cannot step in the middle of an FBI investigation. You understand that, right?"

"I'm not asking you to. Just use your eyes and ears. You've always been so clever. Maybe you'll see or hear something."

"Just tell me one thing, are you asking because of London's death or because of the missing Cézanne?"

"Yes," she said.

CHAPTER 11

Mike's executive assistant, Susan—protector, apologist, and overseer of all things Greggs Allen and Gabretti—expertly fielded questions from the media, but when the call came in from CaMu's underwriters, she turned it over to her boss. Unfortunately, Mike had no answers regarding the museum's culpability in the Cézanne debacle—at least not yet.

He let out a breath and pushed the button on the intercom.

"Yes, Mr. Gabretti."

"Susan, I've had it. Any more calls, tell them I've left the building."

"You mean lie?"

"Absolutely."

"Yes, sir," she said, her voice as clear and bright as the ring of crystal. The woman was unflappable.

Mike leaned back in his chair, eyes sweeping from the custom furniture to the commanding view of the bay. This suite was everything he'd ever wanted. Even had its own bathroom where he could piss and shower at will. Unfortunate that complete privacy, while ideal for fucking his paralegal, hadn't been so great for his marriage. By the time he realized Sophie was the only thing he really wanted, he'd lost her. But damned if he didn't still have this beautiful office. Oh, and Alexa; he still had Alexa.

He rested his forehead in his hands, closed his eyes, and willed himself to focus. The painting, London's suicide, the old fart's alleged confession. It all reeked.

London was constantly on the make for green, but always in support of CaMu. He lived and breathed the museum. Why steal a painting and risk destroying the reputation he'd worked so carefully and so many years to build? And not just any painting, but one lent by trustees to be the centerpiece of London's personal triumph, the most important exhibition ever mounted at CaMu. Was it revenge for his shattered liaison with Hani? Twenty-two years after the fact? Mike didn't believe it for a second. And God help Hani if the FBI—or worse, the press—uncovered the affair. Mike winced at the potential for salacious headlines.

Hani was so different from Mike's own mother. Hani smelled of oil paint instead of perfume. She never worried about her hair or nails, if she had on the right shoes or carried the latest handbag. Whether because of these things or in spite of them, Mike loved her dearly. Growing up, he'd been mortifyingly smitten. It wasn't just that Hani was beautiful, although she had been. Still was, in fact. But Hani, born into old money, had never known need or envy. Instead of inuring her to the outside world, her privileged life made her brave. More than brave, it made her kind.

"I'm spoiled," she'd say. "My life is filled with what gives me joy, my family, my art, my kitchen, *chesed.*" Acts of loving kindness, her heart's true religion.

Now, Mike wondered how much of that kindness was borne of guilt over the affair with London. That was unfair; still, he couldn't help it. Hani loved Samuel, but Mike knew from experience marriage wasn't easy. Sometimes, even in love, we make mistakes. Mike was well-schooled in the art of making mistakes.

There was a knock at the door.

"Come," Mike said.

Susan stuck her head into the room. "Better turn on your television."

"Christ. What now?"

"Autopsy results on Dr. London. News is saying he died as a result of some weird accidental sex mishap. I don't understand. I thought the police found a suicide note." Susan paused and shook her head. "Oh, and before I forget, Inspector Miller is on his way back."

Del sidled up behind her and laid his hands on her shoulders. "No more inspector, Susan."

She laughed. "I remember, but after calling you inspector for so many years, it's hard to—"

Mike interrupted. "Did you hear about London?"

Del nodded. "Yep. Apparently the suicide note isn't a suicide note."

A phone rang in the outer office and Susan stepped out of the room, softly closing the door behind her.

Del sank into the leather chair facing Mike. "I talked to Terry Molina. Cops found no suicide note at the scene. In fact, he still hasn't seen the note. He and Kralmer are waiting for the FBI to grace them with a copy. Terry confirmed someone at Channel Six received the original overnighted via courier—"

"Suede Dunn."

Del raised an eyebrow "What about Suede?"

"She was the recipient. London sent the confession to Suede."

Del was quiet for a moment. "Okay. Anyway, put London's confession together with the autoerotic asphyxiation, and no appreciable physical evidence to suggest the scene was tampered with, and we're left with a confession and a death, and no connection."

Mike laughed. "So sometime after we each met with London about the painting, he wrote out a confession, couriered the note to Suede at Chanel Six, then walked back into his office, decided to have a private jack-off party, and whoopsie-daisy? All one big coincidence? That sound right to you?"

"According to Terry, the FBI is satisfied the confession wasn't written under duress or by anyone other than London himself." Del's eyes narrowed to hard slits. "Not that any of this will matter to my mother. She's convinced London had nothing to do with the theft of the Cézanne."

Mike agreed with Hani, but given the acid in Del's voice, decided not to take sides. "What happened to the theory that London wasn't alone? How can the medical examiner rule out murder?"

"No unexplained trauma to the body. More to the point, simple logic. Why would someone go to the trouble of humiliating the guy? Why not just put a bullet through his heart?"

Mike gave a derisive snort. "London was a far bigger douchebag than you realize. An opportunity to demean him? Volunteers would line up. I'm not saying London wasn't a bastard, but he was a loyal bastard. I agree with your mother, he wouldn't do anything to jeopardize CaMu, not to mention his own reputation. You're positive you can't worm information out of your FBI buddy?"

"The Feds won't talk to me. They'd barely talk to me when I worked Homicide."

Mike fixed his gaze on Del. "So, you're going to pussy out on this?"

"What is it with you? If by *pussy out* you mean not sticking my nose into a federal investigation, then, yeah, that's exactly what I'm going to do."

"And the murder?"

"What murder, Mike? The medical examiner ruled London's death an accident—his death and confession are unrelated." Del scrubbed his hands over his face wearily. "Okay, so I don't believe in coincidence any more than you do, but I'm a security consultant, not a cop. I advise rich, paranoid bastards about how to fortify their pseudo-castles, and assholes in suits how to keep employees from ripping off the supply closet. My hands are tied."

Mike controlled a rush of irritation. "What about the security cameras? They're all over CaMu. The vids would show who went in and out of London's office."

"The cameras are in the public areas, not the administrative offices, and I guarantee the Feds already have the tapes, or to be accurate, the hard drives." Del walked to the window overlooking the bay. "Don't you think I want this over, the painting returned?"

Mike was pretty sure what Delbo wanted was payback for his mother's affair with London. "Sure you want it returned. Especially if it turns out London is guilty. But here's the thing," Mike said, pissed at being put in the position of having to defend a man he could barely tolerate. "I don't think he is."

"Then let the Feds do their job." Del checked his watch. "Enough of this. It's almost six. You up to catching a bite to eat?"

"Can't. Alexa is having a girls' night out with friends. Promised I'd take full charge of Amy." Mike paused, pressed his lips together, then asked, "So how did you end up with Sophie, while I got stuck with Alexa?"

Del sighed. "Come on, Mikey. Let's not get into this again."

"I hope things work out for you two, really," Mike said, certain they never would. Divorce notwithstanding, Mike knew Sophie still loved him. Deep down, Delbo knew it too. "By the way, if you hurt her, I'll cut your balls off and feed them to Casper."

Del stood silent at the window, his back to Mike.

"Hey, are you listening to me?"

"Yeah, I'm listening. You're the only one allowed to hurt

Sophie," Del said, not unkindly. "Why pick on Casper? What happened to Alexa's yapping pile of mange?"

"Alexa couldn't handle a baby *and* a dog. Her mother took Titsy."

"Bitsy."

"You ever check out that dog's undercarriage? Thing was so fat, it had boobs. I'm surprised Alexa didn't give her mom Amy and keep the dog—less upkeep," Mike said.

"Alexa loves Amy."

"Alexa loves the idea of Amy. Dressing her up, parading her around, showing her off. Problem is, Alexa gets tired of her toys fast, and she's already bored with playing mommy. I've got to get a nanny in the house so I can quit worrying."

"You don't think Alexa would hurt the baby?"

"Not on purpose, but I think she might forget about her, run off, and leave the baby while she's sleeping, or stick her in the bath and get distracted. Nothing intentional. Nothing Alexa does is intentional. Deliberate is not my wife's style."

"You sure about that? She *is* the one who told Sophie about your affair."

"Excuse me?" Mike chewed the words, the blood instantly hot in his veins.

"How could you not know that?"

Mike shook his head. "I was sure it was someone from inside the firm but—goddamn bitch."

"Water under the bridge, Mikey. It's done."

"Done is right."

"How about we swing by, pick up Amy, and bring her to dinner? She might enjoy an evening out without her mama."

"Who wouldn't?" Mike said and almost choked on his own joke.

★ ★ ★ ★ ★

Rain began to fall again, a thin steady drizzle blown inland from the bay. Mike held Amy tight, stepping carefully on the slick wet cobbles of the driveway. Alexa trailed behind them with an umbrella.

"If you're taking the Volvo, leave me the keys for the Z4," she said.

"I'm taking the Volvo because the car seat is in the back." Why did he have to explain this? "You're not getting the keys to the Beemer. Drive your own car." Mike smiled down at Amy, leaned into the backseat to secure her in the carrier, and kissed her impossibly soft cheek.

"The Honda is almost out of gas," Alexa said

"Lucky for you, there's a gas station two blocks away."

"Come on, Mike. I don't have time to stop for gas. You were supposed to be home by six. I'm already late."

"Well, standing around whining isn't going to get you there any faster." Mike ran his eyes over his wife. Five-inch heels, skintight leggings, see-through top and no bra. Night out with the girls? Smelled like a steaming pile of shit to him, but he didn't care enough to confront her.

They both glanced up as Del's Porsche rounded the corner and pulled into a space across the street.

"Terrific, Mr. Holier-than-Thou. The evening's complete," she said.

Mike glared at her, rain falling like fine needles against his skin. All she could do was complain. Had she always been like this?

"Don't give me that look, Mike. The guy is a boring, self-important man-whore who uses a too-pretty face and a nice ass to collect women."

"Which you can't stand because he refuses to drool over you. Look, Alexa, I'm tired, I'm wet, and not a chance in hell I'm handing over the keys to the Z. You may as well go."

Anger hardened her eyes, and with an impressive long-legged fuck-you stride, she stormed down the driveway. Del ducked to avoid her umbrella, then turned to watch her climb into the Civic parked at the curb.

"Trouble in paradise?" he called out to Mike.

Mike attempted a smile. The cunt hadn't even bothered to say goodbye to Amy. "Nothing a personality transplant wouldn't cure. Hers, of course. I'm charm personified."

"Goes without saying. You sure you don't want to take separate cars?"

"Affirmative. You're in charge of making Amy smile on the way to Mac's." Mike bent into the car to peek at the baby. She was snoring softly, her chubby legs curled into commas, her tiny fist in her mouth. His heart swelled. He cleared his throat to keep his voice from breaking. "She's asleep."

They drove to the restaurant in silence, the sound of rain and the back and forth rhythm of the wipers as soothing as a heartbeat.

Mac's, formally known as MacNeil's Pub, was a family place with comfort food, televisions every ten feet, and a good-natured rowdiness that wouldn't be disrupted if Amy cried. A Friday night crowd packed the small eatery, and the air was thick with fried food, end of the week affability, and the clatter of dishes. The roar of conversation was deafening. No chance of Amy sleeping through this din.

They squeezed into a booth, Del on one side, Mike and carrier-ensconced Amy on the other.

A round, sulky young woman with hair the color and sheen of cooked beets approached the table with menus. Her nametag read RINA. Mike watched her eyes connect with Del. The girl blinked twice as if faced with something so dazzling, she couldn't quite believe what she was seeing. Her dark red pout curved into a smile.

"Hi. Can I bring you something to drink?" she asked.

Del raised a hand, refusing the menu. "Already have it memorized. I'd like a Lagunitas IPA and pastrami on rye." He smiled at her. "Your name is beautiful. Did you know Rina means joy in Hebrew?"

Del and cooze. It was all Mike could do to keep from rolling his eyes. "I'll have a Pellegrino and a reuben with fries," he said.

The waitress's gaze never left Del. "Rina is short for Katerina. Katerina means pure. Joy sounds like a lot more fun than purity." She giggled.

"Excuse me," Mike said louder than he'd intended.

Rina jerked her head around and studied him through slitted eyes.

He softened his tone and gave her his best smile. "I'd like a reuben with fries and a Pellegrino."

She made a note on her pad, looked up, and seemed to notice Amy for the first time. After lobbing a quizzical glance at Del, she leaned over Mike to get a better view of the baby. "Hi, sweetheart. You're beautiful. What's your name?"

"Her name is Amy," Mike said, stroking the baby's fine dark hair with his fingertip.

Del stood and leaned over the table. "Hi, gorgeous," he said. Amy squealed and gurgled happily, and the three of them laughed.

Rina stuffed her order pad in her pocket. "I'll have your drinks and food up in a flash." She looked from Del to Mike. "You two seem like really great dads, and your little girl is adorable."

Mike and Del watched her walk off, their eyes met, and they exploded in laughter.

It felt sweet, cathartic. Mike couldn't remember the last time they'd laughed together. He rocked in his seat and gasped for breath. "Holy shit. I can't believe she thought we were queer. Dude, you definitely need to work on your eye fuck. You've apparently got some kind of disconnect going."

They howled.

"This *is* San Francisco," Del said, wiping away tears with the palms of his hands.

Mike choked out another laugh. "You better hope Alexa doesn't find out. She's already jealous of our relationship."

Del collapsed against the back of the booth and held up his hands in supplication. "Enough. My face aches." His eyes flicked toward the bar and the smile faded. He pointed to the television. "Hey, they're talking about the painting."

Mike peered over his shoulder at the screen. "BREAKING NEWS" ran in red letters across the bottom of a photograph of the missing Cézanne. "Was it recovered?"

"Don't know. I can't hear."

The screen flashed to an in-studio news anchor, then to a dark, rawboned man, with hair slicked back and wearing sunglasses. He held up an old photograph of an elderly man standing next to the Cézanne.

"Who's the guy with the photo?" Mike asked, and then shouted to the crush of drinkers at the bar, "Could someone turn the TV up?"

"Daniel Shapiro, grandson of legendary art dealer and gallery owner, Yoseph Shapiro, claims the missing Cézanne belongs not to the Millers, but to the Shapiro family."

Del's head shot up.

"In 1940, fleeing the German occupation, Jewish art dealer Yoseph Shapiro left Paris for New York and then San Francisco where he opened a new gallery. Shapiro's Paris collection was confiscated by the Nazis. Until a newspaper article promoting the CaMu exhibit fell into their hands, the Shapiro family believed the Cézanne masterpiece to be among the Nazi-plundered works and held little hope of its return.

" 'The Cézanne belongs to my family,' Daniel Shapiro told special correspondent Lon Laramie. 'According to the description in the exhibit catalog, Samuel Miller acquired the painting from his father, Max Müeller. Records prove my grandfather employed Mr. Müeller as a courier at his Paris gallery. What we believed to be Nazi looting was no more than theft by a trusted employee.' "

Del stood, face flushed, hands curled into fists. "That is a fucking lie!"

The conversation in the room died, and Amy shrieked.

Mike picked up the baby, held her close, and spoke to Del through clenched teeth. "For godsake, shut up and sit down. Everyone is staring, and you're scaring Amy. Is that true? Your grandfather worked for Yoseph Shapiro?"

"You heard my mom. He worked for an art dealer. That's all I know." Del dropped back into his seat, nostrils flared, face radiating anger.

" 'Grandfather kept the Cézanne in his office at the Paris gallery. The painting was part of his personal collection, a treasured favorite. Max Müeller had no right to the painting. My grandfather died in 1958, but my family is in agreement. We owe it to his memory to bring the Cézanne home.' "

Del's voice was low and fierce. "Somebody needs to explain slander to that cocksucker."

"That *cocksucker* is Yoseph Shapiro's grandson. His attorneys—and trust me, I can see from here the guy is wearing Armani—attorneys, plural—wouldn't let him open his mouth if they didn't have something to support the claim." Mike kissed a quieted Amy and laid her back in the carrier. "With your artsy-fartsy parents, you must be aware of who the Shapiros are. Even I recognize the name, and I covet Elvis on velvet."

"Screw the humility, Mike. It doesn't suit you, and I don't

have the patience right now. Yes, I'm familiar with the Shapiros. So what? They just said Yoseph died in 1958, and Daniel Shapiro can't be more than thirty-five. He never even met his grandfather."

" 'It's both sad and coincidental the painting should disappear just as we were about to exercise our right of ownership.' "

Mike rested his elbows on the table, steepled his fingers, and touched them to his lips. "Okay, now I'm pissed. Did you catch that? He's insinuating someone was tipped off about his family's intention to lay claim and purposely made the Cézanne disappear. London's confession aside, he's implicating your parents. Who else would benefit?"

They fell silent as Rina reappeared with food and drinks.

The moment she was out of earshot, Del asked, "What do you mean by *London's confession aside*? Are you saying you believe Shapiro?"

"Relax. I'm only trying to think things through. When did your name go from Müeller to Miller?"

"When my grandfather's brother—Avi—emigrated to the U.S. He changed our name to Miller. More American, or at least less German. You remember Avi?"

Mike smiled. "Oh, yeah, I remember Uncle Avi and his stories about your grandfather. Haven't thought about him in years."

"Shapiro's claim is bullshit, Mike." Del raked his fingers through his hair. "How the hell can somebody refute something that happened seventy years ago?"

"Like you'd refute any lie. You're a trained investigator, a damned good one. Although if you tell anyone I said so, I'll deny it," Mike said around a mouthful of reuben. "Eat your food."

"My grandfather is dead. Yoseph Shapiro is dead. Avi is dead. And I'm no historian."

"Start with your dad."

Del gave a steely crack of a laugh. "No way. Everything I know about my grandfather, I learned from Avi. Dad never talked about his father, the war, the Holocaust. They're tough subjects for him, and I won't press."

"Better you than the FBI. Your grandfather was Jewish. He fought for the Resistance. Shapiro was also Jewish. It's possible they were acquainted through religious or political channels."

"I know my parents purchased art through the Shapiro Gallery here in the city, but whether my grandfather worked for Yoseph Shapiro seventy years ago? I have no idea."

"You can probably take that much of the grandson's story to the bank. If your grandfather didn't work for Shapiro, some other Max Müeller did."

"I don't remember Uncle Avi saying much about Paris. He talked about my grandfather's work with the escape networks and *Œuvre de Secours aux Enfants*—OSE—in Vichy."

"Society for Assistance to Children," Mike translated. Mike had a gift for languages and spoke seven. In school, whenever his GPA flagged, he signed on for another language course.

"OSE ran homes for Jewish kids whose parents were in the camps," Del said.

Mike nodded. "I remember Avi's stories. Like Izieu? Forty-four kids arrested, deported, and murdered. Who the fuck arrests a four-year-old?" Mike tossed his sandwich down on the plate and stared at Amy. He placed his palm gently on her chest to ease the knot in his gut. "I was nine, and the story scared the living crap out of me. Why would Avi tell nine-year-olds that shit?"

"So you'd never forget. You haven't, have you?" Del took a deep breath, his face unreadable.

Mike spoke carefully. "Your mother said the Cézanne was worth a lot of money, even back then. Why would someone give your grandfather such a valuable piece of art?"

"Gee, Mike, I don't know, but I'm pretty sure he didn't steal it."

"I wasn't suggesting he did."

"Sure as hell sounded like you were." Del pushed his plate away, food untouched.

"Come on, eat something," Mike said.

"I'm not hungry."

Rina walked up to the table and touched Del's shoulder. "Is your sandwich okay? Would you like me to bring you something else?"

"Yes, sweetheart," Mike lisped to Del, grinning. "You have to eat. Don't want you turning into skin and boner—uh, bones."

Del threw Mike a black look and glanced up at the waitress. "Everything was fine. I'm not as hungry as I thought. Could we get the check?" He said to Mike, "The report was breaking news. That means my parents haven't heard. No TV on Shabbat."

"Or telephones."

"We're not that far away from the house, and I know my parents would love to see Amy."

"Sure, what the hell." Anything was better than going home to Alexa.

CHAPTER 12

The press hovered outside Del's parents' house like locusts in search of a fresh field. He imagined Mike's Volvo taking out a few of the milling reporters and felt instant gratification. "Damned scavengers. There's an empty space. Pull in. We can walk up to the house and sneak in the back way."

Under the starless sky, they hiked the two uphill blocks. The smell of ebb tide and salt swirled around them, the night so cold they could see their breath, tiny clouds of steam floating in the soft relentless rain.

"This cloak-and-dagger shit is fine for you, but I'm hauling a baby and fifty pounds of infant accoutrements," Mike said, as they slipped in the rear gate.

Del knocked on the service door, then used his key. Shabbat began at sundown Friday. His parents wouldn't answer their phone until sundown Saturday. For them, Shabbat was a time of family, prayer, study, and introspection. For Del, Shabbat was the wet blanket that smothered his teenage social life.

Hanna met them at the door. "I saw you come in through the gate. *Shalom Shabbat.*" Del and Mike followed her into the kitchen. The aroma of the morning's baked challah still hung in the air, and Del felt an unexpected pang of loss so keen, he almost staggered.

Hanna took the baby carrier from Mike, her eyes shining. "She's getting so big, Mike. May I pick her up?" Mike nodded, and Hanna lifted Amy, held her close, and bounced her when she started to whimper.

"Is that my little Amy I hear?" Samuel stepped into the room and broke into an ear to ear grin. He stood behind Hanna and caressed the baby's cheek.

"Isn't she perfect, Samuel? When are you going to give us one of these blessings, Mendel? Children are a *mitzvah.*"

Del rolled his eyes. How many times had they been through this? "Thought I might try for a wife first."

Mike laughed. "You mean a woman? Don't tell Rina. She'll be crushed."

Samuel's brow furrowed. "Who's Rina?"

"No one. Mike, shut up." Del moved toward the breakfast nook. "Let's sit down. I assume you haven't seen the news?"

"We didn't attend *shul* because of the reporters out front, but this is still Shabbat."

Right, Shabbat. As if Del could forget.

"Mike, our precious girl is wet. Hand me the diaper bag and I'll change her," Hanna said.

"Wait, Mom. Sit for a minute, please."

She studied Del for several seconds, then settled into a chair next to Mike. "What's wrong, Mendel?"

"Do you recognize the name Yoseph Shapiro?" Mike asked.

Samuel let out an impatient breath. "Yes, of course. If this is regarding the allegation that my father stole the Cézanne from Yoseph's Paris gallery, the story is rubbish. Some TV reporter—the idiot—called the clinic early this afternoon, told me about Daniel Shapiro's claim, and asked whether I wanted to comment. I don't think she liked what I had to say."

"That's settled. Now may I change this sweet thing's diaper?" Hanna planted a kiss on Amy's cheek, then took the proffered infant paraphernalia from Mike. "Talk to your father," she said to Del on her way out of the room.

"You seem to be taking Shapiro's claim in stride, Dad."

"Why wouldn't I? I knew Yoseph Shapiro. I knew his sons, Jakob and Albert. Jakob and your Uncle Avi were great friends. I'm certain Daniel is convinced the painting belongs to his family or he wouldn't be making these allegations, but if Jakob were alive, he'd have the young man's head."

"So it's true. Del's grandfather worked for Yoseph Shapiro?" Mike asked.

"Absolutely. Yoseph died many years ago, but as a boy, I often spoke to him about my father."

Del's mind turned the revelation over. As far as he could remember, his father never spoke of the past to anyone. "The Shapiros knew you were in possession of the Cézanne?"

"I assume so. Your mother and I purchased a number of works from the Shapiro Gallery. The Picasso in the upstairs hallway, the Bonnard, the Signac. Yoseph was long dead by this time, of course. His son, Jakob, ran the gallery. More than once, Jakob's gallery manager, Lee Dutton, made acquisitions with your mother and me in mind. The Redon in the dining room for one. Until Jakob and then Albert passed, Lee remained manager of the gallery. He manages the Frakansia Gallery now."

"Do you remember ever discussing the Cézanne with Yoseph or Jakob?" Del asked.

"Not specifically, but Yoseph had great affection for your grandfather. They were friends, contemporaries."

Del would have felt a lot better about a friendship if he could confirm Yoseph gave his grandfather the Cézanne. "In his stories, Uncle Avi mentioned two paintings besides the Cézanne. One went to a nurse, the other to the couple who smuggled you out of France. How valuable were the works? How did Grandfather acquire them?"

"Enough." Del's father stood, his chair slamming against the wall. "How dare you come into this house and suggest my father—your grandfather—was a thief."

112

"Dad, I'm sorry, I didn't mean to—"

"You're no better than those investigators."

Mike's head jerked up. "What investigators? I hope you aren't talking to the FBI, Samuel. I strongly suggest you don't—"

"Don't what? Tell the truth about my father?" He dropped back in his chair and glanced from Del to Mike. "The FBI showed up at the clinic today five minutes after the call from the reporter. They implied the disappearance of the Cézanne was a conspiracy between Hanna, that piece of excrement, London, and me. Apparently, Daniel Shapiro has been working on his little reveal for quite some time. Last year the *Chronicle* interviewed Hanna about the upcoming Post-Impressionist show. Despite my reservations about including the Cézanne, it was crowned the highlight of the exhibit. The newspaper photographed Hanna in my study."

"With the painting," Mike said.

Samuel nodded and continued. "Daniel Shapiro saw the interview and contacted his attorneys. The FBI now have it in their heads that London, Hanna, and I were somehow alerted to what was in the wind and found a way to secrete the painting. The situation is so absurd I can't even get upset." His gentle brown eyes, now hard as agates, locked on Del. "What troubles me far more is my son's intimation that his grandfather would steal from a friend."

Del made another futile attempt at an apology.

"Samuel, listen to me." Mike said, grim faced. "If the FBI suspects you of concealing a sixty-million-dollar stolen painting, you should be upset. You should be panicked."

"The allegation I'd collude with London is insulting at best. I detested the man. The world is a better place without him. What reason would I have for stealing my own painting?"

Del got to his feet and began to pace the kitchen. He knew the question would make his father even angrier, but it had to be asked, "Why didn't you want the Cézanne in the exhibit?"

"Well, if you think it was because I lived in fear someone would recognize the painting as stolen, both you and the FBI are sadly mistaken."

There was so much rage in his father's eyes, Del barely recognized him. This man whom he'd loved and respected for thirty-eight years had suddenly turned into a stranger.

"If you want to know the truth, I hated the thought of London benefiting from my legacy. He was responsible for so much hurt to this family. He nearly destroyed us."

"Then why agree to let Mom lend the painting?" Del asked.

"Marriage is a shared partnership, not an autocracy. Your mother understood how I felt but was determined the painting should be included in the exhibit. Despite my resentment, I knew she was right. The Cézanne deserved to be seen. This did nothing to mitigate my dislike of London, however." Samuel shook his head ruefully. "I thought once he was dead that would be the end, but he continues to make my life miserable even from the grave."

I thought once he was dead that would be the end. A chill feathered along the back of Del's neck. He returned to the table, spun a chair around, and straddled it backward.

Samuel eyed Mike. "I apologize for what I said earlier. Of course I'm concerned that Hanna and I are suspect. How could I not be? If the authorities are convinced of a conspiracy, they won't look to the real perpetrators. The Cézanne meant the world to me, and I may never see it again, but far worse is the vilification of my father. He died an innocent man at the hands of the Nazis. Now he's being victimized again, and I have no clue how to stop it. My heart weeps." All his anger played out, he closed his eyes and dropped his head forward.

Del sat silent, not knowing what to say. His father, Samuel Miller, the brilliant, assured physician, sat before him diminished and vulnerable, and Del didn't have the words to make it right.

Mike shifted restlessly in his chair. "Despite Dr. London's confession, Hani doesn't believe he had anything to do with the disappearance of the Cézanne. I'm not convinced either."

"Why would the man confess to something he didn't do?" Del asked, not able to keep the irritation from his voice. "What do you think, Dad?"

Samuel's shoulders rose and fell in a deep sigh. "The bastard loved himself too much for suicide. Your mother described how she found him—autoerotic asphyxia was obvious."

"In my opinion," Mike said, "the medical examiner wanted the death off his plate. Accidental was the easy call. A homicide dick at the scene told Delbo they weren't convinced London was by his lonesome."

"The SFPD and the Feds are satisfied with the M.E.'s ruling. Terry backpedalled on the possibility London wasn't alone. Why not give your murder theory a rest, Mike?" Del's eyes found his father's. "You didn't answer me. Do you believe London's confession was legitimate?"

"I wouldn't put anything past Thurman London, but I don't understand why, if he admitted culpability, no one can find the painting. What was in his confession?"

"According to Channel Six—and they had first dibs—the letter was nothing more than a mea culpa," Mike said.

Del shrugged. "Maybe the station is holding back."

"Right. Television news media is famous for its discretion."

Panic flared in Del's solar plexus, his mind cartwheeling. London was furious when Del insisted CaMu bring in the FBI. What if the director intended his eleventh hour confession as some kind of payback meant to implicate Del's parents?

Del said to Mike, "The FBI is a dead end. Can you think of another way I can get my hands on a copy of the confession?"

"Even if Channel Six turned over the original to the Feds,

you can bet your ass they kept a copy."

Del shook his head. "Channel Six isn't going to release anything the Feds have told them to sit on."

Mike sniggered. "Not necessarily. Like I told you, Suede Dunn was the lucky recipient. My recollection of Suede is that *you* could get her to do just about anything *you* wanted."

"Suede?" Dad said.

Mike scooted his chair closer to the table, a lewd glint in his eye. "Channel Six anchor, the leggy blonde with the perky—"

"Shut up, Mike." Del took a breath. "It's still early. I could swing by her condo on my way home. Unless *you'd* prefer to give her a call?"

Mike held up his hands. "Uh-uh, I have more than enough leggy blonde to keep me busy. Suede's all yours. Should I call Sophie? Tell her you'll be late and maybe a little battle-worn?"

"Fuck you, Mike."

Samuel's eyes flashed fire. "I don't appreciate that language. Not in this house, especially not on Shabbat." His gaze shifted to Mike, then pinned Del again. "Are you seeing Sophie? Is that why you and Mike are at each other's throats?"

"Sophie and I have been friends since college. Now, suddenly, it's impossible to have a conversation with him," Del said, jerking a thumb at Mike, "and not have Sophie slip in as the topic of discussion."

Mike kept silent, an annoying hint of a grin nudging the corners of his mouth.

Del was sorely tempted to wipe the smile off his face. Resentment in overdrive, he angled himself away from Mike, the legs of his chair scraping across the kitchen tiles. "Dad, how did Uncle Avi know so much about what went on during the war? He told Mike and me dozens of stories about Grandfather helping to smuggle refugee children out of France. Where did he get his information?" Del paused, inhaled and braced himself to ask the question. "Could he have made it up? Avi loved his brother. Maybe he wanted to make Grandfather a hero in our eyes."

Del's father fixed him with a calm, level stare. The old man's voice was resolute. "He was a hero, and nothing can ever change that. He not only fathered me, he risked everything to get me out of France at an impossible time. He put me in the trust of a family who raised me as their own. He gifted me with life not once, but twice. It would do you well to remember your grandfather died a martyr and a hero. What you say to others is up to you, but I don't ever want to hear you suggest otherwise in my presence again. Am I clear?"

"Dad, I—"

"Do you understand?"

"Yes, sir," Del said, so caught up in shame, he was incapable of mounting a defense.

Samuel pushed back his chair and stood. "We're done here."

Del told himself to leave it alone, but he couldn't. "About Uncle Avi—"

Again, Samuel closed his eyes and exhaled deeply. "My father wrote letters from Paris and Marseilles. The correspondence slowed only after he was deported to the camps. Avi's stories were not make-believe. They came from my father's letters."

"What letters?" Del asked.

"The correspondence written during the time I was with my father in Paris came to me. The other letters, Avi held on to. I have no idea what happened to them after he passed. Your cousin inherited Avi's house. I always meant to ask Levi for the letters, but never followed up. I suppose I pushed them from my mind."

"You never mentioned any letters," Del said, half-pissed they'd been kept from him but wound tight with the possibility they could hold a clue as to how his grandfather acquired the Cézanne.

"The letters are written in German. Do I need to remind you, neither of us knows the language?"

Mike raised a brow at Del. Mike spoke German fluently.

"If he's willing, would you allow Mike to read through the letters?"

"I'm willing," Mike said at once. "And I'd be happy to transcribe them so you have copies in English, Samuel."

Samuel's voice softened and he looked wistful. "The language doesn't matter. When I hold the letters I hear my father's voice. I study the pages and pick out the one or two German words I recognize, and I remember the content. I know which letter is which because when I was a boy, Avi read them—translated them—for me so often." Samuel went silent for a moment, and then said, his face stricken, "I suppose I'm hearing Avi's voice, not my father's."

The kitchen door swung open and Hanna walked in with Amy in her arms. "She is an absolute angel, Mike. She let me change her diaper without a tear or a fuss." She whispered into the baby's ear and Amy gurgled. "You take good care of this one. She's perfect."

"Don't worry, I intend to," Mike said.

Amy's fingers made a star and reached for Mike. Hanna placed the baby in his arms, then cupped the top of her head and kissed her. "If you ever need a babysitter, you call. Doesn't look like I'm ever going to have any grandchildren of my own."

Del looked up at the ceiling and shook his head. "Mom, for godsake—"

"Mike, you didn't plan to look at the correspondence tonight, did you?" Samuel asked.

"No, I need to get Amy home. It would be hard to translate with her here, anyway. She may be perfect, but she's a little attention hog. Aren't you, sweetheart?"

"I wish I were comfortable allowing the letters to leave the house. It's not that I don't trust you," Samuel said, "but with the painting gone, they're all I have left."

"It's okay, Dad. We understand." Del stood and his mother sidled up next to him and touched his shoulder.

"Don't forget about my purse," she said quietly, slipping her key card into his hand. He nodded and slid the card in his jacket pocket.

"Ready to hit the road, Delbo?" Mike asked. "If you plan to talk Suede into giving up what's in the note—or anything else for that matter—I'd better get you to your car."

"What note?" Hani asked.

London's confession was the last thing Del wanted to discuss with his mother. Once was more than enough. "Dad'll fill you in. If tomorrow works for Mike, we'll come by in the morning to look at the letters. Ten o'clock?"

Hanna shook her head. "No. No work on Shabbat."

Mike shifted Amy to his left arm and with his right hugged Hanna. "Fortunately I'm Catholic, and Saturdays are my free day. Ten sounds good. All billable hours to the museum."

"Mike, CaMu is a not-for-profit institution," Hanna said, her words full of reproach.

Mike winked at her. "I am aware of that, Hani. I was joking."

The trio said their goodnights and exited the back gate. The advantage of the uphill hike to the house was the downhill stroll back to the car. While Mike strapped Amy into her car seat, Del stood on the sidewalk, shifting from one foot to another to stay warm. "Were you really joking about billing the museum?" he asked Mike.

Mike looked at Del over his shoulder and grinned. "Hell, no."

CHAPTER 13

Mike's lead foot got them across the Golden Gate to Mill Valley in less than twenty minutes. Not bad for a half-hour drive, and Del's life only flashed before his eyes twice.

"Who gives a shit about the Feds?" Mike said. "Your Homicide *amigos* haven't shut you out. Well, except that fat fuck, Kralmer. The other guy seems all right, though."

"Terry Molina is a good cop, which means there's isn't a chance in hell he'll talk to me now my parents have been dragged into the muck. Anyway, we're talking stolen art. The Feds are flying the bus on this one, not the SFPD."

"Dammit," Mike said under his breath as he pulled onto the driveway next to Alexa's Civic. He shut off the engine but made no move to get out of the car.

"What's your problem? Afraid of Alexa?"

Mike let out a small, harsh laugh, then sobered. "Yeah, as a matter of fact. You want to come in?"

"Hell, no." Del eyed the Volvo's dashboard clock. What he wanted was for Sophie to call. After feeding her a load of crap about not pressuring her, he'd promised to wait for her to make the next move. It had been two days and he was going crazy, but he couldn't very well show up on her doorstep. He unbuckled his seat belt, leaned forward, and rested his forehead on his palms.

"You okay?"

"Yeah, fine. Slammed. I need sleep. Think I'll skip Suede

120

tonight. I can talk to her tomorrow. You realize it's a waste of time, right? She isn't about to invite me in and hand over evidence in an ongoing FBI investigation."

"If I remember Suede—and believe me, bro, I do—with a little encouragement, she'll hand over a lot more than London's confession. It's criminal Channel Six keeps such a class act behind a desk. Never understood why you kicked her to the curb."

Del wasn't about to discuss Suede with Mike. "Things didn't work out. That all right with you?"

"Fine and dandy with me. Not sure Suede feels the same. And you've been spouting the same *didn't work out* bullshit since you broke up with Cindy Lee Fellowes in the first grade."

"Cindy wanted to play Barbies. I wanted to play doctor. We didn't work out either." His laugh came out flat and mirthless.

"All Suede wanted to play with was you."

Without warning, Del's anger sparked as bright and hard as a new-minted coin. "Why the fuck are you all up in my ass about Suede? As if I didn't know."

Mike grinned acidly. "Just trying to help your parents. Weren't you listening? Children are a *mitzvah*. Samuel and Hani want grandchildren. I bet Suede would make pretty babies—and she's Jewish."

"What's your point? Sophie isn't Jewish? Because we both know this is about Sophie and me. I don't get you, Mike. You have a gorgeous wife and baby." He glanced at Amy in the back-seat and lowered his voice. "You have a life. Sophie deserves the same. Eventually, she's going to find someone."

"That's just it. I don't see her looking anywhere but you."

"I didn't realize you were keeping tabs."

"Well, now you know. Sophie gravitates to the familiar, to people and things that make her feel safe."

Del looked out the windshield toward Mike's house. Alexa

stood at the front door. "Your wife is watching us, probably wondering what the hell we're doing sitting in the car."

Mike smiled and waved. Alexa flashed her middle finger. "You can see why the neighbors find her so charming."

Del reached for the door handle. "I'll meet you at my parents' tomorrow morning. Go inside. You need to get Amy out of the cold."

"Trust me, it's even colder inside the house. Delbo, listen to me. I'm telling you this as your best friend. If you let Sophie's insecurities stroke your ego, you're setting yourself up for a fall."

Without a word, Del climbed out of the Volvo, slammed the door, and walked to his car. Through his wipers, the city skyline shone amber in the distance, the lights mirrored jewels against the flat black abyss of the bay. San Francisco; there was no other city like it. For an instant, the possibility of leaving became reality, and thoughts of the offer letter waiting on his desk replaced his ache for Sophie.

He veered onto Van Ness toward home and the promise of sleep. Not that his loft had ever felt like home. Plus, he was too wired to sleep. He pulled into a vacant lot, turned the Porsche around, and followed Lombard up to Russian Hill. During the gold rush, miners had discovered headstones inscribed with Cyrillic letters at the crest of the hill. The markers were long gone, but the name stuck.

He swerved toward Taylor Street and parked in front of Suede Dunn's condo. Even at night, it was one ugly-ass building, a squatter in America's most beautiful city. It was a ruse. Behind the graceless gray cinderblock façade lived über-chic interiors, multimillion dollar views, and several of San Francisco's most recognizable faces.

Del checked contacts on his cell and punched in Suede's number.

"Is this really Homicide Inspector Del Miller?" Suede said, her voice rich, throaty, and articulate, the voice of a television journalist.

He laughed. "No, this is *former* Homicide Inspector Del Miller. Thought you were up on all the Hall of Justice gossip."

"I heard, but I couldn't believe it. A lot like this call."

"Sorry, I know it's late. Do you have a few minutes to talk?"

"For you, I have all night. Oops, did that make me sound like a slut?" She chuckled. "Ah, what the hell. Talk away."

Del drew in a slow, deep breath and said, "I hoped we might talk in person. I'm parked outside your building. I should have called first."

Her voice was even, noncommittal. "Come on up. You remember the door code?"

"I do." Why would he remember the access code but not Suede's phone number? The thought flitted away before his feet hit the pavement.

He took the elevator to the tenth floor, rapped lightly on the door, and waited. No answer. He knocked louder. He hadn't been in the building for more than a year, but knew he had the right unit. Suede's blue enameled mezuzah hung on the doorframe. The metallic snick of a lock sounded from inside.

Suede opened the door and smiled. "Hi, stranger."

He couldn't stave off the instant rush of familiarity as he stepped into the apartment. The smell of rose and lemon, the slanted shimmer of rain on the plate glass windows, a faint whiff of stale coffee. Suede. On the TV screen, Suede was attractive, her features faultless but unremarkable. In person she was ravishing, long-limbed with hair and eyes like burnished gold and a smile capable of stopping a man's heart. She'd stopped his more than once. Tonight she wore a long satin robe the color of fresh cream, as elegant as her polished maple floors and the Mahler symphonies that scored her life.

"Didn't mean to keep you waiting," she said. "I wanted to freshen up."

"You look exceedingly fresh." He leaned to kiss her cheek.

Born in Israel, Suede struggled to perfect her American accent for television. Whether in spite of this or because of it, she wielded idiomatic English like a weapon. "By fresh, do you mean ripe for the picking or impudent in a sexual way?"

He met her gaze and grinned. "Yes."

She laughed. "Same old Del. Thank God. I wouldn't have you any other way. Come, sit, tell me why you're here. I never expected to hear from you again."

The words were like a splash of ice water. "So, we didn't work out. Aren't we still friends?"

Her tawny eyes widened. "*Didn't work out.* Is that how you say it? Where I come from, we'd say you dumped me. Of course we'd say it in Hebrew, and my name would still be Addi Dunayevsky." She winked.

It struck him as absurd this confident, beautiful, intelligent woman would voluntarily choose a victim role. "I didn't dump you, Suede. I've never dumped anyone."

She sat in the swan-white armchair across from him, legs tucked underneath her, one long, lean thigh exposed, and a tiny twist of a smile on her lips. "Doesn't matter. What's past is past. Talk to me. To what do I owe the honor of your adorable presence?"

"I heard you broke the Thurman London story."

"Not so much broke as it fell into my lap. London messengered his confession to my attention. He must have figured I was hungry enough for a big story to make sure he got air time. Smart man. The FBI would have sat on the confession until they located any co-conspirators or, at the very least, the Cézanne. And if our admin staff had gotten hold of it, the envelope would still be sitting unopened on someone's desk."

"You knew Dr. London?"

"This is a small town. We'd met socially. Charming man, but a definite narcissist." She chuckled. "Takes one to know one."

Del studied her. Assured, definitely. Narcissistic? He didn't think so.

"By the time I received the letter, his death had already been reported, so naturally I assumed the note was a suicide confession. We broke the story on air—first things first—then called the authorities. I understand London also sent a copy to the president of CaMu's board of directors via snail mail. Clearly he wanted it to get to us first."

She pressed her lips together and tilted her head. "Funny, but when I first met you, I couldn't believe anyone who looked like you could be a cop. Now I can't imagine you as anything else. I gather you quit the force after the DA tried to hang the murder of that co-ed on Mike Gabretti?"

"The cluster fuck with Mike was only part of it. My partner died of cancer a couple months ago."

"Barb? I didn't know, Del. I'm so sorry."

"Yeah, me too." His throat closed, and he paused until he could speak. "I'm a security consultant now."

She cocked an eyebrow. "Security consultant? How's that working out for you?"

"Four times the money, half the work, and I have my own office. I hate it."

She burst out laughing, raunchy and uninhibited, her teeth a flash of white against caramel skin. "So why the interest in London? Don't tell me CaMu is one of your clients. That would not be good."

He couldn't tell if she was playing him or she really hadn't made the connection. "Do you know who Samuel and Hanna Rosen Miller are?"

"Of course, they're the well-to-do couple who lent—oh, shit."

125

She swung her legs down, placed her feet flat on the floor, and covered her mouth with her hands. "Your parents? Miller is such a common name, it never occurred to me."

He nodded. "Listen, Suede, I need to know the contents of London's confession."

She rested her elbows on her knees. "London took responsibility for the forgery and replacing the Cézanne in the exhibition. That's pretty much the sum total."

"Nothing about how he managed the switch? Accomplices? Location of the painting?"

She shook her head. "Nothing more than I've told you."

Del released a breath. At least London hadn't implicated his parents. "I'd like to see the note."

"The FBI has it."

"You didn't make a copy before you gave up the original?"

She gave him a sheepish look. "Okay, yes, I did, but I don't carry the thing around with me. The copy is at the station."

"I'm asking this as a personal favor. As your friend, can you get me a copy? Given Daniel Shapiro's claim, the Feds suspect my parents may have had something to do with the Cézanne's disappearance. There might be something in the confession that will help prove otherwise, something the Feds missed."

Suede stretched out her endless, well-muscled legs, dancer's legs. Too tall to be a principal dancer, she gave up ballet. Suede Dunn had no interest in being part of the corps.

She blinked her astonishing eyes. "Has anyone inquired, why, if London was clearing his conscience, he wouldn't name accomplices? Hard to believe he managed the theft alone. And it mystifies me that he'd confess, then stroll into his office and jerk off." She smiled. "I'm not Catholic, but isn't it usually done the other way around?"

"Any thoughts about his death?"

"Are you asking if I buy the M.E.'s ruling? I take it you don't.

You think his death is connected to the disappearance of the Cézanne?"

"I don't know for sure, but I was a cop for a long time. Coincidence doesn't sit well."

"Have you considered the possibility London wrote the confession to protect someone?"

He hadn't, but that would answer a lot of the why, if not the who. Clever woman, this Addi Dunayevsky.

She walked over, sat on the arm of his chair, and swung her legs across his lap. "So what are you going to do for me in exchange for a copy of London's confession?"

She smelled of vanilla and citrus and something warm and earthy. Del ran his palm along the smooth skin of her thigh and down her calf.

She glanced at his hand and asked, "What happened, Del? I thought we were good together. We had fun, laughed a lot. Then poof, you were gone. Was there someone else?"

"No one else," he said, his defenses rising. "I thought our split was a mutual decision."

"I remember the sex was good, very good." She closed her eyes, leaned down, and kissed him, her tongue meeting his. She slid from the arm of the chair into his lap.

Inside her robe he caressed her and cupped a perfect breast, her nipple growing hard at his touch. His mind jumped to Sophie and her bas-relief of scars under his fingertips. He ended the kiss and pulled away.

"Don't tell me you aren't enjoying this, because all signs point north." She fixed on his eyes and stopped. "Oh, God, you're seeing someone? I am such a *sharmuta*."

She tried to climb off his lap but he held her. "You are not a whore and, no, I don't have anybody." He didn't, not really, but the words still felt false. Maybe because he so badly wanted them to be a lie.

"You said we were friends. Can't this be a night between old friends? So what if I mourn for a few days. I'll get over you." A quick flash of her radiant smile. "I did before, didn't I?"

Had she? He hadn't cared enough to find out. *Hadn't cared enough.* One person wanting a relationship didn't make it so. Sophie had proven that to him over and over.

He cradled Suede's face in his hands. She was so beautiful, his pulse skipped. He kissed her, his lips sliding down her neck to the heartbeat in her throat. Her arms twined around him; she relaxed the weight of her body against his as he stood and carried her into the bedroom.

Chapter 14

The shriek of Del's cell pulled him out of a pleasant but forgotten dream. He opened one eyelid. If he didn't switch the fucking ringer off that thing, he'd never get any sleep.

Suede sat next to him holding out the offending phone, sheet clutched to her breasts. "Caller ID says Sophie."

Her words fell like sparks. His heart soared, reversed, and seized with guilt. He took the cell and pressed TALK. "This is Del."

Sophie's voice was hesitant. "Sorry, did I wake you?"

He checked the clock on the nightstand: nine a.m. *Shit.* One hour to get to his parents' house to meet Mike and somehow fit in a stop at CaMu along the way. So much for his museum recon mission.

"I should be up anyway." He laughed. "In fact, I wish you'd called earlier." *Yesterday, before I ended up in Suede's bed, would have been good.*

He glanced at Suede. She held her right palm down and made a walking gesture with her index and middle finger. He wanted nothing more than for her to leave the room, but instead he smiled and shook his head to let her know it wasn't a private conversation.

"I apologize for not calling," Sophie said. "Caught a stomach bug, and I've been a little under the weather, but I'm all better now. I wondered if maybe you'd like to try dinner again? We would actually eat this time, a real meal—food and everything—

129

not this Thursday, but next?" She sounded tentative, shy, as though she thought he might say no. As if he could even if he wanted to.

"Sounds great." Out of the corner of his eye, he watched Suede pick up a book from the nightstand and begin to read. He reached over and caressed her shoulder.

"Well, next Thursday then," Sophie said, and the smile in her voice warmed him.

After they said their goodbyes. Del couldn't make himself hang up, didn't want to break the tenuous connection. The cell remained glued to his ear until he heard a click and silence on the other end of the line.

Suede abandoned her book and looked at him, her head propped on her hand, a long strand of gold hair falling across her face. He reached out and tucked the lock behind the shell of her ear.

"Is that the Sophie who was married to Mike Gabretti? Tiny thing, auburn hair? Didn't she and Mike divorce?"

"They did." Suede's eyes studied him.

"Oh. I see," she said, in a tone brimming with insinuation.

Del bridled. "See what?"

"They are divorced, but Sophie got custody of you. I thought Mike was your friend."

"Mike *is* my friend. Sophie is also a friend. I've known her since college. Don't go making something out of nothing, Suede."

"Gee, overreacting much? I was joking, but I gather it's not that funny. So, Sophie's the one? Somewhere in the back of my mind, I always knew. To quote Somerset Maugham, 'The love that lasts the longest is the love that is never returned.' I have some experience with that myself."

This was not a conversation he intended to have, especially not this morning. "Sorry, no time to discuss English literature."

He threw off the covers, stood, and faced her. "Can you toss my jeans over here? They're on the floor, your side of the bed."

She sat naked with her back against the headboard, tangled sheet around her waist. She was stunning.

Her eyes locked on him. "You're beautiful," she said.

Dammit. He turned to hide his arousal and plucked a shirt off the floor. "Come on, Suede, my pants, please?" he said over his shoulder.

She slid off the bed and walked up behind him. With the length of her body pressed to his, her cheek warm against the beads of his spine, she reached around and took his cock with one hand and gently cupped his balls with the other.

The touch sent a tremor through him, and his knees went weak. He drew a sharp breath. "I don't have time. I don't even have time to grab a shower. I need get to CaMu then drive all the way out to my parents' house in Seacliff by ten. When can I get London's letter? Do you want me to meet you at the station this afternoon?"

Suede's body tensed. She dropped her arms, snatched the robe from the end of the bed, and covered herself. "Oh, right. I forgot this was an exchange deal. Payment for services rendered."

He walked to her side of the bed and picked up his Levis. "Come on, that's not what I meant." Wasn't it though? Would he be here otherwise? He zipped his fly, pulled his still buttoned shirt over his head, and sat on the edge of the bed to pull on socks. "Last night was terrific, really." The words rang hollow, and the air between them shifted and soured.

"That's me, one terrific fuck."

"Please don't do this."

"Do what? Call you on what an asshole you are? Somebody needs to. You're a user, Del, and the worst part is, you don't even realize it. You think you're a nice guy." She wrapped her robe tighter and retied the belt. "Never mind. What's the point? You're a man. You'll never get it."

There it was: the verbal equivalent of checkmate. The way every woman he'd ever known signaled the end of a discussion.

"As for the letter, I don't want you showing up at the station, not given your family's involvement. I'm off until Monday, and no way in hell I'm going into work over the weekend for you."

"I can swing by Monday evening and pick it up," he said, scanning the room for his other shoe.

"I'm busy. Do you have a secure fax?"

"In my office." He met her storm-at-sea gaze. "I really appreciate this, Suede."

"Leave your fax number on the table in the foyer as you leave. And Del?"

He looked up from lacing his boot.

"Next time you want to drop by and *talk,* call first. And I don't mean from in front of my building. Better yet, don't call. Ever. We're done." Her eyes shone with unshed tears.

Another wave of guilt rolled over him and broke against his heart. He took a step toward her, but she moved out of his reach. *Leave it alone,* he told himself. Of course, he didn't listen. "Look, I know I'm a selfish prick. I'm sorry—"

"Save your apologies for Sophie. I'm betting you're going to need them. You know the way out. Use it." She turned away from him, strode into the bathroom, and slammed the door.

Another woman, another slammed bathroom door. He brushed aside a kick of relief, finished dressing, and made his way to the guest bath. The mirror reflected dark moons under bloodshot eyes and an overnight beard. He ran his hand over the stubble, then checked the vanity drawers—nothing but tweezers. He splashed cold water on his cheeks, raked fingers through his hair, and gargled.

A layer of fog choked the day. He flicked a business card

onto the art deco table, and with the scald of dishonor burning his throat like bile, he walked out of the apartment, onto the elevator, and into the cold, gray arms of morning.

Del headed south, away from the bay, toward downtown and the museum. The rain stopped during the night, and the sun lay in wait behind a scrim of fog. By mid-afternoon the murk would burn off and it might begin to feel like summer.

The line to get into CaMu was around the block. Now, instead of the Cézanne and the *Finest Post-Impressionist exhibition ever mounted on the West Coast,* visitors were here to admire the museum where the director died rubbing one out. Nothing like a scandal to generate interest in the arts. He parked in the director's spot at the rear of the building—you could always count on Mike for resourceful thinking—and made his way to the front entrance.

Amos waved him through. Del pushed past the crowds at the elevator to get to the stairwell, slid his mother's key card through the reader, and ran up the five flights to the administrative offices. He was aware there were security cameras in the stairwell, but frankly, he couldn't care less.

Carter was at reception. *Fuck.* Del hoped the regular receptionist would be back. He didn't have the time to mess around with an escort. Walt, the loading dock operator, leaned over Carter's desk, and the two were talking.

"Hey, guys, what's up?" Del said.

Carter squinted at him, then grinned. "Almost didn't recognize you with the growth." He pointed at his chin. "We were just talking about you. Walt said you were going to be working here. Welcome to CaMu."

Good old, Walt. Del nodded and held up his mother's key card as if it were his own. "Thanks, but I'm just here to pick up a few things for my mom." Always smart to go for the truth when possible. "She left her purse Wednesday night. Okay if I go back to the docent office?"

Walt pushed away from the reception desk. "Catch you two later. I gotta bounce if I'm going to pick up the mail *and* handle the dock."

"Don't forget to bring back the keys to the mail van," Carter said.

Walt waved an acknowledgment.

Carter ran an index finger down the clipboard on his desk and looked up at Del. "You're not on my new employee roll yet, but the list hasn't been updated. Hardly any admin staff here today. Everyone's still pretty freaked about what happened. You have a key card, so go ahead and go back. Doubt I could track down an escort even if I had to."

Carter tilted his head and rubbed a thumb along his jaw line. "How's Hani? She was pretty wrecked the other night. Tell her I don't believe what they're saying."

Who were *they*, and what were *they* saying? Del wondered but didn't have the time to get into it. "Thanks. She's doing okay. You were here Wednesday night?"

Carter brightened. "Yeah. I'm the one who called security and nine-one-one. Hani was . . . well, you know, too upset."

"You saw London?" Del asked, surprised no one mentioned Carter had been at the scene.

He cringed. "God, no. Hani wouldn't let anyone but the police into that office. I was here working on my script. I'm a writer. The offices are quiet in the evenings. Dr. London gave me permission to stay until they lock down the sixth floor."

"This floor isn't secured at five when the offices close?"

"The doors lock, but employees still have access via the entry keypads, the keypads in the elevators, too. Security doesn't lock down the building—shut off access to the floors, arm the motion sensors, all that shit—until after the museum closes at

134

seven. That's why staff are required to card in when they arrive and out when they leave for the day. Security can track us through key cards, make sure no one's locked in the basement or up in conservation. And don't screw up. I got busy working one night and didn't realize the time. Quarter after seven, one majorly pissed a-hole of a guard tracked me down in the lunchroom and kicked my sorry ass out."

"If the museum is still open, what's to stop someone from ignoring the rules and coming or going via the front entrance?"

Carter gave him a confused look. "Automatic dismissal. It's okay to use the main entrance to run out for coffee or a smoke during the day, but you damn well better key out at the end of your shift. Security didn't tell you any of this when they issued your key card?"

Christ, Miller, you're losing your touch. Del cleared his throat. "Who's in charge of security while Ray is on medical leave? I'd like to talk to him—or her." He checked his watch. Security offices were in the basement. All he needed was five minutes for a quick look around.

"Jack Haskell is acting chief of security, but he's not in the museum this early. He comes in later so he can be onsite when we close. Why do you care about this stuff?"

The kid's cheek twitched and his voice took on the thready timbre of a witness under interrogation. Del gave him a practiced good-cop grin. "Didn't Walt tell you? I'm a security consultant. That's why Dr. London brought me on board."

Another lie, but London was certainly in no position to contradict him.

Carter's shoulders relaxed back into their usual slump. As luck would have it, the call center lit up before the receptionist had a chance to question why CaMu's newly recruited security consultant didn't know the name of the acting security chief. Del gestured he was headed back to the admin offices, and Carter nodded.

He ran his mother's key card and pushed through the heavy glass doors at the end of the reception corridor. The administrative offices, usually teeming, were deserted; no movement or sound other than the whir of air through the filters. Directly in front of him was a partition wall. To the right was the docent office, to the left and around the corner, the director's office. He peered back at the reception desk through the glass. Carter was still occupied with his call. Del veered left and found himself in front of London's door. Yellow crime scene tape sealed off the entrance. The door handle had a push button lock; above the knob was a deadbolt.

Autoerotic asphyxiation produced a death scene different from that of a suicide. Gaspers don't intend to die. Usually, fabric, extra clothing, or towels are found at the scene—cushioning to avoid ligature marks. Pornography or sexual props are often involved. Another key indicator of autoerotic asphyxiation is a reasonable expectation of privacy. Doors and windows locked *from the inside*. His mother said she knocked, walked into London's office, and found him. Why would London, a man obsessed with appearances, not lock his door if he planned to masturbate at work? Or had someone else been in the office, someone who'd unlocked the door when he or she had left London dead?

To keep out of Carter's line of vision, Del took the long way around to the empty docent office. He pulled his mother's purse from her bottom desk drawer. On the way out, he spotted a row of cup hooks lined up just inside the door. Each hook had a key card. His heart rate went up a notch. Carter had it wrong. Not everyone keyed out at the end of their shift. Keying out required leaving the building with a key card. No way there were a dozen docents in the museum today, yet a long row of key cards hung along the wall, ripe for the picking.

★ ★ ★ ★ ★

"*Shalom Shabbat.*" Hanna kissed Del on the cheek.

"*Shalom Shabbat.* You missed *shul* again?" He handed her the purse.

"Neither your father nor I can bear to be entertainment for those reporters. They're vultures."

"You can't let them make you prisoners in your own home, Mom. There's no way to predict how long this will go on."

She reached up and stroked his stubble. "Please tell me you aren't growing a beard."

He took her hand and kissed it. "I'm not growing a beard. I slept in and didn't have time to shave. Mike here yet?"

"Not yet. Weren't you wearing that shirt yesterday?"

"Why are you so interested in my appearance all of a sudden?"

"Interested isn't the word. Try concerned. I am not stupid, Mendel. It's none of my business if you didn't go home last night. You're an adult. But as your mother, I have to tell you, a shower wouldn't hurt." She patted his cheek and smiled her magic smile. "Now tell me what you found at the CaMu."

"I was only inside a few minutes. One thing bothered me, though. Carter said employees are required to carry their key card when they leave the museum at the end of the day, but I noticed a bunch of key cards hanging in the docent office. Don't the other docents key out at the end of the day? You do. I've seen you."

"I'm a trustee as well as a docent. Trustees, like regular employees, are required to key out on the loading dock. Docents, on the other hand, are volunteers. They use the public entrances. And no, they don't key out."

"Then why have key cards?"

"Because docents need access to stairwells and meeting rooms. Key cards are programmed differently depending on the

137

security level of the employee. Docents, for example, can't access conservation, exhibition storage, or any of the basement offices."

"Wouldn't it make more sense if their comings and goings were tracked the same as regular employees?"

"Absolutely not. That would require docents to pass through the loading dock, giving them unnecessary access to secured areas. Remember, art is unloaded on the dock. The freight elevator goes down to both basement storage and up to the top floor, conservation, and restoration. You can understand why security doesn't want volunteers running all over the building. But that doesn't negate their need for access to certain nonpublic areas. The docent key cards are programmed to allow extremely limited access, which is why the cards are left hanging on the wall and why they aren't assigned to specific docents. Giving a volunteer access to set up AV equipment in a locked auditorium is very different from giving him or her access to basement art storage."

"Are background checks done on volunteers?"

"Of course, but why the interest? No docents were scheduled the evening Thurman died."

"You're certain?"

"I'm in charge of the docent schedule, so yes, very sure. What are you thinking, Mendel?"

"I saw all those key cards hanging there, and they made me wonder."

"About?"

He lifted his shoulders. He didn't have an answer for her—not yet. Del's cell buzzed with a text. Mike was at the back gate. "Mike's here. I'll go out and meet him. Where's Dad?"

"Where he always is these days, in his study."

"Would you tell him Mike is here?"

"Why don't *you* tell him? I'll go meet Mike."

Pain lined her voice and Del's insides turned to ice. "What's going on between you and Dad?"

"Just a rough patch. Happens in all marriages." She squeezed his arm. "We'll talk about it later." She took her cardigan from the back of a kitchen chair, draped the sweater around her shoulders, and moved toward the door. "Don't worry, Mendel."

Right. "Mom, before I forget—"

She looked over her shoulder at him.

"I may have left Carter and Walt with the impression I work at CaMu."

Del tapped lightly on the study door, opened it a crack, and poked his head in. A tiny spasm rippled through him at the sight of the bare wall behind the desk where the Cézanne once hung. "Mike's here, Dad. Are you ready? Do you have the letters?"

"I do." Samuel stood, his compassionate gaze focused on Del. Del had six inches on his father; Samuel had twenty-five pounds on Del.

"How do you want to do this?" Del asked.

Mike stepped into the room. "We ready?"

From the corner of his desk, Samuel picked up a stack of letters bundled with a piece of twine. "Mike, you're the one doing the translations. How will this work best for you?"

"Give me paper and something to write with, and I'll get started. I can't speak for Delbo, though." Mike glanced at Del. "Tell me again why you're here?"

Del had been asking himself that very question since he left Suede's. "I want to see the letters."

"Translating isn't exactly a spectator sport. You planning to watch me? By the way, has anyone mentioned you need a shave and a change of clothes? Weren't you wearing those yesterday?" He threw Del a wicked grin. "Suede?"

"Do you ever shut up?" Del took the letters from his father and shoved Mike out the door. "You can use the table in the library."

"You really ought to be more polite to someone trying to do you a favor," Mike said. "It was Suede, right? If you'd lost your way and ended up at Sophie's, she'd have done your laundry for you. Don't take this personally, bro, but you reek."

"Fuck you."

The library, originally intended as a ballroom, was the largest room in the house. Books reached two stories, floor to ceiling. One end of the room held a small unlit fireplace. At the other end, a row of lancet windows spilled sunlight across the mahogany floor, the scent of beeswax and lemon oil rising like perfume from the warm polished wood.

Del handed Mike the letters and pointed toward the long slab of walnut at the room's center. "You can work there. Pens and paper are in the drawer. Do you need a computer? I can borrow a laptop."

"Only if it comes with a secretary. Tell me again what you plan to do? Between you and me, I'd keep the shower option open."

"Later," Del said, walking across the room and folding his six-foot-two frame onto the five-foot-two settee. "Right now I'm going to take a nap. I'm bagged. Wake me if you find anything."

CHAPTER 15

Although sorely tempted to suggest Del opt for sleep over cunt every once in a while, Mike resisted. He only hoped it was Suede. The thought of Delbo fucking Sophie made him queasy. He shook it off and said, "You learn anything else about London's confession?"

Del lifted himself on one elbow and glared from the settee. "What part of nap wasn't clear to you? Suede is going to fax a copy of the confession on Monday when she gets to her office."

Suede. Mike released the breath he didn't realize he'd been holding and loosened the twine on the bundle in front of him. He didn't believe for one second they'd gain anything by translating this pile of old letters. Why would Max Müeller write his brother in the good old U.S. of A. and confess to ripping off his boss? Mike wanted to do this for Samuel, to give the old man a lifeline to his dead father. If anything were ever to happen to Mike, he'd want Amy to have something to hang on to. Not some crap-ass painting, but something real and personal. He'd started keeping a journal the day she was born. When she was old enough, he'd put the book into her hands. She'd never question how much her father loved her.

He plucked the top envelope from the stack. A thick slice of paper the color of weak tea addressed in black ink faded to gray. The letter smelled of dust and mildew and something darker. Fear, or was he imagining it? The address on the front read, Mr. Avi Miller, Howard Street, San Francisco, but the envelope held no postmark. Strange. Couriered, maybe?

The sheet inside, folded into a tidy square, felt smooth and brittle to the touch. Mike took care to unfold the letter so as not to tear along the razor-edged crease. Translating from German into English, Mike began transcribing on a clean sheet of paper.

Dearest Avi, I hope you are well. As I'm certain you've heard, conditions in Paris are deteriorating . . .

Paris, 18 March 1940

Once war was declared, the government began rounding up German nationals as enemies of the state. It does not matter I am a French citizen; my name and German accent provoke suspicion. I am a Frenchman by choice rather than by birth, an insurmountable failing in the eyes of the French. I fear for both Samuel and myself.

Anti-German propaganda is everywhere now, with Parisians constantly reminded to keep a wary eye for spies and the rumored German-controlled underground operating within the city. It is only a matter of time before someone points a finger at the Boche and his infant son. If that happens, or if German tanks should roll into Paris, citizenship will not protect us.

Blackboards posted at the train stations display itineraries for evacuating the city, and not a day passes I do not think of taking Samuel away from here. My employer, Yoseph, a widower with two sons, has made arrangements to leave should invasion become imminent. He is a Jew, however, and Jews fear the Nazis for good reason. If Yoseph leaves, I will be without work.

Paris was Adèle's city, not mine. Without her, I am a stranger. She was too frightened for the baby she carried to risk a journey, and now little Samuel and I are left to pay the price for her fear. What's done cannot be undone, and to regret our decision

to stay serves no purpose, but Adèle is lost to me, you are in
America, and my heart weeps. I thank God for Samuel.

Mike slowly eased back in his chair. Seven decades hadn't dampened the sadness or foreboding in Max Müeller's words. This was a man who knew something ominous was coming. That Max sought out a messenger rather than send the letter via regular post said much. "Hey Delbo, your grandfather writes he was a naturalized French citizen."

Del growled, "Sleeping here."

Mike paid no attention. "He makes a point of mentioning that Yoseph Shapiro is Jewish but says nothing about himself."

Del sat up with a groan. "He had phony identity papers, Mike. Maybe he wanted to let Avi know without stating it outright." Del scooted to the edge of the chaise. "Does he say anything else about Shapiro?"

"Refers to him as his employer. Says Shapiro was making preparations to emigrate. If Max masqueraded as a gentile, Shapiro would have known the truth. Too bad the Shapiro Gallery was so well known. No way for Yoseph to hide behind phony papers."

"Shapiro didn't need to hide. He had enough money and pull to get his family out," Del said, his voice tinged with resentment. "I know it's a difficult subject for Dad, but I still can't believe he never told me about these letters."

"Like he said, the letters are in German. It's not as if you could read them."

"Whatever." Del lay back down on the settee, facing away from Mike.

Mike translated a half-dozen more letters, all dated prior to the German invasion, all filled with detailed descriptions of Paris after France declared war, all sent via regular mail. He pulled the next envelope from the stack. No postmark.

Dearest Avi, my soul aches as I write this. I've waited too long . . .

Paris, 9 June 1940

The Luftwaffe attack last week killed more than two hundred and fifty, including school children. If their goal was to destroy morale and terrify the people of Paris, the Reich can rejoice in victory.

With the German advance, the government turned tail and ran, and the citizens of Paris followed. The roads out of the city are tangled with families on foot dragging all their possessions behind them. Vehicles of every description crawl south, and the entire population flees. It is as though Paris is in a death throe, her life force, her people, bleeding out of her.

I refuse to wait for Wehrmacht tanks to appear on the boulevards. Samuel and I will move south to Marseilles. I must get Samuel to safety, to his uncle where he can live a safe and happy life.

Yoseph left for America and promised to contact you once he is settled. Like you, he is a kind and thoughtful man. I will miss his friendship.

"Hey, Delbo." Mike called over to the settee. Del responded with a snore. "Dude, wake up."

Del pushed himself up on one arm, blinking and rubbing the back of his neck, his voice muzzy. "What the hell do you want now?"

"Have you ever considered giving your prick a rest and substituting some quality shut-eye? Maybe you wouldn't be so damn cranky."

Del glowered. "What do you want, Mike?"

"Does your father have another uncle? Besides Avi, I mean."

Del's gaze shot upward and he shook his head. "Yeah, Uncle

Malachi. He lives in the attic and only comes out on Jewish holidays. That's why you've never met him. Shouldn't point that finger, Mike—very rude gesture. Something you learned from your wife? No, my father has—had only one uncle."

"Max says he has to get Samuel to his uncle. Why not say he has to find a way to get Samuel to Avi in the States?"

"Think about it, Mike. He had to be hyper-aware of the danger of putting too much in writing. You should know all about that. Aren't you supposed to be an intellectual property attorney?" Del pointed to the small neat stack of papers next to Mike. "Are those done? How many left?"

"I've read through half. Your grandfather's handwriting is as illegible as yours. Who knew poor penmanship ran in families? Why do you ask? Not working fast enough for you, sire?"

"Don't get pissy. Just wanted to make sure I had time to catch a shower."

Mike waved a hand in front of his nose. "Don't let me stop you. Got plenty to keep me busy. Your snoring isn't exactly music to translate by."

Del yawned and stood. Mike watched him leave the room, then picked up the next letter.

Dearest Avi, with what seemed like the whole of Paris, on 10 June, Samuel and I started out from the city on foot . . .

Limoges, 30 June 1940

At least I was on foot. At six months, Samuel was not yet ready to hike the 750 kilometers to Marseilles. Imagine it, four out of every five Parisians on the road out of the city at the same time. I packed a single duffle, wore as many clothes as I could fit on my body despite the warm temperatures, and strapped Samuel to my back.

At first it seemed like a holiday, but the heat, sleeping rough, and lack of food and water, exhausted us all. My soul ached for many of the women along the route, their men at war, bone tired from lugging infants and possessions. The chalk messages lining the roads were heart-rending to read, loved ones searching for loved ones. So many families separated in the chaos.

We were bombed twice on the route to Limoges and strafed by machine gun fire too many times to count. Samuel and I found shelter, but others were not so lucky. I cannot push away the memory of the young father I met along the way, the body of his daughter, not more than three, in his arms. We searched for a cemetery, and I helped him bury her, all the while overcome with guilt because my child survived.

Mike rested his head in his hands, swallowed dryly, and closed his eyes to black out thoughts of the little dead girl and her father. If that had been Amy, Mike wouldn't have survived it. He drew a deep breath and continued to read.

Early on, there was camaraderie . . .

We sought comfort in familiar faces. Eventually the desperation for food, water, and shelter led to pillaging and petty thievery. French soldiers were the worst abusers, a terrible blow to a morale already destroyed by the government's betrayal. Everyone looked for someone to blame. As always it seems, Jews were an easy target.

Now we are safe in Limoges. Samuel and I are staying with a friend of Adèle's, and she's arranged for us to ride with her brother to Toulouse. From Toulouse, we will make our way to Marseilles. Samuel and I are fine but exhausted from our journey.

Del strolled into the room, his face ruddy from a shave, hair still wet from the shower. "What's so funny?"

"Listen to this."

Mike read: " 'Avi, I wish you could see my boy. This morning while I changed his diaper, the little shit peed in my face. Maybe I'm going crazy because I couldn't stop laughing. It had been so long since I laughed, not since Adèle. I didn't know it was possible to love someone as much as I love Samuel.' "

Mike blinked several times and pinched the bridge of his nose. "No wonder these letters mean so much to your dad."

"Does he say anything else about my grandmother?"

"He misses her, that's about it." Mike leaned his elbows on the table and rested his chin on the palm of his hand. "This is a shitty task. It's as if Max is sitting here talking to me. I have to keep reminding myself baby Samuel is in the study down the hall, and at the same time try to forget Max died in a concentration camp. If I were in Max's shoes, I could never give Amy up, that much I know. I'm too fucking selfish. Your grandfather was more of a man than I'll ever be."

Del walked over and squeezed Mike's shoulder. "What have we learned? Anything?"

"Your father was right, Max and Shapiro were friends. I can't believe Max was a thief, let alone one who would steal from a friend, not the way he talks about the looting that went on during the exodus out of Paris. He doesn't mention anything about any paintings, but he must've had the canvases when he and Samuel set out for Marseilles."

Del pulled out a chair and sat across the table from Mike. "Here's what I don't get. Yoseph is long dead, and Dad said Daniel Shapiro's father, Jakob, is also dead. So where are the other Shapiros?"

"Didn't Samuel mention something about Jakob's brother?"

"Also dead. We need to figure out when Daniel says his *family is in agreement,* who exactly he's talking about."

"Something's not right with that guy. What if we were to go after him?"

Del blinked, a quick flick like a wince. "Go after who? You mean Daniel Shapiro?"

"He went after your family, didn't he? *Quid pro quo,* dude. Balls to the wall."

CHAPTER 16

Mike stood, stretched, and eyed his watch. Half past two. "I need to get out of here for a while. What say, Delbo, up for lunch?"

"I could eat a horse ranch. The one day of the week Mom doesn't cook, and we end up at my parents'. Talk about shitty timing. Come on, we can take my car."

Del aimed the Porsche toward Mr. Burr E. Toes for beers, takeout quasi-Mexican, and a stroll down to Ocean Beach.

Other than a few surfers in wet suits clustered at the end nearest Cliff House and Seal Rocks, the beach was deserted. Mike's eyes skimmed the sand. "So much for bikini clad hotties. Middle of summer, the sun's out, and it's still fucking freezing out here. This is why in photographs of San Francisco beaches, the people are always wearing neoprene."

"Better a wet suit than hypothermia." Del bit into his taco and followed it with a slug of beer. "You do realize neither alcohol nor glass containers are permitted on this beach?"

Mike raised his bottle in a toast. "To living life on the edge." He brushed off a rock and sat. "Max's other letters—the ones Avi kept? I want to see them. Your dad said Avi and Daniel's father were friends. I'm thinking we may learn a lot more about the Shapiros from those letters than from your father's. You think Denim still has them?"

"His name is Levi, jackass, and you know it."

"Whatever. He wouldn't pitch the letters without offering

them to your father first, would he?"

"No clue. Levi and I don't talk much. He works with computers, has five kids under eight, and a bitchy wife. I only run into him at funerals and weddings."

"I remember him when we were kids. Guy was a narc. That time we refilled the vodka and gin bottles with water? I know damn well he ratted us out." Mike narrowed his eyes. "The bastard owes us. Call the little shit and find out if he still has Avi's letters. If he does, ask him if we can take them away from the house. Your snoring was bad enough. I don't want five rug rats running around while I'm trying to focus."

"What happened to all those parental instincts you cultivated?"

"Holding them in reserve for Amy. My schedule is jammed Monday and Tuesday, but I can work on translating them later in the week." Mike pushed the last of the taco into his mouth, swallowed, and shuddered. "What do you think Mr. B. adds to the meat to give it such a . . . *unique* flavor?"

"Given the taste and name of the place, I'm thinking *chiffonade de* toe jam."

Mike laughed, spitting beer.

"I'll get Levi's number from Mom and give him a call. Ready?"

"As I'll ever be."

Del pulled the car keys from his pocket. Fifteen minutes later they were back in the library. "Can I read what you've translated so far?" Del asked.

"Knock yourself out." Mike pushed the stack of transcriptions across the table. He glanced down at the remaining letters, yawned, and on a sigh picked up the next envelope. Two hours later he straightened his shoulders and flexed his spine, trying to ease the dull, throbbing ache. "Not much between June of 1940 and August 1941. I mean the letters are fascinating day-to-day stuff. Samuel takes a step. Samuel says his first word. Samuel gets a tooth. But nothing about Shapiro, the paintings, or even what Max is doing for income. All the envelopes are postmarked. Given Max's discretion in the letters not sent by post, I'd say he was extremely wary of anything mailed via official channels."

Mike pulled the next envelope from the pile, held the letter up by the corner, and felt a tiny electric thrill. No postmark. He slid the page from its sheath.

Dearest Avi, it saddens me to say, but Marseilles offers scant hope things will improve before this deplorable war ends . . .

Marseilles 15 November 1941

There is much crime and corruption here. The streets are squalid. The sewers smell of rotten eggs and decay, so different from Adèle's magnificent Paris. Great portions of the city are ramshackle and unsafe. Both the Germans and the Italians have bombed, and it's as if the Marseillaises are afraid to rebuild.

I was so pleased to hear you've been in contact with Yoseph. My mind is eased to know he is safe, especially as the news from Paris worsens. A roundup took place in May—nearly four thousand refugees arrested and interned at Pithiviers and Beaune-la-Rolande. This summer brought word of an internment facility in Drancy, northeast of the city. Where will it end?

My work goes well. At times I'm called to be away from Samuel, and I yearn for the child's company. He is clever, Avi, and such a good boy. Adèle would be proud.

My job as a guide suits me, but the Spanish are not as welcoming as they once were. They, too, are becoming concerned about regulations.

★ ★ ★ ★ ★

Samuel entered the library, and Mike set down the letter. "Samuel, do you know why some of these envelopes aren't postmarked?"

"When he could, my father handed his correspondence to trusted couriers rather than subject letters to the postal censors. More than once Avi answered the doorbell and found a stranger on his doorstep, waiting to deliver a letter."

"Also, Max talks about being a guide in Spain. Makes no sense."

Samuel laughed. "Not *in* Spain, *to* Spain. He led refugees across the French frontier to the Spanish border on foot."

"Refugees?"

"Jews. France stopped issuing exit visas in August of 1940. Which meant it no longer mattered whether a Jew held an overseas visa—a U.S. visa, for example—because without a French exit visa, there was no legitimate way out of France."

"The Spanish border guards didn't stop refugees from crossing into their country?" Del asked.

Samuel eased himself into a leather chair near the library table. "Not at first, not if they carried Spanish transit visas. As long as a refugee held the appropriate transit visa, the border guards didn't bother with French exit visas. What did a Spanish border guard care about French bureaucracy? Refugees presented their transit visas and passports at the border, crossed Spain, and entered neutral Portugal. From the Port of Lisbon, they escaped Europe."

Sudden anger hit Mike like a muscle spasm. "Then why the hell didn't Max cross the border? If he had a way out, why didn't he grab his kid and run?"

Sorrow palled Samuel's face. "It wasn't that simple. The Nuremberg laws deprived him of his German citizenship. He was a foreign Jew, a refugee, living under an assumed identity with false papers. He wasn't one of the lucky ones. He'd waited too long and had neither the cash nor the influence to obtain an overseas visa. He guided refugees who held the proper visas to the border but had no way out himself."

"You got out, Dad. You must have had papers," Del said.

"That was different. I was barely three years old and born into war. My father knew the time would come when he would have to send me away. Remember, he and Avi made it out of Witten just before Germany closed its borders. He recognized the danger long before the Germans marched on Paris."

Samuel's solemn eyes held Mike's. "Don't you sense that in his letters, Mike?"

"Absolutely, even in the correspondence dated before the Reich occupied the free zone."

Samuel waved his hand in a motion of dismissal. "The free zone was a sham. The policies in unoccupied France were every bit as anti-Semitic as those in the occupied North. The Franco-German armistice required the Vichy government—the so-called free zone—to surrender on demand anyone without French citizenship. Forged papers, yes, but my father was without a country."

The men sat in silence, the air charged with something dark and heavy. Finally, Mike returned to Max's letter.

More than anything else, I worry about the children . . .

OSE has abandoned most of the children's homes in and around Paris and reopened them here in the South. Keeping the children out of the camps is the priority. Thank God for kind souls willing to take the little ones in. The internment camps are fit for no one. Holding children in one of those deplorable places is unconscionable.

I accompanied an OSE social worker to Camp Joffre in Rivesaltes, near the Spanish border. She was sent to negotiate liberation for as many children as possible. The sun shone the day of our visit, but the ground was frozen. We showed our passes and the guards allowed us through the camp gate. The children met us, filthy and in tatters, some huddled under thin soiled blankets. The barracks were of cement and without ventilation. The camp had no central sewage, the internees forced to use tubs that tipped in the strong icy north wind. Shit was spread throughout the camp, rodents everywhere, malaria and typhus rampant. No human being, let alone an innocent child, deserves to suffer this. Even now when I think of those children, half of me wants to weep and the other half to rail at the injustice. More unsettling are reports of planned raids on OSE-protected homes. The rumblings grow too loud to be ignored. Even living outside the camps is no longer a guarantee of safety.

"Homes like Izieu," Mike said under his breath, brain snagging hard on the home's nearly four-dozen children deported to Auschwitz and gassed. What had it been like for those kids? An image of Amy flashed into his mind, her sunny smile and huge dark eyes, and he held a hand to his mouth to keep from being sick. The past felt close, as if he could reach out and touch it.

"What's the matter, Mikey? Mr. Burr E. Toes coming back to haunt you?" Del asked.

Mike studied Samuel. So much of the Millers' history was linked to their being Jewish. The savage reality of it struck him like a blow.

Del reached over and rapped on Mike's skull with his knuckles. "Anyone home? I repeat, are you okay? You look as if you're about to recycle your lunch."

"Fine. Confused," Mike said, coming out of his reverie. "Max openly mentions working with OSE. I thought OSE was a Jewish group. Wasn't he worried about being exposed?"

"Many non-Jews worked on behalf of *Œuvre de Secours aux*

Enfants during the war. OSE still exists today," Samuel said.

"Your father was concerned about potential raids on children's homes."

Samuel shifted in his chair and crossed his legs. "Rightfully so. OSE preferred hiding children in plain sight. Whenever possible, they provided children who could pass as gentiles with false documents. The youngsters were placed in Aryan homes, institutions, and communities. I often think how difficult it must have been for those kids, cut off from their families, living with strangers, non-Jews, but at least they were safe."

"What do you mean *pass*? Children are children," Del said.

"Not in the eyes of the Reich. Like other foreign Jews, your grandfather and uncle fled Germany for France seeking asylum. Many refugees arrived with children, who, because of language, culture, or religion, couldn't pass as non-Jews or couldn't readily assimilate. These youngsters lived openly in group homes under the protection of OSE. But here's the thing, statutes required OSE to provide authorities with a record—name, birthdate, country of nationality—of the residents. This put the children at risk. That's why, whenever possible, OSE tried to hide children in private homes and institutions.

"It all came to a head with the Vel' d'Hiv Roundup in Paris. Thousands were arrested, women and children en masse. That same summer, 1942, Vichy—the free zone, remember—was directed to round up ten thousand foreign Jews. Each region had a quota, and OSE-protected children's homes were not spared."

"But that was before the Nazis occupied Vichy, Dad."

"Like I said, the free zone was no more than pretense. The roundups marked the beginning of OSE's *Circuit Garel*, a network to get at-risk children to Switzerland. It became your grandfather's passion. No longer was OSE's purpose to protect and harbor but to find a way of getting endangered children out of France to safety. By 1944, OSE was forced completely underground."

Del locked eyes with Samuel. "Why is it you've never talked about any of this before?"

Melancholy shadowed Samuel's features. "It's painful to discuss, yes, but more than that, I wanted you to learn about your grandfather from someone who not only loved him, but remembered him. That was Avi, not me. And to be fair, Del, you've never shown any interest. Much of this is history you could have discovered on your own had you cared to."

Del winced, and Mike couldn't help but notice the faint flush along his cheekbones. Uneasy with the tension between the two men, Mike spoke up. "I'm sorry we haven't learned anything about the Cézanne."

Samuel pulled himself out of his chair and sighed. "Regardless of whether or not you find any information about the painting, I want to thank you for doing the translations. It means the world to me to be able to read my father's words." He held out his hand to Mike, who stood and shook it.

"My pleasure, sir."

Samuel laughed, deep and infectious. "Sir? Since when do you call me sir?"

Feeling his face flame, Mike smiled. Dr. Samuel Miller deserved respect. The men settled back in their chairs, and Mike slipped the next letter from its envelope.

Dearest Avi, the Germans swarm Marseilles, the neighborhoods, the streets, and the alleyways . . .

Marseilles, 20 January 1943

The roundups in Marseilles have begun in earnest. Over the weekend, the Germans destroyed the old port and the market center. Police, both German and French, scoured the city for Jews. Neighborhoods were barricaded and people stopped in the streets and ordered to present papers. House-to-house arrests separated women from their children and dragged the sick from their beds. Two Gestapo agents removed my neighbor, a French Jew named Singer, from his home. Singer arrived in Marseilles from Nice only two months ago. Early in the war, Nice was rumored to be a promised land because of the Italian occupation, but with the flood of Jews into the city looking for a way out of France, the Gestapo and SS took control and roundups began. Singer fled to Marseilles only to be caught in another net. He was a kind old soul to whom Samuel had taken a great shine.

When I asked the officer in charge, an Austrian with a Nazi Party button pinned to his lapel, where they would take the old man, he demanded to see my papers and questioned me about why I left Germany to consort with Frenchmen and Jews. I told him I didn't know Singer was Juif, that the old man sometimes looked after little Samuel. I explained I was a widower, and it was my beautiful French wife, Adèle, who had insisted on living in the country of her birth. He howled with laughter and said when a man's cock is in the mix, sometimes country loyalty must be put aside. God forgive me, I laughed with him.

Mike laid down his pen. "Max should have left Marseilles, escaped the danger. He should have fled to the countryside, hid."

"His work was in Marseilles," Samuel said. "Getting the children to safety took priority."

"How are you three doing in here?" Hanna asked from the doorway.

Samuel looked up from his book and Mike didn't miss the chill in his voice. "We're fine, Hanna."

Hanna nodded and crossed the room. "What about you, Mike? You've been at it for hours. And Mendel? Speak up."

Del had finished reading the translations and moved on to the *San Francisco Chronicle*. He closed the newspaper. "Fine, Mom."

"Almost finished here," Mike said. He clasped his hands behind his head and stretched his legs in front of him.

Hanna joined them at the table. "May I read a few of the transcriptions?"

"Sure." Mike straightened the stack and set them in front of her. Shaking a cramp from his hand, he unfolded the final letter, and fought back a sudden riptide of fear—one sheet, few words. He inspected the envelope. No postmark. He began to translate, then stopped. "Samuel, you should hear this."

As Mike read aloud, tears rolled down the old man's cheeks. Hanna moved to his side and took his hand. Del sat still, head bowed.

Dearest Avi, yesterday the Gestapo came . . .

22 January 1943

I was betrayed. I doubt I'll ever be sure who informed, but what value in knowing? It may have been the old man from next door, but I never spoke to Singer about my work. Samuel and I escaped via the cellars. As arranged, I entrusted the boy to Cécile. She is a fine nurse and will care for him and see he is taken to the couple who will deliver him into his uncle's arms. It was wrong to keep him with me as long as I have, wrong to put him in danger, but I am weak, and the boy is my life and heart. I will never have the chance to ask his forgiveness for bringing him into this brutal world, without a mother, without a country, without a home, and now without a father. I will never be able to apologize for my inability to protect and shelter him. I will carry that guilt to my grave. Take good care of my son, Avi. Tell him I love him always. Tell him I am sorry.

★ ★ ★ ★ ★

The risks Max took to lead refugees to the border couldn't touch the courage required to give up his child. Mike's eyes burned and he swallowed the lump that rose in his throat. Max Müeller was one brave SOB.

CHAPTER 17

Del rose Monday with a throbbing headache and a mouth that tasted like a litter box, all the benefits of a hangover without the alcohol. The morning was cool and overcast with the signature San Francisco dampness that seeped into the bones. He showered, dressed, and drove straight to his office. True to her word, Suede faxed a copy of London's confession. Handwritten rather than typed, the note was barebones, stripped of emotion, self-reproach, and any details about the crime. Suede's theory that London might be protecting someone made sense.

I, Thurman Alcott London, assume full responsibility for the theft of the Cézanne canvas, Nature Morte au Livre, Fruit Putréfié, et Pyramide des Crânes, belonging to Dr. Samuel Miller and Mrs. Hanna Rosen Miller. I hereby tender my resignation from the California Museum of Fine Art, effective immediately.

Sincerest apologies,
Thurman A. London

What the fuck? Sincerest apologies? Made it sound like London missed a lunch date. If he felt guilty enough to confess, shouldn't there be a hint of contrition? Del re-read the note. Maybe Mike was right, and London simply didn't know how to accept blame. If that were the case, wouldn't he point a finger at accomplices instead of mailing a weird-ass confession, jacking off in his office, then waiting for the FBI to show up at his door?

Del had phoned his cousin the previous evening about Avi's correspondence. According to Levi, nothing had been removed from the old man's desk since he passed. Levi would be at work, but his wife, Ruth, would be home if Del wanted to swing by and take a look at the letters.

He drove south to Excelsior and parked in front of the well-maintained blue, gold, and red Victorian. He rang the bell twice before Ruth opened the door. She was a squat, dark little woman, wound tight as a spring, with a nasal voice that grated on Del's nerves. She carried a baby on her hip.

"Did Levi tell you I'd be by?" he asked.

"He said you were looking for some letters belonging to his grandfather. Come on back. I'll show you Avi's desk."

She led him through three rooms littered with indistinguishable shapes labeled Fisher-Price, Mattel, and Hasbro. Who knew Toys "R" Us had an interior design team?

"Does this have anything to do with the painting?" Ruth asked. "Avi went on and on about what a hero his brother was. Now we find out the guy was a thief? Totally humiliating for the family."

Del bit his tongue, holding back a streak of anger so vicious his whole body throbbed. "There is no evidence my grandfather stole the Cézanne."

"I saw the story on the news. How could they say something like that if it wasn't true? I realize he was your grandfather but—"

Del interrupted her. "Levi said the letters were in the bottom desk drawer."

"Help yourself." Ruth set the baby on the rug and stood at the back of the room with her arms crossed, watching him. A high-pitched scream issued from somewhere in the house. She ignored the racket. "Tell me again what you're looking for?"

"You were right—information about the Cézanne. It's possible my grandfather told Avi where he acquired the painting."

"I never met your grandfather, of course, so I can't speak to what he did or didn't do—"

Del was pretty sure she already had.

"But I don't believe what they are saying about your parents."

They again. Del opened the bottom left-hand drawer and pulled out a yellowed and battered Florsheim shoebox with *KORRESPONDENZ* written in black marker across the side. Even he could translate that much German. He lifted the bulging lid and removed the top envelope—postmark Paris. He drew in a fortifying breath and asked, "Who are *they*, Ruth, and what exactly are *they* saying?"

"That over-tan goy on the news, Suede Dumm, hinted your parents hid the painting so they wouldn't have to give it up. They don't need the money, and they're good, honest people. They'd never do anything like that."

Her kind words softened him. "You're right, they wouldn't."

"Dumm is so full of herself. Probably anti-Semitic."

"Suede *Dunn* is Jewish. Dunn is not her real name."

Ruth released a loud huff of air, brimming with indignation. "So she's ashamed of where she came from? That's worse."

Another earsplitting shriek echoed from somewhere in the house, and Ruth yelled for the responsible party to shut up. The infant at her feet began to squall. She picked up the baby. Boy or girl, Del couldn't tell.

"She's not hiding anything. Suede's surname is Slavic, difficult to pronounce. She changed it when she went into television journalism." Why was he wasting words defending Suede to this woman?

Ruth cocked an eyebrow but let the subject drop. "Levi said you can take the letters. Your father should have them." The baby's cries quieted to a hiccupping whimper. Ruth looked at the child in her arms. "I need to put Adam down for a nap."

Boy. Del thumbed through the stack of correspondence. "You're sure? These aren't all from my grandfather." He lifted an envelope postmarked "New York 1942" and pulled out a single sheet, written in French with an illegible signature. Excitement jagged through him. Did it say Shapiro?

"I'm just telling you what Levi told me," she said, a snap in her voice. "He said take the letters. You want to argue, argue with him."

The baby started to cry again.

Pretty clear Ruth wanted Del gone. "Okay. Thank Levi, and thank you for putting up with me."

"At least you're nice to look at." She smiled for the first time, arching her back and biting her lip, her eyes on his.

Del grinned to mask an involuntary cringe, tucked the shoebox under his arm, and made a break for his car.

He set the Florsheim box in the middle of Mike's desk.

"No thanks. I prefer John Lobb."

"The letters you asked for, ass-wipe."

Mike lifted the cover. "Holy shit. These are all from Max? All this translating and transcribing is going to eat into happy hour. When does Wrangler want them back?"

"He doesn't. It's *all* of Avi's correspondence, not just the letters from my grandfather. Some are as recent as the year of Avi's death. Most are in German, but a few are in French. French isn't a problem, right?"

"Mais absolument non, mon ami." Mike shook his head. "Avi taught French and German for like a hundred years. I can't believe you, let alone your father, who was raised under Avi's roof, came away with nothing. Why the hell did you take Spanish in high school?"

Del gaped at him. "Because I live in California. I also went to Hebrew School."

"Where you learned nothing."

"We can't all have a freakish aptitude for languages." Del picked up one of the envelopes. "The letters dated during the war all seem to be from France except the one postmarked New York."

Mike's head jerked up. "Yoseph Shapiro lived in New York before he moved to San Francisco."

"Exactly, but the signature is impossible to read. Once you translate, we should be able to figure out the correspondent. If not, I can always trace the return address."

"How do you want me to tackle this? There's a butt-load of mail here."

"Put the later correspondence aside. Focus on the pieces dated during the war."

Mike rolled his eyes. "Yeah, genius, I figured that much out on my own. Still going to take time to transcribe all these."

"Don't transcribe. You can provide transcriptions for my dad eventually, but right now, we need to know what's in the letters. Read through them, make a note of anything that even hints at how my grandfather might have got hold of the Cézanne or one of the other two paintings."

Mike's eyes went hard. "Come on, dude, who gives a flying fuck? So what if Max stole a few paintings to pay for his kid to be smuggled to safety? That's good enough for me. He had every right."

"I appreciate that, Mikey. I do. But if the Cézanne rightfully belongs to the Shapiros, when and if we get it back, the painting should be returned to them."

"Any clues about the other two paintings as far as subject or artist?"

"Nope, and if there's nothing in this box, we've hit a dead

end. According to Dad, the nurse—Cécile—died of scarlet fever in a displaced persons camp after the war. The couple that brought him to the States worked with OSE, but Dad was barely three years old. All he remembers is their name—Lambert. You have any idea how many Lamberts reside in this country? Even if we could find a way to get a look at the ship records, there's no guarantee the couple traveled under their real name. Plus, they'd more than likely be dead by now."

Mike pulled the box closer. "I have a client scheduled in fifteen. I'll get on these ASAP, but I'm buried, and unless my calendar clears, we're talking Wednesday. You found nothing at all in London's confession?"

"*Nada*. Think I'm on board with Suede. London wrote the confession to protect someone. Question is, who? Given all the years he hovered around my parents, I know zilch about the guy other than he used to be married, and he had an affair with my mother, or to quote my father, 'took advantage of her when she was most vulnerable.' "

"You sound unconvinced."

"Is vulnerable a word that comes to mind when you think of my mother?"

"I was there. Watching Amy fade, losing her, was hell. We were all vulnerable, especially your mom."

Del felt a sharp bite of conscience. Why was it so much easier to judge than forgive? "If London exploited my mother, wouldn't she resent him? Dad sure as hell does."

"Whatever anyone says about London, he cared about CaMu. Your mother recognized that. Maybe it was enough for her."

"Not enough for me. I want to understand what made that asshole tick. I'm meeting with his ex-wife Friday afternoon in Greenbrae. If I find out London was a regular gasper, it'll go a long way to support the accidental death ruling."

"Ah, Gitte. I remember her."

"Hard to forget. The woman used to scare the shit out of me. She spent a lot of time at the house before Amy died—back when my parents threw parties. I think she'll shoot straight about London." Del heard the excitement in his voice. *Once a cop, always a cop.* "This afternoon I'm meeting with Neil Sobol."

"Thought you weren't going to stick your nose into a federal investigation?"

"I'm not. The Feds want to believe my parents had something to do with the disappearance of the Cézanne. I wish them luck. I'm just making sure other avenues of investigation remain open so when the truth bites 'em in the ass, they're ready to move on it."

Mike studied Del. "You're finally convinced the painting and London's death are connected? Ready to go after Daniel Shapiro?"

"Not yet." Del's cell rang. He eyed the caller ID and smiled. Suede. He knew she couldn't stay pissed. "I have to take this," he said, and flipped open the phone.

"Hi, Suede." Del glanced at Mike, who grinned like a half-wit, jabbing his index finger in and out of a closed fist.

Suede skipped the formalities. "According to the FBI, over the past six months, your father met with deceased CaMu director Thurman London privately on several occasions. Would you care to comment? This call is being recorded."

Shit. Del closed his eyes and exhaled. On the record—Suede wanted a scoop. "Bullshit. My father is on the museum's board, but other than trustee meetings, he and London kept their distance. They weren't the best of friends." *Not the smartest thing to say to a reporter, Miller.* "You already seem to have some idea of why they met. How about *you* sharing with *me*?"

Mike stared, eyes questioning.

"Why, indeed?" Suede said, unable or unwilling to keep the contempt out of her voice. "Were you aware London took several payouts from your father? Big money, as I understand. Odd, since *they weren't the best of friends,* as you so delicately put it."

Del's blood pressure shot up fifteen points. "Suede, I have an idea. Why not pack up your do-it-yourself muckraking kit and go fuck yourself? You continue to insinuate on air that my parents had a role in the disappearance of the Cézanne, and I'll make sure they sue your juicy little ass. Would you like me to repeat the last part again in case your recorder didn't catch it?"

Her voice remained calm and steady. "Why is it whenever people don't like the truth, it's always muckraking?" Click.

"Goddamn it!" Del shoved the phone back in his pocket.

Mike leaned across his desk. "What? What?"

"Suede said the FBI is claiming my father not only met with London, but gave him money."

Mike gave a short clipped laugh. "Why would Samuel give London money?"

"I don't know, but I sure as hell intend to find out."

His father's study smelled of warm, safe things that reminded Del of childhood: old leather, wood, and bay rum aftershave. Professional citations covered paneled walls, with every available flat surface piled high with books. Del cleared a stack of texts from a chair and sat facing his father and the wall where the Cézanne once hung.

"He intended to write his memoirs," Samuel said when asked about his meetings with London.

"And you were coaching him? Come on, Dad, make sense." Del was angry. Angry his dad hadn't been honest. Angry the FBI seemed to know more about his father than he did.

Samuel took a deep breath and wiped a hand over his mouth. "London called me six or seven months ago. Told me he had a literary agent and a publishing deal. He planned to write his memoirs, and as much as he cared for and respected your mother, he couldn't skip over the dissolution of his marriage."

"So?"

"London planned to talk about your mother in his execrable book. *To tell their story,* as he put it. He didn't have the balls to break the news himself. He wanted me to tell her. And he called himself her friend—what a farce. I hoped with him gone, all this evil would be over, but evil begets evil. No escape once it gets a foothold."

Del leaned forward in the chair. His mother always called his father a fixer. He repaired the broken, healed the sick, made things right for others. How far would he go to fix things for the woman he loved? "Why did you pay him, Dad? Did he blackmail you?"

"Not Thurman Alcott London. He was above that sort of thing, but he made no secret he needed money."

"What for?"

"I don't know, but I paid him triple his book advance and he agreed not to publish. I was an idiot to trust the lying bastard."

"How do you know he lied?"

"I read about his memoirs in the 'Lifestyles' section of the *Chronicle* two weeks ago, a big focus piece on how the book would be published next year. Do you have any idea how devastated your mother would be if the affair were to make it into print?"

"What did you tell her?"

"She knows about the memoirs but has no idea London planned to write about their relationship." He shook his head. "I couldn't tell her. The affair happened more than twenty years ago and she still can't let go of the guilt. To make her shame public? It would kill her. The afternoon London died, I went to the museum to confront him, tell him I knew he planned to go forward with the book. I wanted a guarantee he wouldn't mention Hanna by name."

Del's stomach went into free fall. "You went to the museum the day London died?"

"I didn't lie. I wouldn't. The police, the FBI, no one asked."

"You're a museum trustee. Why would they ask? They have a readout from your key card every time you enter and exit the building. No wonder they suspect you plotted with London. You met with him on the sly, paid him a large amount of money. Worse, you didn't bother to mention any of this to the Feds."

"My paying London had nothing to do with the Cézanne. If I had something to hide, why would I hand London a check? I tried to explain this to Agent Sobol."

"Christ, Dad. Sobol? Didn't you hear Mike? You shouldn't be talking to anyone without legal counsel. Did you tell Sobol about Mom and London?"

He looked stricken. "No, of course not."

"You need to prepare Mom. Eventually the FBI is going to press about the money and why you were with London that day."

"I never saw him. I walked back to his office, but his door was closed. I heard voices and didn't have time to wait. He was clearly with someone."

Or jerking off. Or dead. The realization hit Del like a pile driver. He didn't know if his father was telling the truth.

"I'm a trustee. Of course I'm concerned about the negative impact of this publicity on the museum, but I will not say I'm sorry about London."

Del loved his father, revered him as someone whose high ideals were worthy of admiration. But the man sitting in front of him at this moment, Del had no idea who he was.

Neil Sobol didn't look FBI. He wore shaggy hair, a relaxed expression, and a very good suit. Not Mike Gabretti good, but not off-the-rack either. To avoid the security hassle at the Federal Building, Neil agreed to meet Del near Stow Lake in Golden Gate Park. Poor choice. The fog had closed in, and it was so cold, even Del's tongue was numb.

Neil shoved his hands deep into his pants pockets and stamped his feet. "You realize I can't tell you anything about the investigation, so unless your plan is to freeze my balls off, you're wasting both our time."

The heat of resentment thawed the icy knot in Del's chest. "I understand you're investigating my father in the disappearance of the Cézanne."

Neil held up a hand to stop him.

"Dammit, let me finish. I only want to confirm the Feds are exploring other possible scenarios. Consider it a favor. When you figure out my parents had nothing to do with the theft—and you will—you'll be scrambling for new leads. You can thank me then."

"Okay, tell me this. Why was your father paying off London?"

Special Agent Sobol would have to mine that nugget of information elsewhere. "Paying and paying off are two different things."

"Maybe, but you didn't answer me, and big freakin' shock, neither did your father. By the way, did you think we wouldn't notice you running through CaMu, using your mother's key card?"

"I didn't give a shit whether you noticed or not."

"You need to start giving a shit. Daniel Shapiro is pushing hard on this."

Warmth crept up Del's collar. "I don't know how my grand-father acquired that painting. If it belongs to the Shapiros, fine, the painting is theirs. I don't care. My concern is my parents. Why would they offer the painting as the featured work in a major museum exhibition if the piece were stolen, and they

were afraid the Shapiros would turn around and claim ownership?"

"Daniel Shapiro is convinced your parents found out about
the claim too late to pull the work from the exhibit, so they did
the next best thing—made the painting disappear. The insurance company ends up paying, and your mom and dad still
have a priceless Cézanne tucked away safe and secure somewhere."

"That's bullshit," Del said.

"Are you under the impression I'm enjoying this? Because
I'm not. In fact, I think it's majorly fucked."

Sobol's sudden spark of anger sent a jolt through Del, and he
stepped back.

"Your grandfather died in the gas chamber at Auschwitz?
Well, so did mine. What a crap thing to have in common, yeah?
My grandparents fled Warsaw for Bruges. When Germany
invaded Belgium, they were rounded up and sent back to
Poland—their home, the country where they were born—to be
murdered. Think about that. My grandmother was lucky enough
to escape. She died of typhus before the Nazis could gas her."

"I'm sorry," Del said, barely able to get out the words.

Neil dismissed him with a wave. "Here's my point. Nazi-
plundered art is one thing. Jews stealing from other Jews is
something else. Those were desperate times. The war was about
staying alive, people doing things they wouldn't normally do to
survive. The Shapiro family? They had the money and the clout
to get out. My grandparents, your grandfather, they paid with
their lives. I don't like Shapiro or people like him. He can't
conceive your grandfather might have had a reason to take the
painting other than screwing over his employer. Daniel Shapiro
sees only greed, because he perceives a world made up of people
like him."

Neil scoured his hands over his face as if trying to bring back the circulation. Given the cold, maybe he was. "Whether your grandfather stole the Cézanne seventy years ago means shit-all to me. I don't decide who gets the prize; that's up to the courts. My job is to find the painting along with whoever made it disappear."

"What about London's death? You're satisfied it was autoerotic asphyxiation?"

Neil gave Del a look that would strip flesh from bone. "And just so we're clear? Your job is to stay the hell out of my investigation."

CHAPTER 18

Mike ordered the correspondence in piles by decade, year, and day. Envelopes displaying Max's now-familiar scrawl were placed in a separate stack. He experienced a prick of nostalgia for the days when the postman delivered something other than junk mail. *Real* letters, snapshots in time, to be read and savored, appreciated years—no, decades—in the future. Fuck email. Fuck Delete All. He selected a thick, square envelope postmarked Paris and began to read.

Dearest Avi, I hope you are settling well in San Francisco. I miss you, brother. I have much news to share . . .

Paris, 28 September 1939

Adèle and I are to become parents! We are joyful beyond all measure and pray that by the time the child arrives, the war will be over. Adèle, always the most beautiful woman in Paris, is now also the happiest, and I, my brother, am a blathering idiot. Forgive me.

Alas, not all the news is good. The situation in Germany worsens. I learned that riots destroyed the synagogue in Witten. It is impossible to fathom. With both France and England declaring war on the Reich, we've been warned invasion is imminent, yet all remains quiet here. The citizens who first coursed from Paris by the thousands fearing threat of German attack have trickled back to their homes and businesses.

*Since the beginning of the year, I've worked as a courier for
a man who sells fine paintings. His name is Yoseph Shapiro, and
he is well known in the city. Yoseph uses his influence to
safeguard those close to him, for which Adèle and I are grateful.
He is a good friend.*

*Yoseph worries the discriminatory laws passed in Germany
will come to France if Hitler is victorious. He tells me I must
take Adèle and join you in America, but Adèle insists our child
be born in Paris. She doesn't believe France could fall to
Germany even if the Nazis invade. Yoseph is not so naive and
has moved his accounts to Switzerland. He pays me in art
instead of francs and insists if I hold the paintings close, one
day I will be a rich man. That may be so, I tell him, but we
can't eat the damned things.*

"Gotcha." Mike whispered. He squeezed his eyes shut and
rested his head on the back of his chair, trying to remember his
World War II history. September 1939 marked the beginning of
the *Phony War,* an eight-month lull in military operations that
bred French complacency. Germany invaded the following June.
France capitulated and was divided into the northern occupation zone and the southern free zone, Vichy. Max had already
been forced to flee Germany; why didn't he listen to Yoseph?
After what the Nazis did in Poland, did he honestly believe he
and his family would be safe in Paris? *Jesus, Max.*

Mike disregarded the gnawing hollow at the pit of his
stomach, lifted the handset, and dialed Del.

"What's up, Mikey?"

"He gave Max the paintings."

"What?"

"Shapiro moved his money out of the country. He paid Max
in art. Told Max the paintings would make him rich one day.
Shapiro had influence, probably enough to get your grand-

parents out of Paris if they'd been willing to leave."

"What Shapiro had was wealth," Del said, his voice a monotone. He sounded bored.

"I bet Shapiro is the one who hooked Max up with the false identity papers." There was a long silence that Mike finally broke. "Would you say something, please? This is big, Delbo. Shapiro gave Max the paintings."

"Says my grandfather. We can't prove it."

"Shapiro moved his cash out of the country. If he'd left his money in France, and France fell to Germany, the accounts would be frozen because he was a Jew. That didn't happen. The Shapiros showed up on this side of the pond with big bucks. Didn't Yoseph Shapiro open the San Francisco gallery within a year of arriving here? Ergo, he paid Max with paintings."

"I understand what you're saying, but a lot of people sensed what was coming and moved their money out. Doesn't prove Shapiro made a gift of the Cézanne. Speculation isn't going to satisfy Daniel Shapiro."

Deflated, Mike put Del on speaker and picked up the next letter, sliding the time-yellowed sheet from its skin. Del continued to talk. Mike paid no attention.

Dearest Avi, my heart, my Adèle, is gone . . .

Paris, 7 February 1940

After Samuel's birth, Adèle began to bleed. The doctor could do nothing. I watched her precious life ebb away, steeped in her blood, her once rosy cheeks the gray of March snow. She gripped my hand as if touch might keep her with me. I thank God for allowing her to see our fine, strong, healthy boy. The content-ment in her eyes will be with me always, as will my shame. I lied to her, Avi. I told her all would be well. How could I not give her the chance to say goodbye? She deserved so much better than a coward like me.

Max's loss chilled Mike to his marrow. Would he feel such profound despair if he lost Alexa? No, not Alexa—Sophie.

"Mike, are you listening to me?" Del's voice boomed over the phone speaker and Mike jumped.

"Shit. No, sorry. Forgot you were on the line."

"Take a look at the letter from New York. Try to determine if it's from Shapiro. Maybe he'll corroborate what my grandfather said about the paintings."

"I want to finish Max's letters first," Mike said, promising to call Del back if he learned anything more. He replaced the receiver and examined the letter in front of him. Dated more than three years after Adèle's death, Max wrote from Drancy Internment Camp outside Paris. Samuel would have been with Avi in the States by then. The envelope held no postmark.

Dearest Avi, I am entrusting this letter to an angel. If there is a way, she will make certain it finds you . . .

Drancy, 10 June 1943

Margarite is not an inmate but an interné volontaire—a voluntary social worker who lives at the camp. Her job is to see the rights of the internees are protected. She holds little power, but her presence makes a difference. The guards take care not to give free rein to their depravity when she is nearby. She is a bright, pretty girl, and the guards are too busy appreciating her charms to notice what she is up to. Her smile is like honey from the most content of bees, sweet and soothing, and it not only lures the guards but blinds them.

Several nights after I left Samuel with Cécile, I stole back to the house in Marseilles. It was foolish, but I missed my boy and my home. The gendarmes were waiting. They took me into custody and sent me to an internment camp in Hérault, then put me on a train to Drancy. I arrived here in the middle of a scarlet fever outbreak. The other Jews from Hérault were immediately shoved on boxcars and conveyed to Pitchipoi, but because I worked at Necker Hospital when I first arrived in Paris, I was assigned to the quarantine ward to help.

There are so many children here, it hammers the heart. The youngsters are separated from their families upon arrival and the parents immediately deported. The children stay, sometimes for weeks. They are not cared for, even the sick ones. Twice I've found little ones dead in their beds when dumping morning chamber pails. These children without home or family tear at me, and I realize my efforts made little difference.

When time comes for the children to leave the camp, the guards chortle and tell them they are going to be with their parents. Their laughter grips my soul like an icy hand. Where the youngsters are sent remains a mystery, but I know Pitchipoi is not a good place. No one ever returns. The single light in my life is knowing Samuel is safe with you. That he is secure and surrounded by loving family gives me peace. I am so very grateful.

Mike pulled a container of antacid from his bottom desk drawer and swallowed from the bottle. The chalky liquid didn't touch the wringing pain in his gut.

Max lost his country, his wife, his son, risked his freedom and his life to get children to safety, only to be forced to witness their suffering and death under abominable conditions. How was that justice? And what the fuck was *Pitchipoi*? Another camp?

Mike pushed the letters out of the way, pulled his keyboard close, and googled *Pitchipoi*.

"An imaginary place to which French Jews imprisoned in Drancy Internment Camp believed they would be deported.

Most internees believed it to be a forced labor camp. Auschwitz."

Auschwitz. Mike took a deep breath and picked up the last of Max's letters. Postmarked, the outer circle of the seal read *Camp d'Internement de Drancy–Bureau de la Censure;* the inner circle, *Préfecture de Police.*

Dearest Avi, I hope you are well. You are in my heart always as is my Samuel . . .

Drancy, 10 August 1943

Margarite has died. She fell ill one day, and I never saw her again. She is gone, the children are gone, and I've lost my family. I cannot remember the last time I slept or ate. I've become an old man during my months here. The scarlet fever epidemic has passed, and I will soon be on a train for Pitchipoi.

Please tell Samuel how much I love him. There are no words adequate to describe what he means to me. Tell him never to feel guilty that his mother died giving him life. Even before he was born, he brought us such happiness. While Adèle carried him, she never stopped smiling, cradling her swollen belly so often, I was certain Samuel would come into this world recognizing her touch. I know you will take care of him as your own, but that doesn't assuage my emptiness.

Isn't it strange how life can take a turn and we not realize until it's too late? Had Adèle and I joined you in America, I can't help but wonder how different our lives would be. Might she have survived? I torture myself with these thoughts now as the pain is all that's left to remind me I'm still alive.

I may not have the chance to write again, so I will say good-bye. Do not be sad or lose courage. I love you, brother, and can never thank you enough. Be well and know you are in my every prayer. In my dreams we are together again. One day it will be so.

Mike refolded the letter and eyed a small piece of paper left in the envelope. He shook it onto the desk. The note was in English and signed *Lena Weber.*

> *"Here's what I was able to find in the camp logs. On August 14, 1943, one thousand Jewish men from Drancy were loaded into boxcars. On August 16, the train arrived at Auschwitz-Birkenau. All prisoners were registered at Auschwitz, including one, Max Rudolf Müeller, born Witten, Germany, January 15, 1915. Of the one thousand men, only four survived. I'm sorry, Mr. Miller. Your brother's name was not among them."*

Mike sat quiet, unmoving. He looked up at the knock on his office door. Susan stuck her head in.

"It's after six. I'm going to go home." She paused. "Are you all right? You look pale."

"I'm fine Susie. Just tired." *Bone tired.*

She nodded. "I switched the calls over to the service." She held out a handful of pink slips. "A half-dozen messages from different media outlets asking about CaMu."

Mike took them from her. "Any of these urgent or personal?"

She shook her head. "Not a one. Just vultures looking for an exclusive."

Mike crumpled them in his hand and tossed the wad of paper into his wastebasket. "Enjoy your evening, Susie."

"Go home and get some rest, Mr. Gabretti." She turned on her sensible heel and left him alone.

Mike touched the stack of correspondence and thought about Max and Samuel, then about Amy. His Amy. He needed to hold his little girl, tell her how much he loved her. Tell her he'd always keep her safe. He threw the unread letters in his briefcase, pulled on his jacket, and headed for home.

Alexa greeted him at the front door. "You're just in time. I ordered pizza. Should be here in five or ten minutes."

"I'm not hungry," Mike said, hanging up his coat. He set his briefcase on the coffee table. "Where's Amy?"

"Where do you think she is? In the nursery. Please don't wake her up. I just got her down."

"I only want to look at her."

Alexa sighed and followed him upstairs. "Did you ask Del?"

Amy snored softly in her crib. Mike leaned over the sleeping baby and stroked her cheek. He loved her so much. Before Amy, nothing in his life had seemed as simple—or complicated.

"Don't wake her up, Mike," Alexa whispered from behind him. "Did you?"

"Did I what?" Mike asked over his shoulder, voice low.

Another exaggerated sigh. "Ask Del."

"Ask him what?"

"Jesus, Mike. About the boat—if we can use it this weekend. My mom will be here, and she can take care of the baby." Her pitch rose to a fine whine. "I need to get out of this house for a while. I love Amy, but I'm held prisoner twenty-four/seven by that little shitting, peeing machine."

Amy's eyelids fluttered open and she began to squall.

Alexa groaned. "Great."

Mike smiled at his daughter. Amy's soft tuft of dark hair fanned out like a dandelion, and her cheeks were wet with tears. He plucked her from the crib and held her close, the warm milky scent of her an elixir. "It's okay, sweetheart. Daddy's here."

"Mike, did you hear me? My mother is coming this weekend. Did you remember to ask Del about the boat?"

The doorbell rang.

"You'd better get the door. That's probably the pizza," he said.

After dinner Mike escaped to his study, re-sorting and skimming the remaining letters. Only two were postmarked during the forties, both written in the same near-indecipherable hand. Mike opened the earliest. It was a letter of introduction, several pages long. It was from Shapiro.

Your brother is a fine man, Mr. Miller, but not a day goes by when I don't pray for him and his young son . . .

New York, January 5, 1941

Even before the Nazis arrived, the political climate for Jews in Paris was deteriorating. Max, so numbed by his experiences in Germany, couldn't grasp the transformation, but to me, a Parisian by birth, the changes were undeniable.

After the influx of refugees from the Spanish Civil War, the government was worried about national security and insisted on internment camps to detain enemy aliens. Overnight, the focus became foreign Jews. Stateless, destitute, unable to speak the language, refugee Jews were suspect. That was the beginning.

Max was the exception. He spoke excellent French—for which he credits you. He had a French wife and could easily pass as a gentile. But he was still a foreigner. My efforts to coax him into escaping France while it was still possible were for naught. Adèle didn't want to leave her home, which I understood. Abandoning Paris was the most difficult thing I've ever had to do.

Adèle's death nearly destroyed Max. I don't know what he'd have done without Samuel. Had Adèle survived, they might have been persuaded to flee, but Max couldn't bear to leave his memories behind.

Early on, I arranged for false papers for your brother. He insisted on knowing how I came by the documents. Long before I left Paris, I put him in touch with my contacts. Max was soon working with La Résistance. *As the exodus from the occupied North accelerated, anti-Semitism intensified, and Max's work grew increasingly treacherous. Undaunted, he became even more committed.*

According to all who know him, neither his dedication nor his bravery ever wavers. You have every right to be proud of your brother, Avi. I am proud to call him my friend, and honored to be his.

Below Shapiro's indecipherable signature was a phone number. Mike searched the Florsheim box for additional correspondence addressed in Shapiro's cramped hand, but once he relocated to San Francisco, there would have been no reason for him to write Avi. Mike found a single letter, postmarked Paris and dated two years after the war. He pulled it from the envelope.

Dear Avi, my heart breaks for you, for little Samuel, and for me . . .

Paris, 24 October 1947

You've lost a brother, Samuel, a fine father, and I, an ir-replaceable friend. Even realizing we received no correspondence from Max after 1943, I'd hoped for better news. Sometimes hope is all we have, yet at times like this, I wonder if hope is an ally or an enemy. Your gratitude is unnecessary. I would have made every effort to discover what happened to Max regardless. My only regret is the outcome is not what we prayed for. Those who knew his work with OSE tell me his chief concern throughout remained the safety of the children. He never flagged in his devotion, efforts, and support of the cause. Your brother was a true hero, Avi.

At present, I'm in France, arranging for my younger son's emigration to the States. We will return to San Francisco in a month. I look forward to exchanging memories of Max and seeing little Samuel again. When I think of how proud Max was of his boy, how much he loved him, I want to shake my fist at the inequity of the world we live in. My thoughts and prayers are with you and your family.

Mike just finished dialing Del's home number when Alexa strolled into the study.

"Are you going to spend all night in here?" she asked, moving behind the desk to stand beside him. Freshly scrubbed and ready for bed, her legs, long and brown under an oversized t-shirt. She was so sexy when she didn't try.

He reached out with his left hand and ran a finger over her breast, pinching the nub gently. She moaned and leaned into him, her legs opening as his hand traveled high up her inner thigh, lifting the hem of her shirt.

Del didn't pick up. Mike started to dial his cell but stopped. The letters were an interesting read, but Shapiro hadn't written word one about the painting, which, as far as Mike could tell, was all Delbo was interested in. So be it. Mike hung up the phone, reached around, gripped Alexa's ass, and pulled her to him.

CHAPTER 19

London's ex-wife lived in Greenbrae, a small, affluent community made up of hillsides and waterfront just south of San Rafael in Marin County. Del had been a teenager when Gitte Brauer was married to London and hadn't had contact with her in years.

He rapped on the door of the neat stucco townhome, heard footsteps, and a cherubic woman, sixtyish, with cropped curly gray hair greeted him.

"Ms. Brauer?" he said, searching her face for a hint of the familiar.

She laughed, soft features jiggling. Her accent was Eastern European. "I'm housekeeper. You Mr. Miller?"

Del nodded, and she opened the door wide. A willowy, attractive woman with chestnut hair and a knowing smile stood at the far end of a long narrow entry hall. As it turned out, Gitte Brauer had changed little in a quarter of a century.

Her eyes grabbed Del's and held. "Well, well, well, Mendel Miller. Didn't you turn into a pretty one? You must have got that face from your mother's side of the family. Your father was never much to look at." She bit her lip thoughtfully and added, "Nice man though."

Bristling slightly, Del considered telling her he was a dead ringer for his paternal grandfather. Instead he held out his hand. "Good to see you again, Ms. Brauer."

She backed away and shook a finger at him. "Absolutely not.

That's how germs are spread."

Del dropped his arm to his side.

"Shall we go into the parlor? Eva will make us tea."

He didn't realize people still had parlors. She guided him to a small, white tufted room, half-marshmallow, half-padded cell, the stink of rose and bleach so strong, he had to breathe through his mouth to keep from gagging. With a musical sigh, she settled into an upholstered chair and directed Del to the sofa facing her. He sidled behind the dwarf cocktail table separating them.

"You prefer Del to Mendel, no? And you're all grown up now. You must call me Gitte." She reached across the tiny table, squeezed his thigh with surprising strength, and winked. Apparently, thigh squeezing didn't hold the same germ threat as shaking hands.

"Why I'm here, Mrs. Brauer—"

"Gitte. You're here to talk about Thurman. The painting is mine, by the way."

Christ. Somebody else was claiming the Cézanne?

"The copy, I mean. I won't call the canvas a forgery, because forgery suggests I painted it to deceive. You know I'm an artist?"

Del bobbed his head, grateful to see Eva reappear with the tea tray, a welcome distraction while he crawled through his shock. The tea smelled like creosote and hot urine and did nothing to improve the parlor's air quality. Next to the ceramic teapot, the housekeeper placed what appeared to be a small plate of brown wafers with hair growing on them.

"Nothing for me, thank you," he said, relieved to get the words out without retching. Eva nodded and left the room.

Gitte offered him the plate. "Try a cracker. They're flax, carrot pulp, and sunflower seeds, healthy and quite tasty."

He held up a hand, and she slid to the edge of her chair,

leaning over the table, her steady brown eyes less than a foot from his.

"Stop looking at me like that. I had no part in whatever went on at CaMu. The copy happened a lifetime ago, back in the eighties. I was at your parents' house and spotted the Cézanne. The painting was beautiful—inspiring. Your sister told me it was okay to photograph. I took measurements and hundreds of snaps. From the photos, I painted the copy—not an unusual thing for a young artist to do. Copying the masters is how we learn. Eventually we come into our own." She laughed. "Or not."

"Where's the painting been all this time?"

"Thurman was awarded our god-awful house in the divorce. When I moved out, I left some canvases behind, including the copy of the Cézanne."

"You told this to the FBI?"

"Of course, although I'm not certain they believed me when I said I knew nothing about the theft."

"How can you be sure the canvas is yours?"

She laughed again. "There is no question. The FBI had me identify the piece. I recognize my own work. Thurman would have as well. Not that I didn't do an exquisite job. The project involved a lot of experimentation, and I got lucky. I used the right paints, a vintage, stripped canvas. I baked the piece to dry the paint and achieve a craquelure similar to the original. I'm proud to say, it would have been difficult for someone, even an expert, not intimately familiar with the original to spot it as a copy without careful examination."

Del thought about Sophie removing every hint of Mike from the home they shared and asked Brauer, "Why did your ex-husband hold on to your canvases? I was under the impression your divorce was—"

"Bitter? Acrimonious? Unpleasant? All of the above. But San

Francisco is a small city, and the art community is nothing if not incestuous. Thurman and I had to find a way to coexist, and we did. Whenever I ran into him at an event, the topic of conversation always turned to my paintings. He'd mention the canvases and his plan to pack them up and return them. Never happened. Thurman was not much for follow-through unless it pertained to CaMu, and I didn't push him. If he'd given up those canvases, we'd have had absolutely nothing to talk about."

"If the forgery—"

"Copy. And I don't care if it was stored in his attic. Thurman would never do anything to harm his precious museum. Exactly what I told the FBI. Not that it made any difference. Jackasses. As if I'd lie to absolve a man who, quite frankly, I detested with every fiber of my being."

"You've heard the rumors about my parents—my father— conspiring with your ex-husband?"

"They're as bogus as Thurman's confession. I'm sorry Samuel and Hani have to go through this. The mudslinging is undeserved."

Her sympathy threw him. He expected rancor given his mother's role in the breakup of Brauer's marriage.

"The idea of your father plotting with my former husband is laughable. Samuel could barely tolerate being in the same room with Thurman even before his—" Brauer studied Del. "You must know; otherwise, why would you be here? Thurman's indiscretion with your mother."

A wry grin tugged at the corners of her lips and her eyes shone. "Your father and Thurman got into a fistfight once. Did you know that? Thurman lost consciousness. A few teeth, too, as I recall. I thought your father was going to kill him."

Kill him? The words echoed in Del's brain.

"I should never have told Samuel about Thurman and your mother. There was no reason for him to know, and my telling benefited no one. My ego was bruised. It was a knee-jerk reaction."

"You told my father about the affair?"

Her body tensed in the chair, her back a plumb line against the cream fabric. "I told him in part to protect your mother. She was nearly destroyed when she lost her beautiful daughter. Thurman was reprehensible to take advantage of the situation. I'd always thought of your father as a gentle man. I had no idea he had that kind of rage inside." She reached for her cup of tea and said, "Have you thought about what might happen if the media were to find out about your mother and Thurman?"

A warning bell went off in Del's head, and his stomach clutched. He kept his eyes fixed on the woman in front of him. His mother had destroyed Gitte Brauer's marriage. Was this payback? He chose his words carefully. "There's no reason the press should find out."

Brauer's smile reached her eyes. "Wipe that concern off your handsome face. I have no plans to tell anyone about Thurman and your mother, and that includes the FBI. It's no one else's business. I'm not sure what you heard, but Hani had nothing to do with why Thurman and I separated. She wasn't his first indiscretion and certainly wouldn't have been his last. The problem with our marriage was Thurman." She gave Del a sidelong glance and pressed a finger to her open lips as if considering the best way to finish her thought. "His *unconventionality.*"

Another surprise. London always struck Del as an archconservative.

Brauer picked up on his confusion and added, "Let me put it this way. When I heard the details of Thurman's death, I was not surprised."

"Just to be sure we're on the same page, Ms. Brauer: your ex-husband routinely engaged in autoerotic asphyxia?"

She broke into a dry cackle. "You sound like a cop, and I told you to call me Gitte. What I'm telling you is that Thurman didn't hesitate to seek out his pleasures whenever and wherever they arose, if you'll pardon the pun. He had at least one illegitimate child, a boy. For all I know, he may have had a dozen." A muscle twitched in her cheek and she blinked several times.

Del couldn't imagine London as a parent. "Was the boy notified of his father's death?"

"Whether or not Thurman still had a relationship with Brian, I can't say. The boy used to stay with us on occasion—too frequently, if you ask me. Brian was told he was Thurman's nephew, and that's what he believed. This was years ago. He'd be a grown man now."

Gitte moved to the edge of her chair again and Del pushed back into the sofa cushions to maintain personal space.

"Tell me about you, Del. Are you married? Children?"

Whether because of her proximity or determination to change the subject, he found this question more disturbing than anything else said during the entire uncomfortable exchange. "No, not married. No kids."

"Well, you aren't gay," she reached out and squeezed his thigh again. "I can smell heterosexuality from here. I like younger men." She flashed a grin. "Bet I could teach you a few things."

He bet she could, too, but doubted it was anything he wanted to learn. Del checked his watch and got to his feet. "Gitte, thank you for agreeing to see me. I appreciate your time."

She rose and faced him, moving so close, he felt her stale, moist breath on his cheek. "It was my pleasure. If you think of any more questions, don't hesitate to call." Her thin eyebrows arched and she smirked. "Give my best to your parents."

When pigs fly.

Once the door closed behind him, Del gulped a lungful of

fresh air and, with the sensation of having made a narrow escape, jogged to his car.

Gitte Brauer clearly despised her former husband. She conceded he was a philandering sonovabitch who refused to acknowledge his own kid, and she had no difficulty believing he offed himself while jacking the beanstalk. So why defend him over the Cézanne? The forgery—copy—whatever—had been stored in London's house, for chrissake. The woman could be a liar, and maybe that crazy story about his dad knocking London on his ass was another lie. Except as much as Del didn't want to, he believed her.

He grabbed his weekend bag out of the trunk and tossed it on the seat next to him. Before leaving for Greenbrae, he'd swung by the loft and packed the essentials for a couple of days on the boat. The *Wet Dream* hadn't seen anything but her Marina Bay slip in months. *Wet Dream:* how had he let Mike talk him into that? They must have been drunk. They were most certainly drunk when they bought the boat. Del's mind jumped to the way Sophie cringed every time she said the name and he smiled. He desperately wished she were with him.

After inching into a too-small parking space, he collected his bag and sprinted to the dock. A forty-one-foot motor yacht, the *Wet Dream* was sleek as a sports car on the outside, all polished cherry and swank inside. She looked sexy as ever.

Reassured that some things don't change, he hopped aboard, stepped down into the salon, and threw his weekender on the galley counter. Even after all these months, the place still smelled of him and Mike and Sophie, of cinnamon, sandalwood, and leather, the scent as much a part of the boat as the sheen of her brass fittings. Every breath made him ache for the past.

The yacht had two staterooms with private heads, one aft, the master, which led to the cockpit, and a smaller VIP stateroom fore. Lots of privacy, but only one shower. Every woman he'd ever brought on board fell in love with the boat. "Who knew pussies were so fond of water?" Mike asked with annoying regularity.

Del forced his thoughts to the present, brain going full tilt, whirring through slivers of evidence and vague connections. London's death was ruled an accident. The medical examiner was convinced, London's ex-wife believed. Why didn't Del? The bizarre confession for one thing; that damned unlocked office door for another.

If Mike was right, and London was murdered, who the fuck hated the guy enough to want him dead and humiliated?

Dad. The answer came unbidden, and a wave of shame so pure, so overwhelming, rushed over him, he wanted to howl.

Up on deck, he stared at the backs of the houses lined up along the bay. Sophie's place was less than a five-minute walk down the trail. Worst-case scenario, she'd turn him down. He locked the boat and set out on the footpath. Not quite twilight, the sun hung low in the sky, the yellow light shimmying off the water like firelight on crystal. At the rear of her house, he peered through the bars of the iron fence. Her blinds were open, and he watched her work at the kitchen sink. The house lay adjacent to the trail access gate. He entered the security code into the keypad and ran to her front door, knocking, then ringing the bell. Casper barked. For such a small dog, he carried a mighty roar. *Good.* As Del often advised clients, a dog was a far better crime deterrent than any security system.

Sophie laughed when she opened the door. "Aha, I knew it was you because you always knock, then remember the bell. Everyone else rings first. Come in."

He kissed her cheek and inhaled the light clean tang of her sweat.

Casper barreled down the stairs and put his front paws on Del's thigh. "Hey boy, how's my favorite advance warning system?" He scratched the dog's head.

"You're early," Sophie said.

"Early for what?"

"I invited you to dinner next Thursday. I had a peanut butter sandwich. I can fix you one if you'd like." She grinned.

"Right. Didn't come to eat. I'm here with an invitation of my own." His eyes cut beyond her, taking in the living room. "If I'm not interrupting?"

"I'm cleaning the kitchen, but I can spare a few minutes. Sit. You want something to drink?"

He shook his head. "Are you busy this weekend?"

"Not unless you count working on my dissertation and doing laundry. What's up?"

"Didn't you say you'd like to get some distance from your dissertation?"

"What is this? Twenty questions? Get to the point, Mr. Miller."

"I'm going out on the *Wet Dream* for a couple of days. Come with me—no expectations. If you're more comfortable, we can each have our own stateroom. We're finally getting summer weather. Pack a swimsuit and let's take advantage and get away from everything. Just think—peace, quiet, and relaxation. This whole thing with my parents, Dr. London, the painting—I want to talk it out with someone who can be quasi-objective, but mostly I want to get away and spend time with you."

"Sounds incredible, but I can't leave Cas and Lucy."

"What about the girl down the street who pet-sits, the one you and Mike used to use?"

"I don't feel comfortable calling Candace out of the blue and dumping them on her without notice."

"She might be happy to get the work. It's summertime, and kids are always looking to make a few extra bucks."

Sophie narrowed her eyes, her message clear even without

words. Del had never needed to make a few extra bucks or had to work a summer job, so how would he know?

He pushed. "Come on, Sophie. Cas and Lu don't care whether you call a pet-sitter in advance or at the last minute." *Fuck.* He dropped onto the sofa and rested his elbows on his knees. "Sorry. I didn't mean to pressure you. I promised myself I wouldn't."

"You didn't."

"Yeah, I did. I figured you might be uncomfortable staying in the master, but if you took the guest stateroom—"

"Michael has nothing to do with this, Del." Her tone had a splintered edge. "My decisions no longer revolve around Michael. I sleep in the bed I shared with him, and that doesn't bother me. Didn't seem to bother you much either. Why would I feel uncomfortable being on the *Wet Dream*?" Tiny flinch.

Outside the window, the sun almost touched the horizon. "I better go. I walked, and the trail closes at dusk. If I don't get my ass moving, I'll have to hike the long way around. I'm going to spend the night on board, weigh anchor in the morning, and I still need to pick up provisions at Amini's."

"Why don't you stay here tonight, and we can talk? Pick up groceries in the morning." She rose from her chair and sat beside him on the sofa.

"Stay in your guest room?"

She laughed a sweet, light giggle. "I must be less adept at seduction than I thought."

Del arched his brows. "Is this a seduction?"

"Not if you have to ask. You're well versed in the art. Share a few tips."

With his hand on the back of her head, he tipped her forehead against his and the room disappeared behind a tumble of dark red curls. He kissed her, then nuzzled the curve of her neck, her scent replacing all remaining vestiges of the stench from Gitte

Brauer's townhouse.

She sat up, shoulders squared. "Think I've got it." She placed her palm on his neck and drew him to her, opening her mouth over his.

"You're a very quick study." Del pulled her into his lap.

"Whoa, slow down there. I thought you wanted to talk?"

"I do—about my father." He released her and exhaled a long breath.

Concern shadowed her features. "Oh, God, Del. Samuel is all right, isn't he? Not ill?"

"No, he's fine. What do you think of him?"

"What a bizarre question. I think the world of your parents. Samuel is one of the kindest people I've ever known." She cocked her head and twisted one of the buttons on Del's shirt-front. "Like father, like son."

Del wasn't so sure about that. "Do you think my father—aw, shit. Never mind."

"I have no idea what you're talking about, but you're clearly upset. Tell me."

"I think my father may have had something to do with what happened to London. Not the painting, I'm sure Dad knows nothing about the Cézanne—"

Her eyes widened. "Del, you're talking crazy. If anything, Samuel's sense of justice is even more—forgive me—overwrought than yours. You can't believe all the insane gossip. No way your father conspired with Dr. London."

He lowered his eyes. "I know Dad didn't collude with London." He paused, trying to put his doubts about his father into words. "But I'm not convinced he didn't have something to do with the man's death."

CHAPTER 20

Del left Sophie's early Saturday, swinging by Amini's to pick up enough food to get him through the weekend. On his way back to the *Wet Dream,* the sun beat hot on his back, the sky gleamed cobalt. If Sophie had agreed to come along, the day would register a perfect ten.

He yearned for escape and nothing beat the water, high at the helm, the rush of the wind and fresh sting of brine. He had to stop himself from sprinting to the boat. As he approached the *Wet Dream,* he saw a figure in the cockpit sporting what appeared to be a captain's hat.

"Hey, what are you doing? Get the hell off my boat." Del raced toward the yacht.

The man turned, grinned, and waved. Del should have been relieved, but seeing Mike worked through his blood like adrenaline, and he felt an overwhelming desire to throw him in the drink.

"Hey, Delbo, what are you doing here?" Mike called down. A pink satchel and a floppy straw hat ringed with fake flowers lay piled next to the hatch. Mike wasn't alone.

Del swallowed his temper and climbed aboard. "This is my weekend for the boat. What are you doing here?" The hatch opened and Alexa stepped onto the deck. Thank God for small favors. Del had no wish to be privy to any more of Mike's indiscretions.

"Easy, bro. You said you haven't been using her."

195

Alexa's pink lips rounded into a pout. "Mikey, you didn't ask? I thought you were going to ask."

"He said he hadn't been using the boat," Mike repeated.

Del's jaw clenched. "Well, I'm taking her out this weekend."

"We just off-loaded our gear," Mike said.

Alexa smiled, the sun sparking off her blue-white teeth. "This is such a pretty ship. If I'd known, I'd have nagged Mikey more about taking me out."

Mike peered up at the sky and shook his head. "Boat, Alexa, not ship, and there is no possible way you could nag me any more than you do."

Del set the Amini's bag on the deck. "I need to get away for a couple of days. This is my weekend. Didn't you see my duffle in the galley?"

Alexa sidled up to Mike and laid her head on his shoulder, voice pitch set to annoy. "Mikey, you promised. This is the first time I've been away from the baby for more than a few hours since she was born."

Mike looked as if he were in pain. "Come on, Delbo. Alexa's mom is taking care of Amy. The old bag will only be in town for a couple days."

"You are so rude." Alexa laughed and punched Mike in the shoulder.

"We can all go out. It'll be like old times. What say Delbo?"

With Alexa along? Hardly old times. The thought of a full weekend of her alternating brays and simpers made Del's teeth itch. The woman could be the poster child for *looks aren't everything*. He didn't want to argue. "Fine, but next time, ask first. You're damned lucky I got here when I did. If you'd launched, I'd have the fucking Coast Guard out after you."

"We're copacetic. Don't make a big—" Mike stopped mid-sentence, his gaze shifting to somewhere down the trail.

Del glanced over his shoulder. Sophie was running toward

the boat, arms waving, curls flying. He hopped down to the dock and met her.

"Good, I caught you," she said, pink cheeked and gasping for air.

He took her tote and placed a hand on her arm to steady her. "What's wrong?"

"Nothing, I—" She bent over, put her hands on her knees, and struggled to catch her breath. "I changed my mind. I want to go. Candace is sitting Cas and Lu. You were right. She was jazzed to earn some extra cash. Told me I *rocked.*" Sophie's eyes skimmed the boat, widening when they fell on Mike and Alexa watching from the deck.

"Hi, Sophie," Alexa said cheerfully.

Sophie blinked at Del. "You didn't tell me anyone else was invited."

"We surprised him. Didn't we, Del?" Alexa said. For once, Mike said nothing.

Shit, shit, shit. Two days on the water alone with Sophie? Del wanted Mike and his harpy off the boat *now.* "I invited Sophie first," Del said. If there were any justice in this world, Mike would take the hint and pack up.

"Del, you promised. You can't go back on your word," Alexa said.

He hadn't promised anything, and her goddamned whining made his skin crawl.

"No worries," Sophie said, face impassive. "We can go out another time."

Del grabbed her hand. "No, stay, please."

"I wouldn't ask you to go back on your promise," she said. "Another time."

Mike joined them on the dock. He slapped Del on the shoulder. "Thought something was off, you planning to go out alone. Two days without female company? Not like you, bro."

His eyes slid sideways to Sophie. "Too bad the boat has only the two staterooms. If there were a third—"

Sophie's features twisted into a mask of annoyance, her voice sharp as a honed blade. "I know how many staterooms she has, Michael. I was there when you idiots bought her. There's plenty of room for all of us." Sophie's eyes shot fire, and she squeezed Del's hand. "I'll stay."

Del bit the inside of his cheek, fighting to keep his surprise in check. Mike, however, with jaw slack and a frozen stare trained on Sophie, evidenced signs of shell shock.

"This is going to be so fun," Alexa called from the boat.

Trance broken, Mike glowered up at his wife.

Del whispered in Sophie's ear, "You sure about this?"

She showed teeth in what he figured was meant to be a smile. "Why not? Show me where to put my gear."

So much for a peaceful weekend on the bay.

Mike and Alexa had already taken over the master, so Del led Sophie to the smaller VIP stateroom and tossed their bags on the bed.

She hopped up beside the duffles and bounced several times. "Bed is as comfortable as the one in the master."

"Sorry about that."

She cocked her head and squinted at him. "Sorry the bed is comfortable?"

"That you don't have the option of sleeping alone. That was the deal, remember?"

"I remember, and if I wanted to sleep alone, I'd have stayed home. I like it right here." She patted the mattress.

He settled beside her, leaned in, and gave her a kiss.

"Want a beer?" Mike stood in the doorway, two unopened bottles in his hand.

Sophie grimaced and pushed Del away.

Yep, this was going to be a blast. "Can we get under way

first?" Del said. "Want me to take the helm?"

"Relax, everything is under control. Plan is, we go out, enjoy the day, then back to Sausalito, berth at Clipper Yacht, and find dinner."

"Dandy. Just don't get shitfaced before you pull out of the marina."

"Aye, aye, sir." Mike saluted. "Get your suits on and come up to the bridge; the sky is so blue, it fucking hurts."

Mike turned. Before he'd taken a step, Sophie vaulted from the bed and slid the door closed behind him. Remembering the look on Mike's face earlier when she agreed to stay, Del couldn't hold back a laugh.

Sophie climbed back on the mattress. "What's so funny?"

"Mike. When you agreed to stay, he was actually speechless. I don't ever remember him reading you so wrong."

"I surprised him?"

"You did."

"Yay me." She grinned a grin so wide and dazzling, his heart skipped.

He slid his arms around her and closed his eyes, relishing the thrum in his chest, part warmth, part ache. The vibration of the engine beneath them brought the boat to life.

"We better get changed." He let out a breath and stood. Yanking swim trunks from his overnight bag, he pulled off his shirt. Sophie didn't move.

"You plan to watch me?"

"Do you mind?"

He didn't. He peeled off his clothes, enjoying the feel of her eyes. With elaborate care, he folded his slacks, underwear, and shirt in a neat pile.

"I love looking at you," she said, her voice breathy.

He reached for his trunks, slipped them on, and sat on the bed. "Your turn."

She got to her feet and snatched up her bag. "I'm going to change in the head."

"Not fair."

"Can't compete with the likes of you. I feel like a tiny white worm, a tiny *scarred* white worm."

"Sophie, you're—"

She held a finger to his lips.

Exquisite. No point in saying the word; she wouldn't believe him. She walked into the head and closed the door.

He rested his back against the headboard and waited. He'd never seen her in a one-piece. She was stunning, like that pinup from the 'forties—the one with the red hair. *Rita Hayworth?* The suit was cut low, pushing her tits front and forward—a large part of its charm.

She held the flat of her hand over her chest, and her eyes moved nervously around the stateroom.

"What's the matter?"

"Here." She pointed between her breasts and flushed. "The scar—is it obvious?"

He caressed her cheek. "No, it isn't. You ready to go up top?"

"Not really, but it's not going to get any better."

He took her hand and they climbed to the bridge while Alexa applauded their appearance. The boat was already on the bay, the engine powered down.

Mike sat at the helm. He stared hard at Sophie. "What's with the granny suit?"

Her fingers stiffened in Del's.

"She looks great," Alexa said. "Hope I look that good when I'm her age."

"God, Alexa." Mike ran his hands over his face and shook his head.

"She's gorgeous," Del said, guiding Sophie to a chaise.

Mike strolled over. "I didn't say she wasn't, but when a

woman has a fine body, she should show it."

"Show it to you, you mean," Sophie snapped, and Alexa laughed.

Del let out a breath. Maybe it wasn't too late to swim back to Marina Bay.

Mike continued to gape, his eyes riveted to the scar on Sophie's thigh.

"Gee, Michael, take a picture why don't you?"

"I didn't realize he cut you that bad."

She froze. "I was in the hospital for three weeks. Did you think I stayed for the fun of it? You want a better look at these, too?" She held her up her palms.

"Gross," Alexa said.

Mike closed his eyes and let out a moan. "Alexa, would you *please* shut up?"

"I'm only saying—"

"Well, don't. Don't say anything." Mike took Sophie's hand and ran his fingers over the marred flesh. "I'm sorry."

"Wasn't your fault—not totally, anyway." The unspoken accusation hung heavy in the salt air. If Mike hadn't been fucking her student, hadn't gotten himself indicted for the girl's murder, Sophie wouldn't have ended up quarry for a killer. She'd have never been cut.

Alexa stood and stretched. "Mikey, what happened to those chips we brought on board?"

"Who gives a shit? I need another beer."

They anchored for the night in Sausalito, shared a pizza margherita and several bottles of Chianti at one of the trattorias on Bridgeway, and topped off the meal with limoncello shots. Sophie and Del sat on one side of the booth, Mike and Alexa on the other.

"I tried to call you Wednesday night. You didn't pick up.

Don't you ever sleep at home?" Mike's question was to Del, but his eyes never left Sophie.

Even in the weak light Del noticed the color in her cheeks. He gritted his teeth. "I was home. I switched the phone to voicemail because I was sick of telemarketers. You could have left a message or tried my cell. Why'd you call?"

"That letter postmarked New York? It was, indeed, written by Yoseph Shapiro. No new information, though, other than additional confirmation he and Max were close. Shapiro had sources in France. He seemed to know all about Max's work with OSE. Avi wasn't blowing smoke, Delbo. In Shapiro's words, Max was a true hero."

"Nothing about the Cézanne?"

Mike shook his head. "I understand why Avi didn't give all the correspondence to your dad. The letters Max wrote from Drancy nearly ripped my heart out."

Alexa slumped in her seat. "You are such a buzzkill. Can't we talk about something besides a dead guy? Sophie and I are bored to tears, aren't we?"

Sophie crossed her arms, pressed her lips together, and loudly said nothing.

Mike continued as if Alexa hadn't spoken. "After the war, Shapiro pulled strings. He hired some woman to investigate what happened to Max."

"Postwar Europe was chaos. Took years for families to reconnect. Sometimes they never did." Del watched Alexa do origami with her cocktail napkin. She held up what he supposed was meant to be a crane.

"Isn't it cute?"

"Christ, Alexa," Mike said on a sigh.

"How far are you with the letters? Still a chance you might find out something about the painting?" Del asked.

"Been through everything but the most recent stuff. You're

underestimating the power of Max's letters. They prove what a decent guy he was, that Shapiro and Max were friends. Max says straight out that Shapiro was paying him with art."

"Like I said before—"

"Yeah, yeah, it needs to come from Shapiro. All I know is, Max would never steal unless he had a damn good reason."

"If my grandfather stole the Cézanne, the painting belongs to the Shapiros. I have no problem with that. My concern is the Feds believing my parents had a role in hiding the thing."

"No shit. Right before we left the house, I got a call from your mother. The FBI searched your parents' manse this morning."

"Fuck!" Del leaned back against the booth. "Why didn't she call me?"

"Maybe you had your phone set to voicemail?" Mike said acidly. "She should have called me the minute they knocked on her door instead of after the fact. She said the agents were respectful. Of course they didn't find anything, but they took the computers, which made Samuel very unhappy. I'm tempted to call my father."

Alexa borrowed a pen from the waitress and began to decorate her crane with flowers.

"Even Slick Mick Gabretti can't control the Feds," Del said.

"No, but he can make their job difficult, and he's the best litigator in the state if things go south."

Del glanced over at Sophie, who met his eyes, brows arched, face expectant. He gave a slight shake of his head. This was neither the time nor the place to discuss his suspicions about his father, not with Alexa sitting across the table. Instead, he described his meeting with Gitte Brauer and her bombshell about the fake Cézanne.

"Why haven't the Feds arrested her?" Mike asked.

"Either they don't have evidence to connect her to the theft, or they don't believe she's involved. Possibly both. She and London were not on good terms."

"But she believes Dr. London made the painting switch?" Sophie asked.

"Nope, she's sticking to the party line: he wouldn't have risked the museum's reputation."

Mike shot Del a what-did-I-tell-you look.

Del shook his head. "I don't get it. Other than my mother, no one could stand London. Yet, despite a handwritten confession, no one believes he'd do anything to hurt CaMu. Oh, and Brauer also confirmed the guy liked his kink, which included a taste for asphyxia."

Alexa laid down her pen. "Finally something interesting to talk about."

"Shut up, Alexa," Mike said. "Any other revelations?"

"Yep, he has an illegitimate kid."

Mike shivered. "London a father? That's a possibility to chill your marrow."

"Apparently it was Gitte Brauer who told my dad about Mom and London."

"What about your mom and London?" Alexa asked, her tone wheedling.

Mike waved over the waitress. "Can we get another round of limoncellos?"

By the time they left the restaurant, Sophie was wobbly from the alcohol. Del took her hand. Mike veered over, none too steady himself, and snaked an arm around her shoulders. She jerked her hand away from Del, hunched out of Mike's hold, and jogged up to Alexa, who was walking ahead.

"What are you doing, Mike?" Del asked.

"My mistake, I thought we were still friends."

"You're divorced friends. Why don't you go walk with your wife?"

"Why don't you mind your own fucking business?" He sputtered and broke into loud laughter. "Sorry, I'm a mean drunk."

"Since when?" Del ran ahead, put his arm around Sophie, and gave her a squeeze.

The group arrived back at the boat in silence, the air charged with something rank and unpleasant. Del sat across from Sophie at the dinette in the salon.

Alexa lay on the sofa, her head in Mike's lap. "Time for bed, Mikey." She made a little mewling noise, arched her back, and touched his face.

Mike's gaze flew to Sophie, then back to Alexa. "Yeah, let's go," he said, his words slurred. He struggled to his feet. " 'Night, you two. Don't do anything I wouldn't do."

"I can't even imagine what that might be," Sophie said without expression.

Mike and Alexa disappeared into the stateroom, Mike sliding the door behind them as Del tried not to think about how wrong it looked for Mike to be with someone other than Sophie.

The sudden weight of Sophie's foot in his crotch catapulted him into the present.

"How about a foot massage?" she asked, her smile sweet.

"Sure." He cupped her heel in his palm and ran thumbs along her instep, making circles on the ball of her foot. She closed her eyes and sighed, and he felt her relax.

At first Del thought the moan came from her, but it was followed by a high-pitched shriek and grunting.

Sophie's leg went rigid. "I never realized how much you could hear out here. Wow, that is too embarrassing."

Del peered over his shoulder to the stateroom. The door was ajar. He walked over and slid the panel shut with a loud bang. More squeals and a round of giggles, softer now.

Sophie planted her feet on the floor. "I'm going up on deck to look at the stars." She held out a hand. "Come with?"

"Nope, too cold."

"Well I can't sit here and listen to *that*." She nodded her head toward the noise. "I'm sorry, I just can't." She turned away but not before he saw the glint of tears on her lashes.

"Come on. Let's go to our room. We can see stars from the window, and I need to use the facilities."

She pursed her lips as if thinking, then nodded.

When he stepped out of the head, she lay on top of the bed facing the wall, still dressed. He climbed onto the mattress and spooned against her.

She shuddered. "I wasn't going to let him get to me. I'm not jealous, I swear, but there's this vague sense of loss I can't shake."

"No worries," he whispered, holding her tighter and kissing her ear.

She turned toward him, her forehead against his chest. She wouldn't meet his eyes. "Del, I don't want to. I don't want—" She stopped.

"To make love." He finished for her, struggling not to sound disappointed.

"I'm sorry." She touched his erection through his jeans, closed her eyes, and kissed him.

He gently pushed her away, holding her at arm's length. "Don't do that. I don't want you to be with me out of some misplaced sense of obligation. I'm not that desperate."

"Should I sleep on the pull-out in the salon?" she asked in a somber tone.

He laughed and kissed her on the nose. "No. Fact is, I've had about all the excitement I can take for today. I'm ready to turn in. Why don't you get ready for bed?"

She crawled off the mattress, pulled a t-shirt and toothbrush from her knapsack, and slipped into the head.

He closed his eyes for a moment, reopening them to morning

sunshine and screams.

"Get out! Get out! Get out!"

Sophie's voice.

"My God, what did he do to you? You were so perfect."

Mike.

"Get away from me, Michael!" Sophie again, voice broken, hoarse, wet.

Del kicked off the blanket.

Loud sobs, closer, then Alexa's voice, "Are those all scars?"

Del slid open the stateroom door. Sophie, wearing only a towel, slammed into him, her face blotched and puffy, hair hanging in matted strands the color of dried blood. He caught her in his arms, her body quaking against his.

Mike stood behind her. "Sophie, I'm sorry, I didn't know you were in the shower." Then he said again, sotto voce, "You were so perfect."

"That's enough, Mike." Del shut the door in his face and flipped the lock.

Sophie's breath caught in a shiver. Yanking a blanket off the bed, Del wrapped her in it and tossed the sopping towel on the floor.

"I locked the door," she whispered. "I locked the door I always lock, the outer one. I forgot to lock the door from the master because I never had to before. I didn't think."

"And Mike walked in?" Del guided her to the edge of the bed and sat next her.

She nodded, gray-green eyes huge and turbulent.

No way Mike couldn't hear the shower. Had he assumed Alexa was in there?

There was a rap on the stateroom door. "Sophie, I need to talk to you."

She froze and looked at Del, eyes half-pleading, half-terrified. "Don't let him in."

"She doesn't want to talk right now, Mike."

"Dammit, let me in."

Del stood, opened the door, and faced Mike. "Back off. You've caused enough grief." He slid the door shut.

Sophie lay on the bed huddled under the blanket. From her small jerky movements, he could tell she was crying again. He stretched out beside her and held her.

"I disgusted him. You should have seen his face." She inhaled a quick jagged breath.

"He didn't know, Sophie."

"How repulsive I am?"

"You couldn't be repulsive if you tried. He didn't know how badly David hurt you."

"I'm getting off the boat. I'll take the shuttle home. Don't let this thing leave Sausalito. I need a couple minutes to put myself together. Then I'll disembark."

"You don't have to do that. I'll talk to Mike and Alexa. We'll head back to Marina Bay." How had everything gone so friggin' wrong?

"Don't. I'm fine, and I don't want to ruin your weekend."

"Right, because I can't take much more of this fun." Del tucked a strand of damp hair behind her ear. "Believe me, I'm ready to go home."

"I need to be alone for a few minutes. Would that be okay?"

"If you promise to let me know if you need anything."

"Can you get my clothes? They're on the hook outside the shower. I can't go back out there."

"Done." He opened the door, and Mike made a move toward the stateroom. Del blocked his way. "Sophie wants time by herself. Give her some space."

Mike's eyes were puffy and red, as if he'd been crying. *Hangover,* Del thought.

"What that creep did to her—it was my fault," Mike said.

"No shit. And keep your voice down. You think she can't hear you? What the fuck is the matter with you? Why did you walk in on her like that?"

"How many times do I have to repeat myself? There was too much construction noise on the dock to hear the shower. I needed to take a piss."

"He's telling the truth, Del," Alexa said. "I didn't know she was in there either. He didn't do it on purpose."

Maybe, but Del stood ready to accuse. "That's Mike. He never does anything on purpose. That would mean taking responsibility."

"What's that supposed to mean? I never intended to hurt Sophie."

Del poked his index finger in Mike's chest. "You think that maniac would have gone after her if you hadn't been banging her student? She was trying to save your sorry ass. What about knocking up your paralegal? Did you think that wouldn't hurt?" Del looked over at Alexa, who had the decency to flinch. "How about crapping all over Sophie during the divorce? That wasn't on purpose, either?"

"I gave her the house."

"Well, she has nothing to complain about, does she?"

"Get the fuck out of my way, Delbo." Mike made another move toward the stateroom, and Del shoved him back. Mike came at him, fists raised.

The door flew open and Sophie stepped out. "Stop arguing. I can't stand it."

"You're both acting like jackasses—typical men," Alexa said, all bray gone from her voice. She crossed the salon to Sophie's side and said to Mike, "I want to go home."

"Sophie—" Mike took a step toward the two women.

Alexa put her hand on his chest to stop him. "Not now. Just get us back to Marina Bay." She eyed Del. "You, too. Both of you, stop the pissing contest and get us home."

Mike and Del stared.

"I mean it. Quit gawking. I want to go home," Alexa said.

"Let's go," Mike said to Del, his voice low.

Del trailed him up to the bridge. "You sure it's all right to leave her with Sophie?"

"When she's not being pathologically jealous, Alexa likes Sophie. It's *you* she can't stand, although she'd like to fuck you. You want to do the honors, asshole?" Mike asked, gesturing at the helm.

Del did a double take. "Oh, you mean drive the boat. I thought you were offering me your wife."

"Ha, ha." Caustic tone notwithstanding, the corners of Mike's lips twitched. "Why didn't you tell me about the scars? A lot of what's been going on makes sense now."

"Good. Explain it to me, because I don't know what the hell you're talking about."

"Why Sophie is all over you. Any other guy would want to know what happened. With you, she doesn't have to spell it out. You're her free zone, her own little Vichy."

"This may surprise you, but there are women who actually enjoy my company. And for what it's worth, my relationship with Sophie is none of your business. You gave up that right." Del gripped the wheel, his knuckles white as bone.

"You're not fooling anyone. You've had a hard-on for her since college. But face it, bro, for most of the last twenty years you've been at each other's throats. No way it's going to work out. You're the ex-cop who believes all people are basically rotten. Sophie is the sociologist who believes they can all be saved."

"And where do you fall on the rotten/saved continuum, dickhead?"

"Wherever I need to. Wherever gets me where I want to go." Mike inhaled deeply and released the air in a long, even stream.

"How could that bastard do that to her? She was so beautiful."

Del shoved the key into the ignition and pressed the starter button. "She is still beautiful, Mike."

"I know," he said quietly, his gaze fixed on the horizon.

CHAPTER 21

Del, Mike, Sophie, and Alexa stood in a cluster on the dock, awkward and solemn as mourners at a funeral. Del didn't miss Sophie's cringe when Alexa insisted on a hug goodbye.

Mike grabbed his wife's hand and pulled her back. "I want to say again how sorry—"

"Don't even bother, Michael," Sophie said, and without another word, spun on her heel and marched down the trail in the direction of her house. Del ran to catch up, putting a hand on her shoulder to slow her down. "Wait up. Don't I at least rate a goodbye?"

She stopped in the middle of the path, panting. "Sorry, I needed to get away from them." He followed her gaze back to the boat, but Mike and Alexa were already on their way to the parking lot. Sophie set her tote on the ground, wrapped her arms around Del's waist, and lifted her face so he could kiss her. "Bye, you."

"Ha, think you can get rid of me that easy? I'll walk you home."

"You're parked at the marina."

He grinned. "I'm in shape. I can handle the five-minute hike back. Come on." He shifted his weekender to his left hand, picked up her tote, and they strolled toward the gate.

A slender Asian girl in her mid-teens stepped out of the house just as they reached the front walk. Candace's easy smile turned to a frown when she spotted Del and Sophie.

212

"Everything okay, Candace?" Sophie asked.

"Sure. Casper and I had a stroll, and both Cas and Lu had breakfast. I thought you wouldn't be back until late. Hi, Mr. Miller."

Del nodded to the girl. "Change of plans. You'll still get paid for the full weekend."

Her face brightened. "Really?"

He reached for his wallet and pulled out a hundred-dollar bill.

Candace backed away. "I don't have change for that."

"Go ahead, take it. It's worth it to know Cas and Lu were well cared for."

"Del—" Sophie gave him a hard stare.

"You're sure?" Candace asked.

"Absolutely."

"Sweet. Thank you, Mr. Miller. Thank you Ms. Gabretti." She took the bill and sprinted toward home.

Sophie's expression was pained. "A hundred dollars is more than three times her rate for an entire weekend. What if she expects that every time?"

"Don't worry so much. It was nice of her to agree to sit on short notice. I wanted to show my appreciation. If she hadn't been willing, you wouldn't have gone along. Hmm, maybe I should chase her down, get the money back, and give it to you for damages." He attempted a smile, lingering on the steps while Sophie slid the key in the lock.

Casper and Lucy sat waiting on the other side of the door. "Hi, you two. Did you behave for Candace?" Sophie glanced over her shoulder at Del. "Toss the bags anywhere and grab a seat."

"Excellent idea. Is yours available?" He winked at her. Another pathetic effort at lightening the mood, but she giggled anyway.

"I'm sorry it ended up being such a shitty weekend," he said. "Certainly wasn't what I had in mind." The understatement to end all understatements.

"That's reassuring. I'd hate to think any part of that fiasco was intended." She quirked a tight smile.

"So, what's the deal with Alexa? Mike says she likes you. I'm jealous. The woman hates my guts."

"I doubt she likes me, but I understand her pain—and pain, thy name is Michael. *You* are a completely different story. She covets your relationship with Michael. I'm her husband's ex-wife. You're his best friend—best friends are forever. I'm a tiny bit jealous of you myself." She joined him on the sofa and something sad crossed her face, a flash of dark emotion, gone in an instant. "Del, I've said this before, but I really mean it. I don't ever want to come between you and Michael. I've seen you two angry at each other, but never like today. I thought you were going to come to blows. Promise me whatever he does—"

"What? You think he deserves defending?"

"No, but you've always stood by him. Your loyalty is one of the things I admire most about you. One of many things." She bit her lip and raised a suggestive eyebrow. "Now, come upstairs with me."

You're her free zone, her own little Vichy. Mike's words burrowed into Del's brain even as his cock led the way to the bedroom.

Sun flooded the room, rays of light illuminating dust motes floating in the warm, dry air. Sophie faced him and lifted the edge of her tee to reveal the scarring on her taut belly. He tugged the shirt over her head, her mass of curls spilling over bare shoulders as if racing for freedom. Finally, he saw what his touch had only hinted, a road map of her hell. Hundreds of lines the delicate color of a rosebud marred creamy white flesh. He bent his head to kiss the pink vertex of the cross that ran between her breasts.

"You are so beautiful." He dropped to his knees and laid his cheek against her stomach, holding her close, feeling the uneven ridges of her pain.

Later, in the cocoon of an embrace, his face buried in the curve of her neck, he silently mouthed, *I love you.*

"Any chance of getting something to eat?" Del asked. Long past lunch, his stomach screamed for attention.

"I think I can manage food." Sophie bounded out of bed, noticed his stare, and grabbed her robe.

"Don't hide from me."

The bob of her head almost imperceptible, she tightened the belt around her wasp waist. "Sandwich okay? I thawed the roast from the dinner we didn't eat. Not bad on an onion roll with lots of mustard."

"Sounds perfect," he said, gathering clothes off the floor. His cell rang. He dug the phone out of his jacket pocket and looked at the screen. S. DUNN. *Shit.* After their last conversation, he didn't want to talk to Suede, particularly with Sophie in the room.

"Aren't you going to answer?"

He gave a resigned shrug and pressed *talk.* "This is Miller."

"Not even a cursory, 'Hi Suede?' Wait, let me guess—you're not alone and your company is female?"

Del felt the heat of Sophie's gaze. "How can I help you?" he said into the phone.

"You sound like a shoe salesman."

"Is that what you called to talk about?"

"Actually, this was an attempt to make up for being such a bitch last time we spoke. Needless to say, I'm already regretting the urge to atone. But then I regret most of my urges when it comes to you. I tried to call yesterday afternoon. I couldn't get through."

"I was out on the *Wet Dream*."

"I bet you were. So you haven't heard about Daniel Shapiro?"

Apprehension tightened around Del's chest like a steel band. "What about him?"

"He did a television interview—with Channel Seven, the little shit—in which he not only reiterated your grandfather was a thief, but also a liar who had nothing to do with either *Œuvre de Secours aux Enfants* or the Resistance."

Del's pulse ratcheted up a notch. "Bullshit. We have letters from Shapiro's grandfather proving it's bullshit. Is that why you called?" *Some atonement.*

"That was why I called yesterday. Today—" She cleared her throat and drew a breath. "The story is going to break any minute, and I thought you should know. Daniel Shapiro is dead, murdered. He took two bullets to the back of the head. Even San Francisco's esteemed medical examiner can't turn this into an accidental death. There will be questions, Del. Shapiro gets on TV and maligns your grandfather, and within twenty-four hours someone blows his brains out."

Del's mind reeled and unwillingly snagged on an image of his father. Unsteady, he dropped onto the edge of the mattress. "Any suspects?"

"Negatory—at least none the cops will admit to. Well, I've done my good deed. I'll hang up and let you get back to whatever—or whoever—you're doing."

"Wait—thanks for the heads up," he said. The line went dead in his ear.

Sophie squeezed his arm. "You look pale. Everything okay?"

"Daniel Shapiro's been murdered. No details."

She blinked, her eyes a mix of shock and concern. "Who was

that on the phone?"

"A source." The word slipped out before he could bite it back, and his face burned with the lie. Worse, he knew she could see it.

She tilted her head. "The *source* you were with when I called to ask you to dinner? What's with the look? You didn't answer your home phone. I called your cell and woke you up. Doesn't take Sherlock Holmes to deduce you weren't sleeping in your own bed."

"Sophie, I'm sor—"

"Don't—please." She turned away. "I'm sick to death of apologies. I don't own you, Del. I understand that, and I'm fine with it. Really."

Wrong. She did own him, and there was nothing either of them could do to change the fact.

After lunch, he drove back into the city. The afternoon snarl of traffic through Berkeley was expected but no less a pain in the ass. The university, foraging out a way to pay for the new under-construction athletic complex, decided to schedule back-to-back events for the next decade. The result? Protracted mass vehicle chaos.

His cell went off again. He hadn't connected the hands-free and couldn't get to the phone. After the cell rang three more times, he took the Ashby exit, pulled over, and checked missed calls. All four came from Mike's office number; no message. For most people, no message meant an unimportant call. For Mike, no message meant it was important enough he'd keep calling until he got an answer. *Jerk.* Del punched in the number.

Mike picked up on the first ring. "Don't you ever answer your damn phone?"

"Not when I'm on the freeway. I weighed the options. Die a horrible, fiery death or take your call. Guess which I chose? What the hell are you doing at work on a Sunday?"

"Just heard someone blew Daniel Shapiro's brains out."

"Old news. Suede called."

"Did she happen to mention that Danny Boy had pharmaceutical issues?"

"For fuck's sake, I'm parked on a freeway off-ramp. Skip the Jeopardy round and cut to the chase."

"After we left the boat, I dumped Alexa home and drove here—did I mention her mother is staying with us? Anyway, thought I'd read through the rest of Avi's correspondence—the postwar stuff—to find out what we had."

"And?"

"After Jakob took over the Shapiro Gallery, he made extended trips to New York, during which he and Avi corresponded. Avi and Jakob were friends, right?"

A horn blared as a beat-up Volkswagen Golf swerved around Del's Porsche. "And this has what to do with drugs? Spit it out."

"Relax, dude. I'm getting there. In his letters to Avi, Jakob constantly expressed concern over Daniel's drug use. The correspondence is intermittent but stretches over a period of almost two decades. Daniel wasn't some kid experimenting. He was into some nasty shit. Jakob writes about possibly cutting Daniel off, moneywise, so I spent the day doing some research."

Del leaned back in his seat and let out an exasperated breath. "Mike—"

"Just listen. When Jakob died six years ago, he left the gallery, the whole shebang, to his brother Albert. Even though Albert was in his seventies, nearly as old as Jakob. Daniel got bupkis, as your people say."

"And when Albert died, he left everything to Daniel," Del said.

"Bzzz, wrong. Albert is not dead."

"Yeah, Mikey, he is."

"And you called yourself a detective? Albert Shapiro is *not* dead. He's in a home for old farts right here in our City by the Bay. That ritzy place for Jews south of SoMa—is south of South of Market redundant? Neuman House. He's been sequestered for . . . wait for it . . . five years. Dementia." Mike's tone was conspiratorial. "We should talk to him."

Del rubbed his hands over his face. "You said the guy's suffering from dementia. Plus his nephew was just murdered. Not what you'd call an ideal time for a chat."

"You don't think it's a little whack that Albert contracted—or whatever the hell the word is—dementia and ended up in a retirement home within a few months of taking over the Shapiro Gallery? That Jakob noticed his son was a junkie but didn't pick up on his brother's mental illness? Does not compute, my friend. What I hear from my connections is that Daniel ran the gallery into the ground."

"Now you have connections?"

"I specialize in art and literary law. You damn well know I have connections. I told you we needed to go after Daniel Shapiro. The gallery went out of business three years ago. Didn't take Danny long. The Shapiro Gallery had been in business for almost seventy years. Dan-o's in charge for less than two, and the place is history."

"The man is dead, Mike."

"Right, shot through the back of the head, execution style."

"Drug hit you think?"

"What I think is you need to get your ass over to your parents' and talk to them about Albert Shapiro. Samuel knew the guy. And talk to Albert if you can get into Neuman House. Also, confirm your FBI pal is looking into Daniel Shapiro's less-than-distinguished past."

"If the Feds weren't looking into Shapiro before his murder, they sure as hell are now. I'm on my way to my parents'. Straight up, you think any of this has to do with London and the missing painting?"

"Straight up? No question. Daniel Shapiro was a junkie. No money, no fix. Puts a whole different spin on things."

After assuring Mike he'd call if he learned anything new, Del hung up and merged back onto the I-80 toward San Francisco.

He drove through his parents' front gate unimpeded. The press must have found entertainment elsewhere, probably partying over at Daniel Shapiro's place. Apparently, murder trumped conspiracy on the scandal-mongering hierarchy.

Samuel stepped out the front door to meet him. "You're here about Daniel Shapiro."

"In part. Is Mom home?" He searched the old man's face, but for what? Some tell he'd had a hand in Daniel Shapiro's death? In London's? All he saw was his dad.

Samuel pursed his lips and sniffed. "I smell something cooking, so she must be here."

"You don't know?"

They entered the foyer. "This is a big house, and your mother doesn't wear a homing device."

"Why would she need one? She's always in the kitchen cooking too much food." He was pissed at his father; his father was pissed in return; and Del had no clue when or how it happened. "I need to talk to you both."

The three of them circled the table like strangers, sitting as far apart as possible and making small talk until Samuel lost patience. "You said we need to talk, Del. If this is about Daniel Shapiro, talk."

"It's about Albert Shapiro and the Shapiro Gallery."

Hanna leaned forward in her chair. "Your father and I both knew Albert but not well. He took over the Shapiro Gallery—" She glanced over at Samuel. "Right after Jakob died, wasn't it? But only for a brief time."

"He was very much out of his element, but Albert inherited an excellent gallery manager in Lee Dutton and had enough sense to let Lee take care of the business end of things."

"You mentioned Dutton before. He works at the Frakansia now?"

Samuel nodded. "Albert hated the art scene. He died less than a year after Jakob. I always thought stress must have played a role. He never had any interest in running the gallery."

Not quite ready to resurrect Albert for his parents, unsure how they'd take the news that Albert Shapiro was still alive and kicking and living a few miles down the road, he asked, "How did you hear about Albert's death?"

Samuel bowed his head. "Albert was elderly and always somewhat frail. When we heard his nephew took over the gallery so soon after Jakob's death, it was obvious Albert had passed as well."

"What happened to Daniel's mother? No one ever mentions her."

"She committed suicide years ago. Judith suffered from clinical depression. What's this about, Del?"

"First, regardless of what Daniel Shapiro told the media, Yoseph's letters confirm Grandfather worked for the Resistance. Mike has the physical proof in his office. Second, I have no idea under what circumstances the gallery passed to Daniel, but Albert Shapiro is still alive. He's been a resident at Neuman House for the past five years. He suffers from dementia."

Samuel's eyes widened. "Dementia? That's not possible. Albert may not have known much about art, but he had a mind like a steel trap."

"Your father's right. Albert was a keenly intelligent man, although rather unpleasant if truth be told."

"He had scoliosis—born with benign tumors on his spine. He was in some pain and on occasion even relegated to a wheelchair.

He was quite bitter about it. As your mother mentioned, we were not close. I did meet with Albert not long after Jakob's death to express my condolences over the loss of his brother. Jakob had been a good friend to Avi, and we'd done considerable business with the Shapiro Gallery over the years. Albert exhibited no signs of dementia. Are you certain we're talking about the same Albert Shapiro? This can't have been more than a few months before you say he was admitted to Neuman."

"Mike is sure, Dad. Would it be possible for you to contact Neuman House and check on his condition? I want to talk to him—soon, if he's able."

"I don't think a call from me would be wise, given all that's happened with Daniel and this family. Better to have one of my colleagues contact Neuman." Samuel's troubled eyes pinned Del. "If there's a way, we'll get you inside."

CHAPTER 22

Alexa, dressed in loose camo pants and a tight, low-cut tee, stood in the doorway, blocking Mike from entering the house. He focused on the single blond curl nestled between her tits.

"Where the hell have you been, Mike? I appreciated the phone call and all, but when you said you'd be late, I didn't figure on two freakin' days."

"I've been in my office, earning the money required to keep you in the style to which you've become accustomed."

"Bullshit. If you think staying away will make me forget what happened on the ship, forget it."

Again with ship. Christ. "Boat, Alexa. It's a boat." Mike peered past her into the living room. "Where's the baby? Your mom's still here, right?" He'd never have left Amy alone with Alexa for so long.

"Amy's asleep, and Mom went shopping. Don't change the subject. What the fuck was that with Sophie? And quit staring at my boobs."

"I happen to like your boobs." He reached out and lifted the curl, his knuckle trailing the swell of one breast. She was a beautiful woman, no doubt.

"I was there. I know you heard her in the shower."

He smiled and shook his head. "Tsk, tsk. That's not what you told Delbo."

"I didn't want you two to beat the shit out of each other, or more likely, Del to beat the shit out of you. Did you really

223

expect an invitation to join her? With her lover in the next room and your wife a few feet away?"

"Del and Sophie aren't together, Alexa."

"Right, keep telling yourself that. Your plan backfired, Mike. You conned Del, but Sophie wasn't fooled. She knew it was no accident."

He didn't want to get into this, not now. "Look, I saw Sophie in the old lady swimsuit, and I thought—"

"What?"

"For chrissake, we were together for almost twenty years. You think I wanted a peek? Her suit had that skirt," he waved a hand in front of his stomach. "I thought—"

Alexa frowned, then chortled. "Pregnant? You thought she might be pregnant? Del and Sophie, wouldn't that be priceless?"

Goddamn bitch. Why couldn't she ever keep her mouth shut? Did she always have to goad him, egg him on? "Lex, as a personal favor to me, would you just be quiet?"

"Make me." She turned on her heel and headed into the house.

He grabbed her arm and jerked her around.

"Go on, big man. What are you going to do now? Punch me?"

Anger roared through him. He gripped her shoulders, fingers pressing into soft flesh as he backed her into the living room. He pushed her hard onto the sofa, straddled and pinned her.

She looked up at him, her eyes soft and warm and shining. She didn't speak.

He wanted her to say something, to yell at him, to fight back. He wanted a reason to hurt her. He grabbed the waistband of her pants, jerked them down, and shoved a hand between her legs.

She gasped, her arms encircling him. "I love you," she

whispered. "Love me back."

Cunt. He reached for his zipper.

Mike's phone rang just as he pushed off her.

"Ignore it," Alexa said. She bit her lip and opened her legs wider. "Go down on me so I can watch. It's my turn. Pretty please, Mikey?"

He hated it when she whined. He stood, grabbed his jacket from the floor, and dug his phone out of the pocket. "Hey Delbo, whuddup?" He looked over at Alexa and met his wife's black, unflinching glare.

"Hell, yeah, I can meet you," he said into the phone, and Alexa rolled her eyes. Mike ended the call and began to pull on his clothes.

"What does God's gift want now?"

"Asked me to go along when he talks to Albert Shapiro."

"Why do *you* need to go? Swear to God, he can't wipe his ass without you standing next to him holding the roll. Who is Albert Shapiro, anyway?"

"Albert Shapiro is Daniel Shapiro's uncle," Mike said.

"Okay. Who is Daniel Shapiro?" She narrowed her eyes. "Is this about Sophie?"

Mike sighed. "Alexa. Do you ever pay attention to anything outside of your own little world?"

The doorbell dinged three times. Upstairs, Amy began to cry. Alexa's mother, Enid, stuck her big-haired head into the house and called in her stretched southern drawl, "Okay if I come on in?"

"Mom, would you go up and take care of Amy? Mike and I need to talk."

Mike moved toward the front door. "No time, Lex. We'll talk when I get home."

"You just got home. When will you be back?"

"I don't know." He eyed the stairs. Amy was still crying.

"Mi-ike?" Enid always managed to fit an extra syllable into his name. Drove him nuts.

"Mom, will you *please* take care of Amy?"

"I will, Alexa Rose," Enid said, her eyes riveted to Mike's crotch. "I only wanted to suggest your husband close the barn door before he goes out in public."

As the sun dipped toward the horizon, Mike arrived at Neuman House, a Georgian brick mansion with a wide sweep of lawn, sash windows, and drifts of ivy trailing the walls. There was no visible evidence of life. Probably because Neuman House was a place where people came to die. He followed the tastefully discreet signs to visitor parking and slid the Z4 in next to Del's Porsche at the north corner of the lot.

"Thanks for coming, Mikey."

"Looking forward to meeting this guy. You think he's really nuts?"

"Senile dementia is not the same as insanity."

"Whatever. I checked. This place doesn't exactly have an open door policy. How'd you get access?"

"My dad called someone who called someone who called someone. Seems drop-ins are *verboten*. We are *expected*."

They climbed twin flights of stone steps leading to a glossy black door. Del rang the bell.

A leggy young woman with a thicket of brown curls and a body too fine to hide behind a nurse's uniform appeared. She cocked her head, brightened, and gave Del a generous smile.

He grinned back and took a half step toward her. Mike watched, amused.

"Hi, I'm Del Miller. This is Michael Gabretti. We have an appointment to see Albert Shapiro."

"Yes, of course, Mr. Miller, come in. I'm Naomi. If you'll follow me, Mr. Shapiro is out on the screened porch. He enjoys watching the birds and squirrels."

Birds and squirrels? Terrific. Mike raised a brow at Del and asked the nurse, "Does Mr. Shapiro know we're coming? Is he present enough to realize what's going on around him?"

Confusion etched her pretty face. "Oh, yes, he's expecting you. Sometimes he gets a little disoriented from his medication, but he's refused to take anything since he learned about his nephew's death."

Mike exchanged another glance with Del, and they fell into step behind the nurse. The place smelled of alcohol, disinfectant, and sickness. At odds with the doctor's office smell, Neuman was a maze of teeming old people. One room led to the next with no apparent rhyme or reason, and Mike wondered how many of the old farts got lost trying to navigate the place.

Naomi led them first to a television room, through to a computer center, and then to a game room where a bunch of old coots whooped it up over Xbox.

Not a bad way to finish things out, Mike decided. He studied Naomi's white-clad ass. Especially if you got to look at that every day.

They passed through a large open area with an indoor pool and finally out to the screened porch, abandoned except for a tiny bent form seated in a wheelchair, staring out at the twilight.

"Mr. Shapiro, your guests are here," Naomi said.

The figure didn't move.

"His hearing and eyesight aren't what they once were," she whispered. "Mr. Shapiro?" she repeated louder.

The frail body started and twisted around. "Naomi, is that you? Haven't I told you to call me Albert?" The voice was strong, the accent vaguely French. Despite any vision problems, the old man's sharp black eyes flashed as clear and bright as polished gemstone, his gaze focused and steady. Albert Shapiro sure as hell didn't look demented.

The nurse smiled. "I'll try to remember. Let me help you turn your chair around."

"I hope these young men won't mind if I stay seated? Some days are better than others. Today is not a good day."

Del stepped forward, hand outstretched. "Of course not, sir. I'm Del Miller. This is my friend, Michael Gabretti."

A strange look crossed the old man's face, something between surprise and fear. Finally, he smiled and took Del's hand. "Definite family resemblance. I remember you as a boy and your sister—terrible loss. You were a serious child." He studied Del. "You haven't changed much."

Mike sniggered.

Del eyed the old man suspiciously and Shapiro burst out laughing, a sound so full and ripe, it seemed impossible to have come from his withered body.

"Don't concern yourself," Shapiro said. "I wouldn't expect you to remember me. You were young, your sister not much more than an infant, and our meeting was brief." His eyes cut away. "How are your parents? I hope you'll express to Samuel and Hanna how sorry I am for what Daniel has put them through."

It was obvious Shapiro had all his faculties. Mike wanted to know what the hell was going on. "Mr. Shapiro, no disrespect intended, but we were under the impression you suffered from dementia. In fact, your memory seems better than my friend's here." Del shot Mike a warning glance that he ignored. "Unless you're having an uncharacteristically lucid moment—"

"For godsake, Mike—" Del swiveled toward Shapiro. "I apologize, Mr. Shapiro."

The old man held up a hand and looked at the nurse. "Naomi, would you leave us, please? There are things I'd like to discuss with these gentlemen in private. Not that I'd keep anything from you, *mon cher,* but I'm fully aware you have more important tasks than listening to my babble." Shapiro smiled at her.

"Mr. Shapiro—" she said, caution in her voice.

"Albert."

"Albert. I'm not sure I should—"

Shapiro waved her away "Go. We'll be fine. I've known this young man and his family for many years."

After a bit more cajoling, Naomi left the three men alone. Shapiro gestured Mike and Del to the wrought iron settee facing him. His curved backed appeared to grow straighter as he met their eyes. "I agreed to see you. Now I want you to tell me why you're here. I assume this visit has something to do with my nephew."

"We're very sorry for your loss, Mr. Shapiro," Del said.

Shapiro blinked several times and rubbed his lids with forefinger and thumb. "I appreciate that, but I'm sure you didn't come here to express your sympathy, not after the trouble Daniel has caused your family."

Mike focused on Shapiro, trying to gauge his reaction. "We understand Daniel took over the Shapiro Gallery from you?"

"I never wanted the gallery, Mr. Gabretti. My father's wish was that someone with his passion for art take the reins. I had no interest in art or the business end. My brother, Jakob, took over from our father with my blessing, and my nephew loved the gallery every bit as much as his father."

"Then why did Jakob leave the gallery to you rather than to Daniel?" Del asked.

The question seemed to diminish the old man. His shoulders slumped and his eyes misted, settling on the hands neatly folded in his lap. "I won't lie for my nephew. Far too late for that. I assume since you found me, you dug deep enough to know Daniel had issues with narcotics. Jakob always dreamed his son would take over. He left me the gallery to hold in trust until

Daniel was clean."

Del leaned forward. "Forgive me for asking, but was Daniel clean? Not long after he took over, the gallery went belly up."

"No, he wasn't," Shapiro said, his eyes still trained on his lap.

Mike couldn't take any more hedging. "Mr. Shapiro, what are you doing here at Neuman House, and why did you give your nephew control of the gallery if he was still using?"

"Daniel spent his whole life believing the gallery would pass to him. When Jakob left the business to me, well, Daniel was understandably angry."

"Are you saying Daniel put you in Neuman in order to take control of the gallery?" Mike asked.

"No, I put myself here." Shapiro's voice cracked.

Mike couldn't put his finger on what, but something was definitely off here. He stood and began to pace. "Were you looking for a way to get rid of the gallery, looking for a way out?"

Shapiro lifted his head and followed Mike's movements across the porch. "I was afraid."

A chill brushed along Mike's spine. "Of what?"

"My nephew." Shapiro stretched out his arm, and pushed up his shirtsleeve with a gnarled hand.

Mike flinched. The old man's forearm was covered with dozens of small round scars—cigarette burns. "Daniel did that?"

"Not my nephew, the drugs. Daniel was desperate for money. He needed the gallery to support his habit. Like I said, his father promised him the business. Daniel felt he'd been cheated."

"By Jakob?" Del asked.

"And by me. I told Daniel I never wanted the gallery. He wouldn't listen. Although I'd have willingly signed over everything, he found a doctor to attest I was *non compos mentis*. I was too scared to fight. I sold everything and moved into

Neuman House. Control of the gallery passed to Daniel. He
thought he could handle the business on his own. The first
month, he let the gallery manager go."

"Lee Dutton. My parents mentioned him."

"Lee managed the Shapiro Gallery for many years. He knew
his job."

"Mr. Dutton manages the Frakansia here in the city. Have
you spoken with him?"

Shapiro's birdlike eyes raced around the room, his body
trembling as he shifted in the wheelchair. "I didn't realize Lee
was still in San Francisco. We've had no contact. After his
dismissal, he was bitter and wanted nothing more to do with
the family. Not that I blamed him. He'd been a loyal employee
of the gallery for more than three decades. For Daniel to sum-
marily dismiss him was a blow."

"What about Neuman House?" Del asked. "You're obviously
not suffering from dementia. Why are they holding you?"

"This isn't a jail or institution. It's my home. I put myself
here. No one at Neuman House is guilty of anything other than
showing exceptional concern and care for an old invalid. Daniel
wanted control of the gallery. I wanted out. We both got what
we wanted."

Del repositioned himself and leaned forward. "Do you know
who might have wanted your nephew dead?"

Shapiro's shoulders collapsed, and he slowly shook his head.

Mike returned to the settee. "Mr. Shapiro, did your father
ever mention Del's grandfather, Max Müeller?"

A faint grimace crossed the old man's lips. "Because of illness, I stayed in France during the war. I didn't join my family
in the U.S. until 1947."

Mike recalled the letter of condolence Yoseph wrote Avi from
France and the mention of arranging for his son's emigration.

"I have my own memories of those times and of Max

Müeller." Shapiro studied Del, his stare fierce. "I'm sure you've heard this before, but you look exactly like your grandfather. For a moment, I thought I was seeing a ghost."

Maybe it was the old man's deteriorating eyesight, but something about the intensity of his gaze lifted the hairs on the back of Mike's neck.

"Did your father ever hint that my grandfather stole from him?" Del asked.

Shapiro gave a little sigh and almost smiled. "I don't know where Daniel got the idea that Max Müeller stole the Cézanne from my father. Maybe it was the drugs talking, maybe an out and out lie. I can't speak for my nephew, and I'm afraid Daniel can no longer speak for himself."

"You don't believe it then?"

Shapiro's eyes glazed over, his sadness as dark and ineradicable as a stain. "I was ashamed of Daniel, his drug use, but I loved him like a son, and it's a parent's job to protect his child."

What did that even mean? Mike drew in a breath between his teeth. "Were you aware the FBI suspects Samuel Miller of conspiring with CaMu's director to hide the Cézanne?"

"I'd believe anything of Thurman London, but not Samuel."

"You knew Thurman London?" Mike was aware the San Francisco art community was tight, but still, the words landed like a stone.

The old man's laugh was savage. "The sonovabitch killed Daniel's mother. Of course I knew him."

CHAPTER 23

Neuman's exterior lights winked on as they crossed the parking lot.

Del slid his hands in his pockets and leaned against the front fender of Mike's Z4. "What do you think?"

"I think you need to watch my paint job. I just had the car detailed. Tell you one thing, there's something shifty about the geezer. You notice he never answered your question about whether he thought Max stole the Cézanne? I got the impression he didn't much care for your grandfather. How much of that crap about London you figure he spilled to the Feds?"

"None, all, who knows? Judith Shapiro jumped off the Golden Gate, so unless London pushed her—"

"Weren't you listening? London *drove* her to suicide, *lured* her into adultery, then broke her heart. What in the hell did all these women see in that bastard?" Mike grinned. "Of course, I wonder the same thing about you. Did London's ex-wife mention anything about his affair with Daniel's mother?"

"I'd have said. It's possible Brauer didn't know. I had no clue about London and my mother." Del fell silent, reaching for another topic—any other topic.

Mike squeezed Del shoulder, seemed to realize the gesture was out of character, and jerked his hand back. "London split up Daniel's parents and allegedly precipitated Judith Shapiro's suicide. Daniel had plenty of reasons to hate Thurman London. What if this whole shitstorm—the missing painting, London's confession, Daniel's murder—is about revenge?"

"Twenty-five years after the fact? That's one hell of a grudge."

"La vendetta è un piatto che si serve freddo."

"I'm real impressed with your flair for languages. How about a translation?"

"Revenge is a dish best served cold—old spaghetti western starring Leonard Mann and Klaus Kinski."

Del looked to the sky and shook his head. "I don't get revenge. Daniel and London are dead. Albert Shapiro is in an old-folks home. Who's left to get even?" *Apart from my father.*

"How about London's ghost? Next time you screw Sophie, make her drag out one of her tarot decks. She can contact the spirit world. *Scooby Doo, where are you?*"

"Do you practice at being a dick, or does it come naturally?"

"Even better, make her read the cards in bed. She owns a couple of erotic decks that'll curl your . . . whatever you want curled." Mike's laugh was sharp enough to draw blood.

"How about giving Sophie a rest and help me out here?"

Mike's expression softened. "We agree Daniel's death is connected to the Cézanne's disappearance. All we have to do is figure out how."

"Maybe Daniel and London were working together."

"I know you want to believe the worst of London, but you need to face the facts. Unless he acted under coercion, he was not involved in the theft."

"He confessed, Mike."

Mike rolled his eyes. "So I've heard. The question you need to ask is who had reason to want both Shapiro and London dead? And if the theft and the deaths are connected, who had access to Shapiro, London, *and* the painting?"

Del had an answer, one that was killing him. He took a deep breath. "My dad had motive and opportunity."

Mike stayed quiet for a moment, then laughed. "You're joking, right? You don't believe your father could be guilty of anything so dishonorable as hiding a painting from the Shapiros, but you think he might be guilty of homicide? Get real."

Del said nothing.

"Your father is a physician, for fuck's sake. He took an oath. Not to mention he's one hell of a nice guy. What's going on in your head? I realize Sophie can be demanding, but you need to find a way to get some sleep. I said it before, but for the record? You look like somebody kicked the crap out of you from the inside out."

The rent in Del's patience grew. "That's enough about Sophie. I'm sick of hearing it. I told you, Dad met with London, paid him off."

"Big fucking deal."

"Maybe the arrangement didn't constitute blackmail in the strictest sense, but it was damn close. Dad visited CaMu the day London died. He used his key card to get in and out of the building."

"What did he tell the Feds?"

"Nothing. According to him, it was a private matter and had zero to do with the painting. But here's what scares the piss out of me. If it looks to me like he's hiding something, how do you think it looks to the FBI?"

"He hasn't been arrested."

"*Yet.* Eventually the Feds will move in, and now that Daniel Shapiro has two bullets in his head, London's accidental death may not appear quite so accidental. If the FBI takes another look at London's *mishap* and connects it to the theft of the Cézanne, I guarantee that asshole's memoir is going straight to the top of Neil Sobol's reading list, if it isn't there already."

"What did Hani say about the book?"

"Dad doesn't want her to know—as if she won't find out."

"What happened to the theory that London was protecting

235

someone? You can't believe London would cover for your father."

Del shrugged. "Who was there for the guy to protect? You said it yourself. CaMu was the only thing London cared about."

Mike waved him off with a flip of his hand. "I don't give a shit about any of this. Samuel didn't—couldn't—kill anyone. If the FBI had a shred of evidence against him, he'd be behind bars or in an interrogation room."

"You didn't hear him, Mike. How he thought once London was *out of the way,* the evil would be over. How London *got what he deserved.*"

Mike's brows rose. "Are you saying he confessed?"

"No, but he—"

"Can you really blame Samuel for detesting that goddamn pervert?"

"Explain to me again why you took London on as a client if you hated him so much? Why not hand him off to someone else? You're a partner. You have the power to delegate."

"My client is the museum, not the director. Greggs Allen represented CaMu years before London came on board. Greggs turned the museum over to me when he retired. He intended it as a reward." Mike's laugh was mirthless. "I kept hoping London would step down or accept a position elsewhere."

"Or die?"

Mike scoffed. "Oh, please. Didn't occur to me. For one thing, I figured he would live forever. London never demonstrated enough humanity to suggest mortality."

"You're starting to sound like Dad. Granted, London was a douchebag—"

Mike held up his palms in a stop gesture, turned away, and exhaled. "Okay, I never told anyone about this." He pressed his lips together, then continued, his delivery quick and emotionless. "London exposed himself to me when I was a kid."

Del chuckled. "Right, whatever."

A muscle ticked in Mike's jaw. "Happened at your parents' house."

A judder of tension slid through Del.

"We were eight or nine at the time. You, Amy, and I were watching TV. Your parents were throwing a dinner party. London and his wife were there. I needed to take a piss. The downstairs johns were occupied, so I went upstairs to the bathroom at the end of the hall, the one near Amy's room. I knew London was behind me on the stairs but didn't realize he followed me. When I got to the landing I walked straight to the bathroom and shut the door. I had to pee. I didn't even think about flipping the lock. Anyway he walked in on me."

"Accident, probably drunk. He used to drink a lot."

Mike sighed. "You don't get it. He opened the bathroom door, and I'm standing in front of the toilet taking a whiz. The sonovabitch unzips his fly, pulls out his pecker, and starts pumping the python in front of me. Tells me he can't wait. Tells me I can watch, that it's the best way to learn and he's"—Mike paused to add air quotes—" 'a good teacher.' "

"You didn't tell anyone?" Del's head began to throb like a pulse.

"Hell, no. When you're a kid, you think everything is your fault. I was sure I'd done something wrong. The shitbag never ambushed you?"

Del shook his head.

"Fucker figured *you'd* tell your parents. Still makes me sick, the old bastard beating off in front of me."

"Not so old. He'd have been about the age we are now. Did he ever mention the incident again?"

"You mean in casual conversation or during a client consultation? No, he didn't."

"What if you weren't his only victim? You should have told someone, Mike."

"I kept my eye on that SOB. Watched to make sure he kept his distance from children, boys in particular. He went after plenty of adult poon, but I never saw him hanging around kids. Not surprising, given the guy was about as warm and nurturing as a headstone. In case I wasn't clear, he didn't make a move on me. He didn't want me to participate, just observe."

"Martymachlia—it's a form of exhibitionism. He got off on being watched."

"I'm not going to ask how you know that, but for the record, I've enjoyed an audience on occasion." Mike grinned and wagged his brows.

"With another consenting adult, I'll wager. Trap an eight year old in a toilet and you're talking a paraphilia." Del's rage mounted and his mouth filled with a bitter taste. "Gitte Brauer said London's son used to stay with them. If that jackfuck enjoyed *teaching* prepubescent boys, he had a captive pupil."

"What about young Danny Shapiro? London was fucking his mother."

"We sure as hell aren't going to get any answers from Daniel Shapiro. That leaves London's kid."

"While you're out there stepping on the FBI's toes, talk to Lee Dutton. Old man Shapiro seemed mighty put out when you mentioned Dutton worked here in the city. Could be guilt, I suppose. Shapiro gives up the gallery and bada bing, his nephew axes a loyal thirty-year employee."

"I'll catch Dutton tomorrow. Tonight I need enough information out of Gitte Brauer to track down London's spawn. That means back to Greenbrae."

Mike glanced at his watch. "And I need to get home before Alexa throws another bitch fit."

"Mikey, about what happened with you and London . . ." Del faltered, reaching for the words to make things right.

"Yeah, yeah. Blah, blah. For future reference? All the crap the priests feed Catholics about confession being good for the soul? It's a load of horse shit."

Gitte Brauer opened the door before Del's finger found the bell. She wore a duffle slung over one shoulder and carried a rolled mat under her arm. "Well, hi there. Surprised to see you after the way you raced out of here the other day. Thought I scared you off."

She had, but damned if he'd admit it. "I'd like to ask you a couple more questions if you have time?"

"Just on my way to yoga. If I stay, what do I get in return?" She raised her brows and stared at his crotch.

He'd been with older women, but not old. Gitte Brauer was his mother's age. Attractive, yes, but she tried too hard and was veering dangerously close to her sell-by date. The thought turned Del's stomach liquid.

Brauer laughed. "Good God, I'm joking. Don't look so serious. Come in." She led him into the parlor—same stench, same cream puff of a room. She directed him to the sofa. "Ask away."

"Would it be correct to assume you discussed your ex-husband's . . . unusual sexual proclivities with the FBI?"

"Not in any detail, but given the man died of autoerotic asphyxiation, even the FBI should be able to figure out Thurman's tastes landed a little left of center."

"You said the only thing that surprised you about his death was his confession."

"Not quite, I said Thurman would never deliberately hurt CaMu. If the FBI really believes Thurman's confession and death are unrelated, they're idiots."

"What can you tell me about your husband's son?"

"*Ex*-husband and not much. Brian was around twelve when Thurman and I divorced, so he'd be in his early thirties now. His mother—Anastasia—married a man by the last name of

Randolph not long after Brian was born. The family moved to the East Coast, somewhere in Maine or Massachusetts. Considering he lived so far away, Brian visited his *Uncle* Thurman quite often—too often, as I told you earlier. I'm not one for children. After Thurman and I divorced, I never saw the boy again."

"You said his mother worked at the museum?"

Brauer nodded. "Managed public relations. Her maiden name was something long and Italian. Sorry, I'm horrible with names. Ask your mother. I'm sure she'd remember. Maybe she was even aware of the woman's dalliance with Thurman, but I doubt it. Thurman had a talent for discretion."

"Did you mention Brian to the FBI?"

"No, why would I? This all happened years ago. I am curious why you're asking, though."

"I'd like to talk to Brian."

"May I ask why? Is there a hidden will or insurance money I should know about?" She flashed Del a tiny unreadable smile.

He chuckled. "No, nothing like that. Are you aware if your ex-husband ever . . ." Del struggled for a tactful way to frame the question.

Gitte Brauer broke into a deep, raunchy cackle. "Knowing Thurman, the answer is a resounding yes." She shook her head, a smirk still playing on her lips. "Sorry, that was out of line. I didn't mean to interrupt. Did Thurman ever what?"

Del chewed the inside of his cheek. He'd spent most of his adult life asking the hard questions, so why was this so freaking difficult? He shifted on the couch, inhaled, and tried for diplomacy. "Children—boys?"

She laughed again, this time the sound was harsh and angry.

Del stared.

The over-plucked eyebrows arced into her hairline. "My God, you actually think Thurman—? He was a bastard, but he wouldn't, not his own son."

"Someone else's?"

Her composure evaporated, the easy humor forgotten. "That's not what I meant. All I'm saying is if he did . . . anything like that, I wasn't aware. You think I'd allow something like that to go on under my roof? Even I have standards."

Del wasn't convinced.

On his way home, Del stopped at Big Al's. After wolfing a burger in three bites, he tossed the soggy fries in the garbage and pulled his Porsche into a dark corner of the parking lot. Forehead resting against the steering wheel, lids closed, he tried to clear his brain. Was Gitte Brauer lying, defensive, both, or neither? London was probably a paraphiliac. What, if any, was the connection to the missing Cézanne? He glanced at the clock. Ten p.m. and his mind had turned to mush. *Fuck.* When had his instincts gone to shit?

He needed sleep. His thoughts trailed to his empty loft and the familiar ache for Sophie bloomed in his gut. He still hadn't told her about Guardian Piedmont.

He imagined Sophie as a girl, nine years old, tiny and pale under the inevitable river of auburn hair, abandoned by her mother in a tenderloin SRO. The landlord discovered her hiding in the closet, half-starved. Then came the foster homes. Sophie never talked about abuse, but Del knew it went with the territory. Marrying Mike had been an act of faith. Sophie's trust did not come easy, and Mike rewarded her with more betrayal. She'd been left behind so many times: father, grandmother, mother, Mike. Would she even notice when Del left? He crammed his key in the ignition and the engine jumped to life. He pulled out of Al's parking lot, made a U-turn, and aimed for Marina Bay.

Sophie opened the door, rubbing her bare arms against the

evening chill.

"Hi, I'm here uninvited again."

She looked at him with eyes that seemed to see clear through to his soul. A hint of a tremor in her voice, she said, "You look like you need a hug." She took his hand, pulled him inside, sliding her arms around him. "Tell me what's wrong."

"Everything's wrong. Everything but you." He touched her face. He wanted to tell her how much she meant to him, how he wanted her with him always, how she was his home.

"Did you learn something about the painting?"

He exhaled but couldn't find his voice.

"Don't tell me you're still worried your father may be involved in London's death?"

"Can we talk about something else? Tomorrow is another day, but tonight I don't want to think about anything to do with London or that damned painting."

She tilted her head, her voice soothing. "Sure. Are you hungry? Did you get dinner?"

"Stopped for a burger."

"Ah, explains why you smell a little like fries. On you, I like it." She bit her bottom lip and gave him a half-smile. "We don't need to talk at all if you're tired. Casper's already had his goodnight tour of the backyard. Why don't we go to bed?"

She took his hand and led him upstairs. In the bedroom, she pulled his mouth down to hers. She tasted both warm and cool, of yield and toothpaste, and his mind swam.

She unbuttoned his shirt, her lips against the pulse in his throat. "Think I'm getting this seduction thing down."

"If you want, we can just talk," he whispered into her hair. He wanted to talk; he came here to talk.

She traced his erection with her finger and peered up at him. "Your mouth is saying one thing, but your body is telling me something else."

He ran his knuckles along the curve of her jaw and moved to pull off her tank top.

She stepped out of his reach. "I'd rather keep it on."

He exhaled. He thought they were past this. "I've seen you. You're beautiful. I want to feel you next to me."

"It's not about you. It's me. I can't stand to look at myself." She peeled off her sweatpants and panties, glanced down, and gave him a sad smile. "*Voilà*. The only part that matters is uncovered and yours for the taking."

Jesus, she thought he was only here for the sex. The realization slammed him hard.

She climbed on the bed and held out her hand. When he didn't go to her, she closed her eyes and touched herself, moaning softly.

He heard himself say he needed to brush his teeth.

She giggled. "Strange time to worry about your dental health." She met his eyes and her smile evaporated. "I did something wrong, didn't I?"

"No, it's—I didn't come here for sex, Sophie."

Her cheeks colored and she scrambled for the afghan at the foot of the bed; tying it around her hips like a sarong, she got to her feet. "I'm sorry. I thought—I mean, you were hard. God, I'm such a moron. You're tired." She hid her face in her hands. "The guest room is all yours. The linens are clean."

She moved forward, trapping her legs in the makeshift skirt and stumbled. Del caught her, but she wouldn't meet his eyes. He drew her close. "You know I want you." He caught his reflection in the dresser mirror, and a grown man stared back. How could that be? He felt no different from the kid he'd been the day he first laid eyes on her. "I came to talk. You really think the only reason I come here is for sex?"

She pulled away from him, picked up her clothes, and began to dress. "After I got out of the hospital, you didn't bother to call." She'd mentioned this before, but now her tone was shrill and accusatory.

"Sophie, what David did to you was my fault. I thought you might not want me around."

"I wish you would quit with the guilt. You don't have a right to it. You aren't responsible for what happened with David, so get over yourself and quit looking for excuses to act the martyr. Time for a reality check—you got along fine without me. I'm the one who called, invited you over, and seduced you. Now you expect me to believe sex has nothing to do with you being here?"

Without thinking, he blurted out the words. "I love you."

"I love you, too. We've been friends for most of our lives."

He moved closer, holding her gaze. "Sophie, listen to what I'm saying. I'm in love with you. I always have been."

She blinked, studied his face, and then threw back her head and laughed.

CHAPTER 24

A rush of red-hot fury bloomed in Del's chest. She'd actually laughed at him. "It wasn't meant as a joke."

Sophie stared up at the ceiling and let out an exaggerated breath. "For heaven's sake, Del. You're not in love with me. That's crazy."

"Glad we got that straight. As long as you're sure what I feel, that's all that matters. I'm going to bed." He headed for the door.

"Wait, stop. C'mon, don't be mad."

He whirled and faced her, his rage filling the room. "I didn't expect you to fall into my arms and declare your undying devotion, but I didn't plan on providing a comedic interlude either. Fuck this shit."

"You've had a tough couple of weeks with everything that's going on. You're under a lot of stress. I didn't mean to make things worse, but don't you think if you'd been in love with me for twenty years I'd know?"

"How could you? I didn't realize it myself."

"Women sense these things," she said, her smile infuriatingly enigmatic.

Patronizing bitch. How was it possible he hadn't noticed before now? He stuffed his hands in his pockets to keep from shaking the smirk off her pretty face. "Right, you're so intuitive, Ms. Tarot Reader. Like how you sensed Mike was fucking his paralegal under your nose? Then there was your student." His words buzzed through the air like shrapnel.

Suddenly, she was spun glass, brittle, fragile, as if she'd shatter into a million pieces if he blew a hard breath. Her eyes narrowed and her body went rigid. With a voice as taut as a trip-wire, she told him to get out.

And just like that, his anger evaporated, leaving him empty and sore. "I'm sorry. I didn't mean that." He reached out to her, and she slapped his hand away.

"You can sleep in the guest room, on the sofa, or under a BART train for all I care, but get out of my bedroom."

"Sophie—"

"Get. The. Fuck. Out." She grabbed a pillow off the bed and threw it at him. "Get out!"

He backed into the hallway, blinking as she banged the door closed in his face. Lu and Casper glared at him from the landing. He walked down the hall to escape their accusatory stares, but the pair followed him into the guest room. He stretched out on top of the covers, not bothering to undress. Casper jumped up next to him, made two circles, and settled at his feet. Lucy sprawled on the unused pillow. "Guess I managed to get you two booted out, too. Sorry." He closed his eyes, inhaled deeply, and waited for sleep to take him.

The first thing he noticed when he woke was the blanket draped over him; the second was the intoxicating scent of bacon frying. Lucy was gone, but Casper's sawlike snores still rose from the foot of the bed.

Del squinted to read his watch in the sliver of shade-filtered morning light. Already past nine. He threw off the cover and perched on the edge of the bed. A shadow crossed his lap from the open door, and he looked up. Sophie. Fresh-faced, her curls loose, she looked very young.

"Good, you're awake. Breakfast is almost ready," she said

"Thanks for the blanket." His eyes met hers, then jumped to

Casper. He reached down and scratched the yawning dog. "About last night—"

She blinked. "I acted like an ass. I came to apologize, but all three of you were asleep and looked so sweet, I didn't have the heart to wake you."

He crossed the room to her. "I wish you had."

She bowed her head. "Most people hear the L-word their whole lives, from family, from friends, from lovers. Michael is the only one who ever—" She paused, blew out a puff of air, and slid her arms around him, resting her chin on his chest, gray-green eyes staring up, wide and clear. "I love you, too, Del. I do."

He kissed her forehead. "You love me as a friend. I get it."

"No," she whispered, "not just a friend. That's what scares me. I don't want to lose you."

He stroked her hair. "I'm right here. You're not going to lose me." In a couple months he'd be in a new job on the other side of the country. If he kept waiting for the right moment to tell her, it would only get harder. He took a deep breath. Something gripped his lungs and he choked. "What's burning?"

"Crap, the bacon." She let go of him and raced down the hall.

Downstairs, they made their way through a cloud of acrid smoke into the kitchen. Sophie switched on the fan, opened the windows, and emptied the charred bacon from the skillet into the garbage. "How does cereal sound?"

He grinned. "Cap'n Crunch?"

By the time they finished breakfast and cleared the dishes, Del resolved it was now or never. "Come, sit. We need to talk."

She rubbed her forehead. "Why so serious? If this is about last night—"

"It's not." He took her hand, led her to living room sofa, and settled in next to her.

"You're scaring me a little. Just say whatever you have to say."

He couldn't meet her eyes. "I'm leaving San Francisco."

She laughed, relief softening her features. "I thought you had bad news. Good for you. You deserve a vacation."

"Not a vacation. I'm leaving permanently, moving. I've been offered a position as head of security for Guardian Piedmont Global."

She stared at him. "What? You can't leave. Your parents are here. Michael. Me. A few minutes ago, you told me I wasn't going to lose you."

"I'll be working for the good guys again, Sophie. Insurance fraud is big business. GPG has asked me to develop a program to train investigators in surveillance and interrogation techniques company-wide. You and I both know I was never cut out to be a consultant." He took her hand. "I meant what I said. You won't lose me. I'll never be more than a phone call away."

She pulled away from him and stood. "Where is this new position?"

"I'll split my time between the Atlanta and New York offices."

"That's on the other side of the country." Her eyes filled, and she wiped away tears before they fell. "I don't want you to go."

He rose and held her shoulders, forcing her to meet his eyes. "Insurance fraud is an eighty billion dollar a year business. This is an opportunity for me to do something worthwhile, to make a difference. This job is a chance at a new life."

Chin trembling, voice unsteady, she said, "I didn't realize your old life was so terrible."

He stroked her cheek.

She pulled away and choked back another sob. "I'm sorry. I know I'm selfish, but you've only been consulting for a few months. Give it more time."

The agony on her face clawed at his heart like a talon.

"Sophie, this is a once in a lifetime opportunity." He hadn't planned to ask. The answer would be no, so why bother? The invitation spilled out unpremeditated, surprising them both. "Come with me."

"What?" Her breath caught on the word.

He couldn't read her beyond the shock. "Come with me. You can finish your dissertation anywhere. You said the university might not have a teaching position for you in the fall. Come with me, you and Casper and Lu."

"I can't just pick up and leave. This is my home." Her eyes skimmed the room. "What would I do with the house?"

She didn't say no. "Close the place up. Come on a trial basis. If you decide to stay, then we'll figure out what to do with the house. No strings. Having you with me would be—" *What? What would it be?* He was terrified if he stopped talking, it would give her the chance to refuse. He reared back and steeled himself for rejection.

She bit her lip. "You're serious?"

"Absolutely." Where was this conviction coming from?

"I need time to think."

Not trusting himself with speech, he nodded.

On the way to Seacliff, he did his best to squelch the simmer of hope that bubbled inside him. Hope was dangerous. If Mike knew, he'd be on the warpath. Del shoved away doubts, repeating *this isn't about Mike* like a mantra.

The street outside his parents' house was quiet. The media were either getting bored or out gathering more dirt. Yeah, that last part sounded right. He pulled through the gate and parked near the garage. The basketball hoop he'd used in high school still guarded the far end of the drive. He wondered why his parents kept it.

He studied the house. Replete with stone façade, conical

roof, and pointed arches, the place resembled a gothic fortress. Mike once labeled it the *Millers' Mutant Manse,* but hidden from the street by a thicket of oak and pine, to Del it had always been a refuge, untainted by real life and protected from the city's stew of greed, poverty, and violence. He stopped to lay his hand on the trunk of the extravagant white oak where he and Mike once had a tree house.

His father opened the front door. "Saw you fondling the tree through the window."

Del chuckled and stepped into the foyer. "Remember our tree house?"

"I remember you and Mike roughhousing, and Mike falling out of the tree and breaking his arm."

"Good thing my father's a doctor." *Sworn to do no harm.*

The aroma of chicken soup filled the house. "Good, Mom's here. I have more questions."

"If this is more talk about London, the painting, or the Shapiros, I've had enough."

The man's obstinacy was maddening. "Dad, you can't wear blinders and pretend this isn't happening."

He grunted noncommittally but trailed Del into the kitchen.

"Did either of you know London had a son?" Del asked, after he'd described the visit with Albert Shapiro.

"Thurman and Gitte didn't have children," his mother said, wiping her hands on a dish towel. She placed a bowl of soup in front of him and dropped into a chair.

Del pushed the food away. "Smells great, but I just ate breakfast. Gitte Brauer told me London had an affair with a woman who worked at the museum."

Samuel barked a laugh. "Another one?"

Hanna sat silent, staring at her clasped hands.

Del continued. "The woman's name was Anastasia. Gitte Brauer said her surname was something Italian. She married a man named Randolph? Do you remember her Mom?"

Hanna's brow furrowed. "Anastasia Balcazar? That was decades ago, and she was Spanish, not Italian. She only worked at CaMu for about a year. She left when she became pregnant."

"With London's baby," Del said.

"Thurman and Anastasia did not have an affair. Annie eventually married the baby's father, so that much of what Gitte told you is correct, but his name was Tom Randall not Randolph." She glanced at Samuel. "You remember, don't you? Back then, the board considered an unwed pregnancy an insurmountable scandal."

Samuel's gaze rolled to the ceiling. "No, Hanna, I don't remember, but there's little the CaMu board doesn't consider a scandal, including burnt waffles and a martini before sundown."

Del inched forward in his chair. "According to Brauer, London not Randall, fathered the baby, but London never acknowledged the boy—Brian—as his son." Del swiveled toward his mother. "Brauer said the family moved to New England. Is it possible you could get Anastasia's forwarding information from the museum's personnel files? I want to talk to her son, but to do that, I have to find him. An old address would give me a place to start."

His mother looked withered. Her once perfectly tailored jacket now hung loose on her narrow shoulders, and the dark fleshy bags under her eyes stood in stark relief against her gray skin. She blinked. "Gitte is wrong. I remember Brian. He was Thurman's nephew, certainly not his son."

Del puffed out his cheeks and sat back in his chair. "No, Mom, that's what London told acquaintances, but Brian was his son. Why would Brauer lie about it?"

"Let's say this boy is London's son. What does he have to do with the Shapiros or the missing Cézanne?" Samuel asked.

"Motive. London may have abused the boy."

"Abuse as a motive? For what, stealing a painting?" His father's voice was cold. "You're not making sense, Del."

Hanna pushed her chair back, the wooden feet screeching on the tile floor. "Abuse? Thurman may not have been perfect—"

"Now there's an understatement of biblical proportion." Samuel grinned without humor.

Hanna turned toward her husband. "For once in your life be quiet. Thurman had his faults, but I will not sit here and allow you or my son to slander him without proof. I don't know why Gitte told such a vile lie. I'd have thought the years would have eased some of her bitterness."

"I didn't hear about the abuse from Gitte Brauer. The information came from one of London's victims, an eight-year-old London approached. The boy is an adult now."

"Define *approached*, Mendel."

"London exposed himself to the boy."

"I don't believe it." She stood and slammed her chair in hard under the table.

"Mom, wait."

She left the room without slowing.

Del sucked in air. "If I'm going to find London's kid, I need that address. Look, Dad, I realize you don't believe this has anything to do with the painting or the Shapiros, and maybe you're right, but regardless of whether London's death was accidental, you have to realize he is at the center of whatever is going on. The extraordinary confession, the fake Cézanne stored in his attic, the affair with Daniel Shapiro's mother, her subsequent suicide—"

"London had an affair with Judith Shapiro?" Samuel heaved a sigh of resignation. "Why am I not surprised? Give your mother a few minutes. She'll calm down. If she can, she'll get you what you need. That story about London exposing himself, I trust your source is reliable. How did you find him?"

"He found me." Del chewed on the inside of his cheek for a moment before he spoke again. "Mike was the victim. The incident happened here at the house during a party. Don't say anything to Mom until I clear it with Mike."

"She wouldn't believe me anyway. Her precious Thurman could do no wrong. Is there no end to the lives that bastard torpedoed?" He closed his eyes and put his head in his hands.

Hanna reappeared at the kitchen door. "Who torpedoed who?"

"We're just gossiping, Hanna."

"You two are worse than a couple of old women." She marched across the room and slapped a piece of paper down in front of Del, a thick ivory sheet with her initials in burgundy script.

"What's this?"

"The forwarding address Annie Balcazar left with the museum. Isn't that what you wanted?"

He examined the paper. "This is a post office box in Maine."

"Human resources checked the files. It's all they had, and I lied to get it. You do realize personnel files are confidential?"

Del flipped the sheet over. "What's this Alameda address?"

"Annie's address before she moved. It's old, but I thought it might be easier to trace her from a local physical address than from a post office box across the country."

Del eyed his mother carefully. "I thought you were mad at me."

She sat beside him and squeezed his arm. "I'm not mad, Mendel. I'm disappointed. I understand Gitte's resentment toward Thurman. What isn't clear to me is why you continue to vilify him."

"And what isn't clear to me, Hanna, is why you continue to act as the man's defender." Samuel stood, his chair toppling backward.

Hoping to head off yet another full-blown argument, Del said, "This should be enough information to launch a decent, deep web search. I assume the FBI hasn't returned your computers. I'll grab my laptop out of the car."

"No need, I bought another desktop." Samuel looked at his watch. "You can use my study. I should get to the hospital. I have a new patient I need to check on."

"You are supposed to be phasing out patients, not adding new ones. Why do you insist on going to the hospital every day?"

"Because lately, I feel more at home there than I do here."

Weary of their quarreling, Del fled to his father's study. He closed the shutters against the afternoon glare, sat down behind the monitor, and jogged the mouse. The screen sprang to life. The web version of *Time Magazine* stared back at him—an article about CaMu and the missing Cézanne. He bookmarked the page, opened his subscription search service, and entered his ID and password. After clicking on the locater page, he typed in Anastasia Randall's old Alameda address and waited for a response. The current owner's name might prove helpful. It was unlikely, but he or she could have additional information on the Randalls.

The name *Ann Balcazar* appeared on the screen. According to the documents in front of him, Ann purchased the property in 1978 from Thomas Randall.

"Hey, Mom?"

No response.

He walked to the door and called again.

Her bare feet were soundless on the stairs. "What do you need, Mendel? I was lying down."

"Sorry. You said Balcazar's husband's first name was Thomas?"

She paused on the bottom step. "Tom, yes. What did you find?"

"Thomas Randall sold the house back in 1978 to Ann Balcazar for twenty grand. She still owns the place."

"Twenty thousand? Are you sure? Property values were lower back then, but not that low. Ann must be a relative. Maybe she can put you in touch with the Randalls."

"Unless Ann is Anastasia, and she never moved."

"Why would she buy a house from her husband?"

"Gitte Brauer said London's son—*nephew*—was a frequent visitor. That would make sense if Brian lived right across the bridge." London's dirty little secret—especially if he abused the boy.

"I know what you're thinking, Mendel. Thurman did not abuse anyone."

He abused you, Del thought, feeling ill.

"Annie left the museum and married Tom. I think one of them had family on the East Coast. Why would she pretend to move?"

"That's what I intend to find out."

CHAPTER 25

When Sophie opened her door and saw Del, a crease settled between her brows. "I haven't decided yet."

His stomach seized, and he flashed a weak smile. "Not why I'm here. I have a favor to ask."

"*You* asking *me* for something? How can I say no?"

"You might want to hear the request first." He slipped past her and dropped onto the living room sofa, elbows resting on knees, head in his hands, trying to staunch another headache. He'd had more headaches in the last two weeks than in the past two decades.

"You feeling okay?" Her cool hand kneaded the back of his neck.

He looked up and the concern on her face made his heart jump in his chest. "I just left my parents'. I'm not used to their constant arguing. Being around them is exhausting."

"They're under a lot of pressure. Once this mess is sorted out, things will get better. They love each other." She sat down beside him. "So, what favor dragged you to my humble doorstep?"

"I need to track down London's son, a guy named Brian Randall. There's a woman in Alameda who might be a relative or may even be Randall's mother. I hope she can give me a lead on his whereabouts. Here's the thing, I don't carry a badge anymore, and when I did, women were still more willing to talk when Barb was with me."

Sophie shot him a sly smile. "I find that hard to believe. Women fall all over themselves for an opportunity to talk to you."

He narrowed his eyes and pretended annoyance. "Seriously, Sophie, your presence would jack up the comfort level. She's more likely to open up if you're with me."

"I'll go along. Right now?"

He nodded.

She glanced down at her sloppy jeans. "I need to shower and change clothes first. I was cleaning toilets."

"Make it quick? I called to make sure she was home, but she could leave at any time."

"She knows you're coming?"

"No, I didn't want to spook her. Told her I worked for the water utility and asked her to confirm the property owner's name on the water bill."

"Why would she be spooked?" Sophie eyed him and seemed to sense his eagerness to get on the road. "Never mind. I'll hurry."

She reappeared ten minutes later dressed in a pale green sundress and flip-flops, damp hair snaked in a copper braid down her back. "I'm ready, but how about a few more details about why this Randall is so important?"

"I'll fill you in on the way." He jogged ahead of her, opened the Porsche's passenger door, and held out his hand, inviting her in.

"Aren't we chivalrous?" She slid onto the seat, her smoky eyes never leaving his.

Something quick and fine darted through him, a stab of pure, unadulterated happiness. He leaned in and gave her a fierce, quick kiss.

"What was that for?"

"General purposes." He slammed the door and climbed in

the driver's side.

The sun shone white against the solid blue of the sky, the car's leather upholstery warm next to their skin. Del provided her with the details on Anastasia Randall. "A huge leap, but it's possible London abused his son. He accosted at least one other boy."

"Sexually? Someone came forward?"

Del remained focused on the road but felt Sophie's stare drilling into him. "Happened thirty years ago. London exposed himself to the boy while visiting the home of a mutual friend. The kid was too humiliated to tell anyone."

"Michael," she whispered.

With a knee-jerk reaction, Del hit the brake, and the car lurched. "He told you?"

"Ages ago, but no names. I thought I was the only one who knew."

"Until yesterday, you were."

She sighed. "All those years Michael worked for the museum, and he never said anything. No wonder he loathed Dr. London."

"I told Dad, but at this point, my mother isn't willing to believe anyone or anything that impugns London. It might be different if she learned Mike was the victim, and the incident happened in her home, but Mike needs to be the one to tell her." Del sneaked a look at Sophie. She sat with her head bowed, hands clasped tightly in her lap, absorbed in her own thoughts. "What's on your mind?"

"How much I enjoy being with you even when we're doing something as unpleasant as this." She reached over and gave his forearm a gentle squeeze.

"Ditto." He merged onto I-80, took the Nimitz, and crossed over to Alameda Island. "Did you know this island was once a peninsula connected to Oakland?"

She giggled. "And Alameda is Spanish for tree-lined avenue.

A Twist of Hate

How can you move away? This is your home."

"It'll be tough," he said; then, under his breath, "but it would be a hell of a lot easier if you were with me." He gave her a sidelong glance, half-hoping she hadn't been listening. She sat silent with shoulders slumped, her expression unreadable.

He parked across the street from a tiny Victorian cottage sandwiched between two massive Queen Annes and surrounded by a low stone knee-wall. Painted mint green, the immaculate house boasted enough Victorian gingerbread to induce diabetes in a lesser man. "This is it."

"Darling house," Sophie said, climbing out of the car. "Hey, where are you going?"

Del crossed the road and stopped at the foot of the drive. A detached single-car garage sat adjacent to the cottage. Painted in matching spearmint, trimmed with mullioned windows, and draped with hanging vines that crawled over the door and walls like tentacles. Del peered in through the glass. Boxes lay piled floor to ceiling, filling the tiny structure—no space for a vehicle.

Sophie sidled up beside him. "What are you up to?"

"Checking the garage. Balcazar has two vehicles registered in her name. Only one of them is parked on the street."

"Not much parking here. Maybe she garages it off-site? Sure is a pretty neighborhood, though."

"Alameda's gold coast. This little house is worth three-quarters of a million, probably twice as much before the real estate market tanked."

"I sense you have a point."

"How did Ann Balcazar come to buy this place for twenty thousand? The land alone was worth more than that three decades ago."

They climbed the front porch and Del rang the bell. A small woman in her sixties with a cap of blue-black hair and a narrow, haggard face opened the door. She studied Del and Sophie through the screen. Her eyes were red and swollen, and her despair so palpable, Del took a step back.

"May I help you?"

"Anastasia Balcazar?" Del said.

The woman's gaze flicked from Del to Sophie. "I'm Ann Balcazar. Do I know you?"

"No, ma'am, not exactly. This is Sophie Gabretti. I'm Del Miller." He handed the woman a business card. "You used to work with my mother, Hanna Rosen Miller? She's a docent and trustee at the California Museum of Fine Art."

"I knew Hani, but I haven't seen her in decades. Is this about Dr. London? I heard on the news she found his body. Must have been horrible for her."

"Yes, ma'am. Would you have a few minutes to speak with us?" He expected her to refuse.

Instead she said, "Wait here," and disappeared behind the closed door.

Del exchanged a glance with Sophie, who shrugged extravagantly.

A minute later the door opened, and Ann Balcazar stepped onto the porch, a cardigan draped across her shoulders.

Del caught a whiff of stale smoke and noticed a package of cigarettes in her hand.

"We can talk out here. I don't smoke in the house." She settled into a wicker rocker, tossed Del's card, the pack of Marlboros, and a lighter on the table in front of her, and then pointed to a bench painted the same green as the house. "Please, sit. What is it you want to talk to me about?"

"You and Director London were friends?" Del asked.

"For more than thirty years, yes." Her eyes filled with tears. "He was a good man."

Del studied Balcazar. This was the last thing he expected to hear. Caught off guard, he waited for her to say more.

She pulled a tissue from her pocket and dabbed at her nose. "The police were here after it happened, but they didn't come back after his death was ruled an accident."

Why would they? Case closed. "Could you tell us why the police came to see you?"

She raised her chin and glared at him defiantly. "I've heard about your family's missing painting and Thurman's confession. Until you tell me why"—she looked down at Del's business card—"a security consultant is interested in my friendship with a dead man, yes, I would very much mind discussing why the police were here."

Caught off guard, heat warmed the back of Del's neck.

Sophie silenced him with a warning look and said, "We apologize, Ms. Balcazar. The real reason we're here is because we'd like to find your son."

The woman paled visibly. "Brian? Why?"

Her tone was brisk, but Del saw fear in the woman's pinched features, could smell its sulfuric tang. He grabbed the advantage. "We understand Thurman London was Brian's father."

Ann Balcazar's gaze skidded away, her laugh dry and brittle. "Absurd. Who told you that? Tom Randall was Brian's father." Her hand trembled as she reached for her cigarettes and lighter.

"Your husband?" Sophie asked.

"Ex, now deceased." She flipped open the carton and jammed a cigarette into the corner of her mouth. "He married me just long enough to give Brian a name, and that was the last we saw of him. Easy come, easy go."

Del leaned forward, elbows resting on his thighs. "But Thomas Randall sold you this house."

She exhaled a stream of smoke. "He did. Tom felt duty bound to marry me even though he wanted neither wife nor child. In exchange, I agreed to move to Maine. Tom's family lived in Bangor. Unfortunately, our marriage disintegrated almost immediately. He moved back East, and I promised to leave him alone if he sold me this house. I needed a place to raise my—*our*—son. I gave him every penny of savings I had, filed for divorce, and went back to my maiden name. Tom Randall is Brian's father. If you don't believe me, check his birth certificate." Balcazar stared into the distance, her forgotten cigarette sending up a thin plume from between her fingers.

The harder she tried to convince them that Tom Randall fathered her son, the less Del believed it. "Randall never paid child support?"

She ground out her cigarette in a small glass ashtray and lit another. "I didn't want anything from Tom other than this house."

All well and good, but how had she supported herself and the boy? And why the ruse about the move to Maine?

"Why didn't you mention to anyone at CaMu you decided to stay in the Bay Area?" Sophie asked with exquisite timing.

Balcazar scoffed. "As the public relations manager for CaMu, I organized every event under constant media scrutiny. I was excellent at my job but also unmarried and pregnant. It was a different time. The board of trustees didn't think I projected the right image for the museum, so they fired me. I didn't feel I owed anyone at CaMu an explanation of my failed marriage."

"Yet you remained friends with Thurman London," Del said.

"Thurman hired me. He apologized for the way the board treated me, and yes, helped us out financially." She took a deep breath and coughed. "You asked why the police were here? Money. Thurman named me in his will. The FBI was here as well. I'll tell you the same thing I told them. I know nothing about the painting or Thurman's involvement in the theft."

Del nodded. "I understand Brian spent time with Dr. London when he was younger?"

Her eyes skated away from his. "My son had no father. Tom

stepped out of the picture, and Thurman stepped in. It was a kind thing for him to do."

Kind. Yet another description Del had never heard used in reference to London. "Were you aware Dr. London told acquaintances Brian was his nephew?"

She stared at the tabletop, shifting Del's business card back and forth with a nicotine-stained index finger. "A tiny white lie. Thurman didn't want to explain why he was entertaining a former employee's child."

Maybe Gitte Brauer had it wrong and Brian was Randall's kid, but that didn't negate the possibility London abused the boy. When it came to allegations of abuse, Del was sure Ann Balcazar would be even less receptive than his mother. That didn't stop him from asking or Balcazar from expressing the expected indignation.

"That's outrageous. Thurman would never have—"

Tired of listening to women defend the man, Del interrupted. "Ma'am, do you know if Brian was still in contact with Dr. London at the time of his death? Would you be willing to put me in touch with your son?"

Again, her eyes strayed. "I live alone. My son and I are estranged. We haven't spoken in over a year, and I have no idea where he is. He's over thirty, Mr. Miller, an adult. If you can find him, you're free to ask him anything you want."

If she lived alone, why didn't she smoke inside her house? "Do you have a photo of Brian I might borrow?"

"No. I don't keep photographs."

Fuck that; everybody keeps photographs. "What about a workplace or names of Brian's friends?"

"He never introduced me to any of his friends. Look, I've already told you, I have no idea where my son is." She stood up. "If that's all, I'm going inside. It's chilly out here."

★ ★ ★ ★ ★

"The woman was more than evasive, Mikey. She lied," Del said into the phone. "And for the record, she was piss-poor at it."

"Lied about Brian's whereabouts or about London being his daddy?"

"Both. I thought she wouldn't talk because she didn't want me spilling the beans about Brian's paternity, but it took exactly fifteen seconds with the guy's name and Balcazar's Alameda address to ID him. He's on the DOJ's Sex Offender List."

"What did our little Brian do?"

"First degree child rape—Sacramento. The asshole is non-compliant. Never checked in after they let him out of Corcoran. Database says no photo available, and surprise, surprise, Balcazar has not a single photograph of her only son."

"DMV? State ID?"

"Nope. Not under the name Brian Randall or the half-dozen aliases listed in the DOJ database. I requested a copy of his booking photo. A friend of mine with Sac PD is faxing the shot over. I'd bet my left nut that Balcazar knows where he is. I figured because she worked with Mom, she'd want to help. Instead, all I managed was to give Randall a heads up and a chance to run."

"Bet your federal friend could get his hands on Bri-Bri's photo with no wait time."

"Neil finds out I'm nosing around in this, he'll implode. Even if it turns out Randall *is* London's son, there's nothing to say he's connected to the painting."

"The scum is a convicted kiddie fiddler. We have confirmation London accosted at least one boy. A significant percentage of pedophiles come from abusive homes. If London molested him, it's possible Brian wanted revenge."

"Which is why I intend to run surveillance on Balcazar's house." Del pressed two fingers against the pulsing beat in his forehead. "If London was murdered, the killer had to be someone inside CaMu. According to cops, London died after the administrative floor was locked down, but while the museum was still open. That means the killer had access to a key card." Del thought about his father and his stomach turned sour.

"Any chance your FBI homie will give you a peek at the key card readouts?"

Del burst out laughing. "Are you kidding? Wait . . . shit. Remember I told you the docent key cards aren't secured? Anyone with access to the administrative offices could have used one of those cards."

"I thought they only allowed limited entry."

"They don't permit access to art storage or the loading dock, but if someone is already inside the museum, those key cards will access meeting rooms, elevators, stairwells, and the administrative offices. I checked, and the security cameras are in the same location in every stairwell."

"So what?"

Del heaved a sigh. "Someone could have borrowed a docent key card, keyed out on their personal card via the loading dock, passed right by the guard in the cage, then slipped back in the front entrance of the busy, still swamped museum. It would be easy to access the public floors via a combination of elevator and grand staircase, then use the docent key card to slip up the back stairs and kill London on the sixth, leaving no evidence of his or her being in the building. Since the Feds accept London's death as accidental, and the painting was already long gone by the time London went to meet his maker, why would the FBI bother to look at security vids of the sixth floor stairwell on the day London died?"

"Wouldn't security notice if an employee came in via the main entrance?"

"No reason they would if the museum was open. They'd assume he or she snuck out for a smoke break or some fresh air."

"But wouldn't the FBI—"

"I repeat, the FBI believes London's death to be an accident."

"There are cameras all over that damn museum."

"It's easy to turn your face away when you know where the cameras are, and whoever helped London steal the Cézanne would know."

"Delbo, I'm telling you, London did not take that painting."

"Yeah, yeah, yeah. I keep forgetting."

"You plan to run the key card theory by the Feds?"

Del shrugged to himself. "I'll try."

CHAPTER 26

Promontory Pointe had seen few changes over the last sixteen years. Same postage stamp lots, same neat rows of tiny, perfectly maintained cape cods painted in HOA approved neutrals, and perched along the edge of the bay like birds on a wire.

Mike felt his happy hour drinks but wasn't totally wasted. He parked at the end of the block. Better not to give Sophie advance warning. She'd avoid him if given half the chance, he was sure of it. He inhaled. The scent of salt marsh and sea air stirred memories of his life here. God, how he missed this place, missed Sophie. He slipped his hand in his pocket, his fingers finding the warm brass of his old house key. He still recognized it by touch. He knew Sophie had changed the locks after a recent break-in, but he couldn't make himself let go of the key.

Mike reached for the doorbell and a sharp bark came from inside the house. The pang of loss was so profound, his knees nearly buckled. Even Casper realized Mike no longer belonged here. He was a stranger in what used to be his home.

Sophie appeared at the door wearing cut-offs with a loose cotton halter tied at the neck. She never looked more beautiful.

With arms tight at her sides, hands clenched into fists, and her expression fierce, she asked, "What are you doing here, Michael?"

He hesitated, trying to find his voice. Mike Gabretti without words. Who'd have believed it? His gaze strayed to the scar on her thigh.

"What are you doing here?" she repeated, her tone flint.

Casper ran past her and jumped on Mike. He rubbed the dog's back roughly. "Hi, little guy. I missed you."

"If you're looking for Del, he's not here," Sophie said.

Del? Mike was knocked off-balance. It had never occurred to him Delbo might be here. His stomach roiled. "I came to apologize for what happened on the boat. I didn't mean to hurt you. I just—I was unprepared and very stupid." He took a breath, steeled himself, and worked to keep his voice light. "Can I come in so we can talk?"

"I appreciate your coming by, and I accept your apology, but we have nothing to talk about."

When she stepped back to close the door, he held it open with the flat of his palm. "We do need to talk." He paused and added as an afterthought, "About Delbo." Wasn't that really why he'd come? To talk about Del?

"I'm working on my dissertation."

"It'll only take a few minutes."

She sighed. "Fine, but be quick. I have plans this evening. I still need to dress."

He wanted to ask what kinds of plans but decided prying wouldn't win points. With Casper glued to his heel, Mike followed Sophie into the living room. "Smells incredible in here. What's cooking?"

"Roast chicken. You'll be gone before the bird comes out of the oven."

The phone rang, and Sophie walked to the kitchen to take the call. Mike checked the liquor cabinet. Empty except for a near-full bottle of Lagavulin. He wondered if he'd left the scotch behind, or if Sophie kept the booze on hand for Del. He poured himself two fingers, placed the bottle on the coffee table next to his glass, and settled onto the sofa.

Sophie strolled back into the room. "I don't recall inviting you to drink."

He shrugged. No reason to talk around the subject. "Delbo's in love with you."

She set her jaw. "That's why you're here? Good to know up-front, because it's none of your business. Now you can leave."

His memories sprang like feral cats, and he couldn't take his eyes off her. She was his soul mate. Love like theirs didn't disappear overnight. "You're using Delbo to get back at me, and it's wrong."

A flash of fury sparked in her eyes. "You have the balls to come into my home and lecture me about right and wrong? You're drunk, Michael. Get out. I don't want you here."

He had no intention of leaving, not without telling her how he still felt about her. Sometimes the truth sets you free, other times it reins you in tighter. She knew as well as he did they were meant to be together. Alexa was nothing to him. Worse, she was a shitty mother to Amy. He felt helpless, gutted, as his gaze locked on Sophie's. "You're going to end up hurting Del. He doesn't deserve that."

She took a step toward him. "I said, get out, Michael."

"Tell me you don't love me, that you don't still have feelings for me."

A raw shred of laughter escaped her. "Oh, I have feelings for you."

"Love is forever. Isn't that what you always said? Isn't that what your gran taught you?" Mike poured himself another drink.

"You think because love doesn't go away it's indestructible? That love can't break under disillusion and disappointment or morph into something ugly and unrecognizable? All I can say is, more fool you. Let me make this clear, Michael. My love for you is broken, shattered beyond repair. And with all due respect to my dead grandmother, I'm not even sure how much of what I still feel is love. Truth? I think most of it is memory. And as for Del, I do love him."

"Friendship is not love." Mike stood and swayed. They were face to face, and he let himself be pulled into the depths of her sea-green eyes. If he could just hold her, she'd remember. He reached to touch her, and she jerked away.

"I'm going with Del. We're leaving." Cheeks flushed, she dropped her gaze and mumbled something he couldn't hear.

He didn't have a clue what she was talking about and didn't much care. He grabbed her hand to pull her close. When she pushed him away, he roughly gripped her chin, and made her look him in the eye. She stopped struggling. What was the expression on her face? Surprise?

His hands ran up her bare arms and cupped her face. Kissing her temple lightly, he ran his lips along her jaw until he found her mouth, warm and yielding. He savored the familiar heartbeat of satisfaction at his center. She still loved him. He knew it.

Sophie stiffened and twisted to wrench herself free. "Let go. You're drunk."

There was no strength in her, no conviction, and he held tight. "You don't want me to stop." He shoved his hand underneath her waistband, chuckled as his fingers brushed over the soft thatch of hair and pushed into her. Christ she felt good, wet and ready. He pushed her to the carpet, pinning her with his knees, thighs straddling her body. She bucked hard under his hundred seventy pounds.

"Michael, stop. You're hurting me," she said, her voice pitched so near panic, he almost believed her. As if she didn't want this just as much as he did. She actually had tears in her eyes. She didn't realize the harder she pretended to struggle, the more ridiculous she seemed. He smothered her voice with his hand and eased his weight off to see what she'd do. She pushed hard. Reeling from the booze, he nearly toppled. He laughed, trapped her wrists, and held them above her head with one hand. With the other, he unzipped his fly.

A heavy knock sounded at the door. Distracted, he turned and Sophie thrust him off, his arm slamming against the coffee table base. "Fuck!"

She scrambled to her feet and raced to the entry.

By the time Mike had worked his way back through the pain in his arm and the alcohol haze, Sophie stood at the open door with her arms wrapped around Del's waist, face lifted so he could kiss her.

CHAPTER 27

Del caught Mike's eye from the front door. "What are you doing here, Mike?" Despite Del's best effort, it still sounded like an accusation.

"Visiting."

"And you're on the floor because . . . ? Even Casper is allowed on the furniture."

"Michael dropped by to apologize. He was just leaving," Sophie said in a splintered voice.

Del studied her. "You okay? You seem . . . ruffled." Not ruffled. She was flushed and disheveled, like she'd been—what?

Sophie smoothed a hand over her hair. "I'm fine. Michael's not staying for dinner." She took Del's hand and led him from the entry into the living room.

Mike grinned crookedly and grabbed the coffee table leg to haul himself up. The table shifted and he fell forward.

Del held out his hand and pulled Mike to his feet. "How the hell much of that scotch have you had?"

"Too much, and he was drunk when he got here." Sophie's voice quavered. She bit hard on her bottom lip and moved closer to Del.

He glanced from Sophie to Mike, then back to Sophie. Something was definitely going on.

"I started to tell Michael about our move. I'm sorry. I know I wasn't supposed to say anything."

"What move?" Mike directed the question at Sophie.

She pushed Del forward. "Tell him about Atlanta and New York, about Guardian Piedmont. Would you like something to drink? I'll get you a glass before Michael empties the bottle, or a beer if you'd rather." She ran the sentences together without taking a breath.

"Nothing for me. Thanks," Del said, slightly nauseated and still curious about what he'd walked in on.

"I'll take a beer," Mike said, pressing the corner of his eyes with finger and thumb.

"Fat chance," Sophie said.

"Talk, Delbo. What about Atlanta and New York?" Mike slurred the words.

Del's explanation of the GPG job offer was met with the expected reaction.

Anger bloomed on Mike's face, his lips pursed tight as a chicken's ass. "When were you going to tell me? You didn't say word one. Not about the job or your"—his eyes shifted to Sophie—"travel buddy. Nice way to treat a friend, asshole."

Sophie took Del's hand again. "He didn't know about my decision to go along until just this minute. I'd planned to tell him this evening. You knew before he did, Michael."

Mike's fists clenched and opened, clenched and opened. He glared at Del. "Explains why you're acting like you've been smacked upside the head with a two by four." He pinched the bridge of his nose and shook his head as if waking from a nap. "What about the house, Sophie? I gave you the house outright and now what? You're going to sell the place? What about your PhD? Your teaching?"

"I'm All But Dissertation, I don't need to be on campus, and it's unlikely I'll be offered a teaching position in the fall. As for the house, I wasn't planning to sell. The market's in the cellar, but if you'd prefer, I'll call an agent. I understand this place is legally mine, but I never thought it was fair you handed it over free and clear. We can split the—"

"I gave you the house, because it's your home. The first you'd ever known, that's what you told me. I didn't want to take it away from you." Mike inhaled a ripped breath almost like a sob. "How are you going to support yourself? The tarot? Or are you going to be Delbo's whore? I give the relationship three months."

"That's enough, Mike," Del said. A fury as thick and tangled as a web enveloped him, and he worked to keep it in check.

"I want you out of here, Michael." Sophie turned to Del, "Show him the door, and make sure he finds the knob. I'm going to grab a shower before dinner." She ran upstairs.

"You heard her. Get the fuck out."

Mike raked his hand roughly through his hair and eyed Del. "You don't actually think she's going with you? That act was for my benefit. Sophie is exacting her revenge, getting back at me for Alexa, for what David did to her, for everything and anything. She's seen an opportunity and she's running full-bore. She has no intention of going anywhere with you, bro."

"What act, dickhead?"

"You think it was a coincidence she broke the news to me first? She wanted to hurt me. She won't turn her back on her home."

"Why don't you just leave?" Del made a move toward the kitchen.

"Where are you going? We're talking here. I'm trying to help you. This may not be what you want to hear, but it is what it is."

Del whirled around, dropped into a chair, and scrubbed his hands over his face. All the adrenaline banging through him earlier evaporated. So what if Sophie was shitting on him? So what if she ended up breaking his heart? For the moment, she'd agreed to be with him, and nothing else mattered. "What do you want to talk about, Mike? How I'm not Sophie's first choice? You're too late, that ship sailed years ago. Now it's time for you to hit the bricks. I'll call you a cab."

"I don't need a cab."

"Yeah, buddy, you do."

Sophie scanned the room. "Michael's gone?"

"Put him in a cab. Never seen him so drunk. I had to tackle him to get his keys. Asshole tried to deck me. Once he's sober, he can figure out how to get his car home."

Del pulled Sophie to him and she winced. That's when he noticed the red marks on her arms and wrists, the bruise forming along her jaw. He touched her face gently. "What is this?" Again, a dense rage took him. "Did Mike—?"

"Can we please talk about something else?" She lowered her lashes. "I'm okay. It's over. Look around. See? He's gone. No more Michael."

Del suspected there would always be more Mike Gabretti.

"Come help me set the table." She slid an arm around his waist and they walked into the dining room.

"Did you mean what you said about going with me?" he asked, hesitant, a question from someone afraid of the answer.

She set down the plate she was holding and looked up at him. "Of course, I meant it. Why would you even ask that?"

"Mike said you were . . ." *Shit.* "Mike thought it was an act for his benefit."

"*His benefit?* What does that mean? I wanted to make him jealous? What an arrogant jackass. And you believed his bullshit?" She moved around the table and slugged him in the arm. Hard.

"Ouch! Yes. No. I mean, you surprised me—again—I guess—" *Christ.* Why did this woman always leave him tongue-tied?

She eyed him suspiciously, then panic crossed her features.

"Is that why you asked, because you thought I'd say no? Do you want to withdraw the offer?"

He gathered her into his arms. "Uh-uh, no way."

"I drew a tarot card," she said quietly.

Terrific. For one insane moment, he thought she'd made up her own mind, minus arcane cosmic forces and any residual feelings for Mike. He let her go.

"Don't be like that. I drew The Fool. The card symbolizes a new beginning, the need to follow my heart. She reached up and held his face, her palms soft and warm against his cheeks. "That's what I'm doing, following my heart, and that's why I need you to be absolutely sure you want me."

"I'm sure," he said without hesitation. "Question is, are you sure you want to play the fool?"

She laughed. "For you? Always. Let's eat."

CHAPTER 28

"Not that your car isn't gorgeous, but I can't drive a stick, and I need to deliver Lucy to her vet appointment this morning. Take Michael's Z. In Ms. Balcazar's neighborhood, a Z4 will probably be less conspicuous than my twelve-year-old Sentra, anyway."

"Maybe, but I don't have Mike's keys. Stuck them in his pocket once I wrangled him into the cab."

Her brows tilted up and a smile tugged at the corner of her lips. "Welcome to your lucky day. I still happen to have a set of keys for that vehicle. Just make sure to let Michael know, so he doesn't report the car stolen. What do you expect to find at Ms. Balcazar's?"

"Let's just say the woman woke my spidey senses. You'd think someone who used to work PR for CaMu would be better at evasion. I'd lay odds she's protecting her son. Best guess? He's somewhere close by and they're in contact."

"What if she leaves? How can you watch the house and follow her, too?"

"She leaves, and I can get inside. Guarantee I'll find photos of Brian. His booking shot was useless, dark beard, long hair—guy looked like a homeless Sasquatch. His only distinguishing mark is a small rosy cross tattoo on the back of his neck. Not much to go on. I requested an inmate photo through the Department of Corrections. Anybody's guess how long that'll take to come through. Next stop is Brian's high school yearbook. Plus, if I can get inside Balcazar's house, she has a landline. A tap on her phone, a tracker on her car—"

"Del, you can't break into her house, you're an ex-cop. The woman has security, and not just a sign in the yard. I saw the panel behind her when she opened the front door."

"I saw it, too. Security systems are my business, Sophie. The skills necessary to understand how a system works are the exact skills needed to work around it."

"Promise you won't do anything stupid. You really think Brian Randall is important?"

"The only thing I have to go on is London's off-the-wall confession. It's possible he wanted to protect someone, but I don't know enough about the man to guess who that could be. I can't name a single person Thurman London cared about more than he cared about himself. It appears he and Ann Balcazar had a close relationship. She admitted London helped her out financially. He named her in his will. Plus, she lied to us. Right now, I'm looking for anything that points the FBI away from my parents. Brian Randall is likely London's illegitimate son and a noncompliant sexual predator whose mother is shielding him. Makes me want to know more."

Del touched the tip of his finger to Sophie's nose. "Don't worry. Today, the plan is to watch the house and take a few photographs. Nothing dangerous, I promise. This afternoon, I meet with Neil Sobol."

"The FBI guy? To talk about Ann and Brian?"

"I have a key card theory I want to run past him. The Feds have their investigation. I have mine. If I ask the right questions and don't piss Neil off, I may learn something."

She gave him a skeptical look. "Good luck with that."

Despite what's shown on television, surveillance is little more than an exercise in monotony and a test of patience, especially when stuck in a vehicle alone with no one to talk to.

Del parked Mike's car in front of a large Victorian with a FOR SALE sign, half a block from Ann Balcazar's house. If anyone asked, he could say he was waiting for a real estate agent to show him the property. He didn't have optimum sightline to Balcazar's place, but he could see the front door and part of the lawn. He mounted an unobtrusive camera capable of taking both stills and video to the Z's dashboard and aimed the lens at the house. The camera could be easily activated if needed. So far, he'd seen nothing worthy of a capture.

Beneath a marine layer as heavy and claustrophobic as a wet blanket, he sat and waited for something to happen. Apart from the homeowner, no one entered or left the house. Balcazar stepped out on the porch every twenty minutes or so and lit up a cigarette.

At noon, Del called it a day. He had just enough time to get back to the city and meet Neil Sobol for lunch. He'd give it another shot tomorrow.

Neil was seated at the brasserie counter studying a menu when Del walked into Bay by Bay. The agent closed the menu and stood. "Next time you keep me waiting, make it a place with a bar." He pointed to a dimly lit corner booth where a busboy was clearing dishes. "How about over there?"

"Works for me," Del said.

"I need to use the john. If the waitress comes by, order me a burger, cheese fries, and a cola."

By the time Neil slid into the booth across from Del, their drinks had arrived.

Neil lifted his glass in a mock toast. "I remember when I considered lunch with you an opportunity to catch up and a great way to spend an hour. Today I sense we're here for something else. How about filling me in?"

"Any chance of you not getting pissed off?"

"Sure, as long as you don't piss me off."

Del inhaled. "Have you looked at CaMu's key card readout for the night London died?"

"Are you poking around to find out if we know your father was in the museum early that evening? We do. A detail he failed to mention, by the way. Do you realize how fucking lucky he is the M.E. ruled London's death an accident? I reiterate: *accident.* Let it go, Del."

"Any chance I could see the key card printout?"

"You're kidding, right?"

"You say you believe the director's death was an accident, so what difference does it make if I see the card reads?"

"Even if you were still SFPD Homicide—which you aren't—you're too close to this. You need to tell me if there's something I should be looking for in those printouts. Because if I find out you're withholding information, I will personally hang you by your balls over an open flame."

"Answer one question for me. Were there any docents in the museum the night London died?"

"I assume you mean apart from your mother? One, but so what? Docent key cards aren't assigned, and no crime was committed."

Del didn't mention no docents were scheduled that night. If Neil refused to accept the possibility London's death was murder, he wouldn't give a shit anyway.

"Now I have a question for you. Any way you can get your father to be more forthcoming? It would be much appreciated. He can start with why he paid all that money to London."

"Ah, now I get it. You accepted my lunch invitation, so you could pump me for information about my dad. Even if I knew the why, Neil, it's not my story to tell."

"Fine. You want to—" Sobol paused as the food arrived at the table. He waited for the waitress to walk away, then continued. "You want to hear my theory? I think your mother and London had a fling. London was writing his memoirs. Your father paid him to keep quiet about the affair."

Del's pulse jumped. *Shit.* Had Gitte Brauer lied about keeping her mouth shut? "Who told you?"

"No one. I found an early draft of London's manuscript on his computer that detailed the relationship. A later version didn't mention your mother. Not difficult to put two and two together. I assume London showed the first draft to your father. The interesting thing is, London writes about half a dozen women, but the only one he names is your mother. I'd go so far as to say the earlier manuscript was written specifically to extort money. I don't think London ever planned to publish it."

"You haven't arrested my father."

"For what? Trying to protect his wife's reputation? When the crime is blackmail, we try to avoid arresting the victim. I'll tell you this much, London had a lot more money going out of his bank account than coming in. Evidence suggests London the blackmailer may have also been London the target."

"Cash transactions?"

"You know it. Possibly paying off whoever helped him switch out the Cézanne. Want to hear another interesting factoid? London reported a break-in not long ago. According to the police report, the only thing taken was cash, and the perp left no evidence of how he or she got into the house."

"I assume you're looking into the financials of all museum staff, the board—anyone London had ties with, including my parents?"

"We are, but it doesn't make sense London would be paying off the man he was blackmailing, namely, your father. That's why I agreed to meet with you. I want you to understand at this point in time, your father is not the focus of our investigation into the missing painting. That should make you happy."

Perhaps, but it did nothing to ease Del's fears his father had a hand in murder. "Is the SFPD handling the Shapiro homicide?"

"Daniel Shapiro made claims directly affecting an FBI investigation. We're looking into his murder."

"Did either version of London's memoirs mention whether he had children?"

Neil's brows rose. "No, why do you ask?"

"Curious." Del attempted a disinterested shrug and took a bite of his BLT. Did that mean London wasn't Brian Randall's father, or that the director was simply too concerned about his reputation to cop to an illegitimate kid?

"Inspector, stop." Susan moved to block the doorway. "I have to announce—"

Del pushed past her and walked into Mike's office without knocking. "You got my message about borrowing your car?"

Mike looked up from behind his desk and put his fingertips to his temples. "Yeah, I got it. Don't talk so fucking loud. They can hear you in Nevada."

"What's the matter, asshole?" Del leaned over the desk and hollered. "Got a hangover?"

Mike grabbed his head and moaned. "Jesus, what is your problem?"

"I want you to tell me what went on last night between you and Sophie."

"You two have such an *awesome* relationship, ask her and leave me the hell alone."

"I'm asking you, Mike. How'd she get those bruises?"

"What are you talking about?"

Del's temper rose to a boil. "Quit with the bullshit."

"I don't remember anything about last night. I was totally hammered. Alexa was on my case first thing this morning asking where I left my car. I had no clue. When I listened to your message about the surveillance, I assumed I'd left the car at your loft. I left it at Sophie's?"

Mike lied for a living, and Del wasn't sure whether to believe him or not. He was veering toward not. "You thought I pulled your car keys out of my ass? I borrowed them from Sophie. You hurt her, Mike. She's black and blue, finger marks on her throat, arms, legs."

"Come on, bro, I wouldn't do that." Mike's voice rose. "I don't remember what happened, I swear, but I'll call Sophie and apologize—"

"Too little, too late, *bro*. According to Sophie, you were there to apologize. Contrition is not one of your strong suits. Maybe it's time you bowed out gracefully."

Mike's features hardened. "And let you two run off to New York, so you can play corporate hero?"

Del glared at him. "So you remember our conversation about GPG, but don't remember assaulting Sophie? You are some piece of work. Stay away from her, Mike. I mean it."

"Who died and made you Sophie's keeper?"

"Sophie is no longer up for discussion. What I need now is for you to tell me whether you're still willing to work with me on this investigation?"

"You know I am."

"Fine. I met with Neil Sobol this afternoon. The FBI is no longer focused on my parents. Neil still believes London's death was an accident. He read a draft of London's memoir, so he knows about the affair with my mother. The memoir didn't mention any illegitimate children."

"You tell Sobol about Brian Randall?"

"I wasn't in a sharing mood."

"Good." Mike stood, groaned, and gripped the edge of the desk to steady himself, then waved a shaky hand at his chair.

"Sit. I want to show you something on the computer."

"If it's porn, I'm not interested."

"Christ, you're a pain in the ass. Sit down, will you?"

Del settled into the desk chair and stared at the monitor. "Judith Shapiro's death notice. I already know she's dead. What am I supposed to be looking at?"

Mike stepped closer. Resting a hand on the back of the chair, he read. " *Judith Shapiro is survived by her husband and their infant son.*' Infant, get that? We assumed Daniel was a boy when his mother died. Judith killed herself after her relationship with London self-destructed. This suggests Daniel was born during or soon after their affair. What if London, not Jakob, was Daniel's father? Forget about Danny-boy's drug issues, maybe Jakob found out the truth and left the gallery to Albert because Daniel wasn't really a Shapiro."

"If London fathered Daniel, don't you think Albert Shapiro would have said? I doubt much gets past the old bastard."

"Maybe he didn't want us to know. Let's talk to him again."

"You talk to him. I got a definite hostile vibe off the guy. At least he answered your questions."

"I'm tied up the rest of the afternoon. Any way to arrange a visit for this evening?"

"Not on Shabbat. We can try for sundown tomorrow if you're willing to sacrifice your Saturday evening." The clock at the top of the computer screen read 3:00 p.m. Del pushed back the chair. "I have a three-fifteen with Lee Dutton at the Frakansia. Your Z is in the parking garage, level B, south corner. The gallery's only a couple blocks away. I'll walk and take a cab back to Marina Bay to pick up my car."

"Sounds fair. Since I have to meet with that weird old coot by myself, the least you can do is leave me my car."

Maybe so, but the truth was Del didn't want Mike anywhere near Sophie.

Del stepped out of Union Towers South and tilted his head back just in time to see the sun peek from behind the gray, then disappear again. The clouds would burn off early evening. They always did, just in time for a new marine layer to roll in.

Situated in a nineteenth-century Greek Revival building that once housed a bank, the Frakansia was the perfect setting to showcase the early Neoclassical painting and sculpture for which the gallery was known. Del made his way between the massive sandstone columns, pulled open the heavy glass door, and stepped inside. The gallery was an expansive, light-filled rectangle stippled with sculptures and small bronzes. An elaborate circular staircase loomed at the rear, and paintings covered every wall. At the center of the space, a round upholstered viewing couch seemed to sprout from the marble floor.

Del surveyed the nearly deserted gallery. A single customer, a woman, silver-haired, pink-skinned, and immaculately dressed, flitted from painting to painting like a bee seeking nectar. She reminded Del of his mother.

"Mr. Miller?"

Del started and glanced up.

Camouflaged by the creamy marble and black iron of the staircase, the man's dark suit and shock of thick white hair made him close to invisible.

"That would be me. Lee Dutton?"

The man smiled. "Guilty." He descended the steps, held out his hand, and met Del's gaze with steady blue eyes.

The strength in his grip caught Del off guard.

"Come upstairs. We can talk in my office," he said, his voice both warm and precise.

Del glanced at the woman.

"I'll send Tony down to take care of Mrs. Marino." In a stage whisper he added, "She prefers Tony's company to mine, anyway."

Mrs. Marino laughed, the sound lighthearted. "*Tony* is unattached."

He shook his head and said under his breath, "*Tony* is gay and young enough to be her grandson."

Dutton's office was small but as elegant and tasteful as Frakansia's main gallery. Del sat on a dark green velvet lyre-back chair. Rather than hide behind his desk, Dutton settled himself in the matching chair next to Del's.

"I am aware of the situation with CaMu and the missing Cézanne. I've been acquainted with your parents for many years and think highly of them. That's why I agreed to speak with you."

"I understand you worked for the Shapiro Gallery for three decades before Daniel Shapiro let you go?"

Dutton pressed a finger to the groove between his brows and sighed. "Danny did not *let me go*, as you so delicately put it. I quit. I couldn't—wouldn't—work for the Shapiros any longer, but if you think I shot Danny—"

Del held up his hand. "No, Mr. Dutton, I don't think you killed him."

"You're a homicide detective, are you not?"

"The SFPD and I parted ways several months ago."

Dutton stared at him. "I don't understand—"

"I'm here to talk about Daniel, but not because I believe you had anything to do with his death."

A shimmer of melancholy crossed Dutton's face. "Poor Danny. He was a damaged soul. Jakob tried with the boy, but some children need constant supervision. Look away for a second and they sink deeper and deeper into the abyss. Danny was one of those kids. Jakob couldn't handle him. Danny needed a mother."

"You must have known Judith Shapiro?"

"Of course. Another tragedy, Judith suffered postpartum depression and took her own life before Danny was old enough to crawl. Can you imagine what that does to a child? He grew up believing he wasn't worth living for. I always felt sorry for the boy."

"You mentioned depression, but did something specific happen to precipitate Judith's suicide?"

Dutton's brows went up. "I take it you have a theory?"

"No theory, but according to Daniel's uncle, Judith took her life over a broken love affair."

"You spoke with Albert Shapiro?"

Del Nodded. "Several days ago. He's confined to a wheelchair and lives in residential care here in the city."

"I'm surprised to hear that. Despite the scoliosis and a number of other health issues, Albert was always very independent. He used to get around quite well on crutches."

"Were you aware Daniel had Albert declared mentally incompetent so he could take control of the gallery?"

Dutton's eyes widened. "Albert wasn't interested in running the business and Danny stepped in, but I can't believe the boy would do anything to harm his uncle. Danny worshipped Albert. If a conflict existed, they kept it well hidden, and I was around them every day."

"Did you do anything to stop the takeover?"

"Of course not. It wasn't my place to interfere in family matters. The only reason I didn't leave the Shapiro Gallery earlier was because I needed to secure another position. Frankly, the working environment at the Shapiro was untenable from the moment we lost Jakob. Forgive me for saying so, but Albert Shapiro is a very disagreeable man on his best days. I'm astonished he agreed to speak with you. Although courteous enough in your father's presence, behind his back, Albert was blatantly contemptuous. As I recall, he resented Jakob's friendship with your father's uncle, as well."

"Avi? Do you know why?" Del asked, taken aback.

"I believe the acrimony stemmed from a grudge Albert held against your grandfather, but beyond that, I can't say. When Danny announced to the press your grandfather stole the Cézanne, I knew at once the allegation stemmed from Albert. He'd stoked the boy's hatred of your family for years."

The lying old sonovabitch. "Mr. Dutton, did you know Judith Shapiro's lover?"

The man's shoulders slumped. "I didn't know the man's identity, but we all knew Danny wasn't Jakob's son. Not that it mattered. Jakob loved the boy with all his heart."

"Albert Shapiro knew Jakob wasn't Daniel's biological father?"

"There's no question."

CHAPTER 29

"You're set to meet with Albert Shapiro at Neuman on Sunday after lunch," Del said. He heard Amy whimpering on the other end of the phone line.

"What happened to tonight? I already cleared it with Lex."

"It's summer. Long days, long Shabbat. Too late in the day. If you have plans for Sunday, I'll try to work out something else."

"If I had plans, I'd change them. I only live to be at your beck and call."

"Yeah, right. Is Amy with you, or is that Alexa whining?"

"Alexa drove her mother to the airport. I'm babysitting. How did your meeting go with Lee Buttman?"

"*Dutton*. Enlightening. Seems it was common knowledge Jakob wasn't Daniel's father."

"How many bastards do you think London spawned?"

"Just because Jakob didn't father Daniel doesn't necessarily mean London did the deed. According to Dutton, Shapiro knew about Daniel's paternity. Be careful of that old bastard, Mike. I don't trust him."

"He didn't think much of you either."

"According to Dutton, Shapiro had a run-in with my grandfather and holds some kind of grudge against my family. If you can, find out what the beef was about. Call me curious."

"How do you propose I do that, oh wise Swami?"

"Get him talking. Find common ground. Play good cop. He didn't like me. Start there. Tell him you decided to talk to him one-on-one because I can be a pain in the ass."

Mike chortled into the phone. "Ply him with the truth? Clever. Back to London—let's say for the sake of argument he fathered Daniel. What if London believed the Cézanne belonged to the Shapiros, and he wanted the painting in his son's hands?"

"Uh, if London was Daniel's father, Daniel wouldn't be a Shapiro. What happened to the argument London couldn't be responsible for the theft because it was out of character? I was starting to buy into that."

"A parent will do anything for his kid. I go home to Alexa every night, which means I speak from experience."

"Not much evidence to suggest London was Parent of the Year material. If he took the painting—let's forget the why for now—where is it? And who put the bullets in Daniel Shapiro's brain? Problem is, we don't have all the players."

"That's only one of our problems," Mike said on a long sigh.

"I was in London's office when Mom told him about the Cézanne. The look on his face? Pure shock. Sure, it could have been surprise at how quickly the theft was detected, but less than twelve hours later, he sat down and signed a confession. Did he steal the painting? Did he abet? Was he protecting someone?"

"I'll get what I can out of Uncle Albert. Where the hell are you anyway? I hear traffic."

Del hunkered down in the Sentra's vinyl seat and groaned. "Sitting outside Ann Balcazar's house. I have to slam my head against the dash every fifteen minutes to stay awake. Swear to God, she never leaves her house except to sit on the porch and suck on a cancer stick. I'm half-tempted to file a complaint with the Clean Air Board on behalf of her neighbors."

"You don't suppose she was put on alert by the unfamiliar Carrera GT on her block? That car is about as inconspicuous as a turd in a punch bowl. I thought you were better at this shit."

"I'm parked where Balcazar can't see me. Plus I'm driving Sophie's car—quite the thrill. Compared to the Porsche, it has all the power of the Little Tykes pedal truck my parents gave me on my fourth birthday. Until today, I had no idea merging from the I-80 on-ramp qualified as a death-defying stunt."

"If Balcazar never leaves the house, why bother with surveillance?"

"I told you. She lied. She knows where her son is. I can smell it."

"So call in a favor and get her phone records. She's probably talking to him."

"Brian Randall has an outstanding warrant on his head. If he was stupid enough to make a traceable call, he'd be behind bars."

"Then he's probably smart enough not to knock on Mommy's door."

"Checking a phone record is cheap, easy law enforcement. Round the clock surveillance? That takes resources. Department funds are tight, and Randall's been AWOL for more than a year. Case priorities change. If a tip comes in, the hunt will heat up, but I guarantee you, right now, I'm the only one watching Balcazar's house."

"You honestly expect him to show?"

"I think it's more likely Mom will leave the house to meet him."

"You plan to follow her?"

"I put a tracker on her Camry. If she ever decides to leave her porch, I'll be the first to know."

Del could almost hear Mike snap to attention at the other end of the line. "You plan to creep the place when she leaves?"

"*Plan* sounds so premeditated." Del glanced up as a man on a bicycle rode onto Ann Balcazar's lawn. "I gotta go."

Without waiting for a response, Del ended the call with his

left hand and flicked on the video camera with his right. He used his cell to take several stills of the man as he climbed off the bike. Medium height, slender but solidly built, wearing jeans and a long-sleeved flannel shirt. His movements were smooth, suggesting relative youth, but the baseball cap pulled down over his forehead hid his face and hair. If it was Brian Randall, spooking him was the last thing Del wanted. He tossed his cell on the passenger seat and carefully exited the Sentra, shielding himself behind a large sycamore. Bicycle Man stood on the front porch speaking to Balcazar through the screen. Del had a second tracker stashed in the trunk of the Sentra in case Balcazar's unaccounted-for Impala showed up, but he sure as hell couldn't attach it to a bicycle. Balcazar stepped out onto the porch, closing the door behind her, a small suitcase in hand. She passed Bicycle Man without slowing, climbed into her Camry, and pulled away from the curb.

What the fuck was going on?

Bicycle Man peered up and down the block. Seemingly satisfied, he descended the steps.

Del blinked. There was something familiar about the guy, and if Del didn't get his ass in gear, he'd never figure out what. He stepped from behind the tree and called across the street just as the man reached the bike. "Hey, Brian?"

Bicycle Man's head whipped around. He spotted Del and took off running. Del's longer legs ate up the distance between them. All at once the man stopped, swerved, and doubled back toward the Balcazar residence, aiming himself between the garage and house. He tossed something into the backyard and began to shinny over the fence.

Del grabbed at his flailing leg. Bicycle Man's boot caught him squarely above the right eyebrow, knocking him on his butt. Dazed for a moment, Del shook off the blow and scrambled over the fence. Balcazar's backyard was scrubby and barren, grass barely holding its own against dirt. Bicycle Man was at the back gate, working the rusted latch on an ivy covered eight-foot chain-link fence at the rear of the property. Opened, he'd have a clear shot at Washington Park. Not much cover, but a hell of a lot of space. Del dove at the guy, tackling him to the ground and getting a first look at the asshole's face: Walt Wellerman, CaMu's loading dock operator.

A quick knee to the left kidney and Wellerman stopped struggling. Del straddled his back. Using his knees to pin Wellerman's arms, he yanked down the back of the man's sweat-drenched collar to reveal a small rosy cross tattoo. Del patted him down. Wellerman, emitting a banshee wail, lifted his head and began to struggle again. Del pressed his hand against Wellerman's neck and forced his face into the dirt. "Shut up. You want the cops here? Keep screaming like a girl. Count your blessings you've got me on your back instead of a U.S. marshal."

"Like you're not going to turn me in?"

"Brian—may I call you Brian?" Del asked with exaggerated politeness. "Nice dye job. Is it true blonds have more fun?"

"Go fuck yourself."

"Thanks to you, your mother is on some mighty shaky ground. I advise you to talk, or she's going to be in major shit. You love your mom, don't you?"

"She's got nothing to do with this."

"Right, and I'm the Easter Bunny. Let's start simple. How about you confirm your name?"

Silence.

Del ground the man's face into the dirt. "You can talk to me or someone with a badge, your choice."

Wellerman spat grit from between his teeth. "Okay, Jesus. I used to be Brian Randall. Now, ease the fuck up."

Del released his grip on the man's neck. *"Used to be?"*

"I'm Walt Wellerman now. Brian Randall is dead."

"Wrong. Brian isn't dead. He's a convicted child rapist with a price on his head."

"Runs in the family," he said, his voice scathing.

"You're boring me, *Brian*. How about being a little more straightforward?" When he'd met Wellerman, Del hadn't noticed how much the guy looked like London. Now the resemblance was unmistakable: same build, same hawk features. We all see what we expect to see, he thought. "Thurman London was your father, yes or no?"

"What if he was?"

"You should clue in your mother. Seems to have slipped her mind."

"She was trying to protect me."

"She did a shitty job. Here's what I think. Your father abused you. When you got out of Corcoran, you threatened to make the abuse public. You blackmailed Daddy and convinced him to go along with your plan to switch out the Cézanne and—"

"I don't know anything about your fucking painting. After I got out, all I wanted was a second chance. I did my time, paid my debt. Why should I have the past hanging over my head?"

He may have paid his debt to society, but Del doubted the boy he'd raped had been adequately compensated.

"I went to my *father*." Randall said the word as if it tasted bad. "I asked for his help. So, yeah, I got money out of him. He hired me on at CaMu and paid for a new identity. The ID is solid, too. It's held. I'm Walt Wellerman now."

"Until the FBI figures out you're not."

"They won't. I'm out of CaMu. Gave my notice yesterday."

"Not a good idea to call attention to yourself, *Brian*. The Feds will be all over you."

"I'm not running away. I got another job, better pay, right here in the city, a real smooth, reasonable transition. Legit. Nothing to make the FBI suspicious."

"You have any brothers or sisters, *Brian*?"

He flinched. "No, and I told you, my name is Walt."

"Did you know Daniel Shapiro?"

"That guy who got shot? Hey, if you're trying to pin a murder—"

"Where did your mother go?"

"She said you were nosing around. I told her she should get away for a while, visit my aunt up in Oregon until I figure out what's going on. Look man, I don't want to go back inside. I swear I haven't done anything wrong."

"You're a noncompliant sexual predator."

"No worse than my father."

"Again with the cryptic bullshit. Your father is dead. Would you happen to know anything about that?"

"Life sucks and then you die."

Del lifted his weight off Randall, stood, and planted a foot in the middle of the man's back. "I want you to turn over nice and slow, hands where I can see them. We're going to take a little walk to my car." *And my SIG Sauer and cell phone.*

Randall rolled over and sat up, legs stretched out in front of him. "I need my hands to stand up."

"Use your knees."

Randall drew in his legs in and pulled himself onto his knees. Suddenly, his arm pushed forward and something sharp plunged into Del's thigh. The pain was so electric Del dropped to the ground trying to catch his breath, the knife still protruding from the wound. He glanced up. Randall was coming at him with a large boulder. Del instinctively reached for his missing weapon as Randall lunged.

CHAPTER 30

The sun hung bright as a buttercup against the hard cerulean blue of the early afternoon sky. Mike climbed into his car and programmed the GPS for Neuman House.

A former assistant DA, Mike knew how to cross-examine a witness to get the response he wanted, but like any decent litigator, he also knew not to ask the question unless he already had the answer—at least if the answer mattered. Mike had no clue what made Albert Shapiro tick, and he didn't like going up against the old geezer. Shapiro's kindly geriatric façade was thin as onion peel. Behind it raged a cold, malignant hostility that made Mike's skin crawl. Put another way, the son of a bitch gave him the creeps.

Mike jogged up the Neuman House steps and pressed the bell. Shapiro notwithstanding, he looked forward to seeing the pretty nurse again. Instead of Naomi, a twenty-something redhead, with a thick middle, too much forehead, and oversized teeth answered the door. She stared at Mike expectantly but said nothing.

"I'm Michael Gabretti, here to see Albert Shapiro."

She nodded briskly and motioned him inside. "This way."

Like Naomi, the woman wore a traditional white nurse's uniform, but she'd thrown a too-tight cardigan over the top, effectively canceling cool and crisp and substituting overstuffed cushion. Rather than guide Mike through the public rooms as Naomi had, the redhead led him in the opposite direction under an ornately carved archway and down a long hallway lined with doors on either side.

"Usually we allow only family members back here, but Mr. Shapiro isn't feeling tip-top today and asked that I bring you to his room." She rapped her knuckles against a door halfway down the corridor on the right. Without waiting for a response, she stuck her head inside. "Mr. Shapiro, Mr. Grazetti is here."

"Gabretti," Mike corrected.

She threw open the door and directed Mike into a dim, low-ceilinged box. Windows closed, curtains drawn, the room's vinegary tang of rubbing alcohol and piss made Mike's eyes water. He took quick, shallow breaths.

Shapiro sat hunched in his wheelchair beside an unmade bed, a blanket draped over his knees despite the room's swelter-ing heat. He lifted a remote control from his lap, aimed the small box in the direction of a stereo on the bureau, and gestured Mike toward a single worn rocker tucked in the corner of the room. "Sit down, Mr. Gabretti. I'm curious to learn why you've come. I didn't expect to see you again."

Despite Shapiro's smile, his words held a keen edge that skidded along Mike's nerves and put him on alert. The rocker's dusty cover, yellowed with age, suggested Shapiro didn't have many visitors. A pair of crutches blocked Mike's way to the chair. He stood them against the wall, settled into the rocker, and scanned the room, his gaze stopping on the *San Francisco Chronicle* lying on the bedside table. What did an old man with failing eyesight need with a newspaper?

The nurse threw open the heavy drapes covering the glass slider. "I'm going to crack the door and get some oxygen in here. You should sit out on your patio and chat, Mr. Shapiro. Plenty of privacy, and it's such a lovely day. A bit of air would do you good."

Shapiro gave a perfunctory wave of his hand, and with none

of the charm he'd displayed with Naomi said, "Esther, get out. We don't require a chaperone. And flip the lock on your way by. I don't want to be disturbed." The nurse stood unmoving. Shapiro tilted his head and remained silent, clearly waiting for her to leave. Once she'd stepped from the room and the door lock snicked, Shapiro shook his head. "Sad thing about Esther is she's every bit as dull and graceless as she seems upon first meeting."

He aimed an empty stare toward Mike. "So, Mr. Gabretti, why don't you tell me what I can do for you and why you've come alone? I believe anything we two might have to discuss would be of far more interest to your friend, Miller."

The heat in the room was stifling, and Mike pulled at his collar. "The Millers are like a second family to me, but I'd be first in line to admit Del can be a pain in the ass. When he gets something caught in his craw, it's like trying to stop a charging bull with a whistle."

Shapiro laughed. "Ah, so you're telling me he takes after his father and grandfather rather than his lovely mother? Hanna Rosen was too good for Samuel Miller."

Bingo. Tread carefully, Gabretti. "Hani—Hanna—is why I'm here." Not exactly true, but it was a start. "The past couple of weeks have been tough for her. She lends her husband's priceless Cézanne to CaMu, and the painting disappears. The museum's director confesses to the theft, then Hanna finds him dead. To make matters worse, her husband's father is accused of having stolen the priceless family heirloom during the war, and now the FBI suspects the Millers may have played a part in hiding the Cézanne from your family."

"I certainly wouldn't put such deceit past Samuel Miller, but I'm sorry for Hanna. I still don't understand why you're here, Mr. Gabretti. Is there something you expect me to do from my wheelchair?"

"I'm on a quest for the truth, Mr. Shapiro, and I think you may be able to help," Mike said, convinced even as he said the words, Shapiro had little interest in any truth beyond his own. "I understand it was common knowledge that Jakob was not Daniel's father."

Shapiro's brow clouded and his features twisted, turning his bland face ugly and coarse. Mike smelled the heat of his anger like burning leaves. The old man's voice was harsh. "Who told you such a filthy lie? One of the Millers?"

"You told us Judith's broken affair with Thurman London drove her to suicide. Daniel was born only months before your sister-in-law took her life. Did London father Daniel, Mr. Shapiro? Did Jakob know? Surely London suspected."

Shapiro bowed his head, the color leaving his cheeks. "Daniel was Jakob's son—the son of his heart if not his loins. Perhaps somewhere in the back of Jakob's mind he had an inkling, but he never for a single moment let the thought enter his consciousness. After he lost Judith, Daniel was all Jakob had."

Not unlike Max Müeller and Samuel, Mike thought, but kept the observation to himself.

Shapiro covered his face with hands briefly, then raised his chin in defiance. "As for that scum London, I have no idea what he knew. After he destroyed Judith, our paths didn't cross."

"Did Daniel know Jakob wasn't his biological father?"

"How could he?"

"Someone might have told him."

Shapiro's hands lay fisted on the arm of his wheelchair, his expression dark. "Judith is dead. Jakob is dead. My nephew is dead. What does any of this have to do with a missing painting?"

The old man's voice swelled with emotion, and Mike almost felt sorry for him. Almost, except the bastard couldn't quite keep the smirk off his face. Shapiro was playing him, and Mike didn't like being fucked with. He uncrossed his legs and leaned forward in the rocker. "Don't bullshit me, Mr. Shapiro. A connection between Daniel and Thurman London may have everything to do with what happened to the Cézanne."

Shapiro's lips twitched. "Is this how the Millers intend to get their revenge? Malign my family? Make ridiculous accusations?"

"Don't you have that backwards, sir?"

"The Müellers are underhanded, manipulative graspers, all cut from the same cloth. You think my nephew would be dead now if it weren't for them?" Shapiro exhaled in a furious gust.

Mike pushed himself into the chair cushions to get as far away as possible from the man's rage and gaped at Shapiro, the old man's features as bleak and forbidding as scorched earth. The word *evil* flashed in Mike's brain like neon, and he glanced through the open slider, yearning to bolt.

"Max Müeller talked my father into giving him paintings worth far more than the salary of a courier. Müeller took advantage of an old, scared man afraid of losing everything."

Anger slammed Mike like a muscle spasm and he rose to his feet. "You're wrong. Yoseph Shapiro paid Max in art because he'd moved his cash out of France. Max accepted the paintings because he considered your father a friend. Regardless of the value, art couldn't feed or clothe Max's family."

Shapiro didn't seem to hear. "My father was blind to Max Müeller's machinations. Müeller played the perfect hero. He could do no wrong in my father's eyes. I was only ten, but I watched it all. My father more concerned with getting Müeller and his pretty wife out of the country than finding a way out for his crippled son."

This guy was actually jealous. Mike lowered himself back into his chair. "So, you stayed with friends during the war?"

Shapiro scoffed. "Not friends, strangers. I was recovering from pneumonia. Given my other health issues, the doctors told my family I was too weak to make the journey to the States. My father refused to leave me behind. It was Müeller who argued it was folly to wait, that it would be safer for me to go into hiding. He persuaded my father, and so it was done. Because of the chaos after the war, I didn't rejoin my family until 1947. I was a boy when Germany invaded and a man when the war ended. I spent more than seven years with strangers—think about that— all because Max Müeller wouldn't mind his own goddamn business.

"And the Müellers' manipulations didn't end with my father. Jakob became friends with Müeller's brother, Avi, and insisted on selling art to his family at a reduced profit. Can you imagine? I explained to Jakob more than once that Hanna Rosen came from one of the wealthiest families in San Francisco. He said it was wrong to make a usurious profit off a friend. Samuel Miller was no better than his father. He used Jakob's friendship with Avi to cheat my family out of what we were owed. That all ended the day I took over the gallery."

This guy was a friggin' nutcase. Mike steered the conversation back to Max. "Were you aware Müeller worked for the Resistance?"

Shapiro's eyes blazed, his lips tight over his teeth in a snarl. "My father sent me away from Paris to hide with a family in Marseilles. Imagine my surprise when Max Müeller, the man responsible for my abandonment and exile, appeared in Marseilles with his infant son."

Mike's breath caught. "You had contact with Max in Marseilles?"

"Very little." The resentment rolled off Shapiro in waves. "After all, what could a crippled boy do for the great and powerful Max Müeller? He had no time for me."

Right. He was too busy saving lives to deal with this self-absorbed little shit.

"I detested Müeller, and he was a threat."

"What do you mean *threat*?"

"I was a Jew in hiding, disabled, vulnerable, no more than a boy. Max Müeller could have given me up at any time. That's why I had an acquaintance alert the Gestapo about Müeller and his son."

Mike felt sick and made no effort to hide his shock. "I'm sorry?"

"You heard me. I have no regrets. Tit for tat, as they used to say. Müeller used my father to get his hands on valuable paintings belonging to my family. To *my* family. *Mine*. He stole from us."

Thank God Delbo wasn't here to listen to this bullshit. "Then why wait so long to claim the painting? The Millers had the Cézanne for more than seventy years."

Shapiro reddened. "Because I didn't realize the Müellers—"

Mike had had about all he could take. "Miller. Their name is Miller."

Shapiro huffed a breath and grunted. "I read the newspaper article on CaMu's upcoming exhibit. Until then, I had no idea of the Cézanne's location."

"Earlier, you said Daniel didn't consult you before he made the claim."

"He didn't, but we talked."

"You talked?" Mike oozed incredulity. "I thought he abused you?"

"Daniel was my only living relative. Are you trying to catch me in a lie, Mr. Gabretti?"

Mike calmed his breathing. "And if Daniel had sought your advice regarding the painting?"

Shapiro smiled for the first time, revealing a set of yellowed false teeth. "I'd have told him to do exactly as he did."

★　★　★　★　★

Mike shut Shapiro's door and turned left, nearly colliding with the acrylic wall pocket that hung outside the old man's room. The pocket held a single envelope. In the corridor's crap-ass light, Mike had to squint to make out the Bank of America logo. Addressed to Albert Shapiro, the letter appeared to be a bank statement. A paper statement sent snail mail? People still banked without computers? The thought made him shiver. He peered up and down the hall, saw no one, and plucked the envelope from the cubby, sliding it into his jacket pocket. Del was too busy nursing a concussion and the hole in his leg to disapprove. *Candy-ass.* No way he and Sophie belonged together.

Mike ran into the nurse as he passed through the archway into the foyer. He stopped her with a wave. "You have a few minutes, Esther? I'd like to talk to you."

She narrowed her eyes and cocked her head, clearly confused.

"It's about Mr. Shapiro. Won't take long, I promise." He gave her his most charming smile.

Esther smiled back.

CHAPTER 31

From the low-level din, incomprehensible monitors, and questionable food, to the antiseptic smells meant to mask sickness and death, Del hated everything about hospitals. Lying in this bed was intolerable. He threw off the covers and rolled onto his side, never taking his eyes off the chair across the room or its occupant, Neil Sobol.

"I warned you to keep out of my investigation. I should charge you with obstruction," Neil said.

Dick. Del struggled to remain calm. "Drop the hard-ass routine. It doesn't suit you."

"You withheld information."

"I withheld *suspicions.* You'd have done the same thing." Del swung his legs over the side of the bed and stood, testing his weight on the damaged thigh. "Thank God I get to leave this hellhole today. One night was one night too long."

"Unless you can explain to me why the fuck you confronted a suspect unarmed and without backup, I'm thinking you got what you deserved."

"Who was I supposed to call for backup, my mother? I had a choice: confront Randall or watch him ride into the sunset on his Schwinn while I ran back to the car and dug through the glove compartment for my Sig."

"How is the leg, by the way?"

"Why, thank you, Special Agent Sobol. So thoughtful of you to inquire. The leg is fine."

Neil flushed to his hairline. "Sorry I didn't ask sooner."

"Seriously, hurts like a motherfucker, but it's only a flesh wound." Del gingerly touched the goose egg near his temple. "The asshole knocked me in the head, which is why I was imprisoned here overnight. You're right. I got what I deserved. My fault totally. I saw Randall toss something small into the backyard before he climbed the fence. I should have known. He had the blade in his palm the whole time. All he needed was opportunity, and I delivered it on a silver platter. Lucky for me all he had was a pocket knife."

"Lucky for you, your friend showed up. You could have been in Balcazar's backyard a hell of a lot longer than you were."

Del settled on the edge of the bed, bare feet on the floor. "I was on the phone with Mike when Randall showed. When I didn't call back . . . yep, I am lucky. Any leads on Randall?"

"We've got a BOLO out. Searched his apartment and his mother's house. She's staying with her sister outside Portland, Oregon. We're watching the aunt's place in case Randall shows up. Still haven't found the bicycle."

Del sniggered. "You think he's riding his bike to Oregon?"

"He's been a fugitive for over a year. I'm guessing he was prepared to run when the need arose. Probably had a vehicle stashed somewhere, and used the bike to get to the car."

"You radioed the license plate for Balcazar's missing Impala?"

"Yeah, but if he's driving her vehicle, you know he switched plates." Neil pulled himself out of the chair, the rolled newspaper he'd carried into the room still tucked under his left arm. He held out the *Chronicle* to Del. "You're not mentioned, of course."

Gracing the front page: Brian Randall's booking photo and the headline, *"Fugitive Sex Offender Wanted in Stabbing Incident."*

"Why did you use his booking shot? I couldn't recognize him from this, and I'd met the guy."

"Bureaucratic fuckup. The late edition will include this along with Wellerman's—Randall's—museum ID photo. I checked with CaMu personnel. Randall did not give his notice. He wanted you to think he wouldn't run."

"You mean the scumbag lied? There's a surprise. Find anything to tie him to the stolen painting yet?"

"Only what you already know—means and a connection to Thurman London."

"Randall is London's son. That's a little more than a connection. London gave him cash."

"Checked Randall's financials. Other than his CaMu paycheck, there are no deposits. Although why he'd lie to you about shaking down London, I can't begin to fathom."

"You checked Ann Balcazar's accounts?"

"Yep, and found more nothing."

"You get that Randall had motive to kill London, right?"

Neil sighed. "The medical examiner—"

The phone on the bedside table rang. The Feds had taken Del's cell to download the photos of Randall.

Neil tossed the newspaper on the bed. "I'll let you take your call in private, but if you come up with any more suspicions? I want to hear them. We clear?"

Del stretched out on the mattress, back propped against pillows, and gave Neil a brisk salute. After the door closed, he reached for the phone. "Dude," he said into the mouthpiece, certain the caller would be Mike.

The voice sounded confused. "Mr. Miller, this is Lee Dutton. From the Frakansia Gallery?"

Del cleared his throat to cover his embarrassment. "I apologize, Mr. Dutton. I was expecting another call. How did you find me?"

"I tried the numbers on the card you gave me, but wasn't able to reach you. This may be a matter of some urgency, so I called your parents. Your mother told me you were in the hospital for observation and how to contact you. I'm afraid I insisted. I hope you don't mind."

"What can I do for you, sir?"

"When you dropped by Friday, you asked about Danny."

A chill prickled Del's arms.

"On the front of this morning's paper there is a photograph of a sex criminal—Brian Randall?"

Del grabbed the newspaper from the foot of his bed. "Brian Randall is a wanted man, Mr. Dutton. If you have information regarding his whereabouts, you need to contact the FBI, not me."

"I haven't seen Randall in years, not since I worked for the Shapiros, but I recognized his face at once. He was a friend of Danny's."

The prickle became a wave of unease and a single bead of sweat slid down Del's spine. Randall lied about Daniel Shapiro. A connection to the Shapiros meant another link to the Cézanne. "Are you certain the man in the photo is Daniel's friend? It's difficult to see his face through the beard."

"Absolutely, although I assumed he was still in prison. After reading what he did to that boy, I'm not certain why he isn't."

Randall would be back behind bars soon enough. "You were acquainted with Brian Randall?" Del prompted.

"Not really. Not at all, in fact. His only interest was the Shapiros. He never so much as acknowledged me."

Perspiration now ran in rivulets down Del's back. He reached behind and pulled his hospital gown tight to soak up some of the moisture. "When you say Shapiros, you mean both Daniel and Albert?"

"Yes. Albert loved nothing more than talking about the war, and Randall hung on every word. They made an odd pair, Albert and that scruffy young man. Then one day, Randall simply stopped coming to the gallery. At the time, I assumed he and Danny had a falling out. Months later I learned Randall went to prison. Until this morning's paper, I never knew why or what he'd done."

Del kept his voice steady. "Did Randall ever talk about himself?"

Dutton hesitated. "Not as I recall. I do remember Danny's boasts about his friend's father being someone important, which I found hard to believe because Randall was so unkempt. Once Danny mentioned they—"

"When you say *they,* you mean Danny and Randall?"

"Exactly. Danny said they had something on Randall's father. Danny was high at the time, and I didn't pay much attention. He always talked too much when he was under the influence. It's how I could tell."

"Mr. Dutton, the relationship between Daniel and Brian Randall could be very important. You need to call FBI Agent Neil Sobol and tell him what you've told me."

"I have Agent Sobol's card, but I'm not sure I understand. Is Randall connected to the missing Cézanne? The newspaper didn't mention anything about the painting."

"I don't know—it's possible."

Del ended the call, eased himself out of bed, and made his way to the narrow closet. He bent to pull on his underwear.

Behind him a voice said, "Whoa, dude! Have mercy. No one should be subjected to a view like that."

Del grabbed the back of his gown, held it closed, and turned to face Mike, whose lids were squeezed tight.

"You nearly blinded me," Mike said.

"You are a moron. Consider knocking next time. I just got off the phone with Lee Dutton. He said Brian Randall and Daniel Shapiro were friends, and according to Dutton they— I'm quoting here—*had something on Randall's father.*"

"The fact he was a pervert?"

Del zipped his jeans and sat on the bed. "Got me. How'd things go with Shapiro?"

Mike ran down the afternoon's highlights. "Took every ounce of control I had not to beat the living shit out of the old fart. He blames your family for everything bad that's ever happened to him. If Shapiro figured out a way to hold Max accountable for crappy eyesight and scoliosis, he would. My opinion? The guy's not all there. He's not suffering from dementia, he's just plain demented."

"I told you, I don't trust him."

"I talked to the nurse—"

Del smiled. "The lovely Naomi?"

For a split second, Mike looked sad. "No, the not-so-lovely Esther. I asked whether Shapiro had many visitors. She said his nephew used to visit, sometimes with a friend."

Del sat up straight. "What friend?"

"She couldn't give me a name, but he was around thirty, average build and fair-haired. Sound like Randall?"

"Possibly. He bleaches his hair. Did you ask Shapiro about Randall?"

"Why would I? Until I walked in here, I had no clue Randall had any connection to the Shapiros. Esther told me Daniel and his uncle got on well together. Personally, I don't think I'd be so chummy with a nephew who tortured me with lit cigarettes, even if he was my only remaining relative."

"Lee Dutton said Daniel worshipped his uncle. He didn't know anything about Daniel having Albert declared incompetent."

"Good reason for that. I swung by my office and did a little checking. Seems Daniel never filed a petition for a competency hearing. When Shapiro signed over the gallery, no one questioned his mental fitness. I think he wanted a way out that didn't make it look like he'd ignored his brother's will, so he convinced at least one medical professional he was a danger to himself or others. I'd lay odds he gave himself those burns. The bogus intel about him suffering from dementia came from his Neuman House admission record."

"Why work so hard to make Daniel the bad guy?"

"Shapiro gets off on playing the victim. Another interesting morsel: he had a newspaper in his room." Mike grabbed the *Chronicle* off the bed. "This one. How does a man with supposedly failing eyesight read a newspaper?"

"Perhaps the *not-so-lovely* Esther reads to him."

"Or the poor vision is more of his defenseless old man shtick."

"Did Shapiro say anything else?"

"Jesus H. Christ, he gave your grandfather and father up to the Gestapo. That's not enough for you?"

"Shapiro was a kid, Mike, crippled, without family, alone in a country invaded by people who wanted him dead for no other reason than because he was born a Jew. He felt abandoned. No wonder his father's efforts to convince my grandfather to leave France stung."

"You never cease to amaze me. I figured you'd go ballistic when you heard, and here you are defending the guy."

"I'm not defending him. What he did was loathsome, but if Shapiro hadn't forced my grandfather's hand, my father might not have made it out of France in time. Maybe Dad survived, and I'm sitting here today, only because Albert Shapiro dropped a dime on my grandfather."

Mike snorted and rubbed his palms together. "Wouldn't that frost the jackhole's shriveled old balls? Can I tell him?"

Del sighed. "Did you ask him about Daniel's paternity?"

"I asked. He got pissy. Wouldn't admit who Daniel's father was. All he'd say is London made himself scarce after Daniel's birth."

"You know damn well the FBI is digging into the Shapiro family. Any connection between Daniel and London will set off alarm bells from here to Quantico. The Feds talked to Shapiro right before we did, but when I mentioned to Neil about Judith Shapiro's affair with London, he was totally in the dark. Apparently Albert didn't share. Not that it matters. The London-Daniel connection is a dead end—pardon the pun—until we can figure out what prompted London's confession."

"So we're back at square one." Mike massaged his temples. "What do we know?"

"We know Daniel Shapiro and his Uncle Albert were friendly with Brian Randall before he was hauled off to Corcoran. Albert Shapiro holds a grudge against my family and may have transferred his hostility to Daniel. London fathered and probably abused Randall, possibly fathered Daniel, and both Albert Shapiro and Brian Randall despised London."

"But London protected Randall, gave him money, a job, provided him with a brand-new identity—"

"Stop." Del held up a hand. "You just said the magic word. London *protected* Randall. Hasn't that been the question all along, who did London care enough about to protect? Randall had access to Gitte Brauer's painting through London. Plus, he had unrestricted access to CaMu's secured areas. It's possible he smuggled in Gitte's painting and made the exchange while the Cézanne sat in the museum's basement storage. No one would question his comings and goings."

"So you think Randall took the Cézanne?" Mike asked.

"Bet London thought he did, which is why he wrote the confession."

Mike ran his hand through his hair, making it spike. "Randall was a felon. Why would London give him a job with access to priceless art?"

"Because Randall wasn't a thief. He was a sexual predator

just like London. It's even possible London didn't think what Randall had done was wrong."

"Do we think Randall slipped back into the museum and killed London?"

"We do."

"What about Daniel Shapiro? Did Randall put those bullets in his head?"

Del shrugged. "Maybe Randall was afraid Daniel would connect him to London's death."

"Uh-uh, doesn't make sense. Daniel was shot *after* the M.E. ruled London's misadventure an accident. More likely, Daniel and Randall were working together and had a disagreement."

"For example?"

"Let's say Randall, working as Daniel's partner, replaces the Cézanne with Gitte Brauer's copy. Randall and Daniel are now in possession of a priceless masterpiece, which they hide somewhere. If Daniel's claim that Max stole the painting from the Shapiros' Paris gallery is successful, the insurance payout will go to him—well, to the Shapiros—rather than to you and yours, right? Not only would Shapiro and Randall be in possession of a priceless Cézanne, which they might or might not be able to unload, they'd also have the insurance green. The FBI should check Daniel's accounts. Can you think of a better place for Randall to hide the cash London gave him? Although, why bother to hide the money at all?"

"Because once the Cézanne was stolen, Randall knew the Feds would be into everyone's financials. Cash leaving London's account and showing up in Randall's would look suspicious. Forget Daniel, though. I guarantee the Feds have already been over his balance sheet with a magnifying glass."

"That reminds me." Mike patted his chest and pulled out an envelope.

"What's that?" Del asked.

"I'm about to open it and find out, but I'm pretty sure it's Shapiro's bank statement." Mike slid his finger under the flap and tore the envelope open, leaving a ragged edge. "Quaint the way old people still do their banking on paper."

"You stole Shapiro's bank statement? You realize that's a federal crime?"

"I *found* it."

"In your pocket?"

Mike tossed the envelope on the floor and ground his shoe into it. "Address was obscured. I had to open the statement to see where to return it."

"Damn it, Mike—"

"Relax. Well, well, well, looky here." Mike grinned.

Del buried his face in his hands and uttered a long-suffering moan.

"Regular weekly cash deposits up until three weeks ago when London shuffled off to meet his maker—then nothing."

Del grabbed the statement from Mike's hand. "This closed a week ago. That's only two missed deposits. This money could have come from anywhere."

"True, but we know Shapiro wasn't making regular visits to the bank. Someone had to make those deposits for him—they're not electronic. Get Sobol to check the bank's cameras."

"By telling him what? That you stole Albert Shapiro's quarterly bank statement, we found some suspicious deposits, and now we'd like the FBI to take a look at the bank's security footage to see who made the transactions?"

"Come on, Delbo. Dutton connected both Shapiros to Randall."

Del ran his finger down the list of entries. The only debit was a monthly transfer to a company called MoreSpace. *Jesus.* It was right in front of him. He sprinted to the closet, yanking off the hospital gown as he went. He grabbed his shirt and shoes.

"Let's go. Where's your car?"

"Out front. Loading zone. Why? What the fuck is the matter with you?"

"The only cash outlay on this quarterly is for MoreSpace. MoreSpace is a storage company. Shapiro told us he sold everything he owned before he moved into Neuman, so what the hell does the guy need with a storage unit?"

CHAPTER 32

Del ran past the nurses' station, not taking the time to check out, Mike trailing in his wake. He spotted the Z as soon as they stepped through the sliding glass doors to the street. True to his word, Mike parked in the patient loading zone at the hospital's front entrance. *Idiot.* Del made his way to the passenger side. "Open the door," he shouted to Mike over the car's roof. He heard the thunk of the power locks and climbed inside.

"Mind telling me where I'm driving?" Mike asked.

"Daly City. We still have a couple of hours before rush hour. Traffic shouldn't be too bad."

"Daly City is a pretty big target. You have an address?"

"You're the one with the GPS. Program in MoreSpace Storage. Give me your cell. I need to call Neil."

Mike tossed him the phone. "How the hell did Barb work with you all those years? You're a friggin' dictator."

Del squeezed his eyes shut to hold back the pulsing throb in his head. "Shut up and drive."

"Yes, *mein Herr,*" Mike said, punching information into the navigation system. He reached to open the glove compartment and pulled out Del's Sig. "Interested in this?"

Del stiffened. "Where'd you get that?"

"Retrieved it when I saved your life in Alameda."

"I had a flesh wound and a bump on the head."

"Ungrateful bastard. Apparently the blow to your cranium affected your short-term memory. The last thing you said to me before the EMTs shoved you in the ambulance was to pull your piece out of Sophie's car—which I did."

"You don't have a concealed carry permit. It's illegal for you to transport a weapon in the glove compartment."

"Unless you plan to turn me in, make your call so I can focus on getting us where we need to go." The Z's engine growled to life. Mike put the car in gear and burned rubber.

Del entered Sobol's cell number. The call went directly to voicemail. He left a message, dialed the FBI field office, and spoke with a live body who took another message. Del returned the phone to Mike. "Neil is apparently giving a briefing."

"Interesting. Given that he doesn't know anything, it shouldn't take him long. What are we going to do when we get to MoreSpace? How do we know which unit belongs to Shapiro?"

"We don't. That's why we need Neil."

"This is a waste of time. Sobol isn't going to let us join his party, even with probable cause and a search warrant in his pocket—which, I remind you, at this point, he doesn't have."

"He'll get one."

"You sure about that?"

"Albert Shapiro and Brian Randall knew each other. Both men hated London. Randall took—extorted—money from London, but Shapiro is the one with inexplicable cash deposits in his bank account, deposits he was physically incapable of making on his own. What does an old man who *got rid of everything*—his words, not mine—need with a storage unit? And where did the money come from? It's not as if this was done behind Shapiro's back. The statement came addressed to him at Neuman."

"So you plan to hang out at the storage facility until the Feds show up and save the day? You really need me for that?"

"No, but I need you to drive."

Twenty-two minutes later, Mike turned into the rear entrance of MoreSpace Storage, its endless rows of storage bunkers arranged like soldiers on a drill field. At Del's request, Mike cruised the lot twice before he pulled the car into the parking spot nearest the building signed Rental Office. "Now what to do we do?"

"Go to the office and get a price list," Del said.

"Why don't you go?"

"Because some ass-wipe stabbed me in the leg and I have one mother of a headache. Once we figure out what Shapiro rented, we can narrow down where his unit is even if we can't get inside."

"Fine." Mike unbuckled his seat belt and started to get out of the car.

"Leave your phone in case Neil calls back."

"I thought you asked him to meet us here."

"I did. Doesn't mean he will," Del said.

"Look at the statement. What is Shapiro paying MoreSpace?"

Del pulled the crumpled sheet out of his pocket. "Two hundred twenty-five bucks a month, paid by transfer."

Mike stepped out of the car and Del watched him disappear into the office. In the rearview mirror, he caught a glimpse of a vehicle parked in the alley that ran along the drainage ditch behind the MoreSpace property. A tall cinderblock wall separated the alley from the lot and partially blocked his view. Employee parking? Possibility, but weird given the parking lot was virtually empty.

Just when Del began to wonder what the hell was taking so long, Mike burst out of the rental office. Del ignored his protesting leg, and climbed out of the car to meet him, tucking the SIG in his waistband. "Anything?"

Mike rolled his eyes. "I asked for a price list and the *Helpful Storage Associate*—no shit, that was the title on his name badge—

told me I should check online. Lucky for us, they had prices posted on the wall. The only combination of units that add up to two-twenty-five is a ten-by-twenty standard and a five-by-five climate controlled unit."

"Climate controlled means no exterior access."

"Exactly what *Mr. Storage Ass* said. He also mentioned security and individual keypads. All the while I'm thinking, perfect place to stash a priceless masterpiece."

Something electric slid along Del's scalp. "Wonder what's in the larger unit."

"Hell if I know. Ten by twenty would hold a lot of furniture."

Del pulled out his SIG and gestured toward the alley. "Stay here and listen for the phone. I'm going to take a look at that vehicle."

Mike looked over his shoulder. "What vehicle? Would you quit swinging that pistol around? You're making me nervous."

"There's a car behind the cinderblocks," Del said, and began to move toward the wall.

Mike followed him.

Del peered into the alley. A figure was working underneath the car's open trunk lid. When the man stepped from behind the vehicle, Del jumped back and threw himself against the wall. Despite the spiked red hair and sunglasses, Del recognized Randall. "It's him," he whispered to Mike.

Mike stepped forward to look, and Del grabbed his arm and yanked him back. "What are you doing?"

"He's got a gun."

"So do I. I'll approach from the rear. Stay here. If he runs in your direction, get out of his way, but don't lose sight of him."

"Did you catch the part where I said he has a gun?"

Del was already circling the wall. When he had Randall in range, he took aim. "I've got a gun pointed at your ass, so don't fucking move or I guarantee you won't be raping any more little boys."

Randall's body jerked, and he hurled the gun toward the drainage ditch.

Del was on him in two strides. He grabbed Randall in a head-lock and slammed him face first against the wall, the SIG aimed at the base of the man's spine. "I told you not to move, asshole. Think I liked you better as a blond."

Randall moaned.

"Lock your hands behind your head, or I'll make sure you spend the rest of your life in a chair."

Mike ran toward them. Del handed him the SIG. "Hold this on him. If he moves, shoot him. If he breathes too heavy, shoot him." Del patted Randall down hard and fast, pulling everything from his pockets, including a pocket knife that reminded him how much his thigh hurt.

"The gun—it's not mine. I found it," Randall said.

"Save it for the Feds." Mike aimed the SIG at Randall's head. "Move one centimeter and you end your life as a colander, which, by the way, I'd personally love to see. Hey Delbo, turn him around so I can aim this thing at his balls."

A shudder electrified Randall, and he pissed his pants.

Del smiled. Scared was good. Scared meant answers. "Where's the Cézanne, Brian?"

The man shook his head.

Del pulled him away from the wall, then rammed him hard against the blocks. "You killed London. Used one of the docent key cards to access the administrative offices after you'd already exited through security. Did London help you steal the painting?"

"You really think that SOB would steal from CaMu?"

Shit, here we go again. "You knew London had the copy because you were in his house when Gitte Brauer painted it.

You broke in, stole the canvas along with some money, and made the switch. I bet London didn't even notice his ex-wife's painting was missing until it showed up at CaMu." Del decided to go for the bluff. "The FBI knows you and Daniel were pals. They figure you were in it for the insurance money as well as the Cézanne. I mean, really, why settle for one when you can have both, right?"

Randall said nothing.

Del fisted the man's collar and ground his face into the blocks again. "Lose your voice? I asked you a question."

Randall's nose crunched and began to stream blood. His eyes filled with tears. "All right," he said in a half-sob. "Jesus, I think you broke my fucking nose."

Del took hold of his collar again and Randall squealed.

"Wait, give me a chance. The day I met you at CaMu? I saw you and Hani looking at the Cézanne."

"Fake Cézanne," Del corrected.

"The copy was good. We figured no one would notice the switch—not right away—but I could see Hani recognized the painting as a fake. I knew she'd tell London, and he'd suspect me. I should have run, but I wasn't ready. I didn't have time to cover my tracks. I had to convince him not to hand me over."

"So you stole a docent key card, keyed out on your personal card, then used the docent card to get back upstairs and kill him."

"I didn't kill him. I used the docent card because I didn't want anyone to know I was in the building. A meeting between the loading dock operator and CaMu's director would look more than a little suspicious. The docent card was the only way I could get upstairs without leaving a trail. When I got to his office, he was nervous. After I was released from Corcoran, I threatened to out him, tell everyone what he'd done to me. He thought I'd come to make good on the threat, so he played the martyr. Said he'd confess to protect me. Asshole thought a few scribbles on a sheet of paper would make up for all the years of hell he put me through. He left the confession with the receptionist to be messengered. When he came back to his office, he announced we should *celebrate* the way we used to. The freak actually expected me to watch while he played with himself, to save him if things went too far—as if I was still his prisoner."

"London confessed to protect you," Del said.

"Bullshit. He confessed to buy himself time. He'd have retracted everything in the end, claimed he'd been coerced, and everyone would believe him. After all, he was Thurman Alcott London. He didn't give a shit about protecting me. He didn't care about anyone but himself. He just wanted a way to sic the cops on me without revealing the truth about what he was."

"He asked you to watch him masturbate and you killed him," Del said, his voice flat.

"I told you, I didn't kill him. I did exactly what he wanted, and then I let him hang. God, it was a beautiful thing, watching him turn purple, dick in his hands." Randall's Adam's apple jumped as he swallowed, but there were tears in his eyes.

Del took a quick breath. "After what he'd done to you, what made him think you'd save him?"

Randall gave a humorless chuckle. "Boundless ego."

"Your mother won't be happy when she learns you let him die."

"Only because London was her cash cow. That's why the bitch always looked the other way."

Del's stomach clamped tight in revulsion. He'd assumed Balcazar hadn't known about the abuse.

"What about the Shapiros?" Mike asked.

"No more. I'm sick of talking." Randall set his jaw.

"Fuck. Hold on a minute." Mike said, pulling his cell out of his pocket with his free hand.

Del threw him a black look. "Shitty timing, Mike."

"Text from Sobol, 'Units en route.' "

Randall flinched and Mike stepped closer. "Hear that? The Feds won't be near as accommodating as my friend here. You and Daniel Shapiro were buds. He kept your identity secret. Why? Because you agreed to lift the Cézanne in return for his silence? Help him fence the painting? Share the insurance payout once he'd established his family's claim?"

Randall took a fast breath. "Dan was an idiot. All he cared about was his next fix."

"His Uncle Albert is no fool," Mike said, and Del shot him another warning glance. Mike paid no attention. "Albert knew you and Daniel were brothers."

Randall laughed again, choking on blood. "Want to know how I met Dan? I followed him to a bar one night. He thought it was a chance meeting. San Francisco's a small town, right? He didn't blink an eye when he learned his mother killed herself over my so-called *father*. Chalked it up to coincidence. Freaking imbecile. It never occurred to him London might be his father, too."

"You planned to blow the whistle on London. Why didn't you tell Daniel the truth?" Del asked.

"I'd never have exposed London. Admit in public what he'd done to me? My mistake was telling Albert. He wouldn't let it go. Albert wanted me to disgrace London, payback for the way London had disgraced his brother."

"Did you make the deposits into Shapiro's account?" Mike asked.

"Albert's idea. He said if London accused me of shaking him down, there'd be no money trail."

"What about the Cézanne?" Del asked.

"When Albert showed Dan the newspaper piece with the

photograph of the painting, Dan went ballistic. Albert threw fuel on the fire, bitching about the thieving Millers. Dan wanted to call a lawyer right then and make a claim. Albert told him he should wait until the exhibit was under way. More publicity."

"That's when you came up with the plan to exchange the Cézanne for the copy."

"It was my idea to go for both the painting and the insurance money."

Del could hear the pride in Randall's voice.

"Then Dan tried to cut me out. He wouldn't believe London's death was an accident. He blamed me."

"And you killed Daniel because he cut you out of the deal."

"What? No—you think I'd kill my own brother?"

A black sedan pulled up behind the three men. Neil Sobol climbed out, gun drawn. "Lay the weapon on the ground Gabretti, nice and easy, then step away."

"Special Agent Sobol, I'm touched you remember my name." Mike did as he was told and held up his hands to show they were empty. "Just so you're in the loop, Rusty here threw a gun into the drainage ditch."

Sobol kicked away Del's Sig. "What the fuck is going on, Miller?"

"Just holding your suspect until you could get here."

"From the look of him, I'd say you held him too tight. Promise me you gave him a more thorough pat down than during your last tryst, then turn him loose."

Del gave Randall one last shove into the cinderblocks and backed away.

Neil held his Glock to Randall's head. "Think long and hard before you try to run. I won't hesitate to put a round into a kiddie rapist. You listening to me, you piece of shit? This is where I read you your rights, and you get some lovely new jewelry courtesy of the federal government." Neil tossed handcuffs to

Del. "Make him pretty."

"We need to get into those storage units," Del said. "Where's your backup?"

"You failed to mention in your message that you were holding the suspect."

Del's temper flared. "If you'd been available, I'd have filled you in."

"Now, now boys, try and get along," Mike said, and Del nearly decked him.

"Backup is on its way," Neil said. "I put in a call when I pulled into the lot."

"What about the text advising units were already en route?" Del asked.

"What text?"

Del glanced at Mike, who returned a self-satisfied smile. "Oops, sorry. My bad."

CHAPTER 33

"So what was the crap about a text message?" Del asked Mike. They'd been cooling their heels in the San Francisco FBI field office for four hours, and Del's patience was shredded.

Mike shrugged. "Randall seemed to be jockeying for a defensive position. I thought it might keep him talking if he believed the Feds were on their way. In case you didn't notice, it worked. Christ, he's a pitiful bastard."

Special Agent Neil Sobol entered the room, jaw clenched, eyes shooting fire. He pulled out a chair and sat on the side of the table opposite Del and Mike. "Both storage units are empty."

Del's head throbbed, his leg hurt, and he wanted to go home. He made no effort to hide his bad mood. "What do you mean empty?"

"I mean empty, as in, not filled—containing nothing, zilch, *nada*. Randall kept his mother's car in the larger lockup. That's why he went to MoreSpace. He switched out the plates and planned to head out of town."

"Randall stole the fucking painting, Neil. How about asking him where it is?"

"He says he gave the Cézanne to Daniel Shapiro. Shapiro rented the lockups under his uncle's name. Right after Daniel got popped, Randall went to MoreSpace to retrieve the Cézanne, and abracadabra, no painting. Randall swears he doesn't have the Cézanne and doesn't know where the painting is."

"Yeah, and I bet he didn't plug Daniel Shapiro either. You believe his bullshit?" Mike asked.

"The gun we recovered from the ditch is an old Walther PPK, probably made in the thirties. Obviously, we don't have the ballistics, but the weapon has been fired. Damn good chance it's the gun that took down Daniel Shapiro. According to Randall, the pistol isn't his, and he didn't shoot Shapiro."

A shock slammed through Del so intense, his breath caught. His father kept an old PPK locked in a cabinet in his study. He ignored the look Mike gave him and asked Neil, "Did Randall bother to explain how the gun ended up in his hand?"

Neil's lips turned up at the corners. "You'll love this. He says he found the weapon in his apartment the day after Shapiro was shot. Has no idea where it came from. Says he only had the PPK with him today because he wanted to get rid of it. When he spotted you, he panicked and pitched the gun—literally. In his defense, the piece wasn't loaded. Can't say whether Randall shot Shapiro, but he didn't plan on taking out anyone this afternoon."

"Daniel Shapiro tried to cut Randall out of their deal," Mike said. "Instead of sharing in a substantial insurance payout and proceeds from the sale of an Impressionist masterpiece, Randall would get squat. I realize I'm only a lowly attorney and not a special agent of the esteemed Federal Bureau of Investigation, but I'd call that motive."

Del ran his hand over his face, shook his head, and rose. "I don't feel well. I need to get out of here."

"You look like shit warmed over." Mike got to his feet. "I'll take you home"

"We're not done," Neil said.

Mike put a hand on Del's shoulder. "We are for now."

Del turned to Neil. "I want my cell back before the end of the day."

On the elevator down, a cold sweat streamed over Del's brow, and he clung to the handrail to support his shaking legs.

"What happened in there? I saw your face when Sobol mentioned the gun," Mike said.

Del swallowed back a wave of nausea. "My father owns a World War II Walther PPK. What the hell is Randall doing with a gun like that? He strike you as a history buff?"

"Are you suggesting Randall broke in, stole your father's gun, and shot Daniel? Or maybe your father plugged Daniel, then planted the gun in Randall's apartment? Or do you suspect Randall and your father are involved in some sort of conspiracy? For what it's worth, I'm not buying any of the above."

Del exhaled and massaged the back of his neck. "No one could break into my parents' place without them knowing. Their only son is a security expert. I need to see for myself if that Walther is still in Dad's study."

"And what if it isn't?"

"I have no idea."

The study door stood ajar. Del stepped back and knocked softly.

"What is it, Hanna?" Samuel said, his tone decidedly cool.

Del poked his head into the room. "Dad, do you have a minute?"

Samuel laid his pen on the desk. "Of course, come in. When were you released? You realize you shouldn't be driving, Del, not with a head injury. You need rest."

Caught off guard, it took Del a minute to realize his father was referring to release from the hospital and not the FBI field office. "I left the hospital early this afternoon. I'm not a hundred percent, but I'm doing okay."

Mike moved into the room. "Don't worry, Samuel. I've appointed myself chauffeur and keeper for a day."

Del peered at the cabinet where his father kept the PPK,

exchanged a glance with Mike, and gave a little nod. Mike strolled over and picked up a book from an adjacent shelf.

"Intrigued by medical texts, Mike?" Samuel asked.

"Not really." Mike chuckled and replaced the book. "Never noticed this pistol before. Looks old."

"A Walther PPK, SS issue."

Del, who had been holding his breath, exhaled on a fierce rush of near-euphoric relief. He walked over and stood beside Mike.

"You don't strike me as a gun man, Samuel."

The old man laughed. "I'm not. The PPK was a gift from Jakob Shapiro."

Del gaped at his father. "Jakob Shapiro gave you a pistol?"

"He bought the gun at auction. Did you know Adolph Hitler killed himself with his Walther PPK? The gift was meant to symbolize my escape from the Nazis." Samuel eyed Del and Mike suspiciously. "That gun's been in the cabinet since before you two were born. Mind explaining the sudden interest?"

Del lowered himself into the empty chair across from his father. "The FBI believes they have the weapon that killed Daniel Shapiro—a PPK."

"And you came to make sure mine was still on the shelf?" Samuel said, his voice weary and disappointed.

Del bowed his head.

Samuel said quietly, "I'd probably have done the same thing. It's possible Daniel Shapiro was shot with his own weapon. Jakob purchased two nearly identical guns. The other he gave to Albert. I've never fired mine, but back in the day, Albert was quite the marksman. Of course, the PPK is not a long-range target weapon. Maybe Albert never fired his either, but he certainly could have passed the pistol on to Daniel."

"A marksman? Albert could shoot from a wheelchair?" Mike asked.

"Not from a wheelchair. Albert managed quite well on crutches. Even when I met with him after Jakob's funeral, he wasn't confined to a wheelchair. Not that he didn't make use of the chair when it suited him. I always thought it strange how he seemed to revel in the attention the chair brought. He enjoyed having others at his beck and call. Albert had what Jakob referred to as *bad days,* when he claimed to be in so much pain he couldn't stand. Jakob was convinced his brother timed his *bad days* for whenever someone in the family planned an activity, say a tennis match or a hike, in which Albert couldn't participate."

Mike moved a stack of books and settled into the club chair next to Del's. "What if Shapiro still isn't confined to a wheelchair? He has a lock on his door and a private slider that opens to the outside. If he's ambulatory, he could easily get out of Neuman without anyone noticing. He has crutches in his room."

Del nodded slowly, the possibility as true and sharp as the point of a sword. "Albert Shapiro pushed Daniel to claim the painting. He provoked Randall's hate for London. Maybe this is about revenge. What if condemning my grandfather wasn't enough for the old bastard?"

Samuel's brows lifted. "What are you two talking about?"

Mike didn't respond, but said to Del, "Shapiro wouldn't kill his own nephew."

"Except Daniel wasn't his nephew, Mike."

Samuel leaned forward in his chair. "What did you mean, Albert condemned my father? I want an explanation."

"Later, Dad, I promise." Del got to his feet. "Give Mike and me a half-hour head start, then call Agent Sobol. Tell him to get his ass over to Neuman House with a search warrant. The Cézanne is there somewhere, I'd bet my balls on it." Del moved toward the door. "Come on, Mikey, kick it in gear."

"Sure you're up to this?"

Del flashed on his father's Walther locked in the cabinet a few feet away. "I feel a hell of a lot better than I did an hour ago."

Mike had the Z's engine running when Del slid into the passenger seat. Mike floored the gas, and with a long screech of the tires, they peeled away.

"Easy, Mike."

"Thought you were in a hurry. Wasn't the half-hour lag to give you first dibs on Shapiro? How do you plan to talk your way inside Neuman?"

"Get us there in one piece, and we'll find a way in."

Bucking early afternoon traffic, the drive took longer than it should have. Mike pulled up to the curb across the street from Neuman and Del stared at its graceful façade, the quintessence of elegance and placidity. He unlatched his seat belt. "Here's the plan. You call Neuman. Tell them the FBI has Daniel Shapiro's killer in custody, and it's urgent you talk to Allbert. The gunman is a Shapiro family friend, and you want to break the news to the old man gently to ease the trauma."

"What if the old fart won't grant me an audience?"

"He will, trust me."

"He's not going to want to see you."

"Which is why you won't mention I'm here."

Mike made the call and crammed the phone back in his pocket. "I'm in, but apparently Shapiro still isn't well. He's sequestered in his room. Once we're inside, follow me. The residents' rooms are to the left under the arch." Mike opened the car door. "Let's rock and roll."

A barrel-shaped woman in white Del took to be the *not-so-lovely* Esther opened the front door. Mike pushed past her and Del followed him down a long corridor.

"Wait, Mr. Gabretti," the woman called running after them.

"You need permission for your friend to—"

Mike ignored her and burst into Shapiro's room.

The old man glanced up from his wheelchair, face impassive.

"Where's the Cézanne, you sack of shit?" Mike asked.

Shapiro's eyes widened. "What are you talking about?"

Esther stood in the doorway, her voice panicky. "I'm sorry, Mr. Shapiro. I tried to stop them—"

"Shut up, you stupid girl," Shapiro said.

Del grabbed the crutches from against the wall and set them in front of Shapiro. "Stand up, asshole. I know you can walk."

Shapiro laughed and shook his head. "Mr. Miller, I am an invalid."

"You come to Neuman and suddenly you're wheelchair bound? Both my father and Lee Dutton confirmed you were able to walk the last time they saw you."

"What is this? I was told my nephew's killer had been caught."

"You tell us, Shapiro. Do you feel caught?" Mike asked.

The old man sputtered. "Are you seriously accusing me of killing Daniel?" He looked over at Esther, who seemed frozen in place. "Get help, and call the police. I want these men out of here."

"That won't be necessary, Esther, the FBI is on its way," Mike said.

Fear flared in Shapiro's eyes, and Del felt a warm swell of satisfaction.

"I'm a sick old man. Why are you torturing me?"

Del moved so close to Shapiro, he smelled the man's sour breath. "You knew Daniel and Brian Randall were half-brothers. When Randall showed up, he proved the perfect pawn. You not only hatched a plan to destroy London's reputation, you fed Daniel lies about the Cézanne belonging to your family. You pushed him to claim the painting."

"Daniel was a drug addict. He'd do anything for money. He

took the gallery from me."

"Another lie. You signed over the business willingly. Everyone acquainted with your nephew said he was devoted to you, Mr. Shapiro. While Daniel wouldn't have hurt you, there isn't a single doubt in my mind you put two bullets in his head."

"I don't own a gun."

"Not true. Your brother gave you a Walther PPK years ago. Did you forget he gave an identical gun to my father? I hear you were once an excellent marksman, but you didn't need to be a crack shot to murder Daniel at close range, did you?"

Shapiro glared at Del. "You're insane. Brian Randall killed my nephew. I saw him in the newspaper. First day he showed up at the gallery, he told me London was his father and what that sick fuck had done to him. I told him to go public, ruin London, get some closure. Then the stupid little bastard gets sent to Corcoran—"

"You told Daniel that London was his biological father?" Mike asked.

"Daniel was weak, like his mother. I never told him anything unless I had to."

"But you knew about the plan to switch out the Cézanne."

"Brian took a job at CaMu. Daniel brought him to see me here. He went on and on about a copy of the Cézanne in London's house. He had the idea of switching the real Cézanne for the copy before Daniel made a claim for the painting. They'd have the insurance money and the art. I had no interest in either, but replacing the painting with a copy was an opportunity to humiliate London, to get back some of what the Müellers stole from me. Yes, I knew what Daniel and Brian intended, but I was in no position to protest. As I told you before, my nephew terrified me. You've seen the burns."

"We've seen the burns, and they are nothing a compulsive liar with a pathological need for attention couldn't inflict on himself," Mike said.

Del exhaled. They were getting nowhere. "You turned my grandfather in to the Gestapo, Mr. Shapiro. Frankly, I consider you a loathsome, inhuman piece of shit. Max Müeller was a hero. He risked his life and freedom to save others while you sat on your ass in the south of France and pretended to be goyim."

A red flush covered Shapiro's face. "Because of your grandfather, I was cut off from my family for more than seven years. I made certain Max Müeller suffered the same kind of loss. If it hadn't been for your grandfather's interference, my father would never have left me behind."

Disgusted, Del glowered at the old man. "Instead, your father and brother would have stayed in France, and you'd have all been gassed together. Even if they survived, you wouldn't have been so lucky. As a cripple, you were already good as dead to the Nazis." A vein throbbed in Shapiro's temple and his skin turned from red to dark purple. Del wondered if he'd pushed too hard. Maybe Shapiro was having a stroke. The thought made him smile.

"Max Müeller stole the Cézanne just as surely as if he'd walked in and ripped the painting from my father's wall."

"Your father gave my grandfather that painting."

"Müeller coerced him. The Cézanne belongs to my family."

Del shook his head. "What do you know about family? Daniel was your family, Mr. Shapiro, and you shattered his skull with two rounds from a PPK."

Shapiro snarled, his eyes wild, spittle flecking Del's face. "Daniel was the bastard son of a man I abhorred and the woman who cuckolded my brother. Like I said, Daniel was weak. When he was high, he couldn't keep his fucking mouth shut. Brian Randall was my eyes and ears on the ground. He kept watch over Daniel. But when Brian let London die, Daniel was furious. He insisted on cutting Brian loose, and that couldn't happen. I had no choice. I had to stop Daniel from ruining everything."

"Why is Randall protecting you?"

Shapiro gave them a smile so sinister, Del's blood ran to ice. "He doesn't know I can walk. Neither did Daniel, the fool— always so gullible. You should have seen the look on his face when I knocked on his door." Shapiro's awful laugh raised the hackles on the back of Del's neck.

There was a commotion in the hall, followed by footsteps.

Neil Sobol pushed past Esther. "FBI."

Shapiro smirked. "Go ahead and arrest me. I'm a sick old man. What the fuck do I care?"

CHAPTER 34

Del and Mike stood in the center of Sophie's nearly empty living room. The air had an indefinable scent of a place abandoned, the taint of dust and long ago cooking. Moving boxes lined one wall, neatly marked with their contents and future location. Most of Sophie's things would be stored in Del's parents' attic until she was *sure*. Still unconvinced she wanted to be with him as much as she wanted to get away from Mike, Del wondered if *sure* would ever happen. Didn't matter. He'd waited a long time for this and would do what he had to do to make it work. The thought of her by his side every day left him dizzy.

"You're really going?" Mike said, resignation in his voice.

"We are," Del said.

"You can't fix her. Things won't get better."

"I'm not trying to fix her, and if things got any better, I don't think I could stand it."

"You can be there for her, try to convince her she's worth loving, that everything bad that's ever happened to her wasn't her fault. You can be her lapdog, with all the unconditional love and devotion it entails, but after a while, she'll wear you down. It's not possible to love her enough, Delbo. I wanted to rescue her, too. We're a lot more alike than you think."

"I appreciate your help with the move, but I don't want to talk about Sophie." Del dropped his head and took a deep breath. "The property agent said there shouldn't be any problem leasing the house. The location and price are good."

"What if she changes her mind and wants to come home?"

"She can stay with my parents until the renters are given whatever notice is required. I'm not holding her captive. She is free to leave any time she wants."

Mike's lip curled into either a sneer or a smile. Del wasn't sure which. "Have you heard anything else from Sobol?"

"No, but I talked to Terry. The FBI and SFPD are fighting over Randall. The FBI wants him for lifting the painting, and the DA wants him for manslaughter. Randall admitted London expected to be rescued, which established duty of care. That obligated Randall to save—"

Mike held up a hand. "I'm an attorney. I know what duty of care is. Randall was a pawn. The fact London abused him for so many years will carry weight. I'm more interested in Shapiro. Murder one—couldn't happen to a more deserving guy. With any luck, they'll fry the bastard."

"He's in his mid-eighties. He might not survive a trial."

"God, I hope he doesn't get off the hook so easy. Max, London, and Daniel Shapiro are all dead because of that vindictive sonovabitch."

"Shapiro built his life around revenge. His family left him behind during the war, and he substituted my family as the target of his resentment. Judith cuckolded his brother, and Shapiro decided to lay the blame on London. Five years he waited for Randall to get out of Corcoran so he could use him to ruin London's reputation by publicly exposing London's abuse. Then Randall refused to go public. That damned newspaper photo of my mother with the Cézanne gave Shapiro everything he wanted, a means to send my family a killing blow and pay back London at the same time."

"What a miserable excuse for human being." Mike shook his head. "At least the Cézanne is back where it belongs."

"Not quite yet, but soon." Del gave a quick grunt of a laugh.

"In all its depressing glory."

"Your parents doing okay with all this?"

"London's out of the picture, so my father no longer avoids CaMu. He's more involved with the board, spends more time with my mother, but it's been hard for him. He never saw the betrayal coming. He's still working to accept that Shapiro informed on him and his father to the Gestapo."

Sophie appeared on the landing. "What's going on? I locked Lucy and Cas in the bedroom so they wouldn't get in the way while you were loading the van, and you haven't moved a single box. I don't want to keep them shut up any longer than I have to. Across country in a car will be confining enough. In other words, get to work. I told Hani we'd be by with the boxes around dinnertime. She's cooking, and I have no intention of missing my last shot at her brisket." Sophie grinned from ear to ear.

She looked so happy, Del couldn't hold back a smile. "We're on it, aren't we Mikey?"

"You bet, Delbo. Like stink on shit."

ABOUT THE AUTHOR

VR Barkowski was raised ninety miles north of Sacramento in a town nestled between California's Sierra Foothills and the State's great Central Valley. The youngest of five children, smaller and quieter than the rest, VR soon discovered she was better at putting words on paper than making herself heard. She started to write and never stopped. A graduate of UC Berkeley and a recovering sociologist, VR was the 2012 winner of the Al Blanchard Award for her short story, "Out to Sea"; the winner of the Rocky Mountain Fiction Writers' Colorado Gold Award for her manuscript, *Blood Under Will;* and a finalist for both the Claymore Dagger and the Daphne Du Maurier Award for *A Twist of Hate.* She currently makes her home on Boston's North Shore.